THE GORGING OF SOULS

THE GORGING OF SOULS

ORIGIN CODEX BOOK 2

CLAIRE L. FISHBACK

ISBN: 978-1-970121-12-4 (eBook)

ISBN: 978-1-970121-07-0 (Paperback)

This is a work of fiction. Any references to historical events, real people, or real places are used fictitiously. Names, characters, and places are products of the author's imagination.

Cover image and design by Claire L. Fishback

Printed in the United States of America.

First edition. August 19, 2021.

Dark Doorways Press, LLC

PO Box 620514

Littleon, CO 80162

www.darkdoorwayspress.com

For Wissa
The light to my dark
The dark to my light

CHAPTER ONE

FRIDAY

Teresa Hart could tell her meds were wearing off because the voices got louder. *Auditory* hallucinations, as Dr. Andrews put it. He told her to ignore them.

The drug they had her on, something experimental called Thorithium, wasn't as harsh as the Chlorpromazine they'd had her on before when she was stuck inside these walls after the baby died.

Teresa scoffed at herself.

After *she'd* neglected her baby, causing Tiffany to die.

She was in stage two of the pattern this drug followed between doses.

Stage one: she existed in a daze. A gentle, floating kind of daze.

Stage two came around as the Thorithium left her system. Clarity came to her mind. She could think straight and feel. She hated those times because then she remembered what she'd done eight months ago. The events of The Betrayal, and the days leading up to it, the deaths, came racing back to her.

The voices started during phase three. The loudest came from The One Who Betrayed Her, laughing at her. Sometimes he whispered things in her ear. Unsavory things.

He always told her the babies were his. When he spoke to her—when his voice as an auditory hallucination came to her, that is—her scalp tickled, like someone were just barely touching her hair, but from the inside of her skull.

Sometimes her mother's voice chided her for not following the rules. Sometimes all she heard was Ruthie's shriek or Sheriff McMichael's groan. Sometimes she heard Derrick's skin sloughing off. A quiet *plopping* accompanied by the scent of his charred flesh.

Thirty-six weeks seemed like so long ago, and somehow *not* so long ago. Day in, day out, the same routine. The same food. The days blended into each other. The Thorithium didn't help differentiate them at all.

Teresa stared out the rain-splattered window and caressed her swollen belly, huge with twins, and thought about baby names.

Other residents clustered around the common room. A raucous game of Chutes and Ladders carried on behind her. The two eldest residents of Mountain View chattered away at each other, neither one hearing the other. Not because of deafness, but because they both had stories to tell and didn't seem to care the other was talking. Teresa had learned their life stories her first week there just by listening to the constant mumbling drivel coming out of their toothless mouths.

She liked the sound of Pearl for one of the babies. It was elegant and simple. It was also Derrick's mother's name.

The babies aren't Derrick's, a persistent voice hissed.

It was a voice she thought might be some version of herself. She shook her head. Of course they were his. He had been her husband.

Until you killed him.

"Shut up!" Teresa shouted.

The game of Chutes and Ladders ceased. Teresa glared at the two women frozen mid-game play. Their eyes were wide as if she'd personally affronted them.

A nurse—the kind one who had more compassion than many of the others held in their belly buttons—glanced up from what Teresa referred to as the chaperone desk.

"Everything okay?" the nurse asked.

Teresa nodded.

The game commenced once again, although the two players spoke in hushed tones.

They're whispering about you.

"No they aren't," Teresa said in an insolent tone.

Dr. Andrews insisted her auditory hallucinations weren't too concerning. It was when she *saw* Ruthie and Sheriff McMichael and Derrick in her peripheral vision that gave him cause to worry.

The worst was when she saw *him*. The One Who Betrayed her.

You can say my name, my dear. His voice prickled her scalp. She closed her eyes against the slithery sound. How had she ever trusted him? How did she not notice time after time going to see him that he was a monster? A lion-snake-man hybrid, not the sensual half-clad caveman he presented himself as.

A tear slipped down her cheek.

"Mrs. Hart?" a male voice said behind her.

"It's *Doctor* Hart," Teresa mumbled as she struggled to turn in her chair.

A man in a cheap brown suit and a woman in a too-short pencil skirt and gaudy floral blouse stood behind her.

"I'm John Shelly. This is my associate Betsy Wilkes. We're with the Office of Child Services."

The girl leaned forward and held out a business card. Her cheap perfume wafted from her. Teresa eyed the card but didn't move to take it. She returned her gaze to John and raised her eyebrows, indicating he should continue. His Adam's apple bobbed.

"We are here to discuss your upcoming birth."

Teresa encircled her belly with her arms.

Betsy piped in, her voice high and nasal. The kind of voice that struck the ear wrong no matter who you were. Teresa felt sorry for the girl's mother.

"With no family or friends on file—you have none, correct?"

Teresa scowled. With Derrick gone, as well as her parents, and having been an only child, she had no family. As for friends? Ha. She lost touch with any from college ages ago, and Derrick moving her to the middle of the Colorado Rockies and that Godforsaken town—

"We have a few interested parties," Betsy continued when Teresa didn't respond.

"Parties? Interested? In what?"

Betsy let out a nervous laugh—an even more cringe-worthy sound—and cast a glance at John, who nodded at her.

"People—couples—interested in adopting the baby."

The baby. Tiffany.

Teresa squeezed her eyes shut. Not Tiffany.

"Babies," she said in a low voice. She opened her eyes and stared at the linoleum tiles. "There are two."

Betsy laughed again. "Oh, yes, I see here. My mistake.

Do you already have someone in mind? To adopt them, I mean?" Her voice had risen in pitch as if asking these questions caused her throat to tighten. Teresa gritted her teeth and wished the girl would just suffocate already and get out of her business.

"No," Teresa managed to say in a civil tone. "I will be keeping them."

Betsy's mouth popped open. Her eyes shifted to John and back. Teresa turned her attention to the window. She ran her hands over her belly and hummed a lullaby.

"I'm sorry." John gave a nervous laugh now. "Has Dr. Andrews not discussed this with you? We provided the files."

"Files? What files?" Heat bloomed around her eyes. She didn't turn.

"Pictures, applications, backgrounds," Betsy said with a sideways glance at John. "Of the interested . . . um . . . couples?"

"I said . . ." Teresa spoke through gritted teeth. She struggled to her feet and took a step toward the agents. They both stepped back. ". . . I am *keeping* them."

John held up his hands before Betsy or Teresa could say another word.

"We'll be in touch." He slid a business card across the table. Teresa flung it back at him. It drifted to the floor. John cleared his throat and bent to pick it up. They left, casting glances over their shoulders at her.

Teresa lowered herself into her chair again. She knew, of course—now that her meds were wearing off—they would never allow her to raise the babies in this place. It was far too dangerous with all the crazies running around. Besides, her room was too small to house all the accoutrements of a nursery, times two.

She had to get out of here, before her babies were born, before someone could take them from her.

Just like Yaldabaoth took Tiffany from me.

The memory of The Betrayal came rushing back. His promises, his deception, his lust.

They are my daughters, his voice slithered across the room to her.

She turned her head a fraction. In the extreme corner of her eye, he lurked just inside her peripheral vision. She straightened her head.

He's not really there. You know that.

Dr. Andrews had warned her against giving in. "Ignore them," he said. "Or they'll overpower you like they did before."

Like before. What did he know? He thought everything from the night of The Betrayal had been a hallucination. He refused to believe what she told him.

The dead *did* chase her. A lion-snake-man *had* promised to bring her seven-years-deceased baby back to her—and did. Tiffany guided Teresa every night. Teresa held her little girl, touched her, allowed her heart to open to that beautiful child. Yaldabaoth promised to restore her marital bliss, and after Derrick . . . died . . . Yaldabaoth promised to give him back, too.

It wasn't her fault Yaldabaoth lied to her.

The only hallucination she'd ever had was when she talked to her dead mother on the phone. And Derrick had tried to bring her back to this place as a result, sealing his fate.

The nurse from the chaperone desk approached.

"Time to go to your therapy session," Crystal—that was her name—said.

Teresa nodded and rose from her chair, an act that

became more and more difficult each day. She waddled across the room and down the hall to Dr. Andrews's office, where she sat in the wingback chair across from him.

No lounging on leather sofas here. He was a practical man who didn't seem to believe in patient comfort.

"Mrs. Hart," Dr. Andrews said in greeting.

"*Doctor*," Teresa said. He took the correction as a greeting. "What will happen to my babies when they're born?" she asked. "Two people came to talk to me today."

Dr. Andrews looked up from the thick file on his desk. His face flushed.

"I meant to discuss that with you prior to their arrival. I apologize for that. There must have been a miscommunication with the front office staff."

"I don't care about a miscommunication," Teresa said, trying to keep a wrinkle-causing scowl from working its way onto her face. "What are my options?"

Dr. Andrews bit his lips and took a deep breath through his nose.

"Your mental state"—he pushed his glasses up his nose —"does not bode well for raising a child."

"But—"

He held up his hands. "Aside from that, I don't believe you are any closer to any kind of rehabilitation since you joined us back in October."

"I beg to differ."

Dr. Andrews pursed his lips and flipped open the folder on his desk. That fat stack of paper was *her* file?

"Your records indicate you still have nightmares. You are still exhibiting auditory and sometimes visual hallucinations. You still need medication and to be monitored that said medication is working properly." He looked up at her. "Not to mention, you killed several people last fall." He flipped the file shut and tented his fingers in front of him. "That alone does not bode well for any kind of early release. Or any release at all. Ever."

Teresa's mouth dropped open. She looked down at the ragged edge of his cheap desk where the wood-patterned laminate had peeled off.

"Your options, therefore, are limited." His voice lowered, and for a second she heard Derrick's voice. His doctor-voice. The one she hated when he used it on her. "Adoption to a nice family—pre-selected. Or the babies will enter the foster system. We will do all we can to keep them togeth—"

"That's it? I don't have any chance of keeping them?" Teresa covered her belly as best she could.

Dr. Andrews took another deep breath through his nostrils. He took his glasses off and squeezed the bridge of his nose.

"I'm afraid not," he said. "OCS has left a few records for couples looking to adopt." He moved her fat file to the side and pulled a thinner one nearer. "More interest comes in every day."

"May I?" Teresa asked.

"Of course." He pushed the folder closer to the far edge so Teresa could reach it. "Might I draw your attention to the green paperclips? Those are a few I believe hold the most promise."

Teresa snatched the file and opened the cover. As if he would know what she might look for, what her requirements were. None of them would be suitable. None of them would hold any promise. Because none of them were *her*.

Inside were dossiers of the families with all their information: annual household incomes, places of employment, background checks—more than she'd had to supply when she and Derrick adopted Maggie. But that had been a whole other situation, as it turned out. Forgeries and more secrets and more lies.

At the end of their session, Dr. Andrews gave her the next dose of Thorithium. Teresa returned to her room and eased herself onto her bed. She opened the file and flipped through the pictures, ignoring the three with green paperclips.

Too old. Too poor. Too ugly.

She sighed and looked at the three Dr. Andrews had picked out.

The first one was a woman with eyebrows plucked into a constant state of surprise. She wore her brown hair in a fashionable bob. Her husband had graying temples and a wide smile.

The second could have been Teresa herself and Derrick if they needed people to portray them in a dramatization of their lives. Blond woman with blue eyes. The man tall and dark-featured.

The third green paperclip held a woman with a large mole on her cheek and thick, Neanderthal-type eyebrows. The man was a weaselly looking thing with a large nose and a completely out-of-place cleft chin. She tossed the folder onto her bed.

One of the babies kicked. Teresa put a hand on her belly. A little elbow or heel slid across her palm.

She couldn't let anyone take them. She would find a way. She would do anything to keep them safe.

A knock came at her open door.

"You've got a visitor," the nurse said.

Teresa hadn't had a visitor in months. Not since Ann Logan, now the sheriff, stopped in once at the beginning of her stay to let Teresa know she'd be locked up forever. Ann had also mentioned she'd be taking care of Maggie. The visit had been short and not impolite, but not friendly either. Why would it be? Teresa had killed Derrick. Derrick and Ann had been high school sweethearts.

Teresa also had no friends, as Derrick was so quick to remind her when he was still around. Even Louise, whom she'd befriended during the incidents leading up to the night of The Betrayal, was gone.

Killed by you.

Teresa followed the nurse to the visitor's room and looked around. Her eyes landed on the back of a head full of dark hair shot with gray. A canvas jacket covered his shoulders.

"No," Teresa took a step back. "It can't be."

The nurse pressed a hand to Teresa's back. "He's right over here."

Raghib turned and gave her a toothy grin.

CHAPTER TWO

"Go on, dear," the nurse said. "He's been waiting for some time. Arrived before visiting hours."

The nurse placed a hand on Teresa's elbow and guided her to the seat across from Raghib.

The night of The Betrayal, Raghib had kidnapped and delivered Maggie—his own granddaughter and Teresa's adopted daughter—to Louise, who subsequently stabbed him in the back. Literally.

The nurse helped Teresa ease into the seat before walking away. Teresa waited for the nurse to return to her station.

"How are you here?" Teresa asked in a small stunned voice. "I thought—"

Raghib laughed, then winced. "It still aches sometimes, where she . . . you know."

Teresa nodded and crossed her arms as best she could with her belly in the way. Raghib's eyes flicked down to her expansive stomach.

"*Why* are you here?" she asked.

"I'm here to help you." He met her eyes and leaned

forward. "And them." His eyes dipped down to her stomach and back up.

Teresa scoffed. "And why would I trust anything you say? You betrayed your own *granddaughter.*"

Raghib lowered his eyes. "A moment I am not and never will be proud of." His lips tightened into a line. His eyes met hers again. "You mustn't trust anyone who comes to discuss the welfare of your children. Not even your Dr. Andrews."

"And what about you? Are you not here discussing the welfare of my children?"

Raghib grinned and let out a hoarse laugh. "This is not going as expected."

"Tell me what you want to tell me so I can go lay down. I'm very tired. Carrying twins is exhausting."

"I can only imagine." He cleared his throat. "Mountain View is not what you think it is," he began. His voice was so low Teresa had to scoot her chair around closer to him. She couldn't lean forward conspiratorially like Raghib, and she didn't want anyone nearby to hear them talking.

"Go on," she said.

"The Messengers of the Light—the group Louise and I belonged to—have infiltrated this place and are using it for their own purposes."

The Messengers of the Light was an organization who wanted to bring Yaldabaoth—their god—to power. Louise had told Teresa they were like the CIA and FBI in their methods and technology.

Teresa scoffed. "They are using a mental hospital as a front?"

Raghib nodded. He reached into his jacket and withdrew a small stack of photos.

"These are people interested in adopting your babies.

They are all Messengers of the Light." He spread the photos out.

Teresa leaned forward. The woman with the extreme eyebrows. The woman who could have played Teresa herself in a dramatization. The woman with the mole. They all stared up at her. Not the same pictures as the file, but definitely the same women.

She told him about the file of dossiers and the green paperclips. She paused, her hand moving to her stomach. "Why am I telling you this? I don't trust you either."

He laughed. "As well you shouldn't." Teresa never could tell if his grin was a smile or a grimace. "But please, Dr. Hart, hear me out." His eyes held a desperate earnestness she couldn't deny.

"What do the Messengers want with my babies?" There was always a purpose, a plan, a scheme. Some otherworldly secret.

"They believe your babies are the Children of Chaos," Raghib said. "Yaldabaoth's offspring."

Images flashed through her mind. Injecting herself with Derrick's zoe—his life—after she'd extracted it from him with a giant hypodermic needle. Racing through the darkness, chased by the dead, into Yaldabaoth's arms. It hadn't been the first time their flesh connected, but this time it was she who initiated it.

It only takes one time, Teresa's mother's voice sang in her ear.

Teresa wanted to believe the babies were Derrick's, but in her deepest darkest heart she knew they were not. They hadn't made love in months before The Betrayal.

Teresa shook her head and wiped away a tear.

"They aren't his." Her voice shook. "Derrick was my husband. These are *his* babies." Her face momentarily threatened to contort with anguish, but she stopped it and lifted her chin.

Raghib nodded, but his eyes had grown sad. He touched her hand. "Whoever their father may be, the Messengers believe they are the children of Yaldabaoth."

"What will the Messengers do with them? Will they kill my babies? You gave Maggie over to Louise. You knew her plan." Teresa sat back with a gasp. "Are you still working for them?"

Raghib grasped her hand. Teresa jerked it away.

"Please, you must stay calm. Keep your voice low." His eyes flicked up over her head. Teresa knew what he was looking at. There were cameras in this room. "I know you do not trust me, but please, please trust that I no longer work for the Messengers. I have found allegiance with another group. A group who *will* help you."

Teresa scoffed again, bit her lip. "What do the Messengers want with my babies?"

Raghib withdrew his hand. "I do not know the intricacies of their plans. All I know is they will do whatever it takes to bring Yaldabaoth forth, just like Louise. Even if it means harm will come to your children."

"Yaldabaoth is dead." She frowned, recalling that night. His betrayal so soon after she'd attacked him with lust. Her gut clenched.

"I did not know," Raghib said. And why would he? He had been left for dead in Louise's basement. "It will all be in vain, then," he said absently. He met her eyes. "Whatever their plan is, I mean."

"How did you survive?" Teresa asked.

Raghib let out a mirthless laugh. "The old crone managed to miss all of my vital organs when she stabbed me. Perhaps on purpose. Perhaps there was—how do you say?—divine intervention." He grimaced, or maybe it was a pained smile. "No matter."

She should tell Ann. She should call her and tell her he was alive. Maggie could be in danger. Teresa grew faint. She closed her eyes for a moment. It wasn't *her* duty to protect others. Her hands caressed her belly. Except the ones inside her.

"Mrs. Hart," a voice said from the doorway. "Your time is up."

"Don't trust anyone," Raghib hissed. "Not even me."

Teresa moved to stand, but he grabbed her hand. His eyes were intense, and his voice was a harsh whisper. "Tomorrow night, do whatever you must to be put into solitary confinement. I will get you out of here. I will keep you and your babies safe from the Messengers of the Light."

Teresa tugged her hand free. She stood and backed away, shaking her head. He just said not to trust him.

"You can keep your babies," he said, his eyes earnest. He nodded. "You can keep them if you do as I say."

Teresa didn't respond. She hurried out of the visitor's room.

CHAPTER THREE

Teresa woke in the night. She was on her side facing the wall that had a window high up. Moonlight streamed in, giving the room a blue glow. She rolled onto her other side.

A figure stood in the far corner. Dark against the white wall. Teresa sat up.

"Who's there?" she said, breathless. Her mind felt clear and lucid. "Ruthie?" But the shape wasn't tall or scrawny enough to be her. It was too small to be Sheriff McMichael. "Derrick?" Her voice cracked.

Teresa's heart pounded. The door to her room was shut and, as far as she knew, locked every night. She always slept straight through the dark hours and only woke if the nurse came in to give her another dose.

The dark form rushed forward with a hiss. Teresa scrambled backward against the wall and raised her hands.

The thing crawled up onto the bed, hand then foot.

"Get away, get out of here!" Teresa screamed, cringing back and covering her stomach.

It crawled forward and crouched over Teresa's thighs. It wasn't a creature. It was a woman. A woman's face—framed by a curtain of long, dark, straggly hair—peered at her in the darkness. She moved her hands over Teresa's belly as if it were a crystal ball. Her touch was cold through Teresa's cotton nightshirt. Goosebumps broke out over Teresa's body.

"Yaldabaoth." The woman croaked his name. "Yaldabaoth." She pressed her ear to Teresa's stomach. One of the babies kicked. The woman jerked back and smiled at Teresa, then pressed her cheek once again to her bulging belly.

The scent of unwashed hair wafted from the top of her head. Teresa couldn't move. She didn't know what to do. She was afraid if she shouted for help, the woman might become angry.

"Please," Teresa whimpered. "Please go away. Stop touching me." She closed her eyes and turned her head away from the unwashed smell.

Movement jostled the bed. Teresa opened her eyes. The woman was gone.

She sat up and looked around the room, her breath heaving in and out, her heart racing. She peered at the corner from which the woman had come and thought she saw someone, silent and unmoving, still standing there.

Teresa scooted into the far corner of the bed and curled around her belly. She kept her eyes on that darkness.

CHAPTER FOUR

Teresa jerked awake suddenly with a huge intake of breath. The front of her standard-issue nightclothes clung to her legs, cold and wet. Her water had broken.

"My babies—I'm going into labor!" she cried out. But there was no pain. She lifted the wet fabric and sniffed it.

Urine.

Was it hers? She gasped again. Or had that woman *peed* on her?

She got out of bed and cleaned herself up before changing into clean clothes. The usual shapeless top—hers a few sizes too big to accommodate her expansive waistline— and matching scrub-style pants. She slid her feet into a pair of shoes and sat on the edge of her bed, waiting for her door to unlock.

It did so at exactly seven. Teresa got up and went out into the hall. As she made her way to the cafeteria, she scoured the faces of the surrounding women, looking for one who had long dark hair.

There were plenty of women with dark hair, but these were all regulars. Faces she'd seen every day since she got there.

In the cafeteria, she took a tray, got her breakfast, and sat alone at a table—one in the corner so she could observe everyone coming and going. The two oldest residents sat together, smacking their lips and gumming their food. The two who played the board games sat together. Other small clusters of women—friends Teresa thought—congregated at every meal, too, like high school cliques.

Teresa picked up a piece of toast that didn't have enough butter on it. A woman with dark hair Teresa had never seen before came in. But she stood tall and upright. She moved with grace. Her hair was smooth and pulled into a low ponytail. It was shiny and looked clean. But she was a newcomer.

"You." Teresa's voice came out low, like a growl. "You." She stood. Her chair scraped the floor. The Chutes and Ladders duo looked up at her. One of them pointed at herself, even though Teresa wasn't even pointing in her direction. "You with the black hair."

The woman turned and raised her eyebrows at Teresa.

Two orderlies came in. Burly women with mean faces and thick forearms. They were commonly known as the Berthas.

"Hart," one of them yelled, "sit down and eat your breakfast."

Teresa lowered herself back onto her chair. She'd lost her appetite, but her babies needed sustenance, so she ate as much as she could stomach of the goo they called oatmeal and choked down her toast. She drank a plastic cup of watery orange juice to wash it down. The food was awful. She would kill for a stack of pancakes.

Even for dinner.

A brief smile flitted across her lips but quickly crumpled away. "I should have made an effort," she whispered.

Dr. Andrews's eyes were lowered to Teresa's engorged patient records open on his desk.

"A woman came into my room last night," Teresa said. A tear slid down her cheek. "She touched my belly. Her hands . . . her hands were so cold." Her voice shook.

Dr. Andrews jotted a note in her file. "No one was in your room."

"She urinated on me."

His eyes flicked up to her. "Urinated?"

Teresa nodded. "My nightclothes were saturated in it this morning."

Dr. Andrews removed his glasses and pinched the bridge of his nose. "Mrs. Hart. You are eight months pregnant with twins. Do you think perhaps you might have . . ." He pushed his hand at her with his palm up, prompting her to finish his sentence.

"I did *not* wet the bed." Teresa allowed a scowl to form on her face. "I knew you wouldn't believe me."

"Your room is locked every night. It would be impossible for someone to just go in there."

"A nurse perhaps? One of those orderlies?" The woman wasn't big enough to be one of the Berthas, but the dark and the weird light from the moon, plus the fact that Teresa should be doped up at that time could have altered her perception. "I was lucid in the middle of the night when she woke me up. Am I supposed to be . . ." What was she to ask? Was she supposed to feel normal, not hear any voices, have a grip on what was going on around her? But he didn't believe her about the woman, so why should he believe how she felt?

Dr. Andrews eyed her over his spectacles. "I think your pregnancy has you worried."

"How do you mean?"

He sat back. His chair creaked. It sounded like a mewling kitten with each bob. Teresa didn't like it.

"You're pregnant and incarcerated, Mrs. Hart."

"She wants my babies," Teresa whispered. "She wants to take them from me." She scooted forward on the seat. "The way she touched me. She put her ear against my belly like she was listening to them."

Dr. Andrews barely concealed the grumble in his throat.

"I think you need some rest. Why don't you go back to your room and take a nap?" He pressed a button on his desk phone. "Mrs. Hart is ready to return to her room."

"No," Teresa said. "I'm not done here. That woman— what if she comes back? What if she hurts me?" Panic quickened her heart rate. "What if she hurts my babies?"

"You must calm down or you'll put all three of you at risk."

The Berthas came in. They manhandled Teresa out of Dr. Andrews's office and down the corridor to her room. Teresa knew better than to struggle against them. They'd wrenched a struggling woman's arms once while dragging her away.

Oh, how that woman had screamed.

"Calm down or you'll get a sedative," one of them bleated at her.

Teresa stumbled into her room when the Bertha on her right flung her arm forward. Thankfully, she didn't fall.

"You can't shove me around like that!" she shrieked. "I'm pregnant."

"Queen of Sheba over here," one of them said with a laugh. *"I'm pregnant,"* she mocked. The Berthas laughed and slammed the door behind them on their way out.

After stewing for a necessary amount of time, Teresa went out to the common room and took her usual seat by the window.

The sun lit up the grounds outside. The grass glowed like it was radioactive. A few patients from the men's ward were out there. One of them ran around in circles with his arms out to the sides. One wandered the edge of the hedgerow that blocked the chain-link fence topped with razor wire. It hid rows of the stuff on the other side too. Teresa only knew it was there because the last time she was in this place the hedges weren't so tall.

She needed to get out of here.

A nurse—not Crystal—came over and looked out the window. She smiled. "It's a lovely day today. I'm glad the rain stopped, but Lord knows we needed the moisture with all the fires raging." She chuckled for no reason Teresa could discern.

Teresa didn't know or care about any fires. She didn't care that they needed moisture. That was just something people said to justify bad weather.

The nurse went back to the chaperone desk. Teresa stepped closer to the window.

Tomorrow night, do whatever you can to get put into solitary.

She didn't want to trust Raghib—didn't think she could —but he was her only hope right now. With that woman touching her, and the Berthas and their rough hands, she didn't know what the night might bring. In solitary, she would be safe. No one could get her there. Her door was guaranteed to be locked.

Teresa turned around.

The two eldest residents muttered on and on in their shaky and fragile voices. Occasionally, the pitch in their voices would rise as if they just remembered something important to share with the other. A constant commentary of a life they only remembered in snatches.

"Steve brought the new car over yesterday. It's a nice car. Bright red. Shiny. He said I could drive it if I wanted to. But I don't know how to drive a car like that."

"Margret turned six last Wednesday. I got her a teddy bear with a blue sweater. Her mother, that good for nothing wench, got her a full makeup kit. Makeup. At six, if you'll even believe it."

Solitary confinement. Tomorrow night.

Tonight was the deadline. Teresa didn't want to go back to her room. Not after that woman had desecrated her sleeping space with *pee.*

The nurse clicked her pen in and out. *Click-clack, click-clack.* Teresa shifted her eyes to the desk and to the other occupied table.

The Chutes and Ladders duo continued their never-ending game. Up and down the board they played, declaring no winner. If one of them reached the end, she rolled again and went back down, aiming for the chutes. A race to the start.

Teresa touched the back of the third chair at their table.

"Don't touch. Don't touch," one of them said without looking at her. Teresa pulled her hands away from the chair.

The other player looked up at Teresa. "I spy with my

little eye, a woman in front of me," she said. "A big *fat* woman." Her eyes shifted to Teresa's stomach.

"I'm pregnant," Teresa said.

"Me, too," the first one said. She stuck her stomach out and rubbed it grotesquely.

"No, me." The other one did the same.

Teresa grabbed the edge of their game board.

"Don't touch!" They both yelled in unison, reaching toward Teresa's hands.

She flipped the board into their faces.

With only two game pieces and a flimsy cardboard spinner, the effect was mostly lost, but not to these two. One of them started howling in short bursts like a monkey. The other jumped up and raced around from table to table, shoving the chairs and furniture.

The Berthas lumbered into the room, faces red with anticipation.

Was flipping their board enough to get put in the hole? Disrupting the peace—it wasn't enough. She'd get a slap on the hand and sent to her room.

Teresa turned to the two eldest residents.

"Oh, God forgive me," she muttered. She rushed as best she could, angling toward them while the Berthas took chase. She reached the old lady first and shoved her off her seat. The frail thing went down hard. Her head hit the speckled linoleum tile with a hard crack.

Thick fists grabbed Teresa around the biceps. She struggled to get her arms forward to protect her belly and her babies, but the Berthas dragged her out of the common room.

The squeak of Dr. Andrews's leather shoes preceded him down the hallway and came to a halt in front of Teresa and her escorts.

"What is the meaning of this?"

"Caused a ruckus," Bertha One said.

"Hurt one of the other inmates," Bertha Two added. Her grip tightened on Teresa's arm. Pins and needles crackled in her palms, they held her so tight.

"You're cutting off my brachial arteries," Teresa said with a pained gasp.

"She's too big for any of the straight-jackets," one of the Berthas said, her hand tightening further on Teresa's arm.

"We can't strap her down in her condition." Dr. Andrews gave a deep and resigned sigh. "Take her to solitary." He turned to her. "Mrs. Hart."

"It's Doctor Hart," Teresa said and laughed a drunk laugh. She'd done it. She'd really done it.

He only grumbled and must have given the Berthas some sign because they dragged her to the elevator, grips never loosening. They went down a couple floors, and the elevator opened on a putrid-green hallway lined with doors without windows. The lights above flickered with the electric clicking-buzz fluorescents were prone to.

The Berthas shoved her inside. She managed to make out a bunk before the door slammed behind her and darkness enveloped her.

In complete silence and complete darkness, Teresa sat on a cold thin mattress with her head resting against a padded wall. Something bubbled up inside her. She tried to stifle it. She covered her mouth with her hands, but that only succeeded in shooting a bubble of snot out of her nose.

A laugh erupted from her. A big hearty laugh she hadn't heard in, well, probably ever. Maybe she laughed with reckless abandon in the early stages of her relationship with Derrick, but that was so long ago now she couldn't recall for sure.

She laughed because she'd done it. She'd really done it. Raghib would be here tonight and she would be free. Whatever happened after that, she would figure out.

She ran a hand over her belly.

"Yaldabaoth," she whispered. One of the babies kicked under her palm.

I am here.

"Yaldabaoth. Help me keep my babies safe." She closed her eyes. A tear slid down her cheek. "Help me keep *our* babies safe." Another tear. They fell freely now, wetting her cheeks and dripping down into the crook of her nostrils, around her lips, off her chin, onto the front of her shirt.

The feel of his voice caressed her hair, tingled her scalp.

What you seek, you shall receive.

CHAPTER FIVE

The lock on the door to solitary buzzed, echoing in the darkness outside Teresa's cell. She struggled to a seated position. The lock clanked, and the cell opened. Lights from the hallway blinded her. She wasn't sure how long she'd been in there. Couldn't remember if she'd had any meals. Without light, the time blended.

Dr. Andrews stepped in, followed by the Berthas.

"Time to go," he said.

"Go? Where?" Teresa asked.

"Back to your room, of course," Dr. Andrews said with a tight smile. "Enid is okay. Just a goose egg on her noggin, nothing more."

"How long have I been in here?" Teresa asked.

"Just a few hours," Dr. Andrews said. "We wouldn't want to keep you here in your condition for too long, after all. These babies could be born any moment now." He gave her belly a lecherous grin.

"No," Teresa cried, curling back onto the bed and covering her belly with her arms. "No, I want to stay here."

She had to stay. Raghib would come get her tonight. If she wasn't there, he would think—

"No, I must stay, please."

The Berthas looked at each other and laughed. "Never heard no one *want* to stay down here." One of them said.

Dr. Andrews waved them into Teresa's cell. They grabbed her yet again and hauled her back to her room, back to that filthy mattress that likely now reeked of urine.

That night, she didn't change into the fresh pajamas the nurses had left on her clean sheets. She stayed in her day uniform. She didn't even take her shoes off. She sat in the far corner of her bed and stared where the woman had appeared. She fought the drowsing effects of the Thorithium, but succumbed to them before she knew it.

Sounds outside her cell woke her. Clicking and snicking. The door handle jiggled. The door opened.

Four figures came into her room. Two in back held a blond woman by the arms. Her head sagged. She wore the standard-issue pajamas of the hospital. For a moment, Teresa thought she was looking at herself.

Teresa pushed against the corner. The third figure in black stripped off his mask. His bright grin illuminated from the moonlight high up in the window.

"Raghib!" Teresa said. He helped her to her feet. "I tried. I was there—in solitary—but they took me out."

"I know," Raghib said. "You did very good." He took her hand and held it to his breast. "I vow to do everything I can to ensure your safety. And the safety of your babies."

Relief washed over her.

"Who are they?" Teresa indicated the others. "Who is that woman?"

"This is the new you," Raghib said with that grimace. "An impostor to take your place and give us time." He motioned to the other black-clad figures. "These are our allies."

The allies hefted the blond woman onto the bed. Teresa noticed she was pregnant.

"Is she okay?" Teresa asked.

"Heavily sedated. That is a—how do you say—fat suit? To make her look as though she is with child." Raghib took Teresa's hand again. "Please, we do not have time to lose. Let us go." He pulled her out of the room and broke into a quiet jog down the corridor. Teresa quickened her pace, but couldn't keep up. Uneasy suspicion crept into her blood.

"It's okay, Dr. Hart," a female voice said beside her. A gentle hand took her elbow. The voice sounded familiar. "It's me, Crystal." The woman lifted her mask. It was the nice chaperone from the common room.

Raghib eased the door to the stairwell open.

"We must hurry," Crystal said, guiding Teresa by the elbow.

Teresa nearly tripped on the stairs. Raghib lifted her, supporting her as they rushed down. The other masked figure opened the door at the next landing, peeked out, then waved them forward.

Cool air caressed Teresa's face and blew her hair back from her forehead. They approached an SUV. Side doors shot open. Crystal and the other black-clad woman helped her inside and stretched a seat belt across her lap. Raghib climbed into the passenger side up front.

The vehicle turned a tight circle and headed out of the nearly empty parking lot.

She held her breath as the SUV twisted and turned down the hill leading away from Mountain View. If they made it to the bottom, she might be able to breathe again. The driver pressed harder on the accelerator.

He's going too fast, Teresa thought.

It felt out of control. Surely they would crash. Just like Derrick did the night of The Betrayal when they careened down that hill and hit that tree.

The SUV approached the end of the twisting road. The driver turned onto the main road leading in and out of the mountains around Harmony.

Teresa leaned back and rested her head on the headrest.

She let out a breath. She was free.

An explosion sounded. Glass shattered. The SUV skidded and spun across the road. When it stopped, the front end pointed down a hill.

The airbags had deployed. Teresa touched herself all over. Miraculously safe and unharmed.

Raghib lay motionless in the passenger seat. He let out a pained cough. "Run, Doctor. You must run."

"I can't run like this." She indicated her expansive stomach.

"You must go. It is them." He groaned and gripped his ribs. "The Messengers of the Light. Run, Teresa. Run."

Teresa slid out the side door. A white van with a red stripe down the side and a mangled front end sat on the road near the SUV. It looked like an unmarked small ambulance of some sort. The passenger door opened.

Teresa climbed over the bashed guardrail and speed-waddled down the hill as fast as she could with her giant belly. She kept going until the voices behind her drifted away to the silence of the nighttime forest. And still she hobbled, only stopping a few times to get her breath.

She walked for what felt like hours, but with the Thorithium in her system, time could be warped. She didn't realize where she was until she came upon a familiar dirt road. One she'd traveled many times on foot. She hurried across and stepped over what was once a boundary protecting her from the dead who chased her. Ruthie, Sheriff McMichael, Derrick.

Green lights bobbed and bounced, illuminating the area. Teresa had learned what they were last year. Tiffany had told her. They were lost souls.

They were real. They were real all along, just like everything else.

A wash of relief flooded through her, followed by a startling chill.

Maybe this *isn't real.*

Her thoughts warred with each other. She walked farther until the abandoned funeral home loomed into view.

This was the most dangerous place for her. Not only because of what she'd done, but because Ann Logan, former detective, Harmony's town sweetheart, was still in Harmony.

But exhaustion had taken a grip on her. Teresa wanted —no *needed*—to lie down. Her legs shook. Her feet hurt. Her back ached. Her belly felt stretched and heavy.

She sagged toward those wretched front porch stairs and stumbled inside.

The same old couch sat in the middle of a living room. The locals called it the abandoned funeral home, but to Teresa it was just a creepy old house.

Part of her expected—maybe hoped—for the walls to shift into the sand-colored cave of Tartaros. For Yaldabaoth to be there, gazing into his pool. He would turn and take her in his arms and protect her and *her* babies. But the other part of her recoiled at the very thought.

The pungent aromas of this place full of neglect assaulted her nostrils. If it was Yaldabaoth's cave, it wouldn't stink. She grimaced and lowered herself onto the moldering couch. It was surprisingly soft and dry.

Voices jolted her out of a light sleep.

Messengers of the Light.

She floundered for precious seconds, trying to get her feet to the floor, to get upright, to flee to the door.

The voices came from behind her. From deeper inside the house. Laughter, high and excited. Flashlight beams danced on the wall. One struck her face and darted away. Teresa dropped back onto the couch and pressed herself against it.

The voices came nearer.

Fluid gushed from between Teresa's legs, soaking her pants and the couch, followed by pain ripping her womb. Teresa cried out, clamped a hand over her own mouth.

"What was that?" a woman's voice asked.

Teresa breathed and gritted her teeth against the ragged pain ripping through her abdomen. Sweat broke out on her upper lip.

"It came from over there." Flashlight beams bobbed and dipped sickeningly as the group investigated.

She was done for. They'd found her. The Messengers of the Light. Her moments of freedom, of safety, were over. They would kill her and cut her babies out of her—

A young woman's face came into view. A kind face. "It's

okay." She stroked Teresa's forehead, smearing sweat into her hair.

"It's her," a soft but hulking man said. "It's Teresa Hart!" He let out an excited squeal. Others in the group—Teresa wasn't sure how many there were—gasped.

"What's she doing here?" a woman with long red hair asked.

"Is she dangerous?" asked a different man, one with a beard.

"She's hurt or something," said the kind woman next to Teresa's head.

"I'm in labor! I need a doctor." It had been over seven years since she'd experienced childbirth. She didn't remember it hurting this bad. "Something isn't right," Teresa cried out. "I need a hospital. Forty percent of twin births end in C-section."

"We got this." The girl looked away from Teresa's face. "Levi, go get help."

Her babies would be born in a matter of moments. She could feel it.

My children.

Yaldabaoth's voice spoke into her ear. Her scalp prickled. Teresa turned her head to the side, unafraid if she caught a glimpse of him this time. He wasn't there.

She came in and out of consciousness from the pain. Black spots swam at the edges of her vision. In those clear moments, firelight flickered from torches set in stone walls.

For a moment she thought she was back in Tartaros—in Yaldabaoth's cave. Then the musty living room would reappear.

But in those snatches in which she was back in the cave, she searched the shadows for him. For Yaldabaoth.

Figures shifted in the shadows between. Ruthie, Sheriff McMichael, Derrick.

Yaldabaoth laughed.

Why had she come here? Why didn't she go knock on someone's door for help?

It was a nightmare. It had to be.

No, it was the Thorithium holding her in a lucid state between dreams and reality. A place that frightened her. She often saw images from The Betrayal there in that place. Ruthie's soulless eyes, her shrieking mouth. Sheriff's bloody feet stumping along after her. Derrick—

But no. It wasn't the Thorithium. She hadn't had her latest dose. She didn't know when her last dose even was.

Pain tore across her abdomen again. Claws. It was their lion's claws ripping her apart from the inside.

Arms lifted her. When they lowered her again, she was on a crisp sheet. Another was placed over her. Someone cut her pants off.

"Breathe, Teresa," said yet another woman's voice. It was a gentle instruction. "It's going to be okay."

Teresa took a few breaths until the pain subsided. She opened her eyes. A different woman crouched next to her now. A woman with darker skin and unnaturally blond hair.

"I'm Lory," the woman said.

"I don't need a Lory. I need a doctor," Teresa whispered, shuddering with a chill. The contractions subsided for now. She breathed out and closed her eyes.

Raw and ragged pain ripped across her uterus. Teresa woke with a pained cry. She didn't remember the pain with Tiffany. This seemed wrong. Too much. Too intense. Too white-hot.

Teresa screamed. Yaldabaoth laughed. She needed to

wake up. She needed out of this dream. She'd never had such pain in a nightmare before.

You didn't follow the rules, her mother's voice said. *First marriage,* then *children. God will take them from you, just like he took Tiffany because you went to college.*

Her mother stood by her side, a hand on one of Teresa's bent knees. Yaldabaoth came near and put an arm around her. He licked the side of Teresa's mother's cheek. Her mother turned into the lick and kissed him so deeply her mother's throat bulged with his tongue.

Nausea boiled in Teresa's stomach. She squeezed her eyes shut. When she opened them again, her mom and Yaldabaoth were gone.

"Push," Lory's voice said from between Teresa's legs.

Teresa obeyed. Her hips moved as the thing inside of her thrashed its way out, ripping her flesh as it tore through. The pain, the agony, lessened. Teresa lay back.

The cave walls turned back into the peeling wallpaper of the abandoned funeral home.

A figure came forward with a pink blanket. Teresa tried to reach for her baby, but her arms wouldn't move. Had they drugged her? They had. They had drugged her and they were going to steal her babies and turn her over to Ann.

Wings flapped. Teresa blinked rapidly and turned her head. Lory, with her back turned, fought the blanketed form. A tail lashed the air. A clawed foot kicked.

Teresa watched in horror, trying to glimpse the thing. In the blurry haze, she glimpsed a small triangular head. Not a fleshy wrinkled face. Not a tiny fist. No cries. Just guttural hisses.

Yaldabaoth laughed again. His rich, quiet chuckle. The one that used to bring her pleasure and fear at the same time.

Our child is beautiful, his voice whispered in her ear, stirring her hair. She shuddered.

"Wake up!" She cried out, just as pain shot through her womb again.

"The twin is coming," someone called out. Ruthie? The cave reappeared in a rush that made Teresa dizzy.

"Push," Lory said, suddenly between Teresa's knees again.

The pain was even worse this time around. She pushed until she thought her brain would burst, afraid if she stopped pushing to take a breath the resulting pain would be maddening.

When the baby emerged, a purple blanket was brought forth for swaddling. No sounds came from the bundle.

"Is she okay?" Teresa tried to shout, but her voice didn't come out. It was inside her head.

You didn't follow the rules, her mother said in a sing-song voice again. *Marriage, then children.*

The low light and the sudden relief of pain made Teresa woozy.

"Come on," Lory muttered. She lifted her head from the silent bundle. "Bring the twin over."

"No," Teresa groaned. Images of that demon spawn eating the second twin flashed through her mind, adding to the torment and disorder of this nightmare.

One child a monster, the other stillborn. Her mother's rules certainly did have their consequences. Teresa moaned a wail so full of anguish she couldn't stand it.

"Come on little one," Lory whispered, holding the pink-swaddled baby near the purple.

A cry broke the air. A screaming wail. Healthy and full of life.

Teresa sobbed with relief.

"There we go, there we go." The woman turned, beaming. The purple bundled baby's head was crusted with the caul. "She just needed her sister is all."

Teresa reached for the bundle, but the woman turned away again. Pain, though lesser, came again.

After she birthed the placenta, the pressure and pain subsided. She lay back exhausted. The large but soft man who knew who she was knelt down with a blue bucket and collected the placenta.

"What are you doing with that?" she snapped.

He looked up at her. "I'll freeze it for you," he said. "In case you want to do something with it." He scurried away with the bucket.

Teresa yearned to nurse her babies. She looked toward Lory, who held the purple-swaddled baby. She looked for the other one. The winged one. The young woman with long red hair held the pink-swathed baby.

Yaldabaoth drifted across the cave. No, not the cave. It was the living room in this old yucky house. But the cave flickered in and out like it was transposed underneath this image of the abandoned funeral home.

Lory slowly turned, gently bouncing the bundle in her arms. Yaldabaoth approached her. She would give the babies to him. He would take them from her to raise them in that pit of a cave. In Tartaros.

Lory seemed unaware of his clawed hand reaching toward the baby in the purple blanket—the one who had been so still and so quiet. His finger grazed her little neck.

Teresa screamed.

CHAPTER SIX

Maggie Hart sat on one end of the couch watching her last TV show of the night, while Ann sat at the dinner table, head bent over her laptop. Soon Maggie's show would end, and it would be bedtime.

Maggie still had nightmares every night. Weirder than any of the nightmares she had about Yaldabaoth when she used to dream about him stealing her light. Stealing *Sophia's* light.

Sophia had come to Maggie on her seventh birthday last year. She was a powerful entity who needed to be protected or humanity would be lost. She was Wisdom and mother of Yaldabaoth. He stole her light when she cast him from her. He used that light to create the world. Sometimes Sophia came forward in Maggie's brain, and when she did that, Maggie didn't know what went on around her. And during The Night—that's what Ann called that night last year when they all went to Tartaros to fight Yaldabaoth—Sophia had taken over. Maggie thought these nightmares might be memories instead of just dreams.

She would see herself in Yaldabaoth's hands, his snake

tail wrapped around her throat, her legs kicking as he lifted her off the ground. His yellow eyes held hers in their grip. She couldn't look away. Black cracks formed on her skin while the blue-white glow of Sophia's light drifted toward him, wrapping around his fingers in glowing tendrils. That's when Maggie *usually* woke up because it felt weird—like her skin was tight and it made her itch.

But sometimes Maggie saw Ann shoot Yaldabaoth in the tail and her own loose and floppy rag doll body fall onto the ground by the pool. Everything darkened in the nightmare then, until Ann brought her back to life with angel light, which Maggie knew had happened in real life because Ann had her hands over Maggie's heart.

Ann didn't like to talk about The Night, but Maggie knew the things she dreamed came from somewhere deep inside. Maybe Sophia was the one doing the dreaming.

Maggie didn't tell Ann about the dreams, because Ann had stopped coming to Maggie's room when she had them. Ann's Protector mark—which she got on Maggie's seventh birthday, even though Ann didn't know who Maggie was at the time—tingled for a few months after The Night whenever Maggie had bad dreams. It was Ann's duty to Protect Sophia, and the mark told her when Sophia—and Maggie—was in trouble or scared. But it either stopped working or Ann figured out it was just Maggie's dreams. Either way, she stopped coming.

It was okay. When Maggie woke up from the nightmares, her faithful doggie Pinky was there, and Pinky made everything all better.

The ending song of Maggie's show came on.

"Time for bed," Ann said in a snappy voice, finally turning away from her laptop to look at Maggie. "Go brush your teeth." Ann bossed her around like she was an older sister, not a guardian or a mom. Molly at school had an older sister who was super bossy. Molly always said so.

"What were you looking at on there?" Maggie asked as she made her way to the stairs.

"News stuff." Ann closed the laptop lid. "Go brush."

This was how it went.

Ann would tell her to brush her teeth. Maggie always did. Then Ann would sit next to her on the bed and read her a story, even though Maggie knew how to read. Then she'd pull the blankets up to Maggie's chin and pat Pinky up onto the bed next to Maggie. Maggie always hoped for a kiss on the top of her head—the way Derrick used to do it—or even on the cheek, even a hug, before she pulled the blankets up, trapping Maggie's arms beneath them. But Ann never did that.

Tonight she did all of this the same once again and said, "Goodnight, Mags," on her way out without a last look back. Maggie remembered when she lived at the Harts' house, Derrick used to come back after a time and peek in at her. She always pretended to sleep, but she cracked an eye open and saw him smiling at her. He was a good daddy. She missed him and how he used to put her hair in a sloppy ponytail that was always crooked and tighter on one side, but she would leave it because *he* did it. And he would buy her breakfast at the Muffin Store when Teresa forgot, which she did a lot. And he took her for pizza and made pancakes for dinner. And he hugged her. He'd only been her daddy for a little while, but he was a good daddy, and she loved him.

A tear slid down Maggie's cheek.

Teresa never had acted like she was her mommy, but Derrick had made up for it with all his daddy-ness.

Maggie stroked Pinky's head and counted the glow-in-the-dark stars that Ann had helped her put up on the ceiling.

This time, Maggie was thrust into a dream in which two beings waged war. Light against Dark. Screams and flashes and explosions filled this strange and empty place.

In the way of dreams, she suddenly blipped and was in Tartaros again with Yaldabaoth's tail wrapped around her throat, her skin crackling, her life slowly seeping toward him in tendrils and tentacles of light.

The blast from Ann's gun exploded. Maggie fell. She fell and fell and she didn't land, but she somehow slowed until she floated.

She was in an absent place. That's how it felt. Like an absence. Like when Pinky cuddled her, then got up to get a drink of water. That empty spot that cooled after a second of her being gone.

It was the way it felt when her *baba* took her from her parents and gave her to the Protectorate. To keep her safe, Mr. Bram told her. The place in her heart where her parents lived became empty. The same of her *baba* when he tried to hurt her and she understood without understanding that he was not a good person anymore. His spot was also an absence. Holes where happy memories once lived now filled with sadness.

Another empty spot was where Derrick used to live inside her heart. He left a big empty space.

Maggie thought—knew—if she lost anyone else, her entire heart would be like this place. Dark. Empty. Absent.

It was a dark and shapeless place seen only in nightmares like this. It was the abyss.

If you don't land, you don't wake up.

Yellow light appeared. Far away. Four spots.

Sophia stirred within Maggie's heart.

Luminaries.

Sophia told Maggie things sometimes. Things Maggie didn't know about.

The figures moved closer. Two boys and two girls. Tall, bright angels.

"Do not be afraid," the beings said in unison.

Maggie could not speak. She could not move. That was the way of nightmares sometimes.

"You are here now," they said as one. "But you should not be, for you have not yet perished." They came closer still.

One of the girl ones bent toward her. "Your light still shines."

The four were great angelic beings. They had long fine fingers, and faces so pretty she couldn't look directly at them, but she also couldn't stop herself from looking at them. Tears coursed down her cheeks. The Luminary wiped the tear away.

"New dangers alight upon the material realm," the other female said. "Your work is not yet done, Sophia."

"But you have *forsaken* us, Sophia." The taller male swiped his hand and glared at her. "You created that monster, and now look what has happened. You have unleashed more evils, more darkness, upon this realm."

Sophia hid deep inside Maggie's heart. Maggie could feel Sophia's fear of these creatures of light. Her sadness.

Maggie lifted her chin with a sudden need to protect Sophia from them.

"Tell me who you are," she choked out.

The angels leaned away from her and looked around at each other.

"She does not know us," the last female said. "To whom do we speak?"

"I'm Maggie," Maggie said. Then she crumbled. "I want to go home."

"Where is Sophia?" asked the other female, the one who wiped Maggie's tear.

Maggie pointed at her chest.

"A child holds within her the light of the mother of angels?" the taller male said. Maggie didn't like him.

"We are the Four Luminaries," the nice female said. "I am Eleleth. Come, let me see you." Eleleth bent forward and took Maggie's face in her hands. She gazed into Maggie's eyes so deeply that fresh tears leaked out.

After a few seconds, Eleleth pulled away and turned to the others.

"She has known death in others and now within herself." She turned back to Maggie. "You must protect the ones you love. For if you lose another, you shall surely return to the abyss."

Maggie's mark, which she also received on her seventh birthday, lit up with fierce fiery pain.

Ann sat at the table reading an article on Salida's news website, The Mountain Mail. She casually scrolled through it, and almost choked when a blond woman's picture scrolled by.

At first glance, she swore it was Teresa Hart. But it wasn't.

The woman, Carla Johnson, had gone missing. She was last seen heading out for her usual run on Tenderfoot Mountain. The thought of missing persons brought Ann back to the week leading up to The Night. *They* were all dead.

She shook the thought away and scratched absently at the mark on her chest. Once a searing brand, now a faded reminder of who she was.

On Maggie's seventh birthday, a time when Ann didn't even know Maggie existed yet, she had received the mark during a strenuous run in the woods. It was the Egyptian *Sa*. The mark of the Protector. It was her duty—bound by blood and soul—to protect Maggie.

The mark wasn't itchy, though. It was tingling. It used to burn with hot intensity when Maggie was in real trouble, but lately it only tingled if Maggie was upset.

"Probably just a nightmare," Ann whispered. She looked toward the top of the stairs, visible from her station in the dining room. She should go up. She hadn't checked on Maggie during a nightmare in a while. Part of her felt a little guilty about it. But Pinky was up there. Pinky would help her feel better when Maggie woke up. Ann turned back to her computer.

The tingle didn't subside. It intensified to more of a mild burning sensation. Like heartburn.

Pinky's paws thundered down the stairs. She poked Ann in the leg and ran to the landing. She looked over her shoulder.

Ann took the steps two at a time and pushed Maggie's door open.

The blue-white light that came to Maggie's eyes when Sophia spoke through her came from the girl's entire body. Ann rushed to Maggie's side and tried to shake her, but she was frozen stiff.

"Maggie? Maggie?" Ann's voice came out frantic. The pain in her mark sharpened, like a stab. Ann gasped. Then the sensation went away completely.

The light sucked back inside Maggie's body. She gasped awake. Ann pulled the girl into her arms.

"Maggie?" Ann whispered. Pinky nudged Maggie's face with her nose. Snuffled her ear.

Maggie opened her eyes. "Just a nightmare," she said. "It was only a nightmare."

CHAPTER SEVEN

"I'm so sorry," Lory said. She bustled over to Teresa, carefully laying a baby in the crook of each of Teresa's arms. They were so small and so light. Tiny little babies. That's how twins always were.

The baby in the pink blanket—whom Teresa had seen as a demon thing—latched perfectly. Teresa gazed down at her, at her pink fleshy face, at the little pink fists with ten fingers and *no* claws. Tears dribbled down Teresa's cheeks.

"She's just so beautiful," she said, unable to hide the relief in her voice.

The second baby, the one in purple who had been so still and silent, had a little bit of trouble latching at first, but finally did. She was a little smaller than her sister.

They were both so beautiful. They were both hers. She just wanted to nuzzle them and hold them close. Closer still than they already were. Teresa sobbed because of the adrenaline of the escape and the release of having her babies.

"As soon as you're done nursing," Lory said, "we'll get

you to a more comfortable location, something much more private"—she looked around and grimaced—"and clean."

"The cops used to patrol here all the time," said the man who had collected the placenta. He looked at his watch. "In fact, we should get a move on soon—just in case." He looked at Lory, then to Teresa.

"That's why Paul and I do the tours at night." The young woman gestured to the man. "I'm his sister. Patrina." She held out her hand, realized Teresa couldn't shake hers back, gave a sheepish shrug, and lowered it to her lap.

"What exactly are these tours for?" Teresa asked.

Paul grinned. Teresa noticed the edge of the bucket partially hidden behind the end of the couch.

"Teresa Hart Tours." He pulled a wrinkled piece of paper from his back pocket and handed it to Patrina, who unfolded it to show Teresa.

It was a brochure printed on orange paper. It spoke of the abandoned funeral home being the place where it all happened. It touted the Teresa Hart Murders. Come see where the most dangerous woman in Harmony carried out her ill deeds.

Teresa's mouth went dry. "It didn't all happen here," she said.

It happened in Tartaros.

She was suddenly weary and in need of a good hard sleep of the type she hadn't had since before Tiffany came to her back in October.

"This is fantastic." Paul paced. "We have *her*, the *real* Teresa Hart. We can fill in all the blanks of what happened." He suddenly stopped pacing and turned to her. "You'll tell us, won't you?" He crouched at the far end of the couch and touched her feet. She twitched them away. She would never tell him. She refused to relive it.

"Paul, please," Patrina snapped at her brother. "Don't you realize? As soon as the sheriff finds out Teresa's out—no, we have to protect her." She turned to Teresa. "I'm so sorry for my brother's ignorance."

Teresa liked Patrina.

"I need to burp these babies," Teresa said as both something she needed help with and as a way to change the subject. The sheriff. Yes. Ann would blow up the town looking for her.

Hopefully Raghib's *impostor* would help give Teresa more time before that happened.

Lory took the purple baby from Teresa's arms, and Patrina helped Teresa sit up.

After they burped the babies, Lory kept the purple one in her arms.

"You can walk, yes?" she asked.

"I think so." Her legs weren't broken, but she was so tired.

They walked through the cemetery with the lost souls bobbing and dipping around. Teresa nuzzled the baby in her arms. Ahead of her, Lory cooed at the other one.

Louise's old house loomed in the distance.

"We're not going—" Teresa swallowed hard. Louise was gone. That old crone couldn't betray her again. Or make Teresa feed dog food and compost scraps to a prisoner in the basement. Don't forget cauterizing his severed finger stumps.

Teresa held the pink baby closer. Lory waltzed up Louise's steps and opened the front door. "Welcome home," she said, stepping aside. Teresa went in.

It was completely different than the last time she'd been there. The sunken living room held modern furniture that looked comfortable as well as stylish. The Formica table had been replaced by a little wooden one with a split down the middle for a leaf, Teresa presumed.

The heavy door that led down to Louise's basement of terrors had been replaced with a regular door. No heavy bolt to keep it locked.

No cats, not even the clinging pungent odor of them, were anywhere to be seen.

Lory led Teresa down the hallway past the basement door to another room off the hallway. A guest room, it would seem, but the queen-size bed was covered in clothes still on hangers.

"I was cleaning out some old things to donate when Levi came to get me." Lory handed the purple baby to Patrina. "Paul, help me clear off the bed."

Paul lifted the clothes carefully by the hangers.

"Back in the closet, I suppose." Lory waved a hand. He put the clothes back in. "If there's anything in there you'd like," Lory said to Teresa and Patrina. She gave them a little shrug.

"Where will my babies sleep?" Teresa looked around. The room had a rocking chair and a dresser.

"I've heard of mothers putting their babies in laundry baskets while they do laundry," Patrina said, swaying and nuzzling the purple baby. She looked up. "It would at least keep them safe and contained."

Lory bustled out of the room and returned with a rectangular laundry basket. She placed a pillow and blanket from under her arm in the bottom, took the purple baby from Patrina, and nestled her inside. Teresa did the same with the pink baby. They were so small, they fit perfectly.

Teresa sat on the edge of the bed and gazed down at the

two little lives snuggled together. When she looked up, Lory had shooed Paul and Patrina out of the room.

"I'll make you something to eat," Lory said. "Why don't you get cleaned up? Then you can have a rest."

"Thank you," Teresa said. "For helping me, especially knowing who I am." A thought that she should be afraid, that she shouldn't trust this woman, flickered through her mind. "You won't call the police, will you? While I'm in the shower?" Teresa rose to her feet, ready to snatch the basket and make off with her children.

"You're safe here." Lory touched Teresa's arm. "Get cleaned up. I'll keep an ear out for the littles while you bathe." She led Teresa to the bathroom where she ran a bath.

While Teresa bathed, soaking in water hotter than any she'd had on her body in months—the showers at Mountain View couldn't get above lukewarm—she thought of names for her babies. They came to her as she drifted away, immersed in rose-scented bubbles.

Cassie and Amanda. She smiled.

After her bath, she lay in a bed far cozier than the one she'd been sleeping in at Mountain View. The mattress was soft and seemed to ooze around her body in a gentle hug of comfort and safety.

Everything was so much better. She wondered if it would end. How it would end. What would she have to do to keep this comfort and safety? To keep her daughters safe?

Was she even safe?

Lory bustled in with a bowl of steaming soup and a piece of crusty bread on a tray. She set the tray over Teresa's lap.

While Teresa sipped the broth, Lory peered into the laundry basket on the bed next to Teresa.

"Aren't they just the dearest," she said in a quiet voice. "What are you going to call them?"

Teresa watched her warily. With the tray across her lap, she felt trapped. She didn't like that feeling.

"Cassie and Amanda." Teresa liked the sound of the names. They felt right. When she'd named Tiffany, she'd tried a couple of different options before finally deciding. She tested them by introducing her to the nurses who played along as if Teresa hadn't introduced them already. They laughed when Teresa shook her head and told them, "That's not the right name."

Oh, what a different time and a different life.

"What lovely names," Lory said giving Teresa a smile before returning her gaze to the sleeping babies. "It's good to keep them near each other. They've been together since conception."

Teresa dipped some of the crusty bread into her soup to mop up the last bits of broth and observed Lory. She had long, badly bleached hair. The roots were brassy orange, and the lengths were buttery, as if whoever did her dye job —presumably it was box color—didn't realize her hair would not lift to the color she likely wanted. She had a medium skin tone that really did not look quite right with that color, and kind brown eyes. Her skin was beautiful, slightly aged, but in a way that made it difficult to tell how old she was. But her mannerisms and the way she spoke with a lightly accented voice gave Teresa the impression she might be old enough to have children of drinking age at least.

"Who are you?" Teresa asked her. "Why are you helping me?"

Lory turned from the basket. "That is a conversation for tomorrow. We can discuss . . . well, why you're safe here, and you can tell me more. About your escape, I mean.

Tonight is spent." She lifted the tray from across Teresa's lap. "Just know, you are safe."

The way she said it sounded like she wanted to add more to the end of the sentence.

Teresa added it for her. *For now.*

CHAPTER EIGHT

Teresa dreamed about walking through the woods. The sound of flapping wings in the outside world made birds appear.

I need to wake up.

She did.

A figure with a triangular shaped head atop a set of small but muscular shoulders perched at the foot of the bed. A tail curled over its feet and dangled off the mattress.

Teresa scrambled away. She landed on the floor with a sharp jar to her hip and shoulder. She peeked over the mattress and shot a look toward the door. Could she make it, open it, and run out before this thing launched from its perch?

She couldn't leave her babies.

The black shape spread massive wings for such a small body. They stretched the length of the queen bed. It let out a cry and jumped into the air. As it did, the winged form fell away, like a sheet drifting down after being fluffed.

Teresa let out a shriek, lunged for the lamp, and clicked it on.

Cassie lay on the bed, her eyes wide open, staring up at Teresa. Remnants of leathery skin clung to her arms. They slowly disappeared, like the quick evaporation of rubbing alcohol. Amanda was still swaddled like a tiny little package and still asleep inside the laundry basket. Cassie started to cry.

Teresa lifted the baby into her arms.

"Oh, my sweet baby," she said in a soothing voice. "I'm here."

Amanda woke, too, but she didn't cry. The little bundle of her body rocked a little as she squirmed. She just looked up at Teresa holding her sister.

She had hallucinated, she was sure. The Thorithium's last hold on her perhaps. A result of what she *thought* she saw the night of their birth.

In that cave. In Tartaros. But no. Not there. Teresa didn't know. She had no proof of where she birthed these babies. No proof of anything.

For all she knew, she was still at Mountain View and these babies were dolls she'd fashioned out of pillows and old clothing.

CHAPTER NINE

Sheriff Ann Logan stuck her finger through her father's ring on a gold chain strung around her neck. She stood at the edge of the woods with Pinky, a fawn-colored pit bull she'd sort of rescued. The dog stared intently into the darkness between the trees, ears alert, her body rigid with anticipation.

"In position?" Ann spoke into her radio and gave Rachel —the department's dispatcher, and now Ann's close friend —a sideways glance. Rachel held an iPad that was connected to the camera mounted on the back of Pinky's Kevlar vest.

An affirmative response came over their radios.

Ann crouched next to Pinky. The dog turned her head enough to lick Ann's face. Ann held up her hand against the slobber, still unable to allow kisses, knowing what the dog had eaten *months* ago. Then Pinky turned back to the woods.

"Pinky, wait," Ann said. The dog's muscles tightened

even more. Ann unhooked her leash. Pinky trembled and issued a high-pitched whine, like she was a balloon running out of air. "Find."

Pinky blasted into the woods. Ann joined Rachel to watch the camera bounce and jostle along with the pit bull leaping over low bushes and fallen logs, and dodging tree trunks. The camera captured the back of her head and her half-up-half-down ears flopping every which way as she bounded across the detritus on the forest floor.

Finally, Pinky came to a stop, head held high, ears perked. She took off again, and seconds later, Maggie's face and hands came into view. Pinky smothered her in dog kisses. Maggie's delighted laughter followed.

"She didn't even sniff the ground once," Rachel said. "Look." She played back the video.

"That's what I was afraid of," Ann said. She wanted to train Pinky to be a police dog to assist her during arrests, pursuits, and things of that nature—not that there was a lot of that going on in Harmony. But still. The dog was too much of a marshmallow, though. So, Ann thought, maybe a search and rescue dog. The new wave of tourists, who often went off trail, were prone to getting lost in the mountains surrounding Harmony.

Before sending Maggie into the woods, Ann had hid, followed by Rachel, but Pinky couldn't find either one of them no matter how easy they made it.

Maggie, on the other hand, could hide in the back of a speeding car and Pinky would chase it down to get her. On the one hand, great! Maggie could use a little extra protection when Ann wasn't around. On the other hand, there went Ann's goal to have a dog on the small force that made up the Castle County Sheriff's Department.

"She can sense Maggie. She doesn't have to use her nose." Ann peered into the woods.

"Because of Sophia?" Rachel asked with a raised eyebrow and wry expression.

Ann had filled Rachel in on the happenings of The Night and the events leading up to it. Ann needed an ally who knew what had gone down, who knew the whole story, and who could help her in the event of an emergency. Rachel had listened to the details with skepticism written all over her face, but she seemed to accept it enough to help Ann out when she needed a babysitter.

Ann's mark tingled. She jerked her head up to the trees just as Pinky came sprinting out. The dog ran into Ann's leg, bounced once onto her hind feet, made a panicky sort of grumbling whine, and took off again. Ann chased after, all at once reminded of The Night when a similar pursuit ended in finding a small pile of dead bodies.

She sprinted around a large cluster of tightly packed aspens, just as Pinky's tail flicked out of sight.

"Maggie?" Ann spotted the girl cowering by a tree trunk. Maggie pointed. Ann's eyes followed the direction of that little finger.

The smell of it hit her first. Death. Unmistakable. Rotting, putrescent, death. Then the sound. Flies buzzing in and out. She expected a body. A human body. The sight of the bloated deer carcass in the bushes didn't alleviate any of her apprehension. It was still something large and something dead.

She rushed to Maggie's side and put herself between the girl and the deer. Tears stood on Maggie's cheeks. Her gaze focused on Ann. Her eyes lit blue-white. Her skin glowed.

"Light and dark . . . life and death . . . life not life . . .

death not death . . ." Sophia's voice. The light sucked back into Maggie's chest and left her eyes. Words streamed out of Maggie the girl, not the voice of Wisdom.

"I was hiding and Pinky found me, and then—and then I heard the flies." Maggie wiped the back of her hand on her cheek. Her breath hitched as she spoke. "I was just curious. I saw something there. I couldn't stop. I had to look. So I went and looked."

Ann shushed her gently. "It's okay."

"Is it a person? Who is it? Is it someone I know?" Her voice raised a couple octaves. Panic. Shock. Shit.

"Calm down. It's just a deer."

Rachel stepped through the bushes. "Aw Maggie, what's—oh fuck me." Her hand flew to her nose. "Is that a deer?" Unlike Ann, Rachel had no issue using bad language in front of children. Maybe that was one point toward Ann's "acceptable as a guardian" badge.

"My tummy hurts." There was little warning. Maggie threw up her lunch all over Ann's boots. Rachel gagged audibly. Pinky sniffed at the pile of vomit. Ann pushed the dog away.

"Come on, let's get out of here." She helped Maggie to her feet. The girl didn't let go of Ann's hand when they started walking.

Pinky walked next to Maggie with ears perked and with full attention on her well-being to such an extent the dog almost ran into several tree trunks. Maggie kept a hand on Pinky's back—for balance, moral support, or both. Ann did not know.

CHAPTER TEN

Despite the fact that Maggie threw up and wasn't feeling well, Ann stopped at the station. Probably another mark *against* her guardian badge. She got Maggie settled on the sofa with Pinky cuddled next to her.

Ann brushed a stray hair off of Maggie's forehead. "We won't be here long, okay?" She thought Maggie might have felt hot, but she didn't really know temperature by touch like a real mother.

Ann went back out to the bullpen, leaving Pinky to watch over Maggie.

The new deputy, Cindy Hudgins, and Deputy Hank "Sully" Sullivan sat at two of the three desks in the bullpen. Cindy had a stack of case files and a label maker.

"You're making me look bad with all this extraneous work you're doing," Sully said. He tossed a racquet ball into the air and caught it.

"Just trying to get things organized around here," Cindy said. "Besides, since when is filing extraneous? How can you find anything if you don't have a filing system?" Cindy's eyes darted to the lopsided stack of case files on Sully's desk.

Ann didn't think he'd filed since the day he walked into the station responding to the job posting.

Ann smirked and went through the saloon-style doors into the kitchenette. She opened the fridge expecting to find the usual—a mostly empty and fully expired carton of half-and-half and an old box of moldy pizza. Instead, she found the shelves stocked with orange juice, a few different flavored creamers, fresh fruit, sodas, bottled water, and more.

"Who stocked the fridge?" she called out.

"Deputy Hudgins—" Sully said, using Cindy's professional title but with a small amount of sarcastic disdain in his voice.

"Me," Cindy said at the same time, bright and cheery as usual.

"Good work, Deputy Hudgins." Ann grabbed a sparkling water for herself and a ginger ale for Maggie and stepped back into the bullpen. "Keep it up and you'll be head deputy before too long." Ann said it to get Sully's goat. She laughed when he made a sound of disbelief.

"Sully, why don't you go patrol out at the old funeral home." Ann caught his ball before it could land in his big mitt.

He turned to her with a sheepish expression. He was so much like her previous deputy, George Riley, who had been killed last year in the events leading up to The Night. The biggest difference was Sully knew how to do police work. He'd graduated from the academy, but his sick father brought him back home to Harmony. He didn't want his training to go to waste, so he signed on as deputy under Ann. She could understand his position and was more than happy to have him on her team.

"Sure," he said. "I mean, yes, ma'am Sheriff." He got up

and slapped a Castle County Sheriff's Department ball cap on his head.

"Take a radio with you," Ann said, "just in case."

In the eight and a half months since The Night, word of the case in Harmony had spread, bringing tourism back to the little town. Because of that, a cell tower had been erected nearby. Though coverage within the city limits was pretty good, the farther "out the road" one went the spottier it became.

Sully retrieved one of the long-range radios from the locker room where they sat on their chargers. He clipped it to his belt and, with a touch to the brim of his hat, ducked out the door. Literally ducked. Ann thought he was probably taller than George.

She turned back to Cindy, who was dutifully making labels for the case files. In need of a change of scenery, Cindy had moved to town within the past few months. She came from Pine Valley, so the scenery was mostly the same, just . . . smaller. More rural.

Ann slipped back into her office. Maggie snoozed away, light snores escaping her partially open mouth. Pinky snored along with her. Ann opened her laptop and browsed to the Mountain Mail site again to see if there were any updates on the missing woman. She itched to have a case like that. Straightforward. Normal. No supernatural bullshit to get in the way. Hell, she'd take supernatural over nothing at all. There were no developments in the case.

She clicked over to *Harmony's Community Happenings*, which had changed hands and moved online. She hadn't seen anything like Brent's *Local Inquirer* since. At the thought of Pinky's previous owner, Ann glanced at the dog.

The front page of the Happenings had an exposé-style

interview with Duke Westley. Ann scoffed. Pinky lifted her head and let out a grumble, and just then a commotion came from the bullpen. A booming voice asked for Ann Logan.

It was Duke fucking Westley. The guy who planned to run against her for sheriff in the fall.

Maggie lay on the couch curled around her tummy. It hurt. Not a bad hurt, but a soft and fluffy kind of hurt. Pinky's warmth made it feel a little better, but Maggie knew the only thing that would stop the gross feeling was a hug from Ann.

That or her nest of blankets on the couch at home and a Disney movie on the TV. *Frozen* or *Moana*.

The deer frightened her. She hadn't thought of the nightmares about the Luminaries and the abyss until she spotted it. She thought it was a person. She was too scared to move closer to see. And the buzzing flies made her sick.

The worst part was Sophia shifting around in her chest like she was darting in and out of the empty spaces where Maggie's loved ones used to live. It made her heart feel tight and fluttery. It reminded her she had to protect the ones she loved.

"There she is," Duke said when Ann stepped out of her office.

"Can you please lower your voice?" Ann peered over her shoulder. Maggie had shifted a little.

"Why?" He hadn't lowered his voice. "You got a *baby*

sleeping in there?" He gave a derisive snort. "Nice to see you, too, *Ann.*"

Cindy kept her head down, making labels for Sully's case files now. Ann smoothed her fingertips over her eyebrow.

Even with whatever life experiences he'd had since high school, Duke was the same obnoxious teenager he'd been when she used to hang out with him. He had been the gooniest of Derrick's goon friends.

Duke laughed. It wasn't a contemptuous sound like she was expecting. It was a chuckle.

"You are such a goddamn hard-ass. What happened to you to get so hard? I mean, sure, you always had ambition, but damn, girl. You are a hard. Ass." He winked at her. "It's kind of sexy."

"Oh fuck you, Duke."

Cindy lifted her head at that and looked at Ann.

Duke laughed again. "Listen." He took two steps farther into the station. "We obviously got off on the wrong foot." He had a mansplaining sort of tone. "Not sure how or why. Maybe you were in a bad mood, maybe I overstepped my bounds a bit, maybe . . ." He held his hands like scales, weighing back and forth before apparently deciding to leave it at that.

Ann scoffed. Duke had sauntered into town four weeks ago as if he were the prodigal son returned home to lead his people. She'd come into the office to find him *lounging* at the open desk in the triad of desks in the bullpen, shooting the shit with Sully while Cindy diligently went about doing any work she saw needed attention.

He announced then his plan to run against her in the fall. Give the town of Harmony a *proper* sheriff. As if someone with zero law enforcement background could possibly do a better job.

Sully stood up for Ann, of course, telling Duke Ann *was* a proper sheriff. He told Duke about all she'd done in Salida and about the homicide case in Harmony last year.

"Seven people dead or missing? You call that successful?" He laughed that mightier-than-thou laugh she had never grown accustomed to but had learned to ignore when they were in high school.

Ann had stood, silently fuming. She had no come-backs for this idiot. She took the high road and told him to get out of her station, that they had important work to do and he was keeping them from it.

Duke had laughed again, but stood and picked up his ball cap from the desk. He threw one last dig at her.

"Couldn't handle it, could you? Detective work, I mean? Shooting a guy? That's why you're *here*." He motioned around the little sheriff's office that had become home to her.

"Get out."

"Or what? You'll call the police?" Duke laughed heartily at that. He looked at Sully as if Sully would give him a high five.

Instead, Sully had stood. Duke was a big guy, but Sully was bigger. "You're going to have to leave. Now."

Duke had given Ann a mock salute and a sneer before sauntering out. Now, here he was again, wearing that same stupid grin and wasting her time.

Pinky shook off in the other room, tags jangling.

Duke crouched down. "Who's this?" his voice changed completely.

Ann glanced over her shoulder where Pinky stood in the doorway, ears perked curiously.

Oh Pinky, don't you dare.

But it was inevitable. Pinky loved almost everyone. She bounded over to him all wiggle-butt, tail lashing herself in the face. Snorts. Licks. And finally, the collapse —mostly onto her side with her butt in the air. The last betrayal was the final flop and the roll onto her back, exposing her belly.

"Oh what a sweet little thing. What's your name, pooch? Huh? What's your name?" Duke's voice raised a few octaves.

"Her name's Pinky," Ann all but growled.

"Oh Pinky, oh look at you. Of course it's Pinky. Look at your pink mouth and nose." Duke rubbed her ears. "What's your role in this little Podunk department?" he asked Pinky in babying tones.

Ann could actually feel heat rising to her head like a volcano.

"This is some dog, let me tell you. Look how pretty she is. Look at this face." Pinky gave him kisses right on his mouth, which Duke allowed.

"She ate her previous owner's remains," Ann said. Duke got up from the floor.

"You're serious?"

She met his eyes and raised her eyebrows.

Duke looked at her with a smile, then frowned when he apparently saw she was serious. He eyed Pinky, who sat and pawed the air near his leg, mouth gaping in that classic pit bull grin.

Cindy rose from her desk. "I'm going to run across the street for a latte, you want anything, Sheriff?"

Ann didn't blame her for wanting to get out of there. The tension, though broken by Pinky's appearance, could be scooped with a spoon.

"Black drip for me, sweetheart." Duke winked at Cindy who frowned in response. Her eyes darted to Ann.

"I'm good," she said. "Maybe an Italian soda for Maggie? Raspberry?"

Cindy nodded, collected her purse from her desk drawer, and hurried out. Ann quickly texted her to tell her not to get Duke anything.

"Who's Maggie?" Duke asked, looking around as if another deputy were hiding somewhere.

"My . . . daughter." Ann felt weird referring to Maggie as her daughter, but it beat the alternative.

The girl I'm now the guardian of because I'm The *Protector.*

That would probably raise more questions than just calling her *daughter*.

"*You* have a *daughter?*" Duke looked her up and down as if assessing her physical ability to bear children.

Ann scowled and moved to the dispatch desk. "I have a lot to do." She sorted through the mail again. "Was there something you needed other than gloating about how you think you're going to win in the fall?" She didn't look up from her task, even though she was back to the beginning of the stack.

Duke leaned against the wall. "All work and no time for catching up. I see how it is. I used to be that way. Taking myself too seriously. Working hard to prove myself to everyone."

Because it's so hard being a white male in America.

It was hard to see him as anything but a bulky frat-boy type who called himself The Duke and stood on tables in the lunchroom making absurd—and oftentimes lewd —proclamations.

"I'm going to win, Ann," Duke said, his voice darkening. "I'm going to win, and I'll own this town just like I used to."

Ann belted out a single *ha* at that. "You think you owned this town?" She moved to the filing cabinet. "I think this town owned *you*." She opened the appropriate drawer and found his file—all thanks to Cindy's filing system—and yanked it out. It was over an inch thick. She slammed it down on Sully's desk.

"Let's begin, shall we?" She opened the cover. "Petty theft at fourteen, drunk and disorderly at—Oh, Duke— fifteen?" She gave him what she hoped was a condescending look. "Petty theft, petty theft . . . Joy ride? Another drunk and disorderly at seventeen. Need I go on?" She glanced up at him.

Duke lifted his hands in mock surrender and opened his mouth to speak.

"Ann?" Maggie's voice came from the office. Ann turned. Pinky stood next to her in the doorway like a support dog. Maggie's hand rested on the dog's shoulder.

"All good, Maggie?" Ann asked, softening her voice. "Feeling okay?"

Maggie shook her head and cast her eyes downward. Ann could see just from looking at her she didn't feel well.

Ann turned back to Duke. She lowered her voice. "You have no business coming here the way you have been, acting like you own the place, drinking our bad coffee, putting your boots up on our desks, distracting my deputies." She looked him up and down and shook her head. He honestly truly believed he would beat her in the election later in the year.

Pinky gave a whine and a chuff from her position by Maggie. Ann swore the dog could tell when emotions were high, even if it wasn't Maggie who was upset. Her tail was tucked between her legs. She plodded over to Ann and looked up at her and at Duke.

Duke stomped his foot at Pinky for no apparent reason, his big foot thumping against the floor with an alarming *boom*. Maggie gave a startled cry. Pinky skittered back to Ann's office and huddled next to Maggie.

"Big scary-looking dog like that, you'd think she wouldn't be such a *pussy*." He laughed that cocky laugh from high school and left, bumping into Cindy in the doorway so hard she almost dropped their drinks.

CHAPTER ELEVEN

Teresa sat in the rocker, relishing the fact that she had not one beautiful life, but *two*. How could she be so blessed? Two little lives and they were all hers.

Ours, Yaldabaoth's voice prickled. *You admitted it yourself.*

Teresa willed the voice away.

Lory and Paul had brought in a crib and set it up against the wall to the right of the bed. She moved from the rocker to the bed and lay down, but when she closed her eyes all she could see was Yaldabaoth looking at her, as if his eyes were tattooed on the insides of her eyelids.

She blamed it on the Thorithium. She could only imagine how many withdrawal symptoms there might be from it. Every other antipsychotic had been miserable to taper off.

This one she'd quit cold turkey. It was only a matter of time before the voices would get really bad. She would probably start seeing them. All of them. They would crowd around her, close in, hands groping.

She cringed.

Unable to relax, she sat up and looked down into the laundry basket at her babies. Though she had a crib for them now, she liked having them closer to her on the bed during the day.

Amanda's eyes were open. She peered up at Teresa. Teresa stroked her little cheek. The baby made a delighted little sound—the first she'd made since her initial cry in that . . . cave. Was it a cave? She couldn't be sure. Everything was so strange that night.

Had Yaldabaoth really touched Amanda? Or had it been a hallucination? Teresa shifted the little one's blanket aside. She knew there was a mark there on her neck, but she wanted to really look at it. It could just be a birthmark. Amanda looked up at Teresa.

The mark was just a spot on her neck that was a little redder and a little darker than her fair skin. It would probably fade, like Tiffany's stork bite had. Yaldabaoth hadn't touched her. Teresa nodded, agreeing with herself.

If he had, though, what would it mean?

Little Amanda still gazed upward with her gray newborn eyes. Teresa wondered what color Cassie and Amanda's eyes would be—blue like hers, or dark like Derrick's? Or yellow. Like Yaldabaoth.

She frowned.

Both babies had a light fuzzy dusting of blond hair. That could change, too, she supposed.

A knock came at the door.

"Come in," Teresa said.

Lory entered with a tray of breakfast and something under her arm. Teresa sat on the bed but didn't climb in to have the tray placed over her like an invalid. She could very well sit up and eat her meals.

Lory set the tray on the mattress. From under her arm, she pulled a turtle-shaped thing.

"It's a night-light," Lory said. "It plays white noise and casts colorful lights on the ceiling. I thought the babies might like it. It might help you, too. The white noise, I mean."

"Thank you." Teresa placed it on the nightstand.

"Do you mind if we talk while you eat?" Lory asked.

Teresa shook her head and took a bite of scrambled eggs. She was famished after feeding Cassie and Amanda. Producing sustenance for one baby, let alone two, burned a lot of calories.

"Tell me about the escape," Lory said.

Teresa swallowed the bite she'd just taken and told Lory everything, from Raghib's visit to the woman in her room to getting into solitary confinement and beyond. She told Lory about the woman who looked like her whom they'd put in her cell when they'd pulled Teresa out.

"Someone crashed our car off the road."

"Who?" Lory asked, breathless. She'd listened to Teresa's story with rapt attention, eyes wide.

Teresa shook her head. "I don't know. Raghib told me to run."

Lory blanched. "Run? While over eight months pregnant with twins?"

Teresa shrugged. "I got away, didn't I?"

Lory laughed. "Yes, you did."

"It was a van. White with a red stripe. Like it was trying to be an ambulance or something. But it wasn't. It was just one of those big cargo vans." Teresa bit into her toast, chewed it contemplatively, swallowed.

"Who is Raghib?" Lory asked.

"Just someone—a friend I guess." She hoped he got

away. Maybe he would come find her and take her wherever he had planned to take her.

He probably died.

"Why are you helping me? If you know who I am, what I did to all those people?"

Lory brushed at her black pants. She smiled at Teresa, meeting her eyes with a genuine sort of affection. "I believe in you, Teresa. I believe what happened to you was influenced from outside. From beyond our, well, realm."

Teresa nodded, not allowing her eyes to drift from Lory's. Yaldabaoth was definitely from beyond their realm.

"I know you did horrible things, but I also know you did them for a greater good beyond yourself."

Teresa shook her head. That wasn't true. Was it? She killed seven people in an attempt to restore happiness to her marriage. Her life. Nothing more than that. A cold sensation dripped down her spine. Teresa lowered the half-eaten toast to the tray.

"I know, in the end, something terrible happened. Something so terrible it broke you." Lory's expression had moved from kindness to grief-stricken pity.

"He betrayed me," Teresa whispered. "He promised me things, but after I did what he asked, he betrayed me."

"You loved him?"

Teresa scowled and rubbed the lines away from between her eyes with her fingertips. "No."

"You bore his children."

"These are *not* his children." This time Teresa allowed the scowl.

"I'm sorry." Lory held up her hands. "I won't press you. I can see it was a difficult time." She looked at the basket and rose from her seat a little. Her face softened into a dewy and glassy-eyed expression reserved for babies.

Teresa picked up her toast. "Tell me more about yourself."

Lory lifted her chin. "I'm Lory Magan. I recently moved here to Harmony after hearing of Louise Marga's demise."

The chill trickled faster. Teresa looked from her spot on the bed to the basket holding her babies and then to the door.

Teresa wiped her mouth. "Did you know her?" She lifted the glass of orange juice to her lips and took a sip.

Lory nodded. "I did."

Teresa choked on the juice. She spluttered and coughed into her napkin, shaking the tray and the basket with the babies in it. She stood to stop the jostling.

Lory held her hands up in a halting gesture. "Hear me out before coming to any conclusions."

"Conclusions? You're with them, aren't you? The Messengers of the Light?" If Teresa were by herself, she would run. Leap over the bed, maybe kick the tray into Lory's lap, sprint out of there. As it was, her fight-or-flight response had kicked into overdrive. A hot panic coursed into her extremities.

But she couldn't exactly get away with a laundry basket full of babies tucked under her arm. Aside from that, she'd be recognized. Surely everyone in Harmony was on the lookout for her by now. She needed to change her appearance. Dye her hair or get some tinted contacts or something more drastic. A new face.

"Please, Dr. Hart. Please calm down. Just listen to what I have to say."

Teresa did not relax. She pulled the basket closer.

"I *was* a Messenger of the Light. I was." She looked at her hands in her lap, plucked at a white thing clinging to the black fabric. "I fell out of favor with them."

Teresa huffed out a laugh. "How do you fall out of favor with an organization like that?" She moved a little closer, drawn to her half-eaten breakfast still on the tray.

"I don't care to discuss that right now. I just want you to know I am no longer associated with them."

"Are the others part of the Messengers? Paul and Patrina. Levi—"

"No. Not at all." Lory held up her hands. "They know nothing about the Messengers."

"Who are they then?" Teresa lowered herself onto the bed and lifted her toast. The unsettled feeling still lingered there with her. She needed some sort of proof that Lory wasn't working with those wretched people.

"They are kind of like a morbid book club, I guess you could say. They were drawn here by your story. They are fanatics, really. Especially Paul. He started this group." She smiled fondly.

"How did you get in with them?" Teresa asked.

"Paul runs an apothecary and gift shop in town. When he moved here and opened it, I stopped in. We got to talking. His main downfall is easily trusting others. He gave me his life story—his and Patrina's. Their parents passed and left them a sum of money. Paul was always interested in"—she looked down—"serial killers. But all the *good* ones —his words, not mine—already had a following."

Teresa could deduce the rest. He and Patrina had moved to town, opened the shop, and here they were, living Paul's dream.

"What about Patrina? Was she really okay with all of this? What about the others? How did he recruit them?"

"Patrina adores her brother. As for the others? People have secrets," Lory said, "hidden desires, deep-seated hopes and wishes. I don't know how he found the others, but here they are. And with tourists coming to town again—because of your case, oddly enough—the tour gets a handful of takers a couple times a week."

Teresa finished her breakfast. She moved the tray.

"I'm going to need my medication soon," she said in a low voice.

"You don't need it," Lory said. "We need your mind clear of that drug. It was experimental, and we don't really know what it might have done to your babies, nor what it might do to them while breastfeeding."

"Dr. Andrews said it was safe."

"There's no telling what Dr. Andrews would have told you to keep you in a constant state of compliance so your delusions would not come out. But we need your delusions, Teresa. You are the only one who can talk to him."

"To Dr. Andrews?"

"No," Lory said with a laugh. "You are the only one who can talk to Yaldabaoth."

"Yaldabaoth is dead. Besides, you aren't a Messenger, so why do you care if I can speak to him?" The panic began to build again.

Lory lifted her hands and stood. Teresa pulled the basket toward her and scooted away. Lory halted.

"I may no longer be a Messenger, but I still believe, Teresa." Lory sat on the end of the bed. "I lived that life for a long time. I may no longer be a slave to my devotion, but I still believe the scriptures. Your babies are special." She turned and looked Teresa in the eyes. "I will do everything within my power to keep them safe. To ensure they thrive. As long as you are staying under my roof, I guarantee that."

"That doesn't change the fact that he's dead."

"He might not be," Lory said, her voice rising in excitement. "No one knows if you can die in Tartaros. Think about it."

Teresa shushed her.

"Sorry. Think about it," Lory continued in a whisper. "A being in Tartaros is supposedly already dead, correct? Otherwise, why or how would they be there?"

By going through the abandoned funeral home, of course. But she kept quiet.

"You can't really die twice," Lory said. "He might still be there, a shell of himself once again."

Yaldabaoth's laugh—seductive and sickening—echoed in her mind. Her scalp tickled. Teresa closed her eyes. Behind the dark lids, she saw his gleaming yellow predator eyes staring back at her. She opened them and lifted her chin.

"Thank you for breakfast. I need to rest while they're still asleep." Teresa swung her legs up onto the bed.

Lory lifted the tray and moved toward the door.

"Am I allowed to go outside? Get some fresh air? Or are we stuck in here until you get what you need from us? Obviously, you want them to thrive for some purpose. There's always an agenda, Messengers of the Light or not."

"You aren't a prisoner." Lory's mouth tightened into a thin line. "Whenever you want to go outside, just let me know." She backed out of the room, toeing the door closed behind her.

Teresa climbed off the bed and listened until the woman's footsteps dissipated.

"She's out of her mind," she whispered. "Talk to Yaldabaoth?" She sat on the bed again, reached into the laundry basket, and caressed Cassie's cheek. Cassie made a sleepy grunting sound. Teresa stroked Amanda's face to the same effect.

She scooted back, pulling the basket to position it on the bed next to her, and lay back on her pillow. She closed her eyes. There they were. Those eyes staring back into her own.

"Yaldabaoth," Teresa whispered, hating his name on her lips. "Are you there?"

Silence in her mind and only the soft sleeping sounds of the babies. Teresa rolled onto her side. As she drifted off to sleep, his voice whispered like a breeze across her skin.

Always.

Teresa woke in Mountain View. Moonlight came in through the window high up on the wall.

A dark spot lurked in the corner.

"No," Teresa gasped, knowing it was the woman who had touched her belly. The one who'd *peed* on her.

It stepped closer in a normal way, not the strange crawling prowl like before.

Teresa shied away, backed herself into the corner. Her knees pressed against her breasts. No bulging belly to stop them. She was no longer pregnant, and the laundry basket containing her babies was nowhere to be found. How much time had she lost? Where were Amanda and Cassie? How did she end up back in this place?

The woman turned around in jerky movements. All around her a black halo of shadow moved like ink dropped into water, as if the shadowy essence were leaking out of her pores in the shapes of the veins under her skin.

Blood was black in moonlight. Teresa knew this.

"Who are you? What do you want from me? They're gone. The babies are gone," Teresa shrieked, tears jumping to her eyes.

A thin stream of moonlight struck the woman's face. Teresa stifled a scream. Though the woman's hair was black as the night around her, she wore Teresa's face. The woman's eyes filled with darkness, like Ruthie's after Teresa took her zoe—her life. The irises, pupils, and sclera all merged into one black hole in each socket. Black crackles spread from her eyes down her cheeks and from her lips down her chin.

"What do you want?" Teresa shouted. Adrenaline coursed through her system. In the past, she might have run, but here in Mountain View, she could only dash around her room, pinging off the walls. Or bang on the door and scream for help.

"*Logismoi*," the woman said in a whispery voice that sounded like three of her had said it, each a fraction of a second behind the other. She came closer and gripped Teresa's face with the long fingers of one hand. The other raised up and touched Teresa's forehead between her eyes.

Images filled Teresa's mind.

A woman lay on an altar draped in fine fabrics. Tubes emerged from each arm. Two babies thirstily drank from these tubes. The woman shriveled, like Ruthie. The babies cried and vomited the blood. In the aftermath, they lay still and lifeless. A wailing woman, who looked like Teresa herself in a corseted dress with billowing skirts, held their still forms. Teresa's heart broke with hers.

A flash. A similar setting, but in a cave. A cave like Tartaros, with sandy walls, torches on sconces. Another altar, this one of stone. A woman lay there. This time, the woman who looked like Teresa, wore a red robe and she filleted the skin from the arms, legs, and torso of the woman on the stone. She ground it in a copper bowl and fed this to the babies lying on either side of the altar.

The same thing happened. The babies vomited and died. The Teresa-like woman mourned.

Another flash. Another altar. The woman who looked like Teresa stepped forward and withdrew a large hypodermic needle.

"No," Teresa whispered. But the vision would not stop.

The Teresa in the vision plunged the needle into the woman's eye and pulled the plunger.

Instead of filling with the glowing red zoe, the barrel filled with a gelatinous gray substance, shiny like brushed silver. It swirled in the barrel, much like the zoe had. The Teresa in the vision expressed the substance into a chalice and drank it. The vision dimmed and reappeared like a scene-cut in a movie.

Now the babies nursed from the Teresa-woman. She sat in a rocking chair in a dark place, one baby on each breast.

They did not vomit. They did not die.

They grew bigger, stronger. Aging a couple of months before her eyes.

A final flash. Teresa was in the room in Lory's house again with the crib containing her slumbering babies nearby. Multi-colored stars from the nightlight twirled on the ceiling. It was a warm light, but it did not soothe Teresa's nerves.

The woman stood at the end of her bed.

"Souls of the eight." She pointed at the crib. "Logissssmoi." The woman backed away and disappeared into the shadows while Teresa's heart pummeled the inside of her ribcage.

Teresa lunged for the lamp on the bedside table and clicked it on. No sign of the woman. Nothing at all. It must have been one of those dreams within a dream.

Wings flapped to her right where the crib sat. Teresa jerked her head that way and threw the covers back in one movement. She let out a stifled shriek.

The winged creature perched on the crib. No. Not just a winged creature. Her daughter Cassie.

Teresa whimpered. "Why are you here like this?" she asked in a choked whisper.

The triangular head cocked at her. Tiny hand-like paws, like raccoon hands, gripped the railing of the crib.

Cassie jumped down into the crib. Teresa let out a stifled shriek and reached a hand forward.

"Don't hurt her." She jumped out of bed and gripped the rail herself.

Amanda gave the little monster a gummy smile. Teresa reached in and cuddled her close. Her little face rooted at Teresa's shirt.

Teresa turned off the bright lamp, and with her eyes on the winged monster, she nursed Amanda, who grunted like a little piglet.

An icy sensation coursed down Teresa's arm to her elbow, flaring in the joint, then to her wrist and hand. She clenched her fist and opened it. She couldn't feel the movement. She peered over her daughter's purple blanket. The flesh on her hand looked like cracked porcelain in the dark. No. It was just the twirling lights on the ceiling and the strange way the moonlight played with the shadows. Why did she think she'd be able to see her hand plain as day? At least it was still there. She relaxed and tried not to think about it.

But the cold kept going. It spread across her chest to the other side.

Teresa grew weak and woozy, as if she had low blood sugar.

Stop her, Yaldabaoth groaned in her mind.

She pulled Amanda away from her nipple.

Instead of creamy milk, a silvery gray substance dribbled down her chin. Amanda sucked her bottom lip into her little mouth and made a popping sound. She didn't cry, despite Teresa having pulled her off before she was done.

Amanda stared at Teresa with wide eyes—not the wide eyes of a baby—the wide eyes of someone who knew things.

"Who are you?" Teresa whispered. Amanda waved her tiny fists.

The winged creature flapped onto the bed, face-planted, and pushed itself up. Little uncoordinated thing. Teresa let out a strangled laugh.

"Cassie?" she whispered. The little demon cocked its head at her. "How can—"

Because she's mine, Yaldabaoth's voice whispered.

Teresa could almost feel his arms around her and Amanda, holding her from behind the way he did so many times during his coercion toward betrayal.

Teresa got up off the bed and turned to make sure he actually wasn't there. He wasn't. She burped Amanda and lay her on the blankets. The little winged Cassie followed her movements with interest.

"If you're hungry," Teresa said in a trembling voice to the little gargoyle. "You'll have to change back to my little Cassie." Tears welled in her eyes.

Cassie spread her impossibly wide wings and leaped

into the air. When she came down, the leathery skin settled around her as it had before, leaving behind a naked little baby wriggling on the blankets. Teresa, tears coursing down her cheeks, picked up her daughter.

She fed Cassie, fully expecting the same sensation as from Amanda. But instead, feeding Cassie filled her with a warm glow, as if she were being made whole again. The cracks on Teresa's skin disappeared.

Give and take.

She finished nursing, burped Cassie, and lay her next to her sister. They turned their twin bald heads and looked at each other.

She swaddled them and put them in the laundry basket next to her. Teresa listened to their soft breaths, the wheezes, the little grunts. How they looked like little sausages all swaddled tight the way they were.

Or maggots . . . feeding on her life.

Teresa needed to get her hands on a breast pump. Or find whatever that silvery stuff was she was supposed to feed them—based on that weird nightmare.

You know what it is, my sweet. Yaldabaoth again.

She shuddered and waved her hand as if she could dismiss an auditory hallucination that way.

"Quiet," she whispered. "You'll wake our babies." Teresa looked up abruptly. "*My* babies."

A cold dread came over her. He was right. She knew what the silver substance was. Though it was different than the zoes she had taken nine months ago, and that shadow version of herself had told her what it was called—*Logismoi* —she knew what it really was.

She had to feed Amanda souls and would need the first one fast. Otherwise, Amanda would feed on Teresa's soul.

The only problem was, Teresa didn't know who, or how,

or when. She knew there would have to be some kind of process to follow.

She hadn't known with Yaldabaoth. Not really. She just followed Tiffany to the zoe lines to the . . . well, to the victims. She lifted her chin. That's what they were after all. She could admit that. To herself anyway.

CHAPTER TWELVE

Cold hands. Teresa jerked awake and came face to face with Cassie's triangular head and big black almond-shaped eyes.

"What is it?" Teresa asked. She glanced into the laundry basket at Amanda. Still asleep.

Cassie bounded to the door. Her little raccoon-like hands reached for the knob.

Teresa pulled on a robe, shoved her feet into a pair of slippers Lory had left for her, then thought twice. She took the slippers off and put on a pair of sneakers, also left by Lory. She laced them up.

She wasn't nervous. Her hands didn't shake. As she stood, her knees didn't feel weak, her heart didn't pound. She looked at her little demon child, and a heavy resignation settled over her.

"Okay then," she whispered. "We're doing this again."

Teresa took a deep breath and let it out through her mouth. She stepped forward, hesitated, and bent to pick up Cassie.

Her daughter made clicking purring sounds and

nuzzled her strange little head under Teresa's chin. Her head was surprisingly soft. A downy coating of fur covered it. Her wings stayed folded. Her little paw-hands gripped Teresa's shirt.

"Will Amanda be okay?" Teresa whispered. "While we're gone?"

Cassie's little paw-hand stroked Teresa's face. Then she reached for the door again.

Teresa opened it on the dark hallway. She paused and listened. A clock ticked somewhere toward the front of the house. A low light came from that direction, too. She didn't want to encounter Lory while Cassie was in this form. She turned and went the other way to where she knew the back door was.

They slipped out of the house undetected. Cassie struggled in Teresa's arms until Teresa loosened her grip. Cassie's massive wings unfurled. She took to the sky.

Teresa watched with awe. The little monster swooped and dipped with innate ability. Teresa wondered how a baby, only a few days old, could be so good at flying.

Another thought came to her. How could she even be sure this was real?

Teresa pursed her lips to the side. Last year she'd believed her dead daughter had come back to help her bring Yaldabaoth back to power, so why not believe that her daughter—offspring of Yaldabaoth—could be a winged monster?

Cassie swooped down and, at the last second, slowed to hover in front of Teresa. Teresa held out her arms, thinking Cassie wanted to come back to her, wanted Teresa to hold her again, but instead of cuddling close, Cassie grabbed Teresa's hand and pulled, massive wings flapping and stirring up dust.

Her little grip was strong, but most babies had vice-like grips, so it wasn't alarming. In fact, it felt just like when she stuck her finger in Amanda's palm and Amanda squeezed.

Teresa stumbled along behind Cassie toward the woods with the lost souls. Cassie had to let go of Teresa's hand and fly higher because of the trees. Teresa looked up and saw her soaring overhead. A pterodactyl silhouette against the starry night sky. She turned and slid down into the trees, landing a few yards ahead in what Teresa always thought of as the abandoned funeral home's front yard.

Teresa jogged to catch up. Cassie tugged on her hand and pointed at the entry to the abandoned funeral home.

A lump formed in Teresa's throat. What would be waiting for her inside? Was Cassie leading Teresa to her father?

He's dead, Teresa told herself.

Don't be so sure, my sweet, Yaldabaoth said.

It was just Lory's ideas speaking to her through his voice, though Teresa had never considered whether or not someone could die when already in the underworld.

Cassie tugged on her hand again. Teresa lifted her chin and took small deliberate steps. Up those warped smiling steps. To that dark gaping mouth of a doorway.

Someone cried inside.

Teresa took a step back.

"Someone's in there," she whispered to Cassie, who stalked a bunny. Her long tail lashed the air over her back. Teresa turned back to the doorway and peeked in before stepping inside.

"Who's there?" a girl asked in a thick voice. A cell phone light came on, blinding Teresa.

She held her hand out to block it. "I'm sorry," Teresa said. "I didn't mean to disturb you."

The light lowered, and before the light clicked off, Teresa took in a young girl, probably thirteen or fourteen years old, with dark hair so long it had become scraggly at the ends.

"It's okay," the girl said. "I was just leaving."

Teresa stood awkwardly between the door and the moldy couch where she'd given birth. She grimaced.

"No, it's okay, stay. I'll go somewhere else." Yaldabaoth's cave—if that's what was supposed to appear—wouldn't materialize if another person were there with her. Teresa turned.

Cassie peeked in. Her black eyes, shiny with the moonlight, flicked from the girl to Teresa and back. Teresa's eyes had adjusted to the low light. She could just make the girl out.

"Are you okay?" Teresa asked.

The girl shook her head and wiped at her eyes.

"What's wrong?"

"Nothing," the girl said. "I just want to be alone."

Teresa didn't leave. She leaned on the doorjamb. "*Nothing* is what we say when we don't really want to talk about what's bothering us. It usually means we think the thing that is bothering us isn't worth being upset about. Or we're embarrassed of it. Or we're afraid of what others might think."

The girl looked up at Teresa. She sniffled and wiped her eyes again.

"I know you don't know me," Teresa said. "But maybe I can help?"

The girl shook her head and seemed to weigh the odds of confiding in a stranger. "My sister is going out with the guy I like."

Oh, teenage drama.

"Does she know you like him?" Teresa moved closer.

The girl nodded. "Yeah. She totally knows. I only talked about him to her like a million times. Why would she do this to me?"

"I'm not sure," Teresa said. She really wasn't. "Maybe she's just mean."

"But she's not." The girl looked at Teresa. "She's always nice to me. Protective of me, even. Our dad was a piece of shit."

"She's protecting you, then," Teresa said. "From getting hurt by this kid you like, I mean." Teresa did not want to sit on the opposite end of the couch. That's where all the blood and afterbirth would have been.

Did I really give birth here?

"Maybe she knows what kind of jerk he is and wants to prove it to you," Teresa continued.

"Maybe you're right," the girl said. "But it still just makes me so—"

"Mad?" Teresa asked.

"No," the girl shook her head. "I'm just so sad." She burst into renewed tears. Teresa patted the girl's shoulder and sat on the cushion next to her.

"What's your name?" Teresa asked.

"Glory," the girl said with a loud and snotty sniffle. She wiped her nose on the back of her hand. "My sister calls me Morning Glory. We sing that song by Oasis." She started crying again.

Teresa had no idea who Oasis was.

"I wish she would just break up with him." The girl latched onto Teresa, sobbing against her shoulder.

Cassie bounded into the room like a squirrel, her long tail flicking behind her. She jumped onto the couch behind the girl. Teresa patted Glory's back. Cassie yanked Glory's head back by her hair so far, the girl fell back onto the couch with a startled gasp, pulling Teresa with her. Teresa jumped back, and Cassie leaped over the girl's head onto her chest and plunged her little hand-paws into Glory's eye sockets. The sound that ripped out of Glory's throat was like nothing Teresa had ever heard in her life. And she used to deliver babies.

Cassie's little hands came away with an eyeball clutched in each one.

It happened so fast, Teresa didn't have time to scream. She covered her mouth in horror, and then to stop the screams from flying out.

An ounce of relief washed over her when Cassie tossed the eyeballs into the corner. Teresa had been sure the little monster would stuff them into her mouth, chew them up, and swallow them.

The girl passed out from shock or pain or both.

Something silvery glowed in Glory's eye sockets. Silver like the substance in Teresa's dream, the stuff she was supposed to feed her babies. Silver like what had dribbled from Amanda's chin.

Logismoi.

Teresa slid closer. Cassie held Glory's face, presumably so the silver liquid wouldn't leak out from where it was pooled in her sockets.

"The eyes are the windows to the . . ." Teresa covered her mouth as hot bile burned the back of her throat.

Soul.

CHAPTER THIRTEEN

Her first thought was, *I have nothing with which to collect it*. Tiffany had provided a hypodermic needle. Of course, Teresa had to pull the zoe out of the heart. Harder to just rip one's way into the chest cavity now, wasn't it?

She let out an insane sounding laugh, clapped a hand over her mouth, then caught a sob before it erupted.

"What now?" she asked the little monster still holding the poor girl's face. Was she even still alive?

Drink it, Yaldabaoth's voice hissed in her mind, accompanied by that barely-there touch across her scalp. She ignored him.

Teresa leaned over Glory and felt for a pulse. With her face over Glory's, the silvery substance started to move as if some force were pulling at it. It spiraled upward toward Teresa's lips.

Teresa jumped back. The soul slopped back into the sockets. She cast a quick look at Cassie, then back to the dimly glowing soul.

In the dream, she had to consume the silver substance in order to feed it to her babies.

It made sense. What the mother eats nourishes the child through the milk.

Teresa covered her mouth again.

Drink, Yaldabaoth said again.

"I can't." She thought of Amanda back at the house, maybe awake now, hungry but not fussing in that silent way of hers. Cassie wasn't there to cry on her behalf. Teresa thought of the pain nursing her brought to her shoulder and arm and hand. That weakness that overcame her as her daughter sucked her soul. How Yaldabaoth pleaded for her to stop.

"Okay. Okay." Teresa took a deep breath and leaned over Glory. The soul spiraled upward again. Teresa closed her eyes. Her lips pulled inside, teeth clamping them together.

The substance touched her face, hot and soft like the gentle touch of a baby's hand. Or a fat silkworm. Teresa parted her lips. The soul slid into her mouth. She puckered and slurped.

And slurped. And slurped some more.

In the back of her mind, she remembered the time she injected herself with the zoe. How she'd sprinted to this very house, back when it used to change into Tartaros. How she'd hungrily kissed Yaldabaoth. After their indiscretion, he'd gripped her arms and told her to never take what was his again.

Now, for a second, she wondered if this really belonged to someone else. But she knew it didn't.

This wasn't his or anyone else's. It was hers. It was little Amanda's.

She's his.

Teresa opened her eyes as the last of it sucked into her mouth. She swallowed and grimaced.

It tasted like hot brakes and burning leaves. *Why would a soul taste like that?*

"So more people won't eat them." She covered her mouth and almost threw up, but managed to choke it back down. She couldn't waste it.

Glory's body had deflated, like her organs had putrefied and turned to liquid, like she'd been gutted and deboned and hollowed out. Like a bag of empty skin.

Teresa backed away from it. No need to check for a pulse. She couldn't be alive. Just like Ruthie and the others, though ambulatory, had not actually been alive.

She turned to Cassie. "Let's go feed your sister."

<hr>

Teresa sobbed quietly and nursed Amanda, who hungrily grunted and kneaded at her mother's breast.

What just happened? How much of that had been real? How much of any of this was real?

That poor, stupid, heartbroken girl. Teresa was surprised to find she was mad at the girl for being there crying and sniveling over a stupid boy. Why couldn't she just go lock herself in her bedroom and play loud music? She had to sneak out in the middle of the night to a gross and horrible place to feel her feelings? What was she hoping to find there?

Amanda finished nursing. Teresa looked down at her baby gazing up at her with adoration in her eyes. Teresa burped her—Amanda let out a massive belch—and held her a little longer.

Cassie returned to her human form, leaping into the air like she did and collapsing beneath a sheet of leathery skin.

Teresa bounced Amanda while she got up and went to

the crib. Cassie looked up at her and reached her hands—fleshy pink, chubby baby hands, not raccoon-like ones—toward Teresa. Or maybe toward her sister. Teresa lowered Amanda—who had grown heavy with sleep in her arms—into the crib next to Cassie.

Cassie still reached upward.

"Oh, me? You want me?" Teresa lifted Cassie and nuzzled her. She sat on the bed and nursed her. Cassie's little hands gripped Teresa's shirt.

Teresa tried not to think about what those little grabbing hands did to that poor girl in the woods. She pulled a few baby wipes out of the package on her nightstand and wiped Cassie's hands while she nursed, though there was no evidence of her gory crime.

After feeding the babies, Teresa put them in the crib close together. Only then did she start to shake. Only then did a full onslaught of tears spring to her eyes. She covered her mouth to stifle the sob and hurried to the bathroom. A nightlight in the shape of a sun made of yellow and red and orange stained-glass shards provided enough glow. She mopped her eyes and nose with tissues from a small box on the toilet tank.

"Why me?" she whispered. She leaned closer, and the light shifted. Her eyes flashed yellow. She groped the wall for the light switch and flicked it on. Her eyes were blue again.

CHAPTER FOURTEEN

Pinky's head weighed heavily on Maggie's chest, as if the dog were holding her down to keep her from drifting away.

Maggie's stomach hurt, but not in a sick way like she had eaten too much. It was like a flippy-floppy-fluttery feeling. She couldn't really tell if it was in her tummy or her chest.

It got so bad it woke her up. The clock said it was one. She rolled onto her back. Pinky readjusted herself and snuggled closer. Maggie put her hand on the dog's head.

She thought about the Luminaries and how Sophia had reacted to them. The tall male one had said Sophia unleashed more evils. Sophia had felt like Maggie felt when Teresa yelled at her last year—before she ran away and Ann found her and brought her here to this house and wrapped her in blankets. That was the night Ann had discovered her own purpose and found out who Maggie was. Maggie had breathed on Ann's hand, making Ann's veins glow blue-white. That could only happen to Sophia's Protector.

Maggie had run away because Teresa had yelled at her. Teresa hadn't wanted her.

Maybe the Luminaries were Sophia's guardians. Maybe they didn't want Sophia.

Like Teresa. Like Ann.

Maggie knew Ann didn't want kids. Mr. Bram should have just told whoever to put her back in a foster home. She understood why he named Ann her guardian, of course. Because Ann was her Protector.

In the beginning, Ann *had* been really protective of her. Walked her to and from school every day. Took her to the graveyard to talk to Ruthie and Sheriff McMichael and Derrick once a month. But Maggie could tell Ann didn't want to do that anymore.

Maggie was a . . . it was a word she'd learned in school before summer break. A word one of the not so nice girls at the Daycare Place said. Sally Opperheim—a big kid, even for her age. Sally told Maggie everything she touched turned to poop.

Sally Opperheim also told Maggie she was cursed and that all the people she loved would die. Just like her parents. Just like Derrick. Or they would go crazy, like Teresa.

Maggie rolled over on the bed. Pinky's head slid off of her. The dog adjusted her position to press her head against Maggie's stomach and let out a long sigh. Maggie stroked Pinky's ears.

Sally didn't know anything. She was mean. She looked like a stupid doll with her fair skin and yellow hair in ringlets and her freckles. She even had big blue eyes like a doll.

Sometimes Sally was at the Daycare Place, but she didn't like being there because she was ten and felt like she was old enough to be home alone. Maggie had heard her scream that once at her mom at drop-off. Sally took toys away from everyone or claimed them all as hers because she was the oldest one there. Maggie even tried playing with baby toys, like the stack of plastic rings. Sally took them away anyway and called her a baby for playing with baby toys.

Maggie didn't care about that. She liked to draw, and Sally didn't care about the paper and crayons.

But her words were like sharp needles that dug into Maggie's skin. Sally had told Maggie she was a *burden* that one day at school.

Maggie had to look that up. Sally was a fifth-grader and Maggie was only in second. The only reason they even saw each other that day was because they were both waiting to be picked up.

Maggie hadn't reacted when Sally said she was a burden. Sally even got in her face, but Maggie didn't look at her. She wondered if Sophia had helped her do that, because on the inside she wanted to cry and hit Sally or pull her ringlets straight. But she kept her hands gripped on the straps of her backpack.

Sally only stopped bothering her when Ann pulled up. When Ann got out of the truck to help Maggie in—because it was too tall for her to get in without help—Sally wandered off.

"You okay?" Ann asked Maggie.

Maggie nodded. She didn't say anything, because she thought if she tried she would burst into tears, and she didn't want to be a burden, whatever that was. She looked it up in the dictionary in her room, which used to be Ann's old room. There were still some of Ann's books on the little shelf. Maggie found a picture of Derrick in one of them, when he was a lot younger. She kept it under her pillow.

A burden was something that was borne with difficulty.

Maggie didn't think she was difficult. She used the

thesaurus and looked up other words for burden, which lead her to the word *hindrance.*

"A person or thing that hinders," Maggie had whispered to the quiet room. She'd quickly looked up *hinder.* "To prevent from doing, acting, or happening."

She remembered being confused about it. But then a few days later, while they were talking about their days, Ann talked about something called *byourockrasee* hindering her progress in making the department better. All she wanted was a couple of laptops and some new tech so they could do their jobs. Maggie had taken the opportunity to ask Ann what *hinder* meant.

"*Hinder* means it gets in my way," Ann had said. "Bureaucracy and all this damn—darn—red tape."

Maggie was a hinder. And another word for hinder was burden. Sally Opperheim was right. Maggie got in Ann's way. She saw it sometimes when it looked like Ann was going to take off but stopped at the last moment when she saw Maggie on the couch, or at the table, or standing at the bottom of the stairs with her backpack ready for school.

Ann's face sort of drooped, as if Maggie being a hinder had pulled it down.

The same thing happened sometimes at bedtime. It seemed like Ann was doing things she thought she was supposed to do, like reading stories to Maggie, even though Maggie could read them herself.

Maybe the Luminaries felt the same way about Sophia. Maybe Sophia was their burden.

Maggie looked up at the ceiling. Tears leaked out of her eyes and dripped down her temples into her hair. She wasn't crying because of Ann. She wasn't sad for that. She wasn't crying because she missed Derrick either, though she did. She missed his hugs the most. She cried because she felt sad for Sophia.

And because her tummy felt so weird.

And because of what the Luminaries said. The new dangers. The abyss. If anything happened to Ann, or Pinky, or maybe *anyone* she knew, she would return there.

And that scared her the most.

CHAPTER FIFTEEN

MONDAY

Teresa stood over the crib, hand covering her mouth. Morning light filtered in through a crack in the curtains. She pushed them open.

The babies' swaddling blankets had fallen away, and with good reason. Cassie and Amanda had grown by at least a couple of months, if memory about infant development served her right. They no longer had that fragile, wrinkled, bright pink look to them. Their heads were smooth with a soft fuzz of blond hair. They both sucked their thumbs. They'd also cuddled closer, heads nearly touching.

Something black stuck out from under Cassie in stark contrast to the soft pastels of their blankets and sheets. Teresa reached in and pulled it out. It was a thin leathery fleshy—

She let out a stifled shriek and dropped it. It immediately dissolved to nothing on the carpet.

The backs of her knees hit her bed and she sat down hard onto the mattress. The springs creaked. She covered her mouth with her trembling hand again. Hot tears welled and poured over. Grief so deep transformed her shock into immense sadness.

Her baby, her little Cassie, was a monster, and she'd disfigured that poor girl.

Teresa dug her fingers into her closed eyelids, just to feel a fraction of what that girl had felt. She hitched in a gasp.

I ate her soul.

It couldn't have been real.

That stupid girl.

She had to do it, though. Amanda hadn't been thriving. Teresa had struggled with nursing her. The pain. The knowledge that her daughter was sucking her soul—literally. Not just in that figurative way new mothers sometimes joked about their babies being parasites, sucking their lives through their teats.

Teresa stood on shaky legs and peered down again at her babies. Amanda looked up at her. Her eyes were still the blue-gray of most newborns.

Amanda turned her head, smiled at her sleeping sister, and patted Cassie's face with a chubby hand. A very gentle *pat pat pat.* Was it a thank you? Or was she trying to wake Cassie.

Teresa lifted Amanda. She was heavier than yesterday, but Teresa still had to support her head. Amanda smiled up at her with a big toothless grin.

"Let your sister sleep. Let's me and you have some mommy-Mandy time together." She hated the nickname Mandy for Amanda, but pairing it with mommy made it sound extra cute.

Almost too cute. Definitely too cute.

"Mommy-*Amanda* time, I mean." She smoothed a hand

over Amanda's forehead. "You're not Mandy. I'll never call you that. And *you* should never *let* anyone call you that." She brushed her nose back and forth against Amanda's—to her daughter's delight.

Teresa changed Amanda's diaper and thought about the previous night. She needed to go back, see if the girl was still there. But she couldn't just waltz out into broad daylight. And she couldn't leave these babies behind, either.

Teresa gathered Amanda into her arms. Cassie still slept, likely exhausted from flying around.

Teresa paused at the door, hand on the knob. Lory couldn't see Amanda like this, aged months overnight. But if the woman believed in Yaldabaoth and that they were *his* children, why not? There was no hiding it. Lory would be in with breakfast for Teresa soon anyway, still treating her like an invalid.

Or a prisoner.

She wasn't sure which. Teresa turned the knob and stepped into the hallway.

"Lory?" she called.

"In here," the woman called back. Teresa followed Lory's voice to the front room and found the woman sitting on a stylish couch, poring over some old manuscripts. She looked up at Teresa and back at the document, then did a double take.

"How . . ."

Teresa stepped down into the living room.

Lory touched Amanda's chubby cheek. Amanda grabbed for her hand. Lory let her grip her finger. Amanda brought it toward her mouth.

Teresa swiped Lory's hand away. "No, no," she said to Amanda. "Wouldn't want to encourage biting at this early stage." Or sucking on fingers. Just in case.

Cassie's cries came from the other room. Teresa looked at Lory and to the hallway.

"I can hold her while you get—"

Teresa ignored her and scurried back to her room. She placed Amanda on the bed and arranged pillows around her. Lory came in behind her.

Cassie threw her head back. Her mouth opened impossibly wide. The sound of a thousand people or things shrieking and wailing preceded a black cloud that blasted out of her mouth and accumulated at the ceiling. Teresa flew into Lory, and the women clung to each other in mutual horror.

Cassie closed her mouth as the last of the blast left her. It seemed to be made of a million tiny things. They swarmed toward the window. Teresa reached over the crib and opened it. The cloud blasted outside, leaving silence in its wake.

Teresa peered down. Cassie lay back, eyes closed, still.

"What was that? What was that?" Lory shrieked, as if Teresa would know.

Teresa ignored her and reached into the crib. "Please." Teresa touched Cassie. The child's eyes opened. She flashed a gummy grin at Teresa, who lifted and held her.

"Oh my god, baby, what was that?" She sat on the bed and opened Cassie's mouth to examined the inside. One last weird little black thing swarmed out, like a fly—but not quite. It was more like a tiny version of the lost souls. She wondered if the cloud would have glowed had it been dark.

"Is she okay?" Lory asked, voice still high and shrieking. "How are you so calm? What was that?"

Teresa gave Lory a pointed look. "I don't know what it was, so stop asking."

"How are they so big?" Lory asked in awe.

Teresa settled Cassie on the bed next to Amanda, whose little arms reached upward. Teresa thought maybe she was trying to reach for Cassie next to her and couldn't manage the motor function yet.

"They've got to be, what, two months old by the size of them?" Lory reached toward the babies but didn't touch them. She pressed a pillow down to get a better look.

Teresa didn't know what to tell Lory. She couldn't very well tell her she'd fed them a soul.

Lory sat up suddenly. "Excuse me. I'll be right back."

"Where are you going?" Teresa asked.

Lory paused at the door. "I have a book. I think it might explain some things." She dashed away. Teresa played with Amanda's reaching hands. Cassie reached up, and Teresa grabbed her little hands, too. Four little hands, two in each of her own. They gripped with excellent strength.

"Here it is," Lory said, coming back into the room with a big old book. Great. Another book. One of Louise's missions had been to find an old book containing the instructions to harness Yaldabaoth. Weeks after Teresa's incarceration, *another* book arrived—one telling her everything she experienced had been real.

Lory's weight shifted the edge of the bed as she sat, pulling Teresa to the here and now. She showed Teresa the pages. "It's a story about Yaldabaoth."

Teresa waved her hand. "I know his story."

"You may not know this part of it. Bear with me?"

Teresa nodded.

"After Yaldabaoth created the material world, and before he was cast into Tartaros, he created Adam and Eve."

In the past, Teresa might have shouted blasphemy at this statement. But it wasn't anymore, was it? Not to her. Not after what she'd lived through. Not after her faith was shaken to its core, dashed on the rocks in Tartaros, and regurgitated out into her head and heart.

"But the forms were not living. Yaldabaoth did not have within him the spirit in his breath to give them life. Sophia did that, which made him insanely jealous. That's why he stole her light. He wanted to become more powerful than her and destroy her."

"Yes, yes." Teresa rolled her hand in a get on with it gesture. "I know he's jealous. I know he wants to destroy her."

"Sophia hid inside of Eve. When Yaldabaoth saw Eve alive and with Sophia's life and light, he fell in love with her." Lory smiled at Teresa like it was the sweetest love story of all time. "He yearned for her. He wanted to have her, to hold her. He longed to be with her."

"Isn't that sweet," Teresa said. He had longed for *her* too. He wanted Teresa to be his bride, his queen. She often wondered what would have happened if she'd said yes and given up what she had worked toward. Happiness with Derrick and Tiffany. Would he still have betrayed her if she'd said yes?

"But he could not talk to her, for every time he tried, her spirit fled from her, and when her spirit left, she was merely a shell. A shadow of herself. An empty husk." Lory paused and looked at Teresa. "You may not know this, but there were other rulers. Yaldabaoth's seven sons and daughters whom he created. They ruled the seven heavens of chaos— they convinced him to have his way with Eve, to show her how much he loved her. They wanted her, too, and they threatened to take her if he didn't do it himself."

Teresa sat forward. Peer pressure, even in those days.

"Yaldabaoth returned to the material world and did just

as they said. Sophia fled once again. Yaldabaoth made love to Eve's Shadow."

Teresa barked out a laugh. "Usually when someone 'has their way' with someone else, it's called rape. Besides, wasn't Sophia his mother? Did he have some sort of Oedipus complex? This is not the beautiful love story you think it is."

Lory lowered her eyes. "Yes. I know," she said. "I was a Messenger for so long, I often forget myself when recounting the stories." She touched Teresa's arm. "You are absolutely right. He raped her." She shrugged.

"What happened next? After the rape? Surely there is more to it than that if you think it will explain something."

"Eve's Shadow became pregnant. She bore Cain and Abel into the world."

"Are you implying Amanda and Cassie are going to grow up hating each other?" Teresa asked.

"I'm not implying anything," Lory said. "I'm merely telling a story."

Teresa relaxed. Cassie couldn't kill Amanda. Amanda needed her. Cassie cried when Amanda was hungry or needed changed. Amanda was happier with Cassie around. They were both happier. Teresa looked down at her babies. Maybe Cassie would get tired of Amanda needing her. Could that cause them to drift apart? To hate each other? Resentment breeds hate.

She'd named them Cassie and Amanda for no reason other than liking those names. Cain and Abel. Cassie and Amanda. C and A.

They loved each other though. When would that love, that inseparable bond, dissipate? She didn't think it ever would.

"He wandered the earth and died for his sins," Teresa mumbled. "Cain, after he killed Abel." She looked at Lory.

"He wandered the earth searching for that which he lost," Lory continued. "He died not because of his sins, Teresa. He died because he had killed his other half. The balancing half of one whole. Twins have a bond. If that bond is severed through death, through separation, through whatever it might be, the other twin's soul pines for the loss forever. An incompleteness overpowers the remaining half. They are bereft. Forever seeking something they may never find. Forever feeling not quite whole." She stood and tucked the book under her arm. "How many times have there been stories about twins separated at birth who end up living identical lives? Who end up searching for their lost half because they *know* something is missing?"

Teresa had heard of the twin bond. She looked down at her babies again, sleeping peacefully.

"How does this explain that black thing?" Teresa asked.

"It doesn't, but I thought there might be something more." She turned the pages with a thoughtful look on her face. But she shook her head. "I don't see anything else."

"I think I saw her," Teresa said. "I think I saw Shadow Eve." She thought of the woman who came to her at Mountain View and the night before in her dream. It made sense she would be the one to show Teresa what to feed Amanda, especially if she equated these twins to being her own.

Lory looked at Teresa expectantly.

It suddenly dawned on her why Lory was telling her this story. It had to do with Teresa. Yaldabaoth had his way with her. She bore twins.

The woman had Teresa's face. She looked at Lory.

"I think I'm supposed to be Shadow Eve. Aren't I?"

Lory cocked her head, smiled, and gave Teresa a shrug. "It's just a myth, isn't it?" She winked and stood to go.

"Wait." Teresa stood. "I want to go for a walk. I need a hat or something to disguise myself, and a double stroller."

"Yes of course. Patrina dropped off a stroller this morning. She's a doll, isn't she?"

Teresa merely nodded and followed Lory down the hall. In the foyer sat a three-wheeled, double-wide affair with a big red bow on it.

"Thank you," Teresa said. "It looks expensive."

"Patrina did all the research to find the best of the best for you and the littles." Lory's smile faded. She went to the table and retrieved a grocery bag. "I got you a box of hair dye." She held the bag against her chest. "Though it would pain me to see that beautiful blond wasted."

Teresa cast a glance at Lory's brassy roots and the unnatural golden color of her lengths, then at the box of black hair dye in her hand.

"If I want to be able to walk in the daylight without anyone recognizing me, I have to." Teresa hated to dye her hair, too, but it was the oldest trick in the book for disguising oneself. She also knew she looked like a completely different person with dark hair. There was a time during her teenage years, before her mother died, when she'd tried it.

"Maybe you can help me," Teresa said. "Or I can try a hat for now. Or a wig even."

"I'll see what I can do."

Teresa got both babies changed and fed. She was pleased to find nursing Amanda didn't cause as much pain or discomfort as it had before eating the soul.

Lory came back with a straw hat, a scarf, and some sunglasses. Teresa tied her hair up in a bun, covered it with the scarf, and put the hat on top. She donned the sunglasses.

"I look like someone trying to hide their identity," she said.

"I think you look lovely. Why not stick to my property at first, test out the stroller, get some fresh air? We can decide if other more drastic measures are needed." Lory touched Teresa's arm. "Please be careful. If anyone recognizes you, well, I just don't know what will happen." She gazed down at the babies.

"Even if they *think* they know who I am, there's no way my babies would be two months old." Teresa said, deciding that was their approximate age. "No one would put that together."

"Still," Lory said. "Be careful."

Teresa nodded. She loaded the babies into the stroller. It had heavy-duty "off road" wheels on it, so she shouldn't have too hard a time pushing it through the brush around Lory's house.

Lory helped her get it down the back steps. Teresa pushed it across the grass, through the well-tended garden, and toward the edge of the woods.

It was a bright day. She was glad to have a wide-brimmed hat to block her face from the sun. She was also glad the stroller had a hood to block Cassie and Amanda. They cooed at each other—a lovey sound.

The sun warmed her back, chasing away a chill that seemed to have clung to her since Mountain View.

The abandoned funeral home loomed ahead. She hadn't been near this place in the sunshine before. Last October had been particularly gloomy. Oppressive, even.

Teresa jostled the stroller over some fallen logs, checked

to make sure Cassie and Amanda were okay with the movement—they were fast asleep—and kept going.

She had to look inside the house. She had to know what happened was real and not just some figment of her imagination—some massive hallucination from cutting her brain off from the Thorithium.

Teresa rounded to the front of the abandoned funeral home, set the brake on the stroller, and crouched in front. Still fast asleep. She would be two seconds. A quick look inside, and that was all.

She bounded up the stairs, steeled herself for what might be there, and peeked around the doorframe into the murky darkness.

Glory's body was gone.

CHAPTER SIXTEEN

It was Ann's first real day off since she officially became sheriff almost nine months ago. So when her cell rang before nine, she said, "The station better be on fire or someone better be dead," before fumbling it off the nightstand.

Ann peered at the screen with one eye. She didn't recognize the number.

"Sheriff Logan," she said in a grumpy greeting.

"Hi there, Sheriff," a cheerful voice said. "It's Nancy from the bank."

"Has there been a robbery?" Ann jumped out of bed but paused and chastised herself for being hopeful of a crime. The last months had been too quiet. She feared growing complacent.

"Oh no, nothing so dramatic," Nancy said with a chuckle.

"What can I help you with?" Ann lowered herself back onto the edge of the bed and massaged her forehead.

"There seems to be a noise coming from your safe-deposit box," Nancy said.

"A noise?" Ann raised an eyebrow.

"Yes. A thumping sound. I think it's in two-four time." She laughed again. Nancy was Harmony High's music teacher during the school year.

The only thing in Ann's safe-deposit box was Maggie's book. *The Origin Codex*. The one that Ann was supposed to protect along with Sophia. The book had shown her specific passages to help guide her on her mission to protect Maggie back in October.

She'd taken the book to the bank for safekeeping after The Night. After she found Raghib's body had vanished from Louise's basement.

"I'll be there in a bit." Ann found her pair of jeans from yesterday crumpled on the floor, gave them a quick sniff, and pulled them on, along with yesterday's shirt. She needed to do laundry. The most dreaded chore, especially since now she had to do laundry for two people. She hoped Maggie had at least one clean pair of undies left.

She went out into the living room. Maggie and Pinky were on the couch eating dry Lucky Charms from a plastic bowl in Maggie's lap watching something on the TV at a low volume. Every three or four for herself, she gave a small handful to Pinky. Pinky watched Ann cross the room on her way to the kitchen, tail thumping.

"Don't give her too much," Ann said. "It'll give her gas."

The coffee maker could not brew fast enough. Maybe she should just swing by the diner. It wasn't the same without Ruthie though. She hadn't even taken Maggie back there since The Night, afraid it might trigger some sort of PTSD if Ruthie wasn't there to guess what the girl wanted. Pancakes. Always pancakes.

Ann should make pancakes. She dug through the

cupboards and came up with a box of pancake mix that probably had just enough to make a few for Maggie.

She opened the fridge.

"We ran out of milk," Maggie said from the end of the kitchen. Her honey-colored eyes flicked to the pancake box. "And eggs." She grabbed the box of cereal and peered into it. "And Lucky Charms."

Add grocery shopping to the list of chores.

Ann sighed and ran her hands over her face. "Muffin store?" she suggested. "I have to go to the bank."

"The bank?" Maggie's eyes widened. "The book."

Ann nodded. "The book. Want to come with me?" She didn't really have a choice.

A smile replaced Maggie's semi-shocked face. She nodded vigorously.

"Maybe after, we can take Pinky for a hike?" Ann said.

"Yes!" Maggie pounded up to her room. Pinky chased after her. Maggie's giggles and Pinky's grunts and snorts floated down the staircase.

Anything to avoid doing laundry. The grocery shopping could not be put off. She prided herself in providing Maggie three squares a day and a roof over her head. If she took away one of those things, she'd be a complete failure at being a guardian—rather than just a partial failure.

She poured coffee into a travel mug and took a sip of the scalding brew.

"Nectar of the gods," she whispered. "You have thirty seconds," she called up to Maggie while collecting her wallet and phone. She shoved one in each back pocket, found her keys, and twirled them on her finger.

Maggie and Pinky bounded back down the stairs. Maggie was so excited she tripped at the bottom. Ann lunged forward just in time to catch her. The girl wrapped her arms around Ann in a tight hug.

Ann snorted. She gave the girl a squeeze and a couple pats on the back. "Okay, okay," she said, removing Maggie's arms from around her. "Let's get going."

"Can we invite Rachel to go hiking with us?" Maggie asked. Rachel and Maggie had become close over the past nine months, since Rachel sometimes watched Maggie. Rachel took Maggie and Pinky hiking. A lot.

"Sure," Ann said. "I think she's working today, but I happen to know her boss." Ann winked at Maggie.

They entered the bank. Nancy spotted Ann and bustled around to greet her.

"Well hi there, Maggie," Nancy said. "Don't you look pretty today."

"Hi, Miss Nancy," Maggie said with a beaming smile. "Thank you." Maggie looked down when she said thank you. Ann didn't know what that meant in kids. Herself? She hated compliments. Maybe Maggie had picked that up from her.

She read way too much into the girl's body language. Ever since The Night and all the trauma Maggie had been through, who wouldn't? Ann had even considered taking Maggie to therapy. She decided against it when she learned the price tag per session.

Nancy gave Maggie a lollipop and took them to the secret room, as Maggie called it.

In the secure space that housed the safe-deposit boxes, Ann *felt* more than heard the sound. Along with the thumping came a persistent bass. It vibrated in her chest.

She looked down at Maggie, who looked up at her. Maggie nodded.

"What's in there?" Nancy asked.

"Just a book," Ann said with a shrug. Nancy gave her a questioning look and glanced at Maggie, who also shrugged in the same manner. Ann looked toward the door. Nancy took the hint and left.

"What are you thinking, kiddo?" Ann asked.

"I think we should open it," Maggie said, eyes on the box. "Maybe it's just lonely." Maggie's voice was so sad, Ann flicked her eyes to the girl's face, but Maggie stared at the box in anticipation. She looked up at Ann and raised her eyebrows. "Go on, don't be scared."

Ann snorted a laugh. She was terrified. This book making sounds, flopping around inside the box? It could not be good news.

She opened it.

Freed from the confines of the metal box, the book flipped open. Maggie jumped at the same time Ann pushed back from the table. The pages fluttered. She would never get used to that.

The book had a worn leather cover containing yellowed pages warped with age. A portion of the Nag Hammadi codices that didn't quite make the cut for what was typically included in modern-day translations. It did contain the popular "On the Origin of the World," but the rest of the book—at least the portions the book had shown Ann in the days leading up to The Night—were outside of any translation she'd ever seen. And she'd done her homework since. She owned every book she could find on the subject of Gnosticism. The material was hard to read, since a lot of the scriptures were only partial and scholars had filled in the missing parts with what they felt made sense. Besides that, it was a religious text. Up until a few months ago, Ann had only believed in science, facts, and hard evidence. Maggie had been the first to prove to her there was something *other* out there.

The pages stopped flipping about a quarter of the way in. Ann scooted closer, and as her eyes scanned the Coptic Egyptian characters, they translated in her mind.

Ann read out loud to Maggie.

"'Light and darkness, life and death, and right and left are siblings of one another and inseparable. For this reason, the good are not good, the bad are not bad, life is not life, and death is not death.'" She looked at Maggie. "You—er—Sophia said that in the woods yesterday. What does it mean? Do you know?"

Maggie shook her head.

The book's pages flipped and stilled on a different page.

Ann scanned the words, then glanced at Maggie, hoping beyond hope the girl knew what the next passage meant. She read it aloud.

"The Blighted Womb shall birth the Children of Chaos unto the material world. Upon this birth, the mother-father shall choose a path. Should they be fed the eight Logismoi, they shall strengthen by two. Without, they shall perish."

"Children of chaos," Maggie mumbled. If the room hadn't been so quiet, Ann might not have heard her.

"Louise told me Yaldabaoth means Child of Chaos." Ann shrugged and read the text again in her head. "This says *children* of chaos." Teresa Hart was the last known consort of Yaldabaoth, and she was pregnant. However, without a paternity test, there was no telling *whose* babies grew inside her womb. They could be Derrick's, even though Derrick had alluded to Ann that things weren't going well between them and that Teresa could never get pregnant again. Then again, the text said it all. The Blighted Womb. However, Teresa was locked up tight in Mountain View. If something weird was going to happen again, someone else would have to be behind it.

"What are you thinking?" Maggie asked, pulling Ann out of her thoughts.

Ann looked down at the pages. "Eight Logismoi? What are Logismoi?"

"Yeshua cast seven demons from Mary Magdalene," Maggie whispered, her voice changing. Her eyes glowed blue-white with Sophia. "The eighth demon—Sadness—stayed behind." Maggie gasped, and the glow disappeared. She rubbed her chest over her heart. "I don't like it when she does that. What did she say?"

Ann told her. "Do you think those eight demons are the Logismoi?"

"Maybe?"

The book hummed. Ann glanced down. The passage continued onto the next page.

"Two parts of one whole. Together, they shall be inseparable. Balance shall remain. Apart, they shall seek the other. They shall break the realm searching. Seeking. Apart they shall bring Chaos and destruction." Ann paused and looked at Maggie. "Only the Mother of Angels can stop them."

Maggie groaned and doubled over, clutching her chest.

CHAPTER SEVENTEEN

Ann took Maggie home, though the girl insisted she was okay and could still go hiking. Ann could tell just by looking at her that she didn't feel well. When they got there, Maggie lay on the couch and crashed hard with Pinky beside her. The two were practically inseparable. Ann lifted Maggie and moved her into the master bedroom. Pinky followed behind and cuddled next to her.

Now, while she waited for Maggie to get up or Pinky to shake off and scratch to be let out of the bedroom, Ann sat in the living room and flipped through the channels.

She turned the TV off, sat back, and put her feet on the coffee table next to the book. Her head sagged against the back of the couch. Her eyes landed on a cobweb fluttering in a nonexistent breeze. Why did cobwebs move like that, seemingly all on their own?

Her cell phone rang. "Sheriff Logan," she answered.

"Sheriff," Sully's voice said. "Ronnie Masterton just called. She's the one with the two girls that always sing in the church choir. Voices like angels." He said this as if Ann could remember every person in Harmony. Ann didn't go to church. She thought Sully knew that.

"Anyway," Sully said, pulling Ann back to the call. "One of her girls is missing. The younger one. Glory."

Ann sat up straight. Her feet hit the floor with a *thunk*.

"Missing?" Her eyes jolted around the room looking at nothing, as if she was trying to find Sully in her house talking to her. She should be at the station. She should be the one taking calls like this. Did he know how to handle a distraught mother?

"Ronnie said Glory was in bed last night, but when she got up, Glory was gone."

"What's her address?" Ann grabbed the pencil and notebook sitting on the coffee table and jotted it down.

"Do you want me to go talk to her?" Sully asked. "Seein' as you took the day off since little miss Maggie isn't feeling well?"

It felt like a jab at her questionable ability as a guardian. She knew it wasn't. Not from Sully. Rachel maybe, but not Sully. But she still felt attacked in some small way. Probably by her own conscience.

Ann wanted to do this. She desperately needed something *more*.

"Yeah. Go ahead." She rested her elbows on her knees. "Maggie needs me right now."

"Go," Maggie's voice yelled from Ann's room.

"Hold on, Sully." Ann opened the bedroom door and peeked in. Pinky lifted her head. Her tail thumped the mattress. Maggie was awake.

"Was it a nightmare?" Ann asked.

Maggie shook her head. "Go. I know you want to go and help. Just go."

"Maggie, no."

"Just go." Her little voice was rimmed with tears.

Ann stood stupidly in the doorway, poised to dash either in or out—she didn't know which. It felt like a crossroads. Like whatever she decided right now would cause some cataclysmic shift. Stay or go. What would it mean to Maggie if she chose to go? What would it mean for Ann if she chose to stay?

Sully could handle taking a statement from Ronnie Masterton. She knew he could. He could and he would.

Ann took a step into the room toward the bed. She sat on the edge and took Maggie's hand.

"I'm not going anywhere."

CHAPTER EIGHTEEN

Teresa stared blankly at the vacant couch. Gone. Glory was gone. How could she be gone? She was dead. Wasn't she? She was empty. A skin suit waiting for someone to step inside and walk around in it.

What if Glory chases me when I take the next one?

Teresa turned and left the abandoned funeral home. She pushed and jostled the stroller back through the cemetery to the edge of Lory's property.

At the back door, she called inside. "I'm back. Can you help me?"

Lory appeared within a few seconds, hustling down the hall and into the mud room. They lifted the stroller inside.

"I was just meeting with some of the others," Lory said, preceding Teresa down the hallway.

"The others?" Teresa asked. Lory stopped and turned back to her.

"Your, well, sympathizers, I suppose is what we should call them. It's what they call themselves."

Teresa swiped the hat and sunglasses off her head and face. She untied the scarf and let her hair cascade down.

Lory's eyes lingered on Teresa's shoulders. She fiddled with the straw-like ends of her own hair.

"I'm sure one of them can help us with a disguise for you," Lory said hastily. "Then you won't have to ruin that beautiful hair." Lory touched a tendril grazing Teresa's shoulder and smiled at her.

Teresa gazed back at her. The woman had a lovely face. High cheekbones, a glowing golden skin tone. It was just her hair. So unnatural.

"What do you say?" Lori asked.

What was she supposed to say? Thank you? Or was it a different question. She wasn't sure. Her mind had drifted.

"Do you want to officially meet the others?" Lory's eyebrows rose expectantly.

"Oh," Teresa let out a breath of a laugh. "Yes, sure, fine."

Teresa rolled the twins into her room and closed the door without latching it. She fluffed her hair quickly in the mirror above the dresser, swiped her ring fingers under her eyes, even though she hadn't worn makeup in ages, and pinched the apples of her cheeks. Despite her efforts she still looked tired.

Lory was in the hall waiting for her. Teresa followed her to the living room.

Six people sat around on Lory's stylish couches. The young woman named Patrina was there, sitting on the arm of the sofa next to the guy who had taken the placenta in the bucket—Paul, Teresa remembered.

The memory of that came back to her in a flash. She'd forgotten most of what happened that night, other than she had given birth in the abandoned funeral home. But she distinctly remembered him putting the placenta in that blue bucket.

A sudden fire flared in her chest. He grinned stupidly at her.

"What did you do with it?" Teresa asked, looking at him, meeting his eyes. His smile faltered. He glanced at Patrina, the one who'd sent Levi to get help for Teresa. The one who'd researched the stroller. He looked at her quickly as if she had the answer, then back at Teresa.

"With what?" Paul cleared his throat.

"The placenta," Teresa said. "I saw you put it in a bucket." She moved forward without thought. Her mother bear instinct to protect what was hers had taken over.

Paul cowered back against the couch cushions and lifted a knee against her sudden advance.

Patrina touched Teresa's arm.

"It's okay, Dr. Hart," she said. "He disposed of it so as not to cause any alarm if the police patrolled the area." She gave Teresa's bicep a quick squeeze. "I hope you didn't want to save it." Her eyes widened in an oh-no kind of way.

Teresa took a step back. What had overcome her? Why did it matter what he did with her placenta? She had no use for it. She wasn't one of those people who froze it to eat on the baby's first birthday, or dehydrated it to make capsules out of it, or God knew what else.

"No," Teresa's voice came out as a choked sound. She cleared her throat. "No. I didn't want to save it."

"Why don't you have a seat over here?" Patrina indicated an empty chair.

Teresa didn't like Patrina's placating tone, nor the gentle way she guided Teresa to the chair. It reminded her of the nurses at Mountain View. Teresa turned her head slowly and narrowed her eyes at Patrina.

"You," she tore her arm out of Patrina's gentle hold. "You work there, at that horrible place." Teresa backed away from her. She was the nurse who commented on the weather—how they needed the moisture because of the fires. Teresa's eyes darted from face to face. Did she recognize anyone else? Were they all from Mountain View? Was she still at Mountain View and this was some sick joke?

"Dr. Hart," Lory's voice said with level authority. "Please calm down."

"Calm down?" Teresa took a step toward the hallway. She stumbled up that little rise out of the living room and ran. She closed her door quietly and twisted the lock on the knob. Footsteps came after her. The knob jiggled. The person knocked. Teresa flinched and cast a look at her babies snoozing in their stroller.

"Teresa," Lory said, "please come back out."

No, she couldn't. She couldn't be around *Patrina*, a nurse from that place full of Messengers of the Light, according to Raghib, and Lory who swore she wasn't working with them anymore—but lo and behold here was Patrina, who worked there, where *they* were. Did Lory know?

Teresa's knees weakened, and she lowered herself onto the edge of the bed. She put her hand over her mouth.

She needed to leave. She had to get away from them. She needed to find Raghib and go wherever it was he'd planned to take her and get away from Lory and her lies.

Teresa looked down at her sleeping babies. How could she get away with them? They would surely awaken when she tried to get the stroller out of the house down those back steps. Cassie's cries would alert Lory and the others. Six against one. They'd overpower her. Kill her. Steal her babies for their own purposes.

She paced her room, plucking at her lip.

Best to play along, don't you think? Yaldabaoth's voice slithered over her scalp. *Gain their trust. Make them believe you are not who they think you are.*

"You would know all about that, wouldn't you?" Teresa whisper-snapped. She groaned. Why was she talking to the voices in her head? "That's how you know you're crazy." She let out a mirthless laugh. The voice was right, though. For now, her only option was to play along.

She smoothed a hand over her hair. They had to understand her outburst, right? A new single mother raising twins all alone? Withdrawals from her medication? She was bound to be a little on edge, right? She'd heard of new mothers doing much worse, after all.

Like tipping a large stuffed bear on top of their baby? Her mother's voice chided.

Teresa got up, unlocked the door, and opened it a crack. Lory's expectant eyes met hers.

"I can't go back out there," Teresa muttered through the crack. "I've embarrassed myself."

Lory gave a little *tsk* sound. "It will be okay. I promise."

Teresa closed the door. She paced for a second and made sure the babies were still sleeping soundly. Then she smoothed her hands down her shirt and stepped out into the hall. Once again, she followed Lory to the sunken living room.

"She practically attacked me. Did you see?" Paul grinned around at the others.

"You looked so scared," one of the other guys said. "You should have seen your face." It was Levi, the one who went for help.

"Did anyone get a picture? Or a recording?" Paul looked around. His eyes landed on Teresa. He ducked his head and looked away like a shamed dog.

Teresa lifted her chin and stepped down into the living room. She took the seat Patrina had guided her to before and lowered herself onto the edge, her back straight. She avoided looking at Paul and Patrina.

"Right then," Lory said. "Here we all are now." She smiled around at the small group of people. "Introductions?" Lory nodded her head at someone.

"I'm Levi." He lifted a large hand and ducked his head. His cheeks flushed above his full beard.

"You went for help," Teresa said. His cheeks reddened further.

"You know me. I'm Patrina, this is my brother Paul. We are the ones who run the tour."

"The tour," Teresa said in a low voice. She gave the woman a sideways look. "Tell me more about this tour."

Patrina looked at Paul who looked at her. He nodded.

"Well, it's the Teresa Hart . . . um . . . Massacre . . . Tour," Patrina said, her eyes dipping away from Teresa's face at the word massacre, then back up again. "We have people meet us at the edge of town in the dead of night. We take them on a tour to the places where you . . . well, to the victims' . . . that is—"

"Just say it already, Trina," Paul said. "We show them where you killed all those people. Place to place. Ruthie's house, the old Sheriff's house where Olivia and Hunter live."

Teresa cast her eyes to a nice-looking couple who raised their hands in a united wave. They would have made nice adoptive parents for Cassie and Amanda. Olivia had long luxuriously red hair and green eyes. Hunter had a few-days-old scruff and scowl lines between his dark eyes.

"It's a rental," Olivia said with a shrug.

"We take them around to Brent Winter's house, too,"

Paul continued. "We don't know who lives there, so we have to be careful when we stop by."

"And the Berg's house," Patrina said.

The Berg's. Teresa looked up quickly. "What happened to her? The girl—Marcie?"

Patrina shook her head. "She never came out of her catatonic state."

"We really want to know all the details," Paul blurted. "How did you decide? How did you do it? I think it'll add to the whole experience—ow!"

Patrina hit him on the arm with the back of her hand and shushed him. He mouthed *what?* at her.

"We are all just so excited you're here, with us," Patrina said. "That we were going over some new stuff for the tour that night and found you. That we were able to help you. Can you imagine giving birth to twins all alone? Is that even possible?" She looked at Lory.

"How did you happen to be there?" Paul asked, leaning forward.

Teresa told them about her escape from Mountain View. She left out Raghib's and Crystal's names. Just in case Patrina knew them. Just in case they were all Messengers of the Light, despite what Lory told her.

She looked around at them as she spoke. Her eyes landed on someone who had not been introduced.

"You. Who are you?"

"I'm . . ." She looked at Lory, then back to Teresa. "I'm Rachel."

CHAPTER NINETEEN

They sat around looking at her with expectant and smiling faces—except Rachel, who looked uncomfortable. Teresa could see it in the stiffness of her shoulders and the way her hands kept shifting in her lap. She looked like she wanted to bolt. Her phone beeped, and she jumped up.

"That's work." She held up her phone. "I gotta go." She hurried toward the door.

"Bye, Rachel," Levi called after her. She gave him a close-lipped smile and left.

"Anyway, we end the tour at the abandoned funeral home." Paul scratched his cheek. He returned to talking about the tour after Teresa told them her escape story. A short span of silence followed. Paul broke it. "What do you think? Could you walk us through what happened? Validate my theories?"

Patrina smacked his arm again.

Teresa didn't know what to say. A screaming howl came from down the hallway. Cassie. Saved by the baby. Teresa jumped up, muttered a quick, "Excuse me," and all but ran to her room.

She burst in just as a woman with long dark hair lifted Cassie from the stroller.

The woman from her room. And the other night. Shadow Eve.

"Put her down immediately," Teresa demanded.

The woman turned around. She did not wear Teresa's face behind curtains of greasy black hair. It wasn't the same woman at all. Not from her dream, nor from Mountain View.

A massive scar marred half of this woman's face, distorting it. The skin looked melted, yet tight. A burn.

Cassie still howled. Her little hands pushed at this strange woman holding her. Teresa unfroze and snatched Cassie from the woman's arms. The woman left her limbs held out as if she were still holding the baby.

Lory skidded to a halt outside Teresa's door.

"Rebecca," Lory cried in a voice that sounded both surprised and enraged. "What are you doing here?"

"You need to leave immediately," Teresa said in a low but calm voice. Cassie's cries abated. Teresa pulled the stroller behind her, putting herself between Amanda and Rebecca. Amanda was now awake, little fists waving, feet kicking.

"*Lory,*" Rebecca said, spitting the name. "Long time." Her eyes shifted up and down, assessing. "Blond is a terrible color on you." Her lip curled in the childish sneer of a popular high school girl.

"How did you get in here?" Lory stepped between Rebecca and Teresa.

Rebecca, whose unmarred side of her face indicated she was probably around the same age as Lory, threw a thumb over her shoulder.

"The back door was unlocked. You really should be much more careful."

Teresa realized she must have left it unlocked. Completely uncharacteristic of her to not lock a door behind her. She supposed she had gotten out of the habit after being in a place where doors were locked on her behalf.

"You are the one who needs to be careful, showing your face around here." Lory grabbed the woman by the upper arm and dragged her out of the room. Rebecca laughed and looked over her shoulder at Teresa.

"See you around, *Doctor* Hart," she said with a mad cackle.

Teresa tightened her arms around Cassie. "It's okay little one," she said. It suddenly seemed silly to call her that, knowing what she was capable of.

She should have just ripped that woman's eyes out, Teresa thought. *She'd* wanted to rip the woman's eyes out herself. Not for the same purpose as Cassie—to feed Amanda her soul—but because her mother-bear instinct had risen up like a living thing inside her for the second time that day. Seeing someone she did not know holding her baby . . .

Teresa stroked Cassie's cheek with her finger. Cassie squealed with delight and grabbed for it.

Raised voices came from outside the house. Teresa put both babies in the crib, closed the door behind her, and slipped down the hallway to the back door. She pressed her back to the wall and, with a finger, pulled the lacy curtain aside.

Lory and the woman were having a heated argument. Lots of arm waving. But she couldn't hear exactly what they were saying.

Teresa crept back to her room. Before she went in, she glanced down the hall toward the front of the house. Were her so-called sympathizers still out there? She laughed. The babies had fallen asleep again, heads touching. Teresa sat on the end of her bed.

Sympathizers. The idea was ludicrous. How could she have sympathizers? But there they were. Six of them. Unless there were more. Maybe these six were just a welcoming committee.

Lory appeared in the doorway, breathless.

"I'm so sorry, Teresa." She rushed into the room with her hands outstretched. She gripped Teresa's hands and knelt on the floor in front of her in a ridiculous and dramatic act. Teresa pulled her hands away. Lory rose to her feet and held her elbows nervously.

"Who was that woman?" Teresa crossed her arms. "Why was she here? What did she want with Cassie?"

"Let me explain." Lory held up her hands. "Please. I know you're angry and have every right to be." Lory moved to the rocking chair, dragged it closer, and sat. She gripped her kneecaps.

Angry was putting it mildly. Teresa wanted to kill that woman for even touching Cassie.

"Who is Rebecca? You two obviously know each other and obviously have some history."

Lory looked at her hands in her lap. "She's an old acquaintance of mine." She lifted her eyes to Teresa. "She betrayed me many years ago."

"What does she want with my babies?"

"She may still be working with the Messengers of the Light." Lory leaned forward. "I don't want to jump to conclusions, but she may have been here to take them." She looked at the crib.

"What do the Messengers want with my babies?" Teresa demanded. "I'm sick of not knowing the truth. Tell me."

Lory finally looked at her. "They believe your babies can open the gateway to Tartaros."

CHAPTER TWENTY

After Ann decided to stay, Maggie had moved out onto the couch. She was feeling better, but she wanted to watch *Frozen* and eat popcorn and drink some water. She was incredibly thirsty.

Ann made a nest of blankets on the couch, which Pinky promptly took over. She laughed and tried to get Pinky to move, but Maggie told her it was fine. Maggie curled up with Pinky, shifting and jostling her around to get comfy. The dog repositioned against her.

After the movie ended, Ann turned off the TV and turned to Maggie.

"Should we put on our H-boots and have an H?" Ann asked, eyes shifting to Pinky as she said the words. Pinky knew the word *hike* and the word *go* and if Ann said them, she would have jumped up and started zooming around in anticipation.

"Yes, we shall put on our H-boots and have a H," Maggie said in her best English accent, which she thought was pretty good. It made Ann laugh.

"Let's do that." Ann got up. Pinky lifted her head and

watched her go into her room. Maggie struggled out from beneath the warm dog body.

She grabbed the sides of Pinky's face and pressed her forehead to the divot between Pinky's eyes.

"We're going for a hike," Maggie whispered, then squealed when Pinky jumped up, ears perked so much they almost stood up like pig ears. "Let's go," Maggie said in a quiet voice. "You wanna go?"

Pinky jumped around on the couch, then let out a growly howl before racing into the master bedroom.

"Did you tell her?" Ann yelled from her room.

"No." But Maggie laughed, and that gave her away. She pounded up the stairs to get her shoes.

———

Maggie held onto Pinky as Ann swung her big truck into the gravel parking lot out past the abandoned funeral home. When they had passed the old house, Ann had talked to Maggie really fast, asking her questions Ann already knew the answers to. Maggie thought it was because Ann forgot the answers. Or maybe it was to keep her from looking at the house and remembering. Maggie wasn't sure which. But she looked anyway and saw the dark shape of it deep in the trees.

It didn't bother her, though, seeing it like that. It felt like something that had happened to someone else and she'd read about it or seen it on TV.

Only one other car was parked in the lot.

"That's Rachel's car!" Maggie cried. She grinned and clapped her hands.

Ann laughed the way she did sometimes when she surprised Maggie with something. It was a different laugh than when Maggie said something funny. It was a sound Maggie didn't hear very often. She loved it.

Pinky panted with excitement, letting out little huffy grunts that Maggie loved. Ann got out and jogged around to Maggie's side, even though Maggie could open the door herself. But Maggie knew Ann did it because Pinky would explode out of the truck as soon as the door opened. Maggie wrapped her arms around Pinky and squeezed her before Ann opened the door.

Pinky blasted out. Maggie climbed out after her, using Ann's offered hand, even though she didn't need it.

Rachel climbed out of her car. She looked sad or mad or something. But Maggie ran to her, and she smiled. She gave Maggie a big swing-around hug, like always.

"Thanks for meeting us," Ann said.

Rachel was quiet and contemplative as they hiked, which was typical Rachel, but the younger woman seemed more up in her head today than usual.

Maggie and Pinky raced each other up the trail, Maggie's long curly hair flying behind her, Pinky's tail wagging as she bounded beside the girl, watching her as she went, tongue flopping out the side of her mouth.

"How's she been?" Rachel asked.

Ann shrugged. "She's been fine."

"Nightmares?" Rachel asked. "I mean, because of the deer carcass."

"Not that I'm aware of." Ann suddenly felt like she didn't know anything that was going on.

"That thing gave *me* nightmares," Rachel said with a shudder.

"She felt sick after. Tummy ache. But she's better today, obviously." Ann indicated the squealing girl flying up ahead. Pinky paused to sniff something on the side of the trail, then took off again after Maggie.

"That guy running against you—what's his name?"

"Duke Westley." Ann heard the disdain in her own voice.

"He's a dick." Rachel wasn't one to sugarcoat things. She stated everything the way it was, the way she saw it. She called Ann out all the time, whenever her academy training came into play in their little office in their little town. She'd say, "It's *Harmony*, Ann. Not Denver. Not even Salida. People need . . ." Then she'd insert whatever seemingly insignificant thing, from a neighbor playing their music too loud to someone being tattled on for walking their dog late at night instead of during the day like a *normal* person. Not illegal by any means, but people were nosy. And the influx of new folks moving to town had the locals suspicious.

"I've known him since high school," Ann said, looking up the hill toward Maggie and Pinky. They were crouched at the side of the trail checking something out. "He was a dick back then too."

Rachel laughed. "Good to know my judge of character is still as sharp as ever." She made a smug little sound and groaned. "He keeps coming in. Just popping by to try to build rapport with me and Sully. Sully seems to like him." She rolled her eyes.

"Sully's just polite."

Up ahead was a signpost where the trail forked.

"Let's go this way," Maggie cried, pointing to the left. She and Pinky headed in that direction. Ann jogged ahead, leaving Rachel behind.

"Maggie, Pinky, come back," Ann called. "We need to go the other way to make the loop. That way is too far."

Maggie came back down the trail, her brow worried. Pinky bounded back toward Rachel, rounding her up.

"There's something this way," Maggie said. "It's . . . calling me." She rubbed the mark over her chest.

Ann crouched down to Maggie's level. "What do you think it is?"

Maggie shrugged. "I don't know." She looked over her shoulder and back at Ann with wet eyes. "It's making me want to cry."

Ann looked down the trail. It would add too much mileage to their hike to go that way. "I'll check it out later, okay?"

Maggie looked over her shoulder again. "But she's so sad."

No matter how many times Maggie said something weird like this, Ann could never get used to it.

"Who?" she asked, choking the word past her dry throat.

Maggie closed her eyes and cocked her head. "Glory."

The name came out a whisper, and an electric chill zipped over Ann's body.

Maggie opened her eyes. "What?"

Ann realized her own eyes were wide with the shock she felt at Maggie knowing this name. This was one of those moments when Sophia had to be lurking just under the surface, telling Maggie things Maggie couldn't possibly know otherwise. Unless she'd seen the name written in Ann's notebook.

"How do you know it's Glory?" Ann asked, her lips hardly moving. "How do you know that's her name, I mean?"

Maggie looked down at her hands. "Sophia told me."

Rachel came up behind them. "What's going on?"

Maggie looked up at Rachel, the angle of the light making her golden eyes glow. She looked back at Ann. "You have to go to her."

Ann nodded. "Why don't you go ahead and take the loop with Rachel and Pinky? I'll take a look."

"Take Pinky with you," Maggie said. "She can find Glory."

Rachel snorted. "That dog couldn't find a Milk Bone if it was in the middle of the room."

Maggie scowled at Rachel. "This isn't a Milk Bone, *Rachel*," she snapped. She looked at Ann with a softer, pleading expression. "She can do it. I know she can." Maggie stroked Pinky's head and turned to her, pressing her forehead against the dog's. Maggie did that a lot. Ann wondered if she could communicate telepathically with the canine. "You'll find her, right?" Maggie asked in a small voice.

Pinky let out a growl that ended on an up note, like a question. Maggie released her.

Ann's heart double beat in her chest. Pinky stared hard down the trail, ears forward and alert, muscles taut beneath her fur. Ann clipped the leash to Pinky's harness.

"Okay," she said. "I'll take Pinky."

Maggie hugged Pinky. "Find her, Pinky." Maggie grimaced up at Ann. "It might be too late though."

Ann swallowed past the dryness in her throat at those haunting words. *Too late.*

Rachel took Maggie's hand, and they hiked back down the trail to make the loop. Ann watched them go. Normally, Pinky would watch Maggie go, too, but she still stared down the trail.

"Let's go," Ann said.

Half a mile in, according to Ann's GPS watch, Pinky tugged the leash out of Ann's hand and charged into the woods, baying like a hound, though a hound she was not. Ann jogged to keep up, but the scrub oak and low brush, coupled with low branches snagging her hair and yanking it out of her ponytail, slowed her progress. She hoped it wasn't remains.

It might be too late though, Maggie's words said again.

"Pinky!" Ann called doubling her pace. The trees got thicker, blotting out most of the daylight. Ann pushed her way into a clearing and halted.

An electric charge sizzled through her body.

A female, approximately early teens, curled in a ball with her back to Ann, lay in the center of the clearing. She was surrounded by a pool of maybe blood, maybe something else. It was hard to tell in the late afternoon light filtering down through the dense trees. Pinky stood at the outer edge of the pool of fluid, prancing and chuffing.

"Stay back, Pinky," Ann commanded.

The girl moved. Pinky let out a whimper and scurried over to Ann with her ears back. She peeked out from behind Ann's knee.

"Stay still," Ann called to the girl. "I'm going to help you."

"No one . . . can help me . . ." a slow and rasping voice said.

Ann told Pinky to stay. She sidled around the clearing until she could see the girl's face. Ann recoiled.

Gaping black holes where her eyes should have been marred her face. The stuff on the ground around her trickled from the sockets. Her mouth lay open. The front of her shirt was drenched in black.

"Glory?"

The girl jerked at the sound of the name but didn't move otherwise. Ann couldn't even detect respirations.

"I'm coming closer, okay?" Ann duck-walked toward the girl. Pinky whined from the shadows of the trees. Was this who Maggie felt? As she got closer, the smell of burning brakes and rotting leaves assaulted her nostrils. It burned the backs of her eyes. Ann covered her mouth and nose with her shirt.

"Oh . . . kay . . ." the rasping voice said.

Ann halted.

The girl's mouth hadn't moved.

"What's your name, sweetheart?" Ann asked.

"Sadness," the voice said, lips unmoving.

Pinky held steady, but she stomped her front paws and her hackles were up. She stared at Ann with earnest focus. She let out a high three-note whimper Ann had never heard before, followed by a chuff and a rumbling growl. A warning.

Ann jumped when the girl shifted and flopped onto her back, her arms and legs spread out like a starfish.

Glory's chest lifted off the pine needle-covered floor, arching until the top of her head and her toes were all that touched the ground, and still she bent upward, until her hands planted onto the ground with a sickening crack from her shoulders.

"I am Sadness," the low rasping voice said again. "I am Sadness." She began to spin in a circle, her feet and hands propelling her around like a scuttling crab.

Pinky yipped and backed away. So much for a brave dog. She gave one sharp bark. Ann took her lead and backed around to the edge of the circle to Pinky's side. She crouched while the girl spun in circles like a confused compass trying to locate due North, shouting that she was sadness with that horrible low voice.

The girl halted. Her upside-down face pointed in Ann and Pinky's direction. Ann tensed. Deep within those empty black sockets, eyes appeared. From the short distance, they were all white with a pin point of a pupil.

"I. Am. Sadness." The voice deepened further to a gravelly growl.

Ann's duty to find the missing girl and deliver her home to her mother battled with an intense and undeniable desire to get the hell out of there.

No training had ever prepared her for something like this, and despite what she'd witnessed and experienced last year in Tartaros and the days leading up to The Night, the rational side of her tried to make it fit into a box.

Mental illness. Depression. She's sick. It's just vomit—black, weird stinky vomit.

She's not really upside-down crab-walking toward you.

"Oh shit."

Black liquid spewed from the girl's mouth like a fountain. It splattered across the clearing toward them. Some of it got on Ann's boots and pant cuffs.

Ann pulled out her phone, but she had no bars. She was too far from the cell tower.

"Dammit." Ann and Pinky ran back to the trail. Gurgling laughter faded away the farther they got from that hateful clearing.

At the trail, she had a single bar if she stood just right. She dialed Sully.

"Deputy Sullivan," he answered.

"Sully," Ann said, recognizing a sort of panicky breathlessness in her own voice. "I need backup at the trail by mile marker two out past the abandoned funeral home.

The Mountain Muhly trail. Take the left fork about half a mile."

"You actually have cell reception out that far?"

"Do you copy?" Ann yelled.

"You're breaking up," Sully said. "But I copy what you said before, about the trail. I'm getting my stuff. Duke is here."

"He needs to leave. He can't be hanging around the station unsupervised." Ann resisted making a frustrated sound. "This is in relation to the missing girl," Ann said. "Bring a tarp."

"A tarp?"

Ann couldn't think. A tarp wasn't the right thing to request, but it was all she could think to use to restrain someone spewing black ichor out of every visible orifice.

"Sheriff—Ann, is she . . . dead?"

Duke's muffled voice came through on the other end of the line. Ann cringed.

Dammit, Sully.

So much for discretion.

"I said a tarp, not a body bag. She's not dead." She thought of the book. Was this a Logismoi? "I think she's sick —or injured."

"You don't know? Why do we need a tarp?"

"Sully, please. I'll leave a marker for you. Head straight into the woods from it until you find us. Call Flight For Life." It was the only emergency vehicle that could get anyone to a hospital in a reasonable time, the way Harmony was positioned in the middle of nowhere. "Call Ronnie, too. Tell her we found Glory, that she's hurt, and we're calling it in to get her to the hospital in Pine Valley."

"Yes, ma'am. I'll call them both on my way to you."

Ann tore her over shirt off and draped it in the bushes.

She paused before stepping back into the trees and took a deep breath. Her organs felt like they were trembling. She didn't want to go back, but she had to. Her duty was to the people of her town.

"Okay." She took another deep breath and let it out. "Let's go, Pinky." She stepped back into the brush. Pinky whined. Ann looked at her.

"Come on, Pinky."

Pinky backed away and let out another whine.

"Please. I need you." Ann whimpered herself. Her nose prickled. Jesus. Was she that scared of a little girl?

Demon girl.

"Fine, stay." Pinky sat, then dropped into a down. Ann didn't have to command her to stay again. The dog obeyed. Ann jogged back toward the clearing.

Glory no longer pranced around on all fours—upside-down. She just lay in the puddle of black goo.

"Glory?" Ann called to her. She didn't move. Ann's mouth dried. She shifted closer, one slow step at a time. When Ann was a couple of feet away, Glory's head flopped to the side, dark purple tongue lolling from blackened lips. Her eyes, pure white with pinhole pupils, stared at Ann.

Ann crouched down.

"I'm going to check your pulse, okay?" Rapid, sluggish— she needed to know. Ann reached forward. The horrible eyes shifted and watched her hand. The tongue sucked back into Glory's mouth. She bared her teeth and snapped at Ann. Ann jumped back. Glory rolled away the way kids rolled down grassy hills and lay still again.

Ann stayed put and waited. It wouldn't take Sully too long to reach her. He was in good shape. He was a good cop, too. Responsive. Always stuck to his training.

A few minutes later, the bushes crashed behind her.

Sully came panting into the clearing with a kit in his hand and a tarp stuffed under his arm. He flung a thumb over his shoulder.

"What's with Pinky?" he asked. "I tried to get her to come with me, but she just started shaking. Holy mother of mercy." His eyes drifted from Ann to the blackened dirt in the middle of the clearing, then to the girl laying at the far edge. His face paled.

"She's not dead." Ann took the tarp from him but really didn't know what she was going to do with it. She couldn't exactly wrap the girl up in it.

"What's all this black stuff?"

"Vomit." It came out of her mouth, so that was the most plausible *thing* it could be. A creeping anxiety gnawed her gut. It traveled up to her chest and tightened around her lungs.

"Black vomit," Sully muttered. He looked at Ann. "Usually means blood in the belly, right?"

Ann shrugged, afraid to speak.

Sully took a step toward her. "You okay, Sheriff?" he asked, sliding his ball cap off.

Behind him, Glory sat up. She got her feet under her and rose. Ann grabbed Sully's arm and backed away, dragging him a couple of paces with her before he pulled out of her grasp. He gave Ann a strange look and turned back to Glory. He jumped and cleared his throat.

"Ma'am? Are you okay?" Sully held one hand out as if to halt her in case she came closer. Sully angled his face toward Ann. "Is she on drugs or something? Look at her pupils."

Glory lifted her arms over her head and performed a cartwheel. Over and over. A joyous sound issued from her with each hands-over-feet rotation.

"We can catch her with the tarp," Sully said. "Restrain her until Flight For Life comes." He nodded as if agreeing with his own plan. He lifted the tarp and shook it out. Glory stopped cartwheeling and lowered her arms out to the side. She spun in circles. At least she wasn't spewing the black stuff anymore.

"I know this isn't protocol," Sully said under his breath.

"I don't think there is protocol for this kind of situation."

Sully rushed toward Glory with the tarp out. Glory dodged him, twirled around, and jumped onto his back. Sully cried out with the most horrified sound Ann had ever heard come from a human being. She lunged forward and grabbed Glory around the midsection. Glory let go of Sully. She and Ann toppled to the ground. Ann held on. Glory's arms and legs thrashed. She caught Ann in the shin with her heel. Ann let go.

Glory jumped up, crouched, hissed at them, and ran into the forest with a maniacal laugh. Ann took off after her.

"Glory, wait. We're here to help you," Ann shouted. Bushes crashed behind her. Ann whirled around. Sully came up behind her. Together they ran in the direction Glory had gone, though they could no longer hear movement.

"Maybe she finally crashed." Sully's eyes widened. "What if she OD'ed on whatever she's on?" He was still convinced she was on drugs. Ann could understand. Before last October, she would have searched for logical explanations herself. But she was past that. Mostly.

"Let's keep searching," Ann said.

In the distance a helicopter's blades *thwupped* the air.

"Shit," Ann said. "We have to go meet them."

"We have to find her," Sully said. "We can't just leave her out here, can we?"

"I'll keep looking. You meet the chopper."

Sully nodded and ran off toward the trail.

"Glory," Ann called again. "Please come to my voice. We just want to help you." She kept moving in the direction Glory had run, calling her name into the woods until her voice was hoarse. Daylight dwindled, darkening the forest around her.

"Shit," Ann whispered, peering around hopelessly. She met up with Sully on her way back to the trail. "I'll go talk to Ronnie. We need to organize a search party. The two of us can't cover enough ground to find her." Ann rubbed her eyebrow. "We need to call for help."

Pinky still waited for her on the trail. Ann and Sully parted ways at the parking lot.

CHAPTER TWENTY-ONE

Ann pulled up to Ronnie Masterton's house and parked on the street out front. Lights on inside. A curtain swept aside, revealing a woman's face. It closed, and seconds later the front door opened.

Ronnie Masterton stood in the doorway clutching her elbows.

"Here we go, Pinky." Ann took a deep breath and climbed out of her truck.

"Ronnie Masterton?" Ann said as she approached.

"Did you find her, Sheriff? Is my Glory okay?" Ronnie took a step forward, reaching. She stepped back inside the doorway and motioned for Ann to come in.

Ann followed Ronnie into a front room off the foyer. Two floral couches faced each other across an ornate coffee table that held a tea set.

"I found her," Ann said. She hurried on before Ronnie could be too relieved. "But she's not well. She ran away from Deputy Sullivan and myself into the woods."

"Ran? From cops?" Ronnie sank onto the gaudier of the two floral couches.

"She didn't seem well," Ann said. "Do you know if she's been hanging out with a different crowd than usual?"

"Different? Different how? She has the same friends she's had since grade school."

"Maybe there's a bad crowd at school?" Ann chastised herself for pussy-footing around the issue. She sighed. "Do you know if she's gotten into drugs, Mrs. Masterton?"

Ronnie looked taken aback.

"Drugs? My Glory?"

"She was—" Ann searched for words to describe the girl. "Agitated. Her pupils were tiny. Her behavior was erratic. Not to mention she jumped on Deputy Sullivan's back before running off into the woods."

"Where is she now?" Ronnie rose as if to look for Glory.

"She's still out in the woods," Ann said.

Ronnie cried out. "Still in the woods? You left her out there?"

Ann held up her hands. "Please. Calm down. We lost daylight. Deputy Sullivan is organizing a search. We're calling in help from Pine Valley. They have a K-9 search and rescue unit. We'll start fresh in the morning."

Before Ronnie could say another word, the front door burst open.

"Hi, Mama," a voice said. Her other daughter probably.

"Glory?" Ronnie shrieked. "Glory is that you? Oh, my sweet baby where have you been?"

Ann's stomach fell down into her kneecaps. She strode out to the entryway. Glory, covered in black vomit, stood just inside the door. Her eyes were back to normal, not white with pin-prick pupils, but a gray that was striking with her dark hair.

"I was at the abandoned funeral home thinking about things," Glory said. "Then I woke up in the woods, and here

I am." The girl's mouth stretched into a grin so wide, Ann was surprised her lips didn't crack. It was unnatural.

"You had me worried sick." Ronnie ushered her daughter inside, but steered her away from Ann.

"Thank you for your efforts, Sheriff Logan. I have it from here." She gave Ann a pointed look before turning back to Glory. "Let's get this yucky mud washed off."

"I need to ask her some questions," Ann said. "About what happened to her."

Ronnie stopped and gave Ann a vicious look over her shoulder.

"She already said she doesn't remember."

"Look, I know you are protecting her, and that's okay. But I need to know as much as possible. What if she was kidnapped? What if she was attacked? I need to know if there are dangers going on here in Harmony, if there are things I need to warn other parents about."

Ronnie's shoulders relaxed. "Can I at least get her cleaned up first?"

"I'll wait right here."

Ronnie took Glory up a set of stairs and out of sight. Ann walked around looking at pictures on sideboards. Two girls grinned out of the photos, but as they got older their expressions got surlier.

Is this what I have to look forward to?

She peeked out the window at her truck where a dog-shaped silhouette backlit by the streetlight pointed in her direction. Ann gave Pinky a little wave, felt foolish, and let the curtains swing shut. She checked her watch. Rachel and Maggie had been hanging out for a few hours. Rachel would need to get home soon.

Ann settled onto the not as gaudy of the two couches

and leaned back, then forward. Black splatters marred the cuffs of her pants. She'd take a sample of it.

A few minutes later, Ronnie came back into the room with a glass of water.

"Got anything stronger?" Ann asked.

"Haven't kept the stuff in the house since Albert left," she said with a haughty sniff.

"I meant coffee?"

Ronnie's cheeks flushed. "I have some instant mix in the cupboard, if that'll do."

Ann nodded.

Jaunty footsteps on the stairs. A few seconds later, Glory appeared in the entryway.

She wore jeans and a bright pink T-shirt. But it wasn't the clothes that grabbed Ann's attention. It was her smile. It was wide—too wide—stretching her lips until they lost almost all of their color from the strain.

A far cry from the thing Ann had seen in the woods.

"Hi." Ann gave a lame wave and stood. "I'm Sheriff Logan. You can call me Ann. I hope I didn't scare you earlier. In the woods?"

Glory made obscene amounts of eye contact. Her smile never faltered.

"So very pleased to meet you." Somehow the smile remained while she spoke.

"I need to ask you a few questions about what happened." Ann pulled a little notebook from her back pocket and flipped to a clean page. The breast pocket of her shirt had a pen. She clicked it.

Ronnie came back into the room with a steaming mug of coffee.

"Mother?" Glory said in a saccharine voice. "May I please have a cup of herbal tea?" She pronounced the H in *herbal* like it was a joke to say it that way, but something told Ann it wasn't a joke.

"Of course, darling," Ronnie said. When Ronnie disappeared down the hall again, Glory, still standing in the entryway, turned back to Ann.

"Whatever is it that you wish to know, Sheriff Logan?" When she said Ann's title and name, her voice changed. Not a lot, but enough for Ann to pick it up. It was more monotone when surrounded by the cheery way she said the other words.

The girl's skin held faint black cracks under the surface, like her veins contained that black stuff she'd spewed in the clearing.

"Would you like to sit down?" Ann motioned toward the couches.

"I'm perfectly fine standing here." Glory's smile was unsettling.

"Who are you?" Ann asked in a low voice.

"Glory Masterton," she said.

"Where were you last night?'

"I went for a walk out the road. It was a lovely night for walking," Glory said, lips hardly moving from their smile.

"Why did you go for a walk at night?"

"I was so sad," Glory said. Her smile still did not falter. "I had to get away to be alone."

Ann squinted at her. Something was definitely not right about her, other than the insane smile and the strange discoloring under her skin. Was it the unflinching eye contact? Her eyes themselves were fine—pupils normal.

"Do you feel safe here at home?" Ann asked in a low voice.

Glory's eyes flicked away, then back to Ann's.

"Yes." She said through her grinning teeth. She

swallowed, her throat working, but her face, her mouth, remained still. A trickle of black leaked from the corner. She wiped it away slowly. "I'm so very happy."

Ann watched the inky black stuff seep from her mouth again. She met Glory's horrible stare.

"Sadness," Ann whispered.

Glory's eyes widened a fraction. Ann thought she saw the smile falter. Just a flicker where the corners relaxed slightly.

"Happiness," she said. Her smile renewed with vigor. "Pure joy."

Ronnie came down the hall with a mug, keeping a careful eye on the hot liquid. The tea bag tag flapped as she moved.

"Here you go." Her eyes flicked to her daughter's face, and for a moment, she hesitated. Just a half-second hesitation. She cleared her throat and bustled into the room where she set the tea on the coffee table. She motioned for Glory to follow, before flicking her eyes to Ann. Ann gave her a grim nod.

"We were just talking about how sad I was," Glory said, finally stepping into the room. "I was so sad, Mother." She sat on the couch next to Ronnie, back straight, hands on her knees.

It was like watching someone pretend to be a human being—someone who didn't know how a human should behave.

Ronnie stroked Glory's hair. "I know you were sad, darling. I know. But now you're okay."

"Yes. Now I'm perfectly happy."

"Why were you so sad?" Ann asked.

Ronnie waved a hand. "Boy troubles," she said with a laugh and a nervous glance at her daughter. "Right honey?"

Glory nodded one slow dip of her chin, eyes on Ann, smile in place.

"Did you come across anyone while out walking? Did anyone offer you anything to take to ease your pain? Anything like that?"

"My daughter does not do drugs, Sheriff." Ronnie's exclamation lost power at the end when she glanced at Glory. A dribble of black inky fluid coursed down her chin from the corner of her expansive mouth.

Glory reached forward and gripped the hot mug of tea with both hands. She lifted it to her lips and, smile still in place, gulped and all but dumped it down the front of her shirt. It had to burn, but she did not make a sound. Her throat clicked as she swallowed.

Ann met Ronnie's eyes and nodded her head toward the entryway. "Can I speak with you privately?"

Ronnie nodded and led Ann down the hallway and into the kitchen. The door swung closed.

"What is wrong with her?" Ronnie asked. "Something's off. She's not herself. She's strange."

Ann's shoulders slumped with relief. She opened her mouth to tell Ronnie more of what had happened in the woods, but she decided against it. She wasn't honestly sure *what* she saw. She needed to corroborate her story with Sully's account to really get to grips with it.

"She said she went out the road. Do you know where she might have gone out that way?"

"Probably the abandoned funeral home. Isn't that where everyone goes if they head out that way?" Her tone wasn't snappy, but there was an edge to it, like Ann should know this information.

Ann glanced up at her. "What do you mean?"

"Tony Cook-Robin says there's a tour." She crossed her

arms. "He would know. He's the new writer for the *The Local Inquirer*."

"We patrol that area every night and haven't seen anything." Who the hell was Tony Cook-Robin, and why did Ronnie take his gossip rag to be the gospel truth? Ann didn't even know the *Inquirer* was back. As far as she knew, publication of the joke paper had ceased with Brent's demise.

"Well, I'm not sure where she would have gone then." Ronnie suddenly closed up. She toyed with the gold cross around her neck. "Is there anything else you need, Sheriff?"

"Thank you for your time. I recommend you get Glory to a doctor. Get her checked out."

Ann left the Masterton house. She couldn't get Glory's smile out of her head. She glanced at the house before pulling away. There it was again. Glory stood in the window waving, that smile spread across her lips to the point of splitting them.

Pinky let out a wheezing whine from the bench seat next to Ann.

"I know, girl. Something's weird." Pinky yawned and grumbled. "I'm just not sure what yet."

Yes, the black stuff leaked from the corner of Glory's mouth. But more than that—her skin just didn't seem to form to the contours of her face like it should have.

CHAPTER TWENTY-TWO

Ann had to follow the only lead she had. She drove out to the abandoned funeral home to poke around and hopefully come up with some answers, some evidence of what had happened to Glory before she ended up in the clearing. If Ronnie seemed to believe the abandoned funeral home was where everyone went because of some tour Tony Cook-Robin wrote about—well, she had to check it out.

After all, it was Brent Winter's photo of Teresa in *The Local Inquirer* that had led Ann there before.

Ann had gone out there at least once a week for a couple months after The Night. She searched the house top to bottom, including the expansive basement, for some clue or sign that the place had ever transformed into the Gnostic underworld.

She'd found nothing.

Now, she parked her truck on the side of the dirt road and turned to Pinky.

"You have to stay here," she said, giving the dog's head a scrub. She rolled down both windows and pulled a flashlight out of the glove box before getting out. She still didn't trust the dog around potential remains of any kind. Not since Brent.

Ann clicked on the flashlight and swept the beam into the woods. The tombstones from the old cemetery tilted at odd angles, blackened by age and soot from the fire of 1912. The abandoned funeral home loomed into view.

The yellow tape had been torn down since last time she was out here. They would probably have to board up the place to keep folks out of it. She honestly wasn't sure why she hadn't.

Because you want to be able to go in and search it again whenever you want.

It was true. She wanted—no *needed*—to find a way back, to make sure her dad wasn't still there, alive. Even though he had sacrificed his own soul in exchange to get Ann, Maggie, and unfortunately, Teresa out of Tartaros, a small part of her had to believe he *might* still be there, if only because she wanted it to be true.

She shined the light into the gloomy interior.

The pungent stink of blood and something else struck her nostrils the closer she got to the couch. She couldn't be sure, but there might be new stains there. Not that she'd documented every stain on the old disgusting thing.

If Glory came here because she needed to be alone, she would have presumably sat on the sofa. Otherwise, what, she would just stand around?

Ann took a step closer, shining her light along the length of the furniture. She stepped on something soft and squishy. Ann lifted her foot and shined the light down, illuminating a squashed eyeball, optic nerve and all.

She back pedaled several steps before getting a grip and

crouching down to make sure it wasn't some Halloween gag toy. It was definitely real. She pulled the radio from her belt.

"Sheriff Logan to Deputy Sullivan," she said, trying to no avail to keep the panicky sound out of her voice.

"Go for Deputy Sullivan," he said.

"I need a kit and a scene light out at the abandoned funeral home."

A long pause. She was about to key the radio again, but he responded.

"It's not Glory, is it?"

"No." Ann had forgotten to tell him. "She actually showed up at home while I was talking to Ronnie. This is totally different." Maybe unrelated? But she had to wonder, given Glory might have been here before she went to the woods. Given she had no eyes when Ann first saw her.

It was just a trick of the shadows.

"Keep telling yourself that," Ann whispered.

Sully arrived a few minutes later, plodding through the brush and tombstones with the kit in one hand and a scene light in the other. His shoulders were slumped, stooped almost. He looked tired. Ann wondered if he'd been at the station when she radioed, or at home getting some rest.

Unlike George—bless his giant heart—Sully wasn't squeamish. He also jumped at any chance to help with a crime scene, and he was good at it.

"If that asshole Westley gets elected, I'm not staying here," he told Ann as he approached. "He was at the station *again* acting like he owns the place. Walked in right after I got back from sending Flight For Life away. Like he was just waiting for one of us so he could come back in."

That would explain the downtrodden body language.

"I'll talk to him. Again."

They donned nitrile gloves, and Sully set up the light in the doorway to illuminate the interior. It did a fair job. "Adjust it this way."

He did, then came inside. "What do we got?" he asked, hands on his hips.

"At least one eyeball and potentially some new stains on the couch, but I can't be sure. Do you smell that?" Ann asked.

Sully took a deep breath through his nose. "I smell something metallic. Like blood?"

"Spray the couch down with Luminol. Let's see what we can see."

While Sully got to work on the couch, Ann collected the eyeball. She found a second eye a couple feet away, bagged it, and held them both up. They were gray. Sully stepped to her side.

"Who's do you think they are?" he asked.

Glory Masterton's.

But she couldn't jump to those kinds of conclusions, since she'd seen the girl less than an hour ago and her eyeballs were still inside her skull, and Sully hadn't seen Glory without her eyes. Ann shuddered.

"We'll have to send them off for DNA analysis, along with any other samples we collect."

"It'll take a while to get anything back. The lab's backed up. They told me it could be a couple weeks before they get back to us on that black stuff from the clearing."

Ann felt her lips form a grim line. She was afraid of that.

"Moment of truth." Sully held up a black light.

Ann cut the scene light. The right half of the couch lit up.

"Okay then," Ann said. "Time to collect some samples." She turned back to the kit.

Sully cleared his throat. "I was wondering when we're going to talk about what happened in the clearing in the woods." He held the back of his neck like it hurt, but Ann figured it was a mark for discomfort.

"What do you want to talk about?" Ann pulled some swabs out. "Glory's back home safe and sound." She shrugged and hoped he wouldn't press her.

"Do you think it was drugs?"

"Maybe," Ann said. "Her mother didn't seem to think so. Without a tox report, we might never know." *Now leave it, and let's get to work.*

"She was downright frightening, Ann." Sully pulled on his own gloves. "Downright frightening." He paused. "What are your theories?"

Ann searched the kit for nothing while she collected her thoughts. They could theorize and speculate all night about what happened in the clearing, but Ann couldn't tell him what she thought was the truth.

"Drugs would be a good explanation." She made a quick decision, took a deep breath, and on the exhale said, "Demonic possession is another."

Sully laughed. Ann looked up at him with a raised eyebrow.

"You're serious?"

She shrugged.

He laughed again, a nervous sound, and cleared his throat. "Let's get to work."

After a couple hours, they'd collected a long dark hair —*Glory has long dark hair*—and several cotton swabs with various fluids. Sully promised to run them to the lab.

Before he left, Ann stopped him. "Have you been doing patrols out here when you're on night shift?"

His face turned red and his shoulders slumped. "Not lately."

"Why not? I gave you a direct order to patrol out this way. Now someone named Tony Cook-Robin is spreading rumors about a secret tour that operates at night out here."

"I'm sorry, Sheriff," Sully said. "I just don't like coming out here. It gives me the heebie-jeebies. I mean, isn't this where, you know, *that woman* killed all those people?" He looked around as if mentioning Teresa Hart would somehow summon her.

"She killed them all over town." Ann sighed. "I'm not asking you to get out and come search it every night. Just shine your spotlight into the woods from the road. See if you can see any movement. That sort of thing. Chances are, if they see you looking, they'll run."

"Okay." He looked down, his face flushed.

Ann tried not to show how disappointed she was that he'd disobeyed a direct order. He was a good cop. She couldn't risk him leaving over something like this.

Pinky's barks traveled across the distance. Ann ran, leaving Sully in her dust, burdened as he was with the evidence and gear.

Pinky hung out the driver's side, hackles up. Ann looked around for any sign of someone or something dangerous.

"What is it? What's wrong with her?" A breathless Sully flinched when the dog let out a particularly loud bark.

Ann opened the door, expecting Pinky to run out and show her what was wrong, but Pinky backed up to the passenger side of the bench seat and sat.

"I guess I'll see you later," Ann said to Sully. "Get those

samples to the lab." She made a U-turn and headed back toward town.

Once she was within the range of the cell tower, Ann's phone pinged with several missed calls.

All of them were from Rachel.

CHAPTER TWENTY-THREE

Maggie sat by the window looking out at the road, waiting for Ann. She had never left Maggie this long and never this late. A car pulled in and Maggie jumped up.

"It's the pizza guy, kiddo. Sorry." Rachel answered the door and brought in the box. They ate together in silence.

The house was too quiet without Pinky and too quiet without Ann, even if Ann would probably just be sitting at the table looking at her laptop.

"Wanna play a game?" Rachel asked.

Maggie shook her head. A suffocating feeling filled her chest. She thought it was Sophia trying to tell her something. Her mark grew tight and itchy.

"What's taking her so long?" Maggie asked, unable to keep the words inside.

"I'll try calling her again." But Rachel set down her phone after a moment. "Voicemail. How about a movie?"

Maggie shook her head again.

"Well, how about I just put a movie on? If you want to come sit in here with me and watch it, you can."

Maggie only sighed. She didn't want to leave her post at

the window. If Rachel weren't here, she would just go and look for Ann. She could walk to the station, check there, and out the road.

But it was dark, and the thought of being by the woods at night was too scary.

Rachel put on a movie. *Moana*, of course. Rachel knew she loved that movie. But Maggie stayed on the chair by the window, even though it was wooden and her bottom was beginning to hurt. She needed a cushion.

Maggie crossed her arms on the table top and rested her cheek on them.

A voice entered her mind.

Light and dark, life and death. They are siblings of one another and inseparable. For this reason the good are not good, the bad are not bad, life is not life, and death is not death.

"I know," Maggie whispered. "What does it mean?"

"What was that, Mags?" Rachel's voice was far away and muffled.

"Nothing." Maggie's eyes sagged closed.

The darkness lit suddenly, then blasted her backward through space and time. Pinpoints of light fading ahead of her cast lines at the edges of her eyeballs.

Images flashed. Slow-motion stills of a war waging in some unknown land. Like the start of the dream she'd had the other night, before the Luminaries came to her.

Two figures with identical faces, hands raised, faced each other, expressions twisted into angry battle cries. One had palms with a yellowy-orange glow. She wore all white and looked like an angel without wings. The other held a ball of darkness. With wings spread behind her, she hovered a few feet above her twin, her tail lashing.

"In the time before," Sophia's voice said. Maggie had

never heard her directly like this. "Light and Dark warred with one another."

Time normalized. The twins fought, firing light and darkness at each other.

"They were the only two beings in this land, but their power was great. Darkness filled the world with inky blackness, while Light's power created the stars."

When the energy balls hit each other, they merged and erupted like supernovas. The twins both noticed this phenomenon at the same time, halting mid-attack to watch. The stars and darkness existed together. Light and dark together.

"When they finally realized they were not opposing ends of a spectrum, but parts of one whole, they came together."

The twins stopped fighting. They closed the distance between each other and pressed their palms together. They smiled and touched foreheads.

The image filled with so much light, Maggie wanted to close her eyes, but they were already closed. In the resulting silhouette, the twin with the power of light, wearing the light-colored robes, also wore the leathery wings of the being of darkness—as if they'd traded places.

"Light cannot exist without dark. Dark cannot exist without light," Sophia's voice said. "The same for life and death."

Life is not life, and death is not death.

"They are inseparable," Sophia's voice said. "The power created by this union is what gave the spark for the creation of all that exists now." The view blasted backward until the spark became a tiny light. It bloomed outward, expanding with stars and planets.

"Though there cannot exist light without dark, life without death, they cannot *be* at the same time."

The images in Maggie's mind shifted. The two were torn apart. They clung to each other, arms grasping, faces contorted with grief.

Whatever power that tore them apart succeeded. The twins fell away from each other, spinning end over end, until they were far apart.

"They yearn for each other. This yearning created chaos. Chaos that has yet to leave this realm. Chaos that ebbs and flows with time. Waves breaking and mending."

Horrible images of people in pain, wailing and crying out. Bombs exploding. Guns firing. Maggie wanted to cover her ears, but she couldn't move. She didn't exist in here. It was just her mind—and Sophia's. Pictures flashing and flying around. Some of them she didn't understand. Men in uniforms marching. Airplanes dropping things from their bellies.

"Make it stop," Maggie whimpered. They did not stop.

"The twins must be kept together to maintain balance in this realm," Sophia said over the noise of the pictures. "To separate them again will strengthen Chaos once more."

"Make it stop!" Maggie screamed.

Rachel was there at her side, gently shaking Maggie's shoulders.

"Maggie, wake up," Rachel said.

"I'm awake."

The front door opened. Pinky came charging in, wiggling so hard she lashed herself in the face. She came directly to Maggie who dropped onto the floor and hugged her, getting her own whips from Pinky's tail. Ann came in after. Maggie jumped to her feet and hugged her around the waist.

CHAPTER TWENTY-FOUR

"I'm so glad you're home," Maggie said. "I was worried sick."

"It's true," Rachel said. "She didn't leave this spot the whole time. She even fell asleep there at the table." Rachel frowned. "I think she had a nightmare. She yelled 'make it stop,' or something like that."

Ann patted Maggie's head. "Did you have a bad dream?"

"Was it her?" Maggie didn't look up and didn't let go. "Was it Glory in the woods?"

Ann took a deep breath. "Yep. And now she's home, safe and sound."

"Why was she so sad?" Maggie asked.

Ann looked at Rachel standing awkwardly as if unsure if she should go or not. "Thank you for bringing her home," Ann said. "And for watching her so late. And buying pizza. I'll pay you back."

"No worries. You know I've got your back." Rachel grabbed her keys from the table and left.

Ann extricated herself from Maggie's grasp to lock the door behind Rachel.

"Why was Glory so sad?" Maggie asked again.

"Boy troubles." Ann avoided Maggie's eyes. Maggie had learned Ann's tells. "I'm starving. What do we have here?" She lifted the lid on the pizza box.

"Boy troubles?" Maggie looked confused. She closed her eyes and shook her head.

"You want to talk about your nightmare?" Ann took a bite of room-temperature pizza.

"Not right now," Maggie said. "I'm really tired. I think I'll just go to bed." She went to the stairs.

"Don't forget to brush your teeth." Ann peeked around the edge of the kitchen. Maggie was already halfway up the stairs with Pinky plodding along behind her, like she was spotting her.

Ann watched them disappear into Maggie's room at the top and frowned. Tiredness could explain away Maggie's sudden withdrawal, but coupling it with a nightmare? It had to be the dream. Ann finished her slice of pizza, put the box in the fridge, and went upstairs.

Maggie and Pinky sat on Maggie's bed facing each other.

"I don't know what it means," Maggie whispered. Ann wondered how often she confided in the dog. She knocked on the doorframe.

"Want a story?" Ann asked. Maggie shook her head. Ann helped her under the covers. She tucked her in and paused, stopping herself at the last second from kissing Maggie's forehead. She patted Pinky's head.

"Good night." She closed the door but didn't latch it in case Pinky wanted to come down. Ann paused outside the door and smoothed her fingers over her eyebrow, wondering why she'd stopped herself from showing motherly affection. It had felt natural that time, yet she'd stopped.

Ann returned to the kitchen, pulled another slice of pizza out of the box, and sat on the couch. The book sat on the corner of the coffee table. She pulled out her notepad and flipped to the page with the passage from the bank, opened her laptop, and searched a few of the key terms.

She started with, LIGHT AND DARK, LIFE AND DEATH.

Thousands of search results came back. The first one on the list pointed her to the Gospel of Philip and a site that had all of the Nag Hammadi codices available in searchable format. That could have been handy, oh say, last year.

"Why didn't I think of this before?" Then she remembered that not all of the passages from Maggie's book were part of the original codices. They were supplemental material, so to speak.

Ann scrolled down the list and found a blog by someone named Cynthia Kuhli, PhD. She clicked on it.

'Light and dark, life and death, and right and left are siblings of one another and inseparable. For this reason, the good are not good, the bad are not bad, life is not life, and death is not death.' The passage above comes from the Gospel of Philip from the Nag Hammadi scriptures. In today's post, I plan to delve into what I believe this passage means, how it relates to other beliefs within the gnostic faith—again, my own interpretations—and so much more. Let's get into it, shall we?

The Gnostics believe every spirit has two parts—one from above, from the Entirety, and the counterfeit spirit from below. You'll recall from my post on the Entirety that it is all that existed before. It is all inclusive of the Great Invisible Spirit (what some Christians may refer to as

God), Barbelo (also known as Forethought along with four other Aeons), the Self-Originate, and twelve more Aeons led by the Luminaries, including Wisdom, or Sophia, herself—led by Eleleth. For more on the Entirety, please refer to this post.

Ann clicked on the link to the post, but a lot of it was way too far out of her frame of thinking. Especially when words she couldn't pronounce—Eleleth, Harmozel, Oroaiael, and Daueithai—came up in the text. She clicked back to the other post and kept reading.

These two parts of the spirit are what create balance within the whole. As you'll recall, again in my post about the Entirety, each Aeon consisted of a female and male part. Two parts, one whole.

Harkening back to the passage at the beginning of my post, you'll see there are pairs of opposites. Throughout the Nag Hammadi codices, one will find several scriptures discussing opposing forces.

"Thunder," also known as "Perfect Mind" is one of them. This poem of sorts is a list of opposing forces with I am statements preceding them.

Similarly, in the Catholic faith and others, the seven deadly sins are often paired with their opposing virtues.

Ann skimmed the article to the end, but nothing else really jumped out at her. She read the last lines.

For what is light without dark? What is life without death? What is good without bad? Without these opposites, who is to say what is right and what is wrong?

Ann snorted. "The law, that's who." She clicked out of Kuhli's blog and back to the search engine. She typed in her next search term. BLIGHTED WOMB.

Another blog post from Cynthia Kuhli came up. Ann clicked on it, scanned the beginning, and slowed down when her eye caught a familiar name. *Yaldabaoth.*

When Yaldabaoth raped Eve, her spirit fled to live inside the Tree of Knowledge of Life and Death. Yaldabaoth, therefore, did not rape Eve the woman. He raped Eve the Shadow. She became pregnant with Cain and Abel. It is because of the union of Yaldabaoth and Eve's Shadow that Cain ended up killing his brother Abel.

"Some scholars of the Gnostic texts believe Cain and Abel were the original children of chaos, and that the reason Cain suffered after killing his twin was because their single soul—split in two to be shared among them— yearned for its lost half. This yearning led to suffering.

I believe Cain and Abel were not, in fact, the original children of chaos. Light and Dark were the originals. The twin bond is stronger than any familial bond in the Universe.

Ann searched the remainder of the post for BLIGHTED WOMB, but only saw it was tagged in the metadata for the post. Ann jotted in her notebook: *Eve's Shadow = Blighted Womb?*

Even if it was true, what did it tell her? Nothing. Ann had no idea who Eve's Shadow was and therefore did not know who or what the blighted womb was and therefore didn't know who the children of chaos were.

But something told her they were Yaldabaoth's

offspring, since they shared one of his monikers. And only one person on the material realm had consorted with him.

Teresa Hart.

"Why did I push this off before?"

Because she was locked away in Mountain View.

Ann found Mountain View in her contacts list. It rang twice before a cranky female voice answered.

"Mountain View, how can I direct your call?"

"This is Sheriff Logan," Ann said.

"What can I do for you Sheriff," the voice asked with a bored tone.

"I'm calling to check up on Teresa Hart." Ann suddenly felt stupid, calling to ask if Teresa was still in her cell. If the woman had somehow gotten out, Ann would surely have been the first to know.

"We can't give any confidential medical information if you aren't on her HIPAA disclosure form," the woman said.

"I'm actually just calling to make sure she's still there." There. Done.

The line went dead, and for a second Ann thought the grouch on the other end had hung up on her. Then the droning tone of another line rang through.

"Security. This's Douglas."

Ann went through the spiel again.

"Let me check the cameras." Tapping and clicking came over the line. "Yep, she's there. Looks like she's sleeping."

"Is there any way I could get you to physically look in her cell? To make sure she's in there?" Ann shook her head. What a lame request.

"I can't leave my post here, but I can transfer you to the nurses' station on her floor. Hold on just a second." The line clicked before Ann could thank him.

"Women's ward nurses' station, this is Crystal."

"Hi Crystal." Ann told the young-sounding woman who she was and asked for her to check. Crystal put her on hold.

Ann waited, watching the seconds tick by, anticipation building in her chest and gut. If Teresa wasn't there, she'd have to leave, and to leave, she'd need to figure out what to do with Maggie—

The line clicked. "Hello, Sheriff?"

"I'm here." Ann bit the end off of her thumbnail.

"Teresa Hart is, in fact, in her room, snuggled into bed like a bug in a rug." Crystal made a cute little sound as if it were the dearest thing, a homicidal maniac tucked into bed.

"Thank you for checking for me, *Crystal*, was it?"

"Yep. And no problem, Sheriff. Always willing to help the local authorities."

They said their goodbyes and hung up. Ann took a deep breath. Locked away. That was good. But she still had this issue to deal with and zero leads.

She typed CHILDREN OF CHAOS into the search engine. More of Kuhli's blogs came up, followed by several books with that title. Ann perused them, but, like the Blighted Womb post, the phrase was in the metadata tags.

Ann clicked on the CONTACT ME button on Kuhli's website. There wasn't a phone number, but there was a form. She filled it out, asking Kuhli to call her. Ann clicked over to her email for a quick distraction. There was an auto-reply from Cynthia Kuhli. She had apparently died two years ago.

Ann leaned forward, elbows on her knees. *Shit*. She pulled the *Origin Codex* closer.

"Why don't you just flip open and show me what I need to know?"

At that exact moment, the book's cover flapped open

and the pages fluttered. Ann stifled a shriek. That never happened before. In the past when she'd asked the book for help, it just sat there silent and cold. Mocking.

When the pages stilled, she pulled it closer, noting the leather cover had that weird living heat it got when it was . . . active. She wiped her hand on her jeans.

The passage was more like a poem of contradictory pairs. It told her nothing at first. But later in the poem, she realized it was the same one Kuhli's blog talked about. It also jogged her memory about something Maggie said at the bank about Mary Magdalene and seven demons.

Sins and virtues.

The Perfect Whole, the Perfect Pairs, together in twos shall form the Perfect Soul.

I am hubris and humility.

I am one who takes greedily and gives charitably in equal measure.

I am one who envies and one who is grateful for all.

I am one who indulges and one who abstains.

I am one who gives myself lustily and withholds chastely.

I am full of rage and patience.

I am the one who lay idle in the face of hard work and the one who works with diligence.

I am sadness and pure joy.

I am light and I am dark.

I am the one called Life, and the one called Death.

I am right and left.

I am the mother and the father.

I am the perfect whole. The Perfect mind. The Perfect Soul.

The Blighted Womb. The named mother-father of the Children of Chaos. Shall seek the eight Perfect Pairs. The eight Logismoi shall lend the suffering. The Children of Chaos shall resurrect the Perfect Soul.

"Resurrect the Perfect Soul and do what?" Ann flipped the page, hoping for more, but that was it. She let out a frustrated sound and pushed the book off the coffee table like a petulant child.

Always so cryptic. Always parts and pieces to a full puzzle, parceled out like she was a child wanting candy. She needed the candy goddammit!

She snatched the book off the floor. She flipped it to the page and wrote down the passage as fast as she could into her notebook.

Her mind wandered back to Teresa. She might be locked up inside, but someone was out here doing something to the townsfolk. If it had anything to do with bringing Yaldabaoth back, the Messengers of the Light had to be involved.

Raghib sprang to mind. His body had been missing after the events of The Night. He and Teresa might have been working together back then. Maybe even now.

Ann smoothed her fingertips over her eyebrow. As thin as it was, she had a hunch, and the only way to satisfy it would be visiting Mountain View and talking to Teresa in person.

CHAPTER TWENTY-FIVE

Cassie woke Teresa, though Teresa knew before the little gargoyle had patted her cheek that it was time. When she had tried to nurse Amanda earlier in the evening, the pain in her arm had come again. The black cracks crawled down her shoulder and arm to her hand.

Stop her, Yaldabaoth's voice had said. Teresa had jerked her nipple out of Amanda's mouth. The silvery substance dribbled from her lip again. Amanda hadn't cried. She'd looked at Teresa with half-closed eyes and a somewhat satisfied look on her face.

The black marks remained on her arm, cold to the touch. They disappeared under the short sleeve of her pajama top. Teresa lifted the front. The black marks went all the way up her arm, across her shoulder, and down to her breast. She had hoped the time between . . . feedings would be longer than twenty-four hours, but this was less.

A foolish thought. Hadn't last time been the same? Tiffany had shown up every night last year with her chilly presence and delight.

Mommy. It's time.

Teresa was grateful Cassie didn't speak. It was always her little hand on Teresa's cheek.

Cassie flapped her huge wings and hopped around like a little monkey.

Teresa rubbed the sleep from her eyes, though she'd only been out for a couple of hours. She checked on Amanda. Sucking her thumb in the bottom of the crib. Her eyes were open, but she did not make a sound.

Cassie jumped up and down at the door knob again, desperate to get to the next one to help her hungry sister.

Teresa pulled on a pair of pants and her sneakers again. She shoved her arms into a sweatshirt and pulled it over her head. She glanced at the clock. It was only ten. Early yet for some people. She would have to be careful.

Like the previous night, they went out the back. As soon as Teresa opened the door, Cassie burst upward into the night sky.

"Be careful, little one," Teresa whispered, watching her daughter wheel and spin and swoop high above the nearest trees.

"Off again, are you?" Lory's voice asked behind her.

Teresa blocked the doorway to prevent Lory from seeing Cassie. She wasn't ready for anyone else to witness this transformation.

"Yes," Teresa said. She rubbed her arm through the sweatshirt sleeve. The marks were still there beneath the material. She could feel their chilliness through the fabric.

Lory nodded. "What can I do? To help you, I mean?"

Teresa took in a quick breath. She hadn't had help before. She probably didn't need help now. Except—

"It's earlier this time than last," she said. "I still need a disguise—if you don't want me to dye my hair." She lifted one shoulder and gave Lory the smallest smile. She felt no mirth, no camaraderie. Nothing like that. It just felt like something she should do.

"It's in the works," Lory said with a secretive smile. She touched Teresa's arm in motherly affection. Teresa looked at the hand. Lory pulled it back.

Teresa glanced over her shoulder in time to see Cassie land in Lory's garden and give her what could only be an impatient look with her strange little head and large almond eyes.

"I have to go." Teresa hurried down the back-porch steps.

"Good luck, and be careful," Lory whispered to Teresa's back before closing the door.

They went through the old cemetery again, with the lost souls. Teresa didn't like them. She wished Cassie would go a different route, but just like Tiffany and the zoe lines, this was how it had to be. She trusted her daughter was leading her down the correct path.

Because killing people is the right path.

Glory wasn't dead. If she was, her body would be on the couch.

Images of that horrible empty bag of skin flickered into Teresa's head. Perhaps she imagined it. Perhaps Glory had been fine. Her stomach started to sour. She'd thought the same of Ruthie.

Teresa tripped over a small branch and fell onto her hands. Cassie swooped down and tugged at Teresa's shirt to help her up. Flapping wings threw Teresa's hair every which way.

In the moonlight, it was almost magical to see this winged creature. Her dark oily skin refracted the light, giving her a glow.

She is beautiful, is she not? Yaldabaoth's voice purred, caressing Teresa's scalp.

Cassie took to the sky again. Teresa jogged along, glancing up for the winged creature and straight ahead to dodge the lost souls.

They made it to the dirt road. Teresa paused to catch her breath, but Cassie flew off toward town. Teresa hurried after her. At the square, she swooped to the left, down Evergreen Avenue into the newer residential district. Where Brent Winter once lived.

Cassie did a loop the loop and landed in the middle of the street. She hopped, waiting for Teresa to come closer. She pointed at one of the ranch-style homes typical of this neighborhood. A light was on in the front room.

"I can't go in there," Teresa whispered. "They're up. They're awake."

Cassie tugged on her hand and bounded down the side yard to the gate leading into the back. The place was just like Brent's.

Hopefully, if they snuck in the sliding glass door, a large pit bull named Pinky wouldn't come running out to slobber all over her. She pulled the gate open and slipped inside, not bothering to latch it in case they had to make a quick escape.

A backyard light cast everything in a halogen glow.

A girl sat on a rusty old swing set. The chains creaked and groaned. She had curly blond hair like Shirley Temple. Her back was to Teresa. She looked big for her age.

Cassie stared intently at the girl.

"Is it her?" Teresa asked.

Cassie leaped into the air, straight up like a rocket. She flipped and came straight down onto the girl so fast, she knocked her off the swing. The girl let out an *oof* as the wind was knocked from her lungs. Teresa wondered if that was Cassie's intent. The girl couldn't get enough breath to scream. Cassie tore her eyes out and cast them aside. They hit the sandbox. One bounced to the side. The other made it in and rolled a few inches, coating itself with sand.

Cassie retreated to the shadows.

The girl's chest heaved. With each exhale, she whimpered. Her hands flew to her face, and when her fingers touched her cheeks and fumbled their way up to those now-empty sockets, her breath hitched and trembled even more.

Teresa rushed toward her, aware of how exposed she was in the bright lights from the back porch. If the girl got her breath back and screamed—well, Teresa just hoped her parents were asleep in front of a TV.

Teresa leaned over her trembling form, just like she had with Glory, and slurped the soul into her mouth. It tasted the way old paper money smells—a dirty oily scent, like unwashed hair and socks that had been worn too many days in a row. Teresa choked it down. Better than hot brakes and dead leaves, that was for sure, but it still lingered on the back of her tongue the way a mouthful of dirt might.

The little girl looked empty like Glory had. Teresa pushed at the deflated leg with the toe of her sneaker. It folded over on itself like a spent inner tube. She backed away from it, her stomach souring.

Teresa and Cassie left quickly through the side gate. Shouts and screams came from inside the house. A woman shrieked. Something shattered. Teresa stood on her toes and peeked in the window. A woman stormed past the doorway to what looked like an office. A shouting man, arms waving, pursued her.

That's why the child was outside.

A strange feeling of satisfaction came over her. It sickened her, but she also thought they deserved what they got.

Then she felt guilty.

The girl had been miserable on that swing—barely moving, toes brushing the wood chips beneath her, head bowed. Were all the children going to be sad? Were all the Logismoi going to be children?

Teresa hoped not. Though children weren't as strong as adults.

Another sickening thought. Teresa blamed the Thorithium leaving her system. Antipathy could be a withdrawal symptom from the anti-psychotic. So could detachment.

She hurried back to the safety of Lory's house, tears coursing down her cheeks. She didn't feel anything but guilt, even as she fed Amanda the life-giving sustenance she needed.

CHAPTER TWENTY-SIX

Maggie was in the abyss searching for the lost pieces of her heart. The ones shaped like her parents and Mr. Bram and Derrick. A desperate feeling filled her chest. She saw the shapes in the distance, but she couldn't reach them no matter how long she ran toward them.

One was shaped like Ann, and one like Pinky.

That's why she was there in the abyss.

"I warned you," said Eleleth, in a voice that sounded like Sophia but different.

The dream shifted. A figure clad in white hovered in the distance. He looked like he was hovering because there was nothing around to tell her he wasn't. The abyss was an empty place, after all.

"I'm looking for my brother," the man said. "Have you seen my brother?"

"I don't know your brother," Maggie said with Sophia's voice. "But you have been sent here by him."

"Where am I? I cannot see."

"You are here with me," Sophia said. "You are safe here. Your brother will find you soon." She opened her arms and comforted the man. It was a cold and desperate feeling when she touched him. A feeling of incompleteness as if her heart had been ripped in two.

Maggie woke up. The clock said it was four. Her heart ached. Her mark throbbed. Maggie wished she knew why. Maybe it was from the dream, telling her the nightmare was a warning in real life.

She rubbed her eyes and settled one hand on Pinky. Her mark stung.

"Why is it hurting?" Maggie whispered at the ceiling.

Logismoi, Sophia's voice said in her mind. *Light and dark.* The voice was an echoey whisper.

"I don't know what that means." Maggie's mark burned more. Her ears filled with pressure, followed by static. Pinky licked Maggie's hand. The mattress jostled. Pinky's steps retreated down the stairs.

A few minutes later, Ann's cool hands touched Maggie's. "What's happening? Your mark. It's glowing."

Maggie could barely hear Ann past the buzzing in her head. It was the sound of a million flies and a thousand people wailing in pain or fear or some kind of agony.

"It's so loud. Do you hear it? It hurts." Tears squeezed out of her eyes. "My heart." She opened her eyes.

Ann sat on the edge of the bed. Pinky remained at Ann's feet staring at Maggie with perked ears. She let out a breathy whimper. The sound stopped. Maggie's ears popped.

"Are you okay? What do you need?" Ann asked.

"I'm tired." Maggie lay back on her pillows, her body weighing a thousand pounds.

Ann smoothed a hand over Maggie's forehead. "Get a few more hours of sleep."

"Will you stay with me?" Maggie's breath came faster, and she knew she would cry in a second if Ann didn't stay. The pressure in her heart would force the tears out.

Ann moved around Maggie's bed, sat with her back against the headboard, and pulled Maggie close, wrapping her arms around her.

This is what it feels like to have a mother. The thought came to her from Sophia. *You mustn't let anything happen to her.*

CHAPTER TWENTY-SEVEN

Cassie cried at four—a horrific screaming cry, like the sound might rip her vocal chords. Along with the scream, a black cloud poured out of her mouth.

Teresa wasn't sure if the scream was the cloud or Cassie, but the second Cassie closed her mouth, the sound stopped.

It was replaced with a buzzing, like a million flies. Teresa opened the window and let it out. She considered leaving it open to let fresh air in the stuffy little room, but she thought of Rebecca coming back and closed it tight.

"Ba," a tiny voice said.

Teresa whirled around.

"Ba."

She whirled back and looked down into the crib. Cassie held her feet in her little hands. She was bigger. Both of them were bigger. They'd aged another couple of months at least. Cassie giggled. Amanda opened her eyes and reached for her sister. She rolled over onto her tummy.

Rolling over. Holding their heads up. Teresa held a hand to her mouth. Tears welled. Was she happy or sad that they were aging so quickly? She didn't know. She'd worried so much about postpartum depression while she was pregnant, but she hadn't had time to even consider how she was actually managing.

Fine. She was just fine. They were on opposite feeding schedules, and Amanda was such a good sleeper, and Cassie, well, Cassie was just something else entirely. She gazed down at them and her heart filled with adoration.

"Ba," Teresa said back. "I'm mama. Say ma-ma."

"Ba," Cassie said again with a gleeful laugh. She turned her head and reached for Amanda, who laughed the most joyous sound, it made Teresa want to cry.

Their voices sounded alike, but Amanda's was a tiny bit huskier. Perhaps because it wasn't used as much as Cassie's.

Cassie reached for Teresa, and Teresa lifted her. She changed her diaper and settled in the rocking chair to nurse her. She looked out the window, wondering once again what that black cloud was and where it had gone.

CHAPTER TWENTY-EIGHT

When Maggie woke again, the clock on her nightstand said it was seven-thirty. She was sandwiched between Ann and Pinky, with Ann's arms around her. Maggie closed her eyes and relished the feeling, the love, of being cuddled between her two favorite people.

"What time is it?" Ann asked her in a sleepy voice.

Maggie pretended to sleep so she could stay in this sandwich of love and warmth a little longer.

Ann shifted and groaned. She gave Maggie a squeeze and got up, leaving a cold spot at Maggie's back. "How're you feeling?"

"I'm fine."

"Okay, good." Ann yawned and ruffled her hand through her long straight shiny hair. It rippled like silk. Maggie loved Ann's hair. She wished Ann would let her braid it and play with it, or at least brush it, but Ann never had time for that kind of thing. "I need you to go to the Daycare Place today."

Maggie rolled onto her back into the warm spot Ann left behind. Dread sank into her stomach and coiled there.

She closed her eyes against the heat of oncoming tears. Their time together yesterday had been so nice. She enjoyed spending time with Ann so much. And she hated the Daycare Place. Sally Opperheim went there sometimes.

"My tummy hurts," Maggie groaned, curling into herself. She made it a small and quiet groaning. It really did hurt though. Like fluffy and fluttery. Her tummy made her heart feel like there wasn't enough room in her body for both organs.

"You said you were fine a second ago." Ann poked Maggie's ribs and dug her fingers into Maggie's clamped armpits. Maggie squealed with laughter. Darn it. She didn't like being ticklish. Pinky stood, shook off, and flopped back down, half on top of Maggie.

"Brush your teeth, get dressed—you know the drill. I gotta go somewhere today. Come on, Pinky." Pinky left with Ann before Maggie could ask where Ann had to go.

Maggie did as Ann asked and went downstairs. Ann wore her uniform, which always made her look so cool. A stack of pancakes sat on a plate. Usually the sight of pancakes would make Maggie forget all about the bad news of having to go to daycare, but today they made her tummy fluffy again.

"Do I *have* to go to daycare today?" Maggie slid into her seat at the table. "Can't I just stay here with Pinky? I'll be okay! Pinky will protect me."

At the sound of her name, Pinky trotted over to Maggie and poked her in the leg with her nose. Maggie tore off a piece of pancake and gave it to her.

"Just because I let you stay home alone that *one* time, doesn't mean it's going to happen again."

Maggie slumped. "Where are you going, anyway?"

Maggie forced a bite of pancakes into her mouth. Ann was going somewhere besides the station. If she was just going to the station, Maggie and Pinky could go with her. And she wouldn't be wearing her uniform. Ann didn't wear her uniform very often. And when she did, it meant serious business.

"Um . . ." Ann got up. Maggie watched her move to the coffee pot and refill her mug. "Just somewhere." She shrugged.

Maggie narrowed her eyes. "You're avoiding eye contact."

Ann's lips formed a half smile. She seemed to think about what she would say next. Maggie knew Ann's body language. Ann put her mug on the counter and came over to Maggie. She crouched, took Maggie's hands, and stared at them.

"I have to go to Mountain View to talk to Teresa." She flicked her eyes up and held Maggie's gaze.

At the mention of her adoptive mother's name, a chilly sensation skittered down Maggie's back.

"Why?" Maggie swallowed hard. It felt like pancakes were lodged in her throat. But if they were, she wouldn't be able to breathe. Or swallow.

"I have a hunch. I just want to talk to her to see if she knows anything relating to it."

Ann held back. But Maggie didn't want to push. Sophia's voice came to her again.

You mustn't let anything happen to her.

"You'll be okay, though, right?" She looked up at Ann.

Ann's eyebrows scrunched down, but not in a mad way like Maggie had seen before—usually directed at Sully or Pinky or whoever she was on the phone with maybe talking about the byourockrasee.

Ann squeezed Maggie's hands. "I'll be fine. Nothing's going to happen. We're just going to have a chat. I promise."

Maggie pulled her hands from Ann's grasp. "Don't say that. Don't promise that. On The Night, you promised *nothing* would happen—"

And look what happened.

Maggie rubbed her fists in her eyes to get rid of the tears before they fell and she was a crybaby again.

When she lowered her hands, Ann had a sad look on her face.

I'm being a burden.

"It's okay." She put her hand on Ann's shoulder and gave it a squeeze. "I'm okay. I'm sorry. I'll go to the Daycare Place so you won't have to worry about me being here by myself." She got up to go potty and get her little backpack.

"Maggie," Ann said.

Maggie turned and looked at her.

"*I'm* the one who's sorry."

Ann parked the big truck at the Daycare Place and walked Maggie inside. At the front desk she signed Maggie in.

Ann went down on one knee. "I'll be back to pick you up around four. If you need me, have these nice ladies call me, okay?"

Maggie nodded. Ann gave her a quick hug and dashed out of the building.

"Well hello, Maggie, welcome back," Olivia, one of the daycare people said.

Maggie almost didn't recognize her. She used to have long red hair. It was so pretty the way it draped over her shoulders. Now her hair was so short, it stuck up all over in little spikes.

"What happened to your hair?" Maggie asked.

Olivia touched the short spikes near her neck and turned red. "I cut it," she said in a low and sad voice.

"Why did you cut it if you didn't want to?" Maggie asked.

"She had lice," the other daycare lady said quickly. Maggie could never remember her name, so she called her "Not-Olivia" in her head. "You have to cut all your hair off if you get lice."

"That's not true," Maggie said. "Bradley and his sister Janet from my class got lice before summer break. All they did was use some special shampoo and comb out all the eggs." Maggie imagined lice looked like tiny chickens. They were itchy because the little chickens hatched and pecked your head.

"Well, aren't you Miss Smarty Pants." Not-Olivia came around the desk and took Maggie's hand. "Let's get you all settled in, shall we?"

Maggie followed her. The first kid she saw inside the playroom was Sally Opperheim.

Only, she didn't quite *look* like Sally Opperheim.

Ann parked the truck in the Mountain View lot and went inside. A toadish-looking woman at the front desk hardly gave her the time of day. Her name tag read EVELYN. She was likely the voice from the call last night.

"I'm here to see Teresa Hart," Ann said. "Sheriff Logan, Castle County Sheriff's Department." She was so used to introducing herself that way when she wasn't in uniform. She realized after the fact she likely didn't need to do it while wearing it.

Evelyn looked up at her. She lifted the phone receiver and punched a few buttons.

"Hart has a visitor." She replaced the receiver. "You can head on back." She pressed a button, and the lock on the door into the hospital proper disengaged.

Ann boarded the elevator. She knew where to go. She'd been there a few times in the past months. Usually to just ensure Teresa was still where she was meant to be. This visit was different. She needed answers and hoped to everything holy or not that Teresa would have some. But if Teresa didn't know anything about what was going on, Ann would hit another wall. One made of brick and reinforced concrete.

On the second floor, she pushed the helpless feeling away and approached the visitor's room. The nurse signed her in, and Ann took a seat with her back to the wall so she could face the room's entry.

A nurse ushered Teresa in with a gentle hand on her elbow. Teresa's head hung, her blond hair obscuring her face. She took shuffling and wobbly steps. The nurse helped her into her chair.

"Nice to see you again, Teresa," Ann said without friendliness. "I have a few questions."

The woman lifted her face. Ann pushed back from the table and stood.

"Nurse," she shouted. The nurse paused in the doorway. "Get Chief Administrator Smith in here immediately," Ann ordered. "And call Salida PD. This is *not* Teresa Hart. This woman was reported missing from Salida four days ago."

***

There was something strange about Sally Opperheim. Maggie could feel it. Unlike Glory, though, there wasn't a particular feeling she could really pin down. But Maggie knew just by looking at her. She didn't need any other feeling.

Sally's skin was weird—with a gray tinge. Her eyes were sunken and the skin didn't fit the bones underneath. Dark lines marked her mouth and jaw.

Also, instead of snatching toys away, this Sally handed them out. She was sharing with the other kids. She lifted her gaze. Her face lit up.

"Maggie," Sally cried, as if they were bestest friends who hadn't seen each other all summer. "I put some paper and crayons on the table over there for you." She pointed. Maggie looked at the finger. A crooked finger. Was Sally's finger always crooked? It was like she wore gloves that didn't fit right. Maggie followed the pointing finger.

On the table was a stack of paper and a box of a thousand crayons. Sally lumbered over as if her arms and legs had forgotten how to operate properly.

"I sharpened all of the dull ones." She flipped open the lid of the crayon box and smiled so all her teeth were showing—the way little kids did sometimes when you told them to smile. Before they really knew what a proper smile should look like. Her teeth were too big. And she smelled. Maybe it was her breath.

"Th-thank you," Maggie's voice caught in her throat.

"If you want to play dolls later, you let me know, okay?" Sally moved like she was going to give Maggie's arm a light and friendly punch, but she stopped at the last second. Sally, still smiling, backed away to the toy corner, where she continued to hand out toys to the littler kids and new arrivals like she was the welcoming committee.

The nurse nodded and rushed out of the room. Ann turned to the other nurse, the one staffing the desk.

"Initiate the protocol for escaped prisoners."

The nurse's eyes froze wide.

"Lock the place down," Ann shouted.

The nurse picked up the phone and dialed. Ann stormed back to the table.

"Carla? Carla Johnson?" Ann remembered the name from the Mountain Mail website just the other day.

The woman's eyes focused.

"Ms. Johnson," Ann said, trying to get the woman's attention. "Are you okay? What happened?"

"Druuuugged . . ." the word was slurred and thick. It had been days. How was she still so sloppy?

"What's the last thing you remember?" Ann asked.

"Hhhhhiking. T-Tenderfffoot."

The nurse who'd brought Carla into the room came back. "The Salida PD is on their way. What else can I do to assist?"

"Why is this woman so out of it?" Ann asked.

"She's been taking the same drugs that were prescribed to Teresa Hart." She ducked her head. Her cheeks went crimson. "I think Dr. Andrews might have upped her dosage after the incident."

"Incident?"

"Hart flipped out in the common room. She injured one of our eldest residents."

Twenty minutes later, Chief Administrator Smith skidded into the visitor room. He was a tall lanky man with slicked-back dark hair. He had the look of a used car salesman. Ann didn't like him. He always spoke in condescending tones, never wavering from his calm clinical demeanor. Until now.

"What's going on?" he demanded. "Why is my hospital on lockdown? Why is my staff running around like headless chickens?" He thrust a finger toward the door where a couple of nurses rushed by.

Ann strode over to him in three quick strides. She was too short to get in his face, so the effect was mostly lost, but he did take a step back, which satisfied her need for him to understand she was in charge now.

"Sheriff Logan. What are you doing here?"

"I came to visit Teresa Hart, and *this* woman was brought to me." Ann went to Carla. Smith joined her.

"Oh dear, that is not Teresa Hart." He cleared his throat. "Certainly this is no cause for alarm. The nurse who brought her must have made a mistake. No reason to lock down my hospital—"

"Teresa Hart is missing." Ann was sure of it, but a small measure of doubt squeaked in. She had been a little rash to have the hospital locked down. If Teresa was sitting somewhere else in the hospital and it was a mistake—

"Missing?" He took a step back and laughed. "I assure you, she is likely in the common room. She likes to sit there and look out at the grounds."

Ann wanted to strangle him.

"Even if she is," Ann said, realizing she may have jumped to conclusions. "This woman was reported missing in *Salida*. Over fifty miles away. How the *hell* did she get all the way here?"

Maggie did not like being at the Daycare Place. No, she didn't *not like* it. She *hated* it. Not only because when Sally was there it was usually horrible, but also because all the kids seemed to have some sort of cloud over them, like none of them wanted to be there.

She could relate. She'd rather be at home with Pinky. She'd rather be with Ann, even if Ann was just at the station. She would prefer being there, bored out of her mind, than here. This place, with its bright colors and bright lights—she couldn't figure out how everyone could just be here under these bright lights with all this stuff going on around them like it was all okay.

She realized what it was. None of them had been through what she'd been through.

Her gloomy cloud had been earned.

She pulled a black crayon out of the box. Usually black was broken in the middle and taped back together, never the same again. But this one was sharpened and not broken. She started drawing and wondered what Ann was doing. She hoped Ann was safe. Maggie had a weird feeling in her stomach.

Maybe if she pretended she was sick Ann would come back for her. She tried coughing into her elbow. A little cough at first, then a louder one, but it just sounded like a fake cough.

"You okay, Maggie?" Sally asked from across the room with her too-big smile and her too-cheery voice. It was high-pitched, like she was pretending to be a child.

Maggie nodded. She glanced out the window.

Maybe she could escape during outdoor time. The Daycare Place was like being at school, except they didn't teach anything. They had recess in the morning and nap time in the afternoon. She didn't need naps anymore, so she usually read books quietly while the little kids lay on mats.

Maggie looked down at the drawings. She'd let her hand draw what it wanted. It was sort of like when she'd drawn Yaldabaoth last year to get him out of her head. Her hand had taken over. She had drawn a girl with black hair and dark scribbly spots for eyes in a weird backbend. She flipped the page over. It was too scary to look at. Another one showed the same girl, but with a big smile.

"What are you drawing, Mags?" Olivia asked.

Maggie jumped and looked up at Olivia, who came closer and sat next to her. She lifted the drawing and dropped it.

"Oh . . . that's a cute . . . little girl?"

Maggie looked at it. It was Glory. The way Sophia had shown her on the hike. But instead of looking sad, Glory had a wide grin on her face. Maggie's stomach got fluffy again.

"Well, it's an interesting drawing. I'll put it with your things to take home later, okay?"

As Ann suspected, Smith knew nothing about how or why Carla Johnson was in Teresa Hart's cell. Ann figured he knew fuck all about what even went on in *his* hospital.

Salida PD arrived, confirmed the woman was their missing person, and called for a transport to take Carla to the hospital in Pine Valley—the nearest medical facility—for treatment. The officer in charge called in the K-9 unit to search the surrounding area.

Meanwhile, Chief Administrator Smith took Ann to security to review video surveillance.

"I'll leave you here in the capable hands of Douglas, my head of security." He nodded to the man inside. "Douglas, Sheriff Logan is here to see any applicable footage surrounding the disappearance of Mrs. Hart. Please show her anything she wishes in relation to this unfortunate circumstance."

"Yes, sir." Douglas was a middle-aged male in a baggy security uniform and a ball cap that was a size too big. His ears squashed out to the side. The room smelled like ham sandwiches. "You can sit there." Douglas pointed to a chair.

Ann sat. "How far back do you want to go?" Douglas asked, hands poised over the keyboard.

"Let's start with a week ago," Ann said.

Ann expected a poor-quality video feed, but the image was surprisingly crisp. Ann watched the camera. It showed a low-lit hallway outside of Teresa's room, and the interior.

She reviewed hours of footage of nothing but Teresa coming and going from her cell. Every time the woman left the room, heat boiled under Ann's collar. Teresa should not have been allowed such free range of the facility in the first place.

Finally, three nights previous, at 3:05 a.m., the feed went dark. And when it came back up later, Teresa Hart appeared to still be in bed, snoozing away. The time stamp indicated approximately twenty minutes had passed. If she'd been missing for three days, Salida PD wouldn't find anything in the woods. She was long gone by now.

"Was there a power outage that night?" Ann asked. Harmony hadn't had one, and she figured they were likely on the same grid, but it was worth asking.

Douglas flipped through some reports. He shook his head. "Looks like just the cameras." He clicked through some other files, bringing up still videos of the same time and closing them in rapid succession. He left three open. All screens were black.

"The cameras on her floor and the stairwells and outside." He pointed at each one. "All of the others were fine."

"Someone cut the feed," Ann said in a low voice. She narrowed her eyes. "Were you working that night?"

Douglas shook his head. "I'm day shift. That would have been"—he flipped through some pages in a binder—"Thomas Littleton." Douglas looked at her. "He quit the next day. Only on staff long enough to train and take over the night shift." He gave a speculative *hmm* at the same time Ann did.

"I'll need his contact information to get in touch with him."

Douglas nodded.

Ann turned back to the monitors. "Can I see footage of any visitors Teresa had before this event?"

Douglas nodded and found the file on the computer. The moment Teresa's visitor walked in, cold prickles raced over Ann's body.

"No," she whispered.

It was Raghib.

Ann took a second to collect herself.

"Is there audio?"

Douglas turned the volume up all the way but they couldn't hear anything except susurrations. "The cameras don't have great mics." He raised a shoulder.

Whatever they had discussed, their body language indicated they were making plans. Probably escape plans.

Ann reviewed the remaining surveillance footage leading up to the previous night when the nurse had checked on Teresa at Ann's request.

Ann stopped at Dr. Smith's office and pounded on the door. He opened up.

"Teresa Hart has likely been missing for at least three days," she said through her teeth.

His eyes widened, then darkened. His eyebrows lowered. "Three? How can that—" His demeanor changed. "What can I do to help?"

"I need a space to interview members of the staff. Everyone who was there that night, anyone who interacted with Teresa Hart, the nurse who answered the phone last night when I called—Crystal, that was her name."

"There is an empty office at the end of the hall you may use. I'll send someone to assist you."

Ann took a seat behind the desk in the empty office. She opened the drawers anyway, just to see if anything had been left behind. Empty. She pulled out her notepad and pen from her breast pocket and set them on the desk.

A few minutes later, a petite brunette came in with a thin manila folder in one hand and a paper cup in the other.

"Dr. Smith asked me to bring this to you, and to help you as much as I can." She handed Ann the piece of paper. The woman's name tag read PATRINA.

"Thank you, Patrina. That's an interesting name."

"My parents couldn't decide on Katrina and Patrice, so they combined them. Not sure why they didn't go with Katrice, but here we are." She gave Ann a big grin.

Ann pulled the coffee closer and took a sip. "Thanks for not bringing donuts." She winked.

Patrina's eyes widened. "Oh gosh, do you *want* donuts?"

"No. I'm kidding. I actually hate them."

Patrina ducked her head and smiled. "Me too. I prefer muffins."

Ann had Patrina bring her the personnel files for everyone on the list. She came back a few minutes later, arms laden with red and green folders.

"What's the deal with the different colors?" Ann asked.

"No idea. Maybe they ran out of red or green one day?" Patrina shrugged.

"I'd like to speak with Crystal first," Ann said.

Ann perused Crystal's file while she waited. She'd only been at Mountain View for a couple of months. She was young. This was her first job out of nursing school.

A knock came at the door followed by Crystal poking her head in.

"You wanted to see me, Sheriff?" she asked. Ann nodded and indicated the chair opposite the desk.

"It's a madhouse out there," Crystal said with a quick glance over her shoulder.

Pine Valley's search and rescue team had shown up before Ann had started the interviews. Ann had briefed them on the situation before they went out to search the surrounding woods. They also searched the hospital interior again, just to be certain.

"I understand you were working the night Teresa Hart went missing?" Ann said.

Crystal slid into the chair and nodded. After gathering the pertinent information—name, date of birth, address, phone number—Ann said, "Take me to the nurses' station."

Crystal led Ann to the wide window and counter. The station was currently unstaffed. All of the prisoners were in their cells because of the lockdown. A few of them were yelling inside their rooms, pounding on the doors to be let out.

"We are short staffed here and have been for a while. During the day there are two nurses at the station. But at night, since everyone is in their rooms, there's just one of us."

She walked Ann down the hallway. "We do routine rounds to look in on the patients."

Ann peeked in one of the rooms where a woman sat in the middle of the floor curled in on herself rocking.

"This is Teresa's room." Crystal stopped outside. Teresa's room was not in sight of the nurses' station.

Ann went into the room and looked around, noting a window high up on the wall. "Does that open?"

Crystal shook her head.

"Did you notice anything about Teresa Hart the night she went missing?"

"She'd been in solitary, but they brought her back up, you know, because of her condition—being pregnant, I mean. She said she wanted to stay down there. She claimed someone had come into her room and threatened her."

Ann didn't recall seeing anything on the surveillance footage that indicated this.

"The rooms are locked at night," Crystal said, answering Ann's next question before she could ask it. "There's no way anyone could have gone in. We aren't supposed to unlock them unless there is an emergency, like a fire or the patient is at risk of harming themselves."

"Did you leave the desk at any time other than to make your rounds?" Ann asked.

"Only to use the restroom."

"I don't suppose you know what time you might have left the desk to do that?"

Crystal shook her head again. Ann finished looking around Teresa's room and went back out to the hallway.

"Was there anyone on your floor who shouldn't have been there?"

Crystal thought for a moment. Ann perked. Crystal looked up. "Dr. Andrews," she blurted. "He walked by like he was in a hurry. He was here, and he shouldn't have been. I mean, he can be here whenever. He's the head therapist on this ward. But he doesn't usually come here at night. He has set hours. Usually nine to five. Sometimes he stays later, but never past eight."

"What time did you see him?"

"It was around two or three in the morning?"

Around the same time as the outage.

"Did you ask him why he was here?" Ann asked.

Crystal's chin dropped again. "No. I didn't think it was any of my business."

"When I called last night—"

"I did as you asked." She looked up. "I went to her room and I looked in. She was in there, sleeping. I didn't know it wasn't her. I should have gone inside, I know, but protocol—I'm so sorry, Sheriff." Crystal broke down then, covering her face with her hands, shoulders heaving with sobs. "This is all my fault."

"No, no it isn't. Not entirely," Ann said. "You followed protocol by not unlocking the door. I'm sure there are more people at fault here than you." Lack of staffing, as Crystal mentioned, for one. Maybe even inexperienced staff. For two, an incompetent chief administrator. Not to mention lackadaisical protocols and policies.

Teresa Hart should have been locked inside her cell at all times with minimal outdoor time and should have been under strict surveillance. All activities logged. Someone to escort her to and from her room. Documentation. Records indicating where she was and when.

"Have you spoken with Dr. Andrews?" Crystal wiped her eyes with a tissue she pulled from the pocket of her scrubs.

"Not yet," Ann said. He would be next on her list.

"Maggie," Sally called later that afternoon. "Come play dolls with us." She smiled and waved Maggie over to a circle of younger girls, each with a Barbie Doll in various stages of undress. Maggie never understood why the little kids always stripped the dolls.

Maggie looked at the tabletop. It was covered with pictures she had no remembery of drawing. Most of them were black scribbles. She hitched in a breath and stopped her lungs from heaving. A tight panicky feeling started in her chest.

Why did I draw the abyss?

All she could think of were Eleleth's words. If anything happened to anyone she cared about, she would return there. She didn't know if Eleleth meant *her* or Sophia, but Maggie also knew Sophia wasn't from the abyss. She was from the Entirety. Whatever that was.

"Maggie?" Sally's too-high voice called. "Come on! Come play with us. Please?" Sally dragged out the please.

Maggie plodded over, not really into dolls, but she didn't feel like drawing anymore. Not after seeing what her hand had drawn while she wasn't paying attention. She didn't feel like doing anything—except getting out of there, finding Ann and Pinky, and making sure they were okay.

Why else would she have drawn the abyss? It was like when someone knows something bad is coming. She couldn't think of the word.

Sally handed Maggie a doll. She reached for it. Their fingers touched.

Maggie shot backward—but not her body. Her mind. She saw a figure out of the corner of her eye. Someone familiar. But then a creature with wings knocked her back. Small hands snatched forward. Pain filled her face. Hot liquid coursed down her cheeks. She felt like something was sucking the breath out of her lungs—no, not her lungs—her *being*. Her whole body.

She gasped and pulled her hand back. The doll fell to the floor.

"Whoops-a-daisy," Sally said with that big smile. She

bent to pick it up, smoothed the hair, and handed the doll back to Maggie.

Black fluid dribbled from the corner of Sally's grinning mouth. Up close, the smell of her grew stronger. She slurped. Eyes locked on Maggie's, Sally's hand lifted, as if in slow motion, and she wiped her mouth on the back of it, lowered it, and wiped it on her skirt, leaving a black smear behind.

"Let's play." She pushed the doll closer to Maggie.

Maggie pulled her hands back, afraid to touch the doll. Afraid to touch Sally's hand again.

"I have to go." Maggie got up.

"I think you should stay." Her voice dropped lower. Sally made that horrible slurping again and swallowed. Maggie *heard* her swallow.

Maggie backed away out of Sally's reach and ran for the front desk.

"Where are you going?" Sally called after her.

Maggie needed to find Ann. She needed to know Ann was okay. The drawing of Glory. That smile. Sally. Something wasn't right. The abyss. It felt like a warning.

"I need to go," Maggie said to Olivia. "I don't feel good. My tummy hurts." Touching Sally, seeing and experiencing those weird sensations. Her chest tightened. Her lungs—she couldn't get a full breath. She gasped for air. Her stomach lurched, flopped, and flapped inside her body.

Olivia was saying something, but Maggie couldn't hear her. Maggie's head grew hot and full. Black spots flickered on the edges of her vision. The room tilted. Things happened in slow motion. Olivia running around the desk toward her, hands outstretched, fear on her face, her mouth open, yelling.

Ann's interview with Dr. Andrews was uneventful. He claimed he'd misplaced his cell phone and came back to the hospital to look for it. He hadn't been there during the time of the event, like Crystal had said.

"She must have been mistaken." He shrugged. "I was here no later than ten to retrieve my phone."

He also filled Ann in on a few details of Teresa's stay without divulging any details that would break HIPAA laws. He made it sound like she was a guest in a hotel, not an incarcerated prisoner.

Ann worked her way through the rest of the personnel files and several cups of bad coffee. At one point, she had to switch to water because of a burning in her chest. Acid reflux probably. Too much coffee, not enough food. She couldn't find anything that would differentiate the red from the green folders. She did notice Dr. Smith, Dr. Andrews, Deanna and Tasha Dunlop—a pair of thick women who insisted on being interviewed together—all had green folders, along with a few others. Patrina and Crystal were in red folders.

Ann wrote this down, but she wasn't sure it meant anything.

On her way out, she asked Dr. Smith about it.

"Green folders for our hardest workers," he said. "A-plus employees." Funny his own file was among them.

Ann left Mountain View with zero leads. The dogs hadn't found any scent. All staff stories were a mixture of, "I wasn't working that night" and "nothing happened that I can think of." They all mentioned Teresa had flipped a Chutes and Ladders game—and you don't mess with the Chutes and Ladders ladies, according to everyone—and pushed Enid Brewer, one of the oldest residents, off her chair. Enid had hit her head, but she was okay.

Before leaving, Ann used the phone at the front desk—much to Evelyn's dissatisfaction—to call Thomas Littleton. The number was no longer in service. She dialed the officer who had taken charge of Carla.

Carla was more coherent but still drowsy. She didn't remember much from when she was kidnapped. She had been hiking Tenderfoot Mountain when someone ahead of her on the trail—she didn't recall what they looked like—had stopped her to ask for directions. Someone else had grabbed her from behind and injected something into her neck. Her next coherent memory was the officers from Salida talking to her and getting her out of the fat suit that made her look pregnant.

Ann's only lead was Raghib. She had a feeling the old man had everything to do with Teresa Hart's disappearance.

As she navigated the winding road down from Mountain View, Ann's phone buzzed with several missed calls. All of them were from the Daycare Place.

CHAPTER THIRTY

Ann glanced at her phone, checking for bars, while traversing the winding road. Her mark hadn't ignited or anything, so whatever might have happened must not have affected Maggie too much. Then she remembered what she thought was acid reflux.

Shit.

She looked at her phone again—no bars—then back up. She swerved to avoid hitting a fallen branch jutting into the middle of the road. She slowed a little. Enough to not kill herself.

At the sign welcoming visitors to Harmony, a couple bars finally appeared. She dialed the daycare.

"Is Maggie okay?" Ann squeezed the phone.

"Yes, she's okay. She fell and bumped her head, but she's okay. We walked her through the concussion protocol. She didn't lose consciousness and she's coherent and remembered where she was and all that. She's been in the quiet room ever since."

"I'll be there soon." She hung up before the woman said anything else. She stopped at the house to collect Pinky, knowing Maggie would want her dog if she wasn't feeling well.

At the Daycare Place, Ann jumped out of the truck, Pinky on her heels. They hurried inside.

"I hope it's okay if my dog comes in. We're only here to collect Maggie."

The short-haired redhead's face lit up. "Oh, I just love dogs." She hurried around the desk, dropped to her knees in front of Pinky, and looked up at Ann. "My husband won't agree to get one." Her face fell for a second, then brightened as she stroked Pinky's head.

Pinky didn't wiggle or pay any attention to the pretty redhead. She stared stoically toward a door off to the side of the front desk. It opened, and the other young woman who ran the place came out with Maggie.

Pinky wiggled over to her, sniffed her all over, and bounded back to Ann. Only then did she wiggle for the redhead.

Ann crouched to Maggie's level. "What happened?" She ran a hand over Maggie's hair.

Maggie looked into her eyes and, in a flicker-flash, shook her head. She didn't want to talk there.

"Go get your things," Ann said. "Pinky, heel." Maggie shuffled off, and Pinky plopped her butt right at Ann's shoe. "What happened, and when did it happen?" Ann asked the women.

"It was a couple of hours ago," the not-redhead said. Ann heard some sort of disapproval in her voice.

Where were you where you couldn't respond to our call?

"She came out here and said she needed to leave. She was breathing really fast. I think she just got light-headed or something. She fell backwards. She hit her head on the floor, but we have this spongy flooring. I think it helped." The redhead bounced on her toes to demonstrate.

Maggie came back out with her backpack. She shoved a handful of papers into it before zipping it and pulling it on.

In the truck, Ann glanced at Maggie when she reached her arm across the bench seat to back up.

A tear coursed down Maggie's cheek. Ann put the truck in neutral and engaged the e-brake again.

"Hey, what's going on?" she asked.

Maggie stared straight ahead, stroking Pinky's noggin in her lap.

"Sally Opperheim," she said. "Something happened to her."

"Today? At daycare?"

Maggie shook her head. "No. Last night. Or recently." She brushed away the tear on her cheek. No more followed. "Something wasn't right about her."

Ann's throat turned to cracked dry earth. "What wasn't right?" she asked, trying to keep her tone light and curious, while simultaneously thinking of Glory and how *she* wasn't quite right.

Maggie screwed up her face the way she did when the words she needed weren't there for her to use. "It was like . . . her skin—"

"Didn't fit right," Ann finished for her in a low voice.

Maggie nodded. "How did you know?"

Ann wasn't sure what to tell her. If she should tell her anything. But the kid had a knack for reading people's faces. Maggie stared at Ann from Ann's peripheral vision. Ann flicked her eyes over. Maggie's eyebrows were furrowed, her mouth set in a tight line.

"Okay, fine," Ann said. "It was Glory." She backed out

of her spot. "She was weird. Even her own mom said she wasn't herself."

"She had a big smile," Maggie mumbled. "And black stuff coming out of the corner of her mouth."

Shit.

Just like Glory. They had to be linked. Ann glanced quickly at Maggie and back to the road. She needed to change the subject. She didn't want to tell Maggie anything just yet, not until she had more information, or figured *something* out. Maggie would have questions, and Ann wanted to have answers for her.

"Did anyone else notice? The black stuff I mean, or Sally being weird?" She figured the Daycare Place staff would have sent the child home or something. What if it was contagious? Could Sally have contracted something from Glory?

It's not an illness, Detective. You know that.

"I don't think so," Maggie said. "The ladies there don't really watch us like guardians or anything. They just make sure none of us get hurt, or cry, or fight, or whatever. If no one is doing any of those things, Not-Olivia reads magazines and goes outside a lot. Olivia—she's the redhead—hangs around, but in the corner. Like from a distance. Until nap time. Then she rounds up the little kids and reads them a story."

Ann frowned. Perhaps the Daycare Place needed a visit from the Department of Human Services to whip those women into shape.

"Does anyone ever get hurt there?" Ann killed the engine in the driveway.

Maggie shook her head. She slid off the bench seat on her belly until her toes touched the ground.

Maybe I should get a lower vehicle.

She snorted, imagining herself driving a minivan like some soccer mom—wearing her workout clothes everywhere and drinking expensive lattes with extra frap or whatever.

No thanks.

Pinky jumped out after Maggie.

"Your backpack," Ann called, but Maggie leaned her weight into the door and forced it shut. She and Pinky ran around to the backyard.

Ann grabbed Maggie's bag. One of the papers was sticking out of the not-quite-closed zipper. She unzipped it and pulled out a stack of drawings.

Her heart triple beat when she saw the first one. It was obviously Glory, with the way she was posed in that crab-crawl and the big black spots for her eyes and mouth. The drawing was crude, but Maggie was pretty good with her crayons. She'd drawn pictures of Ruthie and Sheriff after they'd gone missing last year.

After they died. After Teresa Hart killed them.

"I can't be as stupid as I was back then," Ann whispered. She hadn't been stupid. She'd been distracted. Pulled in various directions. Wanting but not wanting to help on the missing persons-turned-homicide case.

She'd returned home to Harmony last year to recover from the psychological trauma of the Salida Stabber case and her first use of deadly force. Though she'd found the courage to use her gun again to defeat Yaldabaoth, she still didn't carry one unless absolutely necessary. Like if there was a call that required it. And this was Harmony. There never was a call that required a firearm. So she never carried it.

Ann flipped to the next drawing. Glory again. This time with a big wide smile, her face lopsided.

Ann riffled through the remaining drawings, wondering if she might come across another person depicted in crayon. Instead, she found pages full of black scribbles, each one darker and more filled in than the last.

The abyss.

The last one was entirely black except for four person-shaped yellow spots in the middle of the page.

Who were they? She thought maybe Sophia was one, but the other three? No idea. She wondered if Maggie had had some sort of vision or something. A premonition. Maggie loved to draw, but her typical drawings these days were of all three of them together with the house on one side and a tree with a swing they didn't have on the other. Maybe they needed a swing.

Ann deposited the drawings on the table and walked through the house to the backyard. Maggie threw a ball for Pinky, who retrieved it faithfully every time, but would not drop it. Maggie had to wrestle it out of her big mouth.

"Maggie," Ann called. Maggie looked up, startled. "Can I talk to you about your drawings?"

Maggie's eyebrows shot up. "My drawings?"

"The ones you drew at the Daycare Place."

Maggie threw the ball, but Pinky didn't chase it, like she knew Maggie wasn't going to play anymore.

Ann spread the drawings out on the table.

"Who is this?" Ann asked.

"Glory," Maggie said in a small voice so quiet only a part of it came out. "I saw her like that. At the hike yesterday. I think Sophia showed me."

"What is this?" Ann pointed to the black page with the four figures in the center. "Who are these people?" She stabbed the drawing with her finger.

Maggie sighed and pushed the pages away. "I don't

know." Her chin tilted down and her shoulders slumped inward.

She's not a suspect, Detective. She's a kid. Don't be so hard on her.

Ann crouched by Maggie and took one of her hands. Maggie looked down at her.

"You can tell me."

The tears in Maggie's eyes spilled over. Ann wiped them away and cradled Maggie's face in her hands.

"Don't cry," Ann said, her tone harsh even in her own ears. She softened her voice. "I'm not mad or upset. I just want to know. Will you tell me? I think it's important."

"Those are the Luminaries," Maggie said.

Luminaries. Like from Kuhli's blog post Ann had glossed over.

"Eleleth"—Maggie pronounced it Ee-lay-layth—"and the others. They came to me when we were in Tartaros. Before you gave me the angel light." Maggie hitched in a breath. "One of them scares Sophia. He's mean."

"You never told me," Ann said, her voice small now, choked. "About in Tartaros."

Maggie shook her head. "I didn't know until the deer in the woods." She swiped a wayward hair off her cheek. "I've been having nightmares about it, but after the deer, I figured out they weren't nightmares. They were memories." Maggie's face saddened. "Ann?"

"Yeah?"

Maggie's honey eyes met hers. "Why don't you come anymore? When I have nightmares? Doesn't it tell you?" She pointed at Ann's chest, at her mark.

Ann rubbed at it as if Maggie's calling her out had made it itch.

"I—it tells me, but it's only ever just a tingle, so I didn't think they were that bad." Her growing ineptitude as Maggie's guardian grew ten sizes. "Why didn't you come get me if they scare you?" She felt like an asshole for deflecting the blame.

Maggie looked at her hands. "I didn't want to bother you."

"Maggie." Ann lifted Maggie's chin. "You don't have to worry about bothering me. Okay?"

Maggie nodded. She picked up the picture of Glory. "Sophia showed me these. It's Glory. She's scary. Something is wrong." Maggie's voice hitched. "Sally Opperheim was the same way." Maggie wiped her nose on her hand. "She's usually mean and takes all the toys away from everyone, even the little kids."

As if Maggie wasn't a little kid at seven years old. Almost eight, as she would remind Ann.

"Today she was handing them out. She was sharing. She wanted to play dolls. And when we did, I accidentally touched her hand and—" Maggie sucked in a breath of air and grabbed her stomach. "I keep getting a weird feeling in my tummy." Maggie wrapped her arms around her midsection.

"Do you feel that way now?" Ann asked.

Maggie nodded.

"What happened when you touched Sally's hand?" Ann asked.

"I saw what happened to her. I felt it. I think something happened to her face. Maybe her eyes?" Maggie lowered her arms. "There was someone there first. Someone familiar." Maggie winced. "My mark." She pulled her collar down.

Ann gasped at the sight. It looked like a brand. "When did this happen?" Ann asked.

Maggie shrugged. "The other night. When I had that nightmare."

"I'll get you some burn salve." Ann climbed the stairs to the linen closet where she kept cleaning supplies and medicine and bandages and all sorts of things. She grabbed a tube of expired topical pain reliever and hunted for anything else that might help ease Maggie's pain. She knew, though, that it wasn't the *actual* mark that hurt. It was under it. The meaning of it.

She stood facing the interior of the closet for a few minutes, looking at the towels above her head on the upper shelves. The last person to fold them was probably her mom. Her dad likely had had no reason to use more than one towel. Ann and Maggie only used one each. Ann washed them and put them back out. Probably not often enough.

What would Mary Logan do in this situation? Ann barely remembered her own mom. Ann was younger than Maggie when her mom died. She remembered black hair and tanned skin like her own, and sparkling brown eyes looking down at her with a smile, the sun making a halo behind her head. Ann knew it was just one memory of her, but it was the moment before her mom was struck by a car and killed. For some reason, it was the only memory she had of her mom. She didn't remember baking cookies together, or going to parks, or anything like that. Just that fleeting moment before she was struck by a car.

Ann liked to think her mom had been caring, loving, comforting. All because of that one smile. Because of those sparkling eyes. Because of the feel of her hand around Ann's.

How had Derrick done it? He had treated Maggie like a biological daughter. Sure, his own biological child hadn't lived very long, but how had he done it? How did he love a little person he just met? One he didn't raise from infancy. Was he just that good of a man? A father?

Ann was surprised to find tears in her eyes. She hastily wiped them away, cleared her throat, and closed the closet door.

Get it together, Logan.

She put some expired ointment on Maggie's mark, knowing it probably wouldn't help. But if she didn't do something, she'd feel helpless. After, she got the girl set up on the couch with a blanket and pillows. Pinky, who finally gave up on them coming back out to continue the game of fetch, came in and gave Maggie a sniff and a lick on the forehead. Then she jumped up to cuddle with her, letting out a blasty sigh.

Ann shuffled the drawings together. What was she missing?

A heart that wasn't cold and stony and shriveled . . . a warm, caring soul—

Ann's thoughts stopped short when she remembered last year's thing was seven souls. This was eight Logismoi, but she had to think if it was related to the book, plus mention of the Perfect *Soul...*

She went to the coffee table and grabbed her notebook. She'd written down the perfect pairs from the poem the book had shown her.

Glory had called herself Sadness in the clearing. When Ann saw her again, she was—what did she say?

Pure joy.

Ann ran her finger down the list. Her heart thumped hard.

I am Sadness and Pure Joy.

She jotted Glory's name next to that pair and read the

rest of the list. She took a deep breath. Maggie said Sally took the toys from the other kids, but today she gave them out.

I take greedily and give charitably in equal measure.

Two down, six to go.

Time to get serious. Ann couldn't be made a fool. She needed to step up her game as a former detective and as Maggie's guardian and especially since Duke was trying to unseat her as sheriff.

CHAPTER THIRTY-ONE

Teresa followed Cassie down the dirt road toward town, fiddling with the scarf hiding her hair. It was even earlier this time. The sun had disappeared behind the big mountains—she never bothered to learn their names, though Derrick had known every mountain peak in the area. He tried to point them all out to her once.

Cassie floated effortlessly in the twilight sky overhead. At one point, a flock of birds distracted her. She swooped after them, letting out a joyous shriek. Well, it sounded joyous to Teresa. To the casual observer, it probably sounded frightening.

Teresa looked around, expecting people to be out enjoying the nice summer night. The evening hadn't cooled off the way it usually did after the sun went down. The day must have been hot. She wouldn't know. She'd been indoors.

Once Lory finally got her a real disguise of some sort, she fully expected to get out more during the day, even if it was just for a walk down the dirt road. She'd never been past the abandoned funeral home away from town. That way seemed safest.

Cassie swooped to the left again, down toward the old residential district. The neighborhood where Sheriff McMichael had lived. Now Olivia and Hunter lived there.

The paved road turned to dirt. Teresa jogged farther into the neighborhood, casting quick glances up at Cassie overhead. Her little gargoyle liked to play on the updrafts and vortexes. Sometimes she swooped left, then veered right. It kept Teresa on her toes.

Finally, Cassie dove. She landed on the road ahead. Teresa ran to catch up, then bent over, hands on her knees. She wasn't used to all this running, and if she remembered anything about post-natal exercise, running was definitely not on the list. She was probably doing damage to her joints.

Cassie bounded into the creeping twilight toward a small cabin tucked away in a stand of dense pine trees. Teresa crept up on the house and peeked in the window to see a tidy, bordering-on-sparse home. A woman on her hands and knees scrubbed the floorboards with a smile on her face, seeming to enjoy the work.

She was a young pretty thing. But definitely a grown woman. Teresa had it in her head they would all be children. Easy to overpower. Easy to manipulate or coerce into trusting her.

She ducked. Last year, when Tiffany had led her around in the middle of the night, all of the people had been sleeping. Or high, in Brent's case.

The only one who had been awake was Derrick. And, she supposed, Sheriff McMichael counted, but he only woke up after she'd already stabbed the oversized hypodermic needle into his chest.

Cassie hopped around in impatient agitation.

"I know, I know," Teresa whispered. "I don't know what to do. She's awake." Teresa peeked again. The woman was gone from the immediate area. Teresa was sure people locked their doors now. She couldn't just break in.

They crept around the house looking for another way inside. People should have their windows open, air out their stuffy houses, get some fresh air, for Pete's sake. They made it all the way around to the front door without finding a single way to get in. There wasn't even a back door. It was the smallest cabin she'd ever seen.

She touched the doorknob. Just as she suspected. Locked. She would have to knock. She would have to be seen.

"Stay behind me," Teresa said to Cassie. She smoothed her shirt, adjusted the scarf covering her hair, and rapped on the door.

"Coming," a sing-song voice said from inside. The door opened.

Teresa was about to say hello, but before the greeting could form in her throat, Cassie blasted past her and tackled the woman to the floor.

Teresa screamed with the suddenness of it, then quickly lurched inside and closed the door.

The woman and Cassie wrestled on the floor. The woman's eyes were wide and frightened as she held Cassie back by her madly flapping wings. Cassie's hands reached toward the woman's face. The woman grunted and strained.

Teresa lunged forward and pushed her weight against Cassie's back, hoping she wasn't hurting her baby. The wings flapped. The whooshing air from them knocked pictures over on side tables, and a vase spilled water onto the floor, the flowers bursting in an array of colorful petals. The vase rolled off the edge of the table and bounced on the rug without breaking. Still, Teresa pressed Cassie forward, groaning with the effort, hoping their combined weight and the unruly wings would get Cassie to her goal. The woman was strong.

"Oh, god, what is this?" the woman screamed. She tossed her head back and forth. Cassie's little hands groped the woman's face and found purchase, hooking into the occipital bone, gouging around the closed eyelids. Teresa leaned back, taking her weight off of her daughter.

The woman screamed. Cassie's hands came away with the eyeballs. She held them aloft like small prizes won. The eyelids were still attached.

Ragged flesh rimmed the woman's empty eye sockets.

"What is this!" the woman shrieked.

"Your worst nightmare." Teresa grabbed the vase. She hit it against the side of the woman's head, tinging the crystal with blood. The woman stopped screaming, but a slow and horrible groan came from her. Teresa hit her again with a sickening smack, rendering her unconscious.

Silence filled the cabin, save for the ticking of a clock and Teresa's ragged breaths. She took a second to collect herself. The clock rang out the first notes of the Westminster chime. Teresa shrieked. Cassie hissed and coiled back onto her haunches, ready to attack.

"Just the clock," Teresa said. "Just the clock." She stroked Cassie's strange little head, which pressed against her palm with a vibration like a purr. Teresa leaned over the woman and, in a matter of seconds, ate the third soul.

It tasted of sweat and rusted metal. As with the other two, the woman's body had lost substance, leaving behind empty skin.

Teresa retied her scarf and turned to leave when someone knocked on the door. She dropped to the ground, her stomach lurching with fear and the residual taste of the soul. If this visitor had heard the woman's screams, they probably wouldn't knock and wait. They'd try to come in.

Cassie bounded over to Teresa and huddled close, one little hand-paw on Teresa's shoulder, almond eyes staring at the door. Teresa had seen the woman who lived here on her hands and knees. If anyone looked in the windows, they'd see Teresa and the little gargoyle beside her.

Not to mention the dead woman skin suit on the floor.

"Cindy?" a man's voice called from the porch. He knocked again. "Are you home?"

It was only a matter of time before he started walking around, looking in the windows.

"I'm sorry about earlier," he said. "Can I come in? Can we talk?"

Teresa remained silent. She had to get out of there. She had to get back to Amanda to feed her, but there was no back door. She hoped to anything holy that still might be on her side that this person wouldn't come in without an invitation. She hadn't locked the door.

"It's okay," Teresa called without thinking. "Just go away. We can talk tomorrow."

"It's not okay," the voice said. "I shouldn't have made fun of you for being a hard worker."

Teresa frowned.

"I guess . . . I guess I just . . . I don't know. It's like in grade school when boys tease the girls they like."

Teresa imagined this man leaning against the door with his forehead touching it—all sappy and sentimental, like in the movies.

She looked around. Her eyes landed on a belt on the table from where the vase fell. A belt with a gun in a holster, handcuffs, a night stick. Next to it was a badge.

She'd killed a cop. Again.

"What I'm trying to say is . . . I like you. A lot." A pause. "Did you get the flowers?"

Teresa looked at the blood-stained vase. She didn't know what to say. She crawled over to the nearest table and used her scarf to turn off the light. Mustn't leave fingerprints. Cassie stayed in the middle of the area, clutching the eyeballs in her paws, cocking her head at Teresa.

Could they take another?

The thought sickened her. Her stomach was full of the cop's soul. She didn't think she could consume two in one night. The thought made her gorge rise. She covered her mouth.

"I understand if you don't feel the same way."

Teresa crawled to the next table and turned off that lamp in the same way, too. One lamp remained.

Why so many damn lights?

"I'm tired." Teresa called. "I'll talk to you tomorrow."

"Is everything okay in there? You sound strange."

Crap.

Teresa scrambled to the door and twisted the lock on the handle as quietly as possible, then wiped it off. Half a second later, the knob jiggled. She held out her hands to Cassie who bounded to her. Teresa retrieved the vase, and she and Cassie crawled to the darkest corner and huddled there. Cassie deposited the eyeballs into the vase and held onto Teresa's shirt.

He thought something was wrong. He would look in and see them.

She thought she saw movement outside the window across the room. A face pressed against the glass between cupped hands. She swore they made eye contact. The figure moved past the other windows.

Teresa counted to three, held Cassie and the vase close, and ran to the door. She covered her shaking hand with the scarf, opened it, slipped out, and took the time to close it behind her as quiet as she could. Together, she and Cassie sprinted into the night.

Teresa came in the back door of Lory's house and locked it behind her and Cassie. She slogged down the hall, legs trembling, body aching, lungs burning, and stumbled into their room. She hid the vase in the back of the closet to deal with later. Cassie hopped onto Teresa's bed, leaped into the air, and shed her leathery skin. She bounced on the bed on her back with a delighted giggle and reached for Teresa.

"I need to feed your sister first," Teresa said. But Amanda was still sleeping.

"Ba," Cassie said, tiny hands reaching. "Ba ba."

Teresa shrugged. "Okay. You first then. You better not take all of it. Amanda needs it most. I think."

She'd fallen asleep nursing Cassie. She only woke when a tiny hand patted her cheek. Cassie made a popping sound with her lips. Teresa got up. Amanda was awake, her thumb stuffed in her mouth.

Teresa briefly wondered if she could suck her own soul through her thumb. What a silly thought.

I'm so tired.

She lay Cassie gently in the crib and lifted Amanda. This time, she fell asleep for good, cuddling Amanda in her arms.

Teresa woke when the shrieking started. She jerked back as the black cloud blasted out of Amanda's mouth this time. Buzzing and shrieking. It rushed past her face, stinging her cheek and blowing her hair. She flinched.

The cloud collected in the corner of the room where it swarmed, trapped.

She jumped up and opened the window. The cloud blasted outside.

Teresa wondered if she would eventually get used to it. She closed the window and glanced at the clock. Early— only three. Everything was getting earlier. She hoped Lory would follow through with a wig, otherwise Teresa would be forced to dye her hair black. The scarf just looked too much like she was trying to hide her identity.

Amanda hiccupped, tears in the outer corners of her eyes. She'd grown another couple months. She was sitting up on her own, though she tried to grab her foot and fell over with a joyful giggle.

"Mama," she said.

Teresa let out a sob and covered her mouth. She huddled close to her smaller baby.

"That's right," she said. "Mama."

Amanda squealed with glee.

CHAPTER THIRTY-TWO

WEDNESDAY

Teresa came out of her room a few hours later to a silent house. The clock ticked in the living room.

"Lory?" she called. No one returned her shout. "Are you home?" No response. She wandered out to the front of the house and stood at the top of the basement steps. She did not want to go down them. Doing so would probably trigger some PTSD response. Like the acrid stench of burned meat likely would. Luckily, she hadn't been subjected to that scent since she cauterized Bram Logan's severed finger stumps.

Teresa shuddered.

"Lory, are you down there?" she called. Again, no one answered. She sighed with relief. Nice to have the place to herself. Not that Lory was a nuisance. Just that over the past months she'd hardly had any alone time, having been surrounded by crazy people—and now by her *sympathizers*.

She turned and spotted a gift bag on the dining room table with a note. Teresa read it.

For the littleuns. I'll be back soon. —L

Teresa opened the package. Inside were several little stuffed animals. Teresa took the bag to her room and deposited it inside, peeked in at the babies—slumbering away—and wandered down the hall toward the back. She passed a junk room of some sort. Across from it, she found Lory's room.

Teresa would have loved to have had the room as a teen. Four poster bed with canopy, white furniture, a hope chest at the foot of the made bed.

Lory had arranged a few decorative pillows along the headboard. The bedspread looked to be one of those bed-in-a-bag deals with matching shams and coordinating sheets in a gaudy pink floral pattern.

A beautiful white vanity sat to one side. Teresa had always wanted a vanity like that. She pulled the little chair out, sat, and clicked on the light. It lit up the entire mirror. Teresa gazed at the bulbs with awe until her eyes landed on her reflection.

She cringed at her appearance. Bags under her eyes, dull and pale complexion. She shouldn't be surprised. She hadn't had her usual creams and serums in that place. It had been months since she'd had a proper skin care regimen. Months since she needed one. Since she needed to *make an effort* to look good for anyone. Even now, who did she need to look good for?

She sorted through the bottles arranged on a mirrored tray, tilting each one to read what they were. Toners and serums and moisturizers.

First wash your face, her mother's voice said. It was from a time before everything went to hell. Her mother giving instructions on proper skin care.

"It's never too early to start an anti-aging skin care

regimen," Teresa whispered, mimicking her mother's voice. Her mother had told her that when she was fourteen. "A fresh and beautiful face is the first thing your husband should see when he wakes up."

She rolled her eyes and went into the *en suite* bathroom where the girly motif extended. Pink everything. Countertop, sink, shower, toilet. The wallpaper shined white with light pink undertones and horrid pink flowers.

Teresa found a bottle of expensive-looking face cleanser. She tied her hair up with a scrunchie and headband she found in a drawer and washed her face before returning to the vanity in the bedroom.

She sat in the little chair and opened the drawer to her left. She wasn't sure what she was looking for. A hair brush perhaps? It's where she would have put one. Her motions had been on autopilot.

Instead of a hairbrush, however, there was a smashed and mangled looking cardboard box.

Teresa used the tip of her finger to lift the lid. A wedge of light from the mirror illuminated a newspaper clipping. Curious, Teresa pinched the edge and pulled it out.

It was a newspaper photo of the Denver Police Academy graduating class. Teresa didn't care what year, because her eye landed on the list of names. One name specifically.

Ann Logan.

She pushed the lid off to uncover another clipping. This one of the Salida Stabber story. Wasn't it the Salida Slaughterer? She shook her head. The article praised Detective Ann Logan.

Teresa frowned.

Under that was a stack of photos. All of them were

Ann. Surveillance shots or something like that. Candid. Secretive.

Teresa could only assume Lory had taken the photos. But why?

The last picture, however, told the whole story.

It was a Polaroid of a young woman with dark hair holding a baby. Her face looked familiar. The smile, something in the eyes.

Sitting next to the woman was a familiar man, though healthier looking than when Teresa had seen him. The unmistakable blue eyes and the deep dimples tugging his grin upward solidified the familiarity.

Ann's father. Bram Logan.

Teresa used her hair to put a blond wig on the woman's portrait.

It was Lory. The woman was Lory. The man was Bram. The baby had to be—

Teresa gasped. Lory was Ann's mother.

CHAPTER THIRTY-THREE

Ann called Rachel a few times to see if she could watch Maggie, but Rachel didn't answer. Ann left her a text to call her as soon as possible. She was not comfortable leaving Maggie home alone, though she had a security system installed a few months ago. Plus her mark would tell her if anything went wrong. And Pinky. Pinky would give her life to protect that girl. But no. With Teresa at large, her only option was taking Maggie with her.

Her phone rang. Ann answered it without looking at who it was.

"Rachel?" she asked.

A few seconds of labored breathing before Cindy's voice came on the line. "Hi . . . Shhhherifff . . ." she said.

"Cindy? Are you okay?"

"I'm . . . not . . . feeling . . . well . . ." Her voice came out long and drawn, as if the very act of speaking took everything out of her.

"Take the day off. Get some rest. Feel better, okay?" Ann said.

"Oh . . . kay . . ." Cindy hung up.

Ann hoped Rachel was at the station. But when they arrived, the dispatch desk was empty. Sully smiled at Maggie.

"Hey, girlfriend," he said. Maggie blushed, but hurried forward and gave him a high-five. Pinky also wiggled over to him for pets.

"Where's Rachel?" Ann asked, weaving around the bullpen desks toward her office.

"Day off," Sully replied, still rubbing Pinky's ears.

"Cindy called in sick," Ann told him.

"Oh?" Concern arched his eyebrows. "Should I take her some soup or something?" He moved to grab his keys.

Ann shook her head. "Probably a typical summer cold." She took Maggie to her office. "You need to be on your very best behavior," Ann said. "Because I'm going to ask Sully to look after you today."

"Why can't I go with you?" Maggie asked. "What are you doing?"

"Boring police work," Ann said. "Besides, it's going to be too warm for you and Pinky to stay in the truck most of the day."

"When will you be back?" Maggie asked.

Ann didn't know. She crouched, her belt creaking. She rarely wore her uniform, since pretty much everyone knew who she was, but official police business, like visiting a mental hospital and canvasing neighborhoods, required it. Besides, enough new people had moved to town in the past nine months who might not know she was the sheriff.

"I'll be back as soon as I can. Don't worry. I'm just knocking on doors and asking questions." She smiled, and Maggie lunged forward and hugged her. Ann could feel her rapid little heartbeat. "There's a ton of stuff to eat in the fridge here. In case I'm still out at lunchtime."

She pulled away from Maggie's embrace.

"Would you rather go to the Daycare Place?" Ann asked, knowing the answer.

Maggie shook her head.

"You can watch videos on my laptop," Ann said. "And you have your backpack with crayons and books and stuff."

Maggie nodded.

"And you have Pinky to keep you company." She smiled. Pinky thumped her tail on the floor at the sound of her name.

Ann left the office and sidled over to Sully.

"Hey," she said. She looked over her shoulder and lowered her voice. "So, Teresa Hart is missing from Mountain View."

Sully's head shot up from his computer. "Out?"

Ann held up her hands to quiet him. "I haven't told her yet." She jerked her head over her shoulder.

Sully opened his mouth to say something but closed it without saying a word. Probably something about how keeping that information secret was a bad idea. Ann knew it was, but for some reason, she couldn't bring herself to tell Maggie. Not yet.

"I'm going to canvass the neighborhoods, see if anyone has seen anything. Would you mind just keeping an eye on Maggie while I'm out?"

Sully gave Ann a look she couldn't read.

"I can take her back home, leave her there alone with Pinky." It wasn't meant as a guilt trip, but she couldn't help but think Sully would see it that way.

"No, it's fine." He turned back to the folders on his desk. "Not sure how you're going to canvass the entire town by yourself, but, hey, I'm sure you can manage it." The tips of his ears turned red.

"I'll do my best." She went to the door. "She's easy. You won't have to do anything. Just make sure she doesn't leave or anything like that."

"What about the dog?" He'd never referred to Pinky as "the dog" before.

Ann frowned. "She'll be fine, too."

"What if nature calls?"

"Look, I'll just take them back home." Ann headed toward her office.

"No, no." Sully let out a long breath. "It's fine. Really. Go do your thing. The Hart case was yours. It's only fair you get to do the legwork for this new development." He paused. "I need the whole story, though. You can't leave me out of this sort of thing. We all need to know what's going on."

Ann knew he meant more than just the Teresa Hart development.

"I will." Ann nodded. "Thanks, Sully." She paused at the door. "Can you organize a town hall for later this afternoon? We need to set a curfew and inform people of the Teresa Hart situation. Draft a communication to go out to all residents, that sort of thing. Set it for five. Please."

"Teresa?" Lory's voice called from the front of the house. Teresa scrambled to shove everything back in the box and into the drawer. She pushed it closed and grabbed a bottle off the vanity. She collided with Lory on her way out of the master bedroom.

"What were you doing in there?"

"Looking for some face wash," Teresa said with a laugh she knew sounded fake. "Found it." She held up the bottle.

Lory's eyes shifted to the bottle in Teresa's hand.

"That's not face wash. It's toner." Lory cocked her head and narrowed her eyes.

Teresa looked at the bottle and back at Lory. She didn't know what repercussions there might be if Lory found out she'd been snooping. She couldn't afford to lose Lory's trust, one-sided as it might be.

"Um—"

Lory's eyes shifted over Teresa's shoulder, and Teresa followed her gaze. One of the newspaper clippings stuck out of the drawer.

Lory's eyebrows lowered. She opened her mouth, probably to chastise Teresa for snooping, for abuse of her trust, for who knows what else that would likely shatter whatever friendship they might have built. Teresa opened her mouth to explain, but someone knocked on the front door.

Lory whirled around at the sound. They both stared down the hall.

Ann started her questioning at the most logical place. The eyeballs at the abandoned funeral home had sent her to Louise Marga's old house first. It was the closest to that place. Perhaps the woman who lived there now—Lory Magan—had seen or heard something.

She considered the two names—Louise Marga and Lory Magan—with the same initials as if there was some sort of connection. Nothing she could see right off. Probably just a coincidence.

She parked out front and climbed the all-too-familiar

porch steps. Amazed at what a fresh coat of paint could do. She knocked on the door and waited.

Another knock came. Louder.

"You need to hide in the basement." Lory's eyes were wide and frantic. She grabbed Teresa's wrist and pulled her down the hall.

In Teresa's room, Lory released Teresa and reached in for one of the sleeping babies.

"They're asleep, what are you doing?"

"If it was one of your sympathizers, they would have knocked a certain pattern and come in." Lory reached again, but Teresa grabbed her arm. Lory looked at her, face stricken. "Teresa, I don't know who it is at the door."

"If you wake them up, they'll cry, and whoever's at the door will hear them," Teresa snapped. "Be reasonable, Lory. It's better if we stay in here." Teresa blocked Lory from reaching for the babies.

"The basement would be safer," Lory said in a pinched whisper. Her eyes were full of fearful tears.

When no one answered right away, Ann paced along the porch, wandered back, and knocked again with the side of her fist.

The door opened. A woman with bleached hair and tanned skin poked her head out. She wore large sunglasses that obscured half her face, despite the gloom around her house.

"Lory Magan?" Ann asked.

"That's me," the woman said in what sounded like an exaggerated — bordering on ridiculous — Southern accent. "Now, what can I do for you, Sheriff?"

"Ms. Magan, We have a suspect at large," Ann said. "She may have been in the area. Have you seen this woman?" Ann held up a photo of Teresa.

"Not that I can think of." Ms. Magan shook her head. "She's pretty. What's she suspected of doing?"

"Have you seen this man?" Ann held up a picture of Raghib, just in case. Might as well ask around after both of them.

Lory peered at the picture. "Are they in cahoots?"

"Have you noticed anything suspicious or out of the ordinary the past few days? Anyone lurking around?"

"There was a woman with long dark hair creeping around my property," she said. "I forgot to lock my back door, and she came right inside."

Ann wrote this down in her little notebook. "Any other descriptors? Approximate age, height, eye color?"

"Her eyes are dark brown, almost black. She's about your height, I think?" She looked Ann up and down. "She has a big scar covering half of her face."

"Be sure to keep your doors locked, okay?" Ann said. "Mind if I take a quick look inside?" Ann asked.

"Of course not." Lory stood aside. "Wouldn't want to obstruct justice or nothing like that." She flashed a big beaming smile, and for a second, she looked familiar.

Ann paused and looked at her. The sunglasses obscured so much of her face. But her smile. Ann stepped inside.

The woman had made some amazing upgrades to Louise's cramped little home. Or maybe it was just the lack of stacks of magazines and books and whatever else. The place seemed brighter and more open.

"You've really cleaned this place up nicely," she said, making chatty conversation. "Before you moved in, an old woman lived here. I think she was a hoarder." Ann turned around. "What brought you to Harmony anyway?"

"I lived here when I was younger," Lory said. "It's been around thirty years or so." She gave Ann a close-lipped smile.

"Any reason you're wearing sunglasses inside?" she asked as she casually looked around.

"Migraines," the woman said. "The light sensitivity is the worst. That's why it took me so long to come to the door. I was holed up in the dark trying to ride it out."

"I won't keep you too long then." Ann's eyes drifted to the door to the basement. It had been changed out with a normal door. No bolt. She suddenly had an urge to see the basement. To see if there were still signs of what had happened in there. A prickly desire tugged at the back of her mind.

"Basement?" she asked, pointing at the door. Her throat went dry.

Lory nodded. Ann thought the woman's smile faltered, if only for half a second.

"Can I take a quick peek down there?" Ann cleared the hitch from her voice. Louise used the excuse that all she kept were Christmas decorations and other stored things. Hot and cold flashed over Ann's scalp.

Lory had every right to deny Ann access to the basement, of course. She didn't have a warrant and no probable cause to even try to obtain one. If Lory had nothing to hide, why wouldn't she let Ann take a peek?

Lory touched her forehead. "Sheriff, I'm sorry—this migraine."

"Just a quick look?" Ann gave Lory a big smile. "Then

I'll be out of your hair and you can finish riding out that headache."

Lory's smile returned, though not as beaming. "Of course." Lory waved Ann toward the door.

"After you." Ann copied Lory's gesture.

Lory stepped toward the door and opened it. She looked over her shoulder at Ann before going down the stairs. Ann followed.

The stained concrete had been carpeted in a plush white. The walls had been paneled with white shiplap. The main part of the room had a rocking chair, a loveseat, and a playpen in the middle. A table that looked like it was made of stone with a decorative cloth and bowl of plastic fruit stood at the back.

"Do you have kids?" Ann asked, nodding toward the playpen.

"My daughter . . . grandbabies." Lory winced.

"I'm sorry, Ms. Magan." Ann suddenly felt like a jerk. "I can see you're in a lot of pain. I'll get out of your hair." She followed Lory up the stairs.

"Thank you for your time." Ann started to leave. "Oh, there's a town hall at five. Please try to attend. If you're feeling better."

"Certainly," Lory said, her accent suddenly gone. Ann detected a different accent, but couldn't place it with just the one word. She gave Lory an appraising look, wondering where she'd seen her before. Her roots were an odd orangish color while the rest of her hair was a strange and unnatural yellow.

"Have we met before?" Ann asked.

"I don't believe so." Her Southern accent magically reappeared. "You have a nice day now, Sheriff."

"You, too. Feel better." The door closed behind her. The deadbolt engaged.

Ann climbed into her truck and drove down into the older residential district where Sheriff McMichael had lived. No one had seen anything unusual or suspicious, and no one had seen Teresa in that neck of the woods.

If Teresa truly was back in town stealing Logismoi, Ann was certain someone would have seen her.

Of course, last year no one had known she was doing something similar. That was the problem with Harmony. People knew everyone's business, but no one wanted to be held liable. Bystander apathy. They were private people, but they did love their gossip.

Ann kept trying. She moved on to Evergreen Avenue and got a hit. Maybe.

"There was some noise over at the Opperheim residence," said the older woman who answered the door. Ann thought her name was Jean or Joan. "Oh, but they've been fighting a lot. That poor little girl. I see her outside on her swing set sometimes at night looking so forlorn."

"Opperheim? As in Sally Opperheim?"

The woman, Jean, Ann decided, nodded. "A pretty little girl. Like a big Shirley Temple."

"Have you ever seen her parents involved in any sort of domestic—"

"Oh no. They don't hit. They just yell. You'd think they'd keep their windows closed if they're going to do that."

"Is the yelling the only noise you heard?"

Jean shook her head. "Two nights ago, the little girl, she was there on the swing. Her parents were fighting. I went and brushed my teeth and when I came back, she was gone."

Sally had probably just gone back inside. "What time was that?"

The woman pondered. "Well, my evening program had ended, so it must've been just after ten."

Ann jotted this down. "Thank you. If you think of anything else, please give the station a call. And please try to attend the town hall at five today."

The rest of the neighborhood had evidently turned a blind eye to the Opperheim argument. No one saw anything, or they reported they'd been asleep. No one had seen Teresa Hart, either.

CHAPTER THIRTY-FOUR

Cassie and Amanda had woken up — quietly, thank goodness — while Lory occupied the visitor. Teresa had changed their diapers as silently as she could. They sat on a blanket on the floor in the corner, huddled like the fugitives they were.

The front door closed. Teresa let out a relieved sigh. She put the babies on the bed with pillows arranged around them, as well as a few of the stuffed toys Lory had purchased.

Teresa opened the bedroom door a crack and heard Lory let out a huge sigh. Her footsteps came down the hall.

Lory came into Teresa's room, swiping at a stray hair on her forehead. Her face looked drawn.

"I'm so glad I listened to you," Lory said in a daze. "That was the sheriff. She wanted to see the basement."

Teresa sucked in a quick gulp of air. Ann Logan had been within yards of her. What if she'd wanted to look in other areas of the house? It would have meant the end.

"How was it?" Teresa asked, nonchalant.

Lory seemed to stir, as if she hadn't known Teresa was there. "It was . . . okay."

Teresa raised one eyebrow. "Are you sure?" She turned back to the babies and danced a little stuffed kitty between them. They squealed with delight when she bopped Cassie on the nose with it, then Amanda. Their poor reflexes had them grabbing at the air as she moved the toy away. "Aside from hiding me, I would imagine seeing your *daughter* after all this time had to have been, I don't know, weird?"

Teresa swore she head Lory swallow hard.

"I wondered if you'd seen that," she said with a frown. "It isn't nice to snoop, you know. A less understanding person might consider it a betrayal of trust."

"So, it's true then? I didn't imagine that dark-haired woman sitting with Bram Logan in the picture was you?"

Lory sighed. "It was me."

"Ann thinks you're dead." It was a recurring theme with the town's sweetheart. First Bram—surprise! He wasn't. Well, now he was. And now Lory.

"I know," Lory said.

"She didn't suspect anything?"

"She was six when I . . . left," Lory said. "I doubt she remembers much of me, and if she remembers anything, I would have had dark hair." She fingered the frayed ends of her hair.

"You look too young to be her mother. She's, what, in her thirties?" Teresa always figured she and Ann were around the same age.

Teresa kept bopping the babies back and forth with the kitty until Cassie finally snatched it from her. She held it up triumphantly and tipped over backward with a squeal of startled delight.

Amanda leaned forward and patted her sister's chubby

knee. Teresa reached down and propped Cassie back up, handed her the kitty, found a similar stuffed puppy, and gave it to Amanda. She stood and turned to face Lory.

Lory had a thoughtful look on her face. "Let's just call it . . . Divine Intervention." She waved her hand mystically.

"Let's call it what it is and tell me the truth," Teresa said. "How am I supposed to know you aren't going to turn me over to your daughter?"

Lory's mouth opened and closed like a landed fish. She laughed nervously again.

"You better start spilling, Lory, or I will take these babies and I will find somewhere else to stay. I'm pretty sure Paul or Patrina would *love* to have me." She didn't want to leave. She felt at home here. The babies were happy and comfortable. And it was nice having a friend.

She is not your friend, Yaldabaoth's voice slithered across her scalp. *She is a means to survival.*

It was nice having someone willing to look after her then.

Lory stood in silence for a few seconds, as if contemplating what she should tell Teresa.

"It all started when I was around eighteen years old," Lory said with a wistful voice.

"I don't need your life story—just give me the highlights."

"Okay, fine. There was a time when the Messengers of the Light and their rival organization were one. Leadership quarrels split them up, and over time, the beliefs they fought for changed. There is a book that has additional secret texts within it, and in this book was a doctrine about reuniting the two factions through a contractual marriage and subsequent conception of a child."

Teresa frowned, but she took in Lory's medium skin

tone and horribly fake hair color, plus her slight accent. She was from somewhere else. Who was Teresa to pooh-pooh another culture's ways?

"The contract stipulated that we—Bram and I—"

"The book actually told you to marry Bram?"

"No." Lory laughed and looked down. She fiddled with her earring. "We were the most likely candidates for this ceremony." She appeared wistful. "We were already in love. Secretly. We volunteered." She lowered her chin and smiled, but when she lifted it, the smile had vanished. "We were to marry and bring the two factions back together by conceiving The One."

"The One what?"

"The One who would protect Sophia—you know, Wisdom? Yaldabaoth's mother?—upon her manifestation. We had a small ceremony attended only by our parents and the four Luminaries."

"Luminaries?" Teresa asked.

"I'll spare you an entire lesson on the Gnostic faith. Just know, they are powerful beings from the Entirety. They are god-like in their powers, but they are not omniscient like god."

Teresa nodded in understanding. Cassie and Amanda were playing quietly with their stuffed toys, showing each other the different ones over and over as if discovering them for the first time. Their coos and giggles warmed her heart.

"The Luminaries came to us bearing the rings we were to use in our marriage ceremony. The rings contain within them light from the Entirety." She looked at her left hand where a band encircled her ring finger.

Teresa couldn't see what was special about it from where she stood.

"The rings would keep us alive until the completion of

the contract. That is what I meant by Divine Intervention. I haven't aged for many years."

"How old *are* you?"

"Fifty-three." She looked at her hands.

Teresa waved her hand. "Fifty-three isn't *that* old." That's why Lory had started her story with her age of eighteen. She'd been so young when they married.

"We had trouble, though. Conceiving, I mean. I-I couldn't . . ." She looked down. "I had two miscarriages, and after that, nothing."

Teresa knew the feeling. She and Derrick had struggled to get pregnant with Tiffany. When it had finally happened, it had seemed a miracle.

"What happened, after you and Bram couldn't conceive? You must have eventually, since Ann is here." Teresa's voice had softened.

"My twin sister—identical—offered to help. She said the Luminaries came to her. They told her *she* was the one to carry The One. She said they saw within her the light of the Barbelo—the primary Aeon, higher in power than even the Luminaries. But again, I won't bore you with a lesson."

"Why did they allow your marriage to Bram if your sister was the one who held this power?"

"The Luminaries are not all-seeing gods. They are limited in their power. And, you know, identical twins." A soft laugh whispered from her lips. "I guess even the Luminaries were confused."

This scandalous secret had Teresa's attention now. Though curious, she didn't want to ask how things were done between Bram and Lory's twin, and she didn't have to.

"We did this in secret," Lory said, her voice soft and sad. "Without doctors, I mean. It wasn't to be a surrogate pregnancy. We share one hundred percent the same DNA."

Under the veil of darkness, Lory and her sister had exchanged places in the marital bed.

"Did Bram know?"

Lory shook her head. A tear slid down her cheek. "My sister and I agreed we would switch places until the conception and birth of The One." She wiped the tear away. "I did not know my sister loved Bram before this deal was made."

While Lory had watched her twin's belly swell with life, and Bram's attention and loving gaze turn to her, a rabid jealousy began to swirl in her chest, breaking her heart.

"But didn't he think she was you?" Teresa asked. "Did you ever tell him?"

"Yes. After Ann was born, we told him." She frowned. "He was not happy about the arrangement, but we had fulfilled the first part of the contract, so he let it go. The only issue was—"

"He had fallen in love with your sister," Teresa knew it was coming. How could a man spend over nine months with someone—even if she *did* look just like his wife—and not develop feelings for her.

"He fell in love with her." Lory nodded. "We are alike in many ways, but though we share the same physical appearance and DNA, our personalities are not identical."

"So, what did you do?"

"Bram, Ann, and I moved stateside to raise her away from my sister—"

"Why didn't Bram and your sister just take Ann and do the same—before you took your place back?" Teresa asked.

"It would have broken the contract. It stipulated Bram

and I were to raise Ann. Bram was a stickler for following rules. Especially when higher powers were involved." Lory brushed at her cheek. "Anyway, I had hoped he would learn to love me again as he had before, but I'm not sure he ever really did." She looked at her hands. "Six years later, I was hit by a car."

Teresa looked up at Lory.

"In Crested Butte. I woke days later in a hospital room at the Messengers of the Light headquarters in Egypt."

"That's why Ann believes you're dead," Teresa said in a soft voice. Oh the scandal. Oh the secrets. Oh the pain and suffering Ann went through. It was delicious.

"She was here looking for you, by the way," Lory said.

Though she knew it was likely the reason for Ann's visit, Teresa's stomach soured.

CHAPTER THIRTY-FIVE

Teresa had spent most of the day in her room. Nervous to go out, knowing Ann was out and about searching for her. She paced for a little while. Lory came in with a stack of magazines for her to peruse while the *littleuns* slept.

"You can come out to the living room, if you want," Lory had said.

But Teresa didn't want to. She felt safer in her room with the door closed.

While she'd flipped through some of the home decorating magazines, her mind wandered to Lory's story. So many secrets in that family.

Now she ventured out, palming the door closed behind her. Teresa's *sympathizers* were gathered in the living room again. The curtains were drawn, and lamps were stationed on tables at the ends of each couch.

"Oh, Teresa, there you are," Patrina said from the arm of the couch next to her brother. It was as if they all had assigned seats. Olivia, Hunter, and Levi sat on the other couch, Olivia in the middle. The only one missing was Rachel.

"Your hair," Teresa said, her eyes on Olivia.

Olivia toyed with the short spikes at the nape of her neck. "I know. It's a little too short isn't it?" She let out a nervous laugh.

Hunter made an aggravated grumble in his throat. "I hate it. I hate it when *straight* women have short hair." He scowled so fiercely, deep lines formed between his eyebrows and around his mouth. Teresa opened her mouth to tell him if he kept doing that the lines would become permanent, but Paul piped up.

"I love it, Olivia," he gushed. "I think it makes you look cute and edgy. Like a rock star."

Olivia blushed.

Hunter snorted. "A *lesbian* rock star." His arms tightened across his chest.

"What's wrong with lesbian rock stars?" Levi asked.

"My *wife* is *not* a *lesbian*," Hunter hissed through his teeth. The skin around his eyes turned red.

"Well, *I* like it. *I* know she's not a lesbian." Paul looked away with wide eyes, and his face flushed. Hunter gave Paul a narrow-eyed look.

"I think you look cute," Teresa said. She shrugged, hoping to dispel the awkwardness. "Besides, it's just hair. It'll grow back." Olivia looked like someone had cut her hair with a steak knife of questionable sharpness.

Lory appeared at Teresa's elbow, a paper-wrapped package in her hands. She motioned for Teresa to step down into the living room and take a seat. Teresa did so, sitting in the chair at the end of the room. Her assigned seat, she supposed.

"I finally got a disguise for you," Lory said.

"That was fast," Olivia said. Teresa caught a glimmer of a smile on her lips.

Lory handed Teresa the package.

Teresa opened it and lifted a beautiful brunette wig.

"Brown?" Olivia said, her voice aghast. "What about—"

Lory shushed her. "There wasn't enough hair from your *donation* to make a proper wig, but I sent it to Locks of Love. Someone will really appreciate your gift. I bought this one from Mrs. Rose. She has a whole collection of wigs. She calls them her girls. Anyway." Lory waved a hand. "She retired this one a few years ago. Her name is Samantha."

Olivia's face paled. She touched her short hair and sniffled. Hunter rolled his eyes and crossed his legs away from her and didn't do anything to help his wife feel better. Teresa didn't know if Hunter was the type to show affection in public, but she thought he would at least put his arm around her or touch her knee. Instead, he seemed to be eyeballing something across the room. Teresa tried to follow his gaze and thought that some*thing* might be some*one*. Paul.

Patrina's grin caught Teresa's eye.

"Put it on." Patrina motioned to the wig in Teresa's lap. "Let's see how it looks. I just love wigs. You can become a completely different person with the right styling." She looked around at the others and back at Teresa.

Teresa positioned the wig and flipped it on. Patrina jumped off the couch arm and helped her.

"You do look completely different," she whispered in awe. "The darker color really brings out your beautiful blue eyes and your fair skin." Patrina gasped and lifted her hand to her mouth. "You look like Elizabeth Taylor." She grinned and moved from in front of Teresa so the others could see. "Doesn't she look like Elizabeth Taylor, you guys?" She turned back to Teresa. "Oh, with a cat eye and mascara." She clapped her hands and held them by her mouth. She looked desperate to do Teresa's makeup. She let out a breath. "You look stunning. Blond or brunette." She fiddled with the ends, fluffing them over Teresa's shoulders, flicking the bangs to the side.

"Stop fussing, Trina." Paul's voice had a tenseness in it that hadn't been there when he'd told Olivia he loved her hair. Patrina returned to the arm of the couch.

The brown hair felt real in Teresa's hands, soft and natural. It draped over her shoulders, curling slightly at the ends. It had to be real human hair based on the quality. It didn't have that extreme shiny sheen of cheap costume wigs.

"I hope this didn't cost too much," she said. "You all have done so much for me and my babies."

"Oh, the babies," Patrina said, her voice going all gushy. "I hope they are awake next time I'm here. I just want to pinch their chubby little cheeks. And hold them. Oh, Teresa can I hold them?"

Patrina seemed to be one of those people who found everything to be just so delightful. As if she found gratitude in every little thing. She probably turned all negative incidents into something positive, finding silver linings in everything bad that ever happened.

"Jesus, Patrina, can you stop talking for two seconds?" Paul seemed to be trying to block Hunter's evil eye with his hand.

"She's fine, really. I like her positivity. It's a breath of fresh air," Teresa said. Patrina squeezed Teresa's hand and gave her a smile that scrunched her nose. Then her face fell.

She turned to Lory.

"Um, the sheriff was at Mountain View." Her eyes shifted to Teresa and back to Lory. "She's looking for Teresa."

"Yes, we know, dear," Lory said. "That's why the curtains are drawn. Sheriff Logan came to the house today." Lory moved closer to her and stroked her arm. "We'll need to be careful and more diligent in protecting her now." She looked around at the others.

They all nodded. Except Hunter who still glared in Paul's direction.

Lory clapped her hands once. "Who's ready to get started? I think we've kept Teresa long enough." Lory lifted a hand toward Teresa as if asking the group to give her a round of applause.

"Get started with what?" Teresa asked.

"Our weekly meeting," Levi said.

"What are you meeting about?" Teresa asked.

Paul cleared his throat. "The tour. And the shop. I run a shop in town."

"He sells bullshit," Hunter growled.

"If you don't want to be here, maybe you should just go home," Olivia said in a low voice. She lifted her hand as if to tuck her hair behind her ear, but there was no hair to tuck. She dropped her hand.

Hunter got to his feet. "Fine by me."

Lory tried to stop him with a hand held up toward his chest. "Now, Hunter."

He glowered at her palm. "Don't you say a word to me." He smacked her hand away and thrust a finger at her chest. "You did this to her." He looked over his shoulder at Olivia. His eyes flicked around the group. He shoved past Lory, knocking her to the side so hard she had to grab onto the half wall separating the dining room and kitchen from the sunken living room.

"Hey!" Paul jumped to his feet. "Don't talk to her that way, and take your aggressive mannerisms out of here."

Patrina grabbed his arm. "Paul, no. He's not worth it."

Hunter spread his arms out, as if inviting Paul to hit him. Paul was a big guy, but Hunter had at least fifty pounds of muscle over him, with broad shoulders and big hands. Paul sank onto the couch.

"That's what I thought." Hunter glared around at all of them and stomped out. He slammed the door behind him so hard Teresa cried out and looked toward the hallway, toward the babies.

Levi went to Lory to make sure she was okay.

"Just a little shaken is all," Lory said. Levi helped her to a vacant chair in the living room. "Olivia, I'm so sorry. I didn't mean to cause strife—"

Olivia lifted her hand and shook her head. "It's fine. He'll stew and get over it. He always does." She looked up with a shaky laugh. "Let's just get on with the meeting."

Teresa looked at Olivia studying her lap, and Paul staring intently at Olivia as if willing her to look at him. Something was definitely going on between them.

CHAPTER THIRTY-SIX

After exhausting all avenues, Ann returned to the station. She parked out front when her cell buzzed on her hip.

"Ann," a familiar voice rasped across the line after she answered. "Ann, don't hang up."

"Raghib."

"Listen to me, Ann." His voice was tight and strained. "Teresa is out."

"I know. Four days ago." She gripped the steering wheel with her free hand. "What have you done, Raghib?" she asked through her teeth.

He didn't answer right way. His wheezing breath came over the line.

"I saw the footage. You were the last person to visit her." Ann tried to keep her voice calm, but she couldn't stop her jaw from clenching.

"Yes, yes, I know. It was me. But I no longer have her." He swallowed so hard Ann heard it over the line. He took a breath. "We got her out. We were on our way, but a van crashed into us. A white and red one. Teresa got away."

"Who crashed into you?" It always felt like pulling his teeth to get information out of him.

"Someone on the inside—Mountain View. Probably more than one."

"I interviewed everyone who was on staff that night," Ann said. "All of their stories matched up."

Raghib laughed. "They likely took the time to get them straight."

Ann clamped her lips shut and growled deep in her throat.

"I believe several nurses, a couple orderlies, and her very own Dr. Andrews may have been in on this."

Ann's mouth loosened its grip on itself. "Dr. Andrews?" She had interviewed him. He'd seemed like a weak little dweeb of a man—incapable of any scheming like this. Then she remembered the colored folders. Red and green.

Chief Administrator Smith is probably the one in charge of this.

"Where is she now?" Ann asked.

"I can't tell you that."

"Obstruction of justice," Ann blurted.

"I do not know where she is, I mean," he hurried on.

"Why did you want her?" Ann asked.

"That is of no importance," he said. "The important matter is the Messengers of the Light are once again operating in Harmony, at Mountain View. They have other motives. Motives I am unsure of. But what I know is, the Messengers believe Teresa's babies are the keys to opening Tartaros."

Ann lifted her head from her hand. "And why would anyone want to open Tartaros?" Her throat had suddenly gone dry.

"Because, Ann. Yaldabaoth is still alive."

She shook her head. "No. No he isn't. He was torn to shreds. I killed him. The seven killed him. He's dead."

I fucking shot him.

Seven times.

"The thing with Tartaros is the rules are different there. Souls are souls. Your father exchanged his to save you and Teresa and Maggie. How is my Magdalene?"

"You do *not* get to call her *yours* ever again." Ann's voice growled, but her stomach flip-flopped.

"Fair enough." His voice held a hint of sadness. "The book says, '*A sacrifice. A vessel*'." He paused. "Those may or may not be separate entities. There is no way to tell unless Tartaros is opened."

Ann pulled in a deep breath through her nose. "What are you saying? Give it to me straight, Raghib. I'm sick and tired of your cryptic bullshit, just like I was months ago when you came to me and betrayed not only me, but your *grandchild*, too." She clenched her jaw and looked out the windshield.

He was quiet for a few seconds. A heavy sigh. "Your father—he might live."

Ann didn't react, but inside her heart triple beat painfully. She rubbed her breastbone.

A part of her believed her dad might still be alive. That's why she kept going back to the abandoned funeral home. That's why she'd looked for a way back in. Her dad's body hadn't been there when she and Maggie had come back. She'd felt it dissipate beneath her, leaving him behind, and Ann had learned, during the events leading up to The Night, that not everything made sense and not everything fit in a tidy box and not everything could be proven. Her black-and-white-evidence-speaks-the-truth-no-nonsense   mindset from before had been shattered when she'd gone for that run in the San Isabel National Forest and had seen Maggie's silhouette against the backdrop of the Royal Mountains. It had shattered again when the mark of the *Sa* seared into her flesh—and countless times after, including the past few days.

Raghib continued. Ann almost missed what he'd said. She asked him to repeat himself, just to be sure.

"Your father may be alive in Tartaros, and he may have the soul of Yaldabaoth inside him."

May and *maybe* were wishy-washy words. According to Raghib's logic, her dad sacrificing his soul, staying behind, would mean he was both the sacrifice *and* the vessel, which is what Ann wanted to believe. But that was *Raghib's* logic. In reality—though she wanted to believe her dad was still alive in Tartaros—Yaldabaoth could be in any one of the people who had made it in and out of Tartaros that night. Bram, Teresa, Maggie—

She jerked her head up. Were these Luminaries somehow related to this?

Ann got out of the truck and went into the station. Maggie and Pinky were in the bullpen ready to go.

"I knew you were out there," Maggie said. "I could tell by the way Pinky's tail wagged in a circle like a helicopter." She laughed. "She probably heard the rumble of your truck."

"I wouldn't let her go look," Sully said, not looking up from the case file on his desk. He had the label maker out. "I called Cindy to check up on her," Sully said. "She sounds just awful. Super lethargic." He narrowed his eyes at Ann.

"Speaking of sick . . . We never really finished talking about the incident in the woods."

"Glory is home with her mom," Ann said. "Case closed." She cleared her throat and avoided looking at him while he shuffled the stack of files together into a neater pile.

"That's not what I meant. I'm talking about the way she was. In the clearing."

Ann did not want to get into Glory's situation right here and now. She didn't even know what to tell Sully. She hoped he would be content to keep on believing Glory had been on drugs or sick or something. If she told him the truth —that she was Logismoi and someone was stealing souls for some ill purpose—he would cart her off to Mountain View.

Ann's phone rang.

"Rachel."

"Hi Ann," she said. "I'm so sorry I didn't answer your calls earlier. I went to Pine Valley to just get away from . . . whatever. Disconnect, you know? I just turned my phone back on."

"That's okay," Ann said. She hadn't realized it, but she'd been thinking that perhaps the next time she saw Rachel she'd have ill-fitting skin and black goo dripping out of her. Relief replaced those thoughts. "Hey, we're having a town hall at five. Do you think you can watch Maggie for me? It'll just be an hour or so. I'll pay you since it's your day off."

Silence on the other end. A heavy sigh. "Okay. I'll come watch her. No worries."

"Thank you. See you around four-forty-five?"

Rachel agreed and they hung up. Ann turned to Sully.

"We'll talk about Glory later." She rolled her eyes over to Maggie, indicating now was not the time with a child present. "Thank you for watching her," Ann said. "I know that's not on your list of duties, and I really appreciate it."

"Yeah," Sully said. "You're lucky she's an easy kid."

Ann thought it was meant to be a lighthearted comment, but his tone betrayed him.

At the house, Ann threw her keys on the table. She yearned to get out of her uniform and into her favorite jeans and a T-shirt, but she had to keep it on until after the town hall.

"How are you feeling?" she asked Maggie.

"I'm okay," Maggie looked at her hands clasped in front of her. "But . . ."

"But what?"

Maggie raised her eyes to Ann's. "You're not."

Ann managed to keep her face stock still. Even the barest flicker of an expression would give her away. She really did not want to tell Maggie what Raghib had told her or that she'd even spoken with Maggie's traitorous grandfather. The secrets were piling up. She opened the fridge and pulled out sandwich fixings.

"You never told me about your trip to Mountain View yesterday." Maggie stood at the end of the counter, just tall enough to hook her arms on it and rest her chin on top of them.

"Sandwich okay? Or crackers and cheese?"

Maggie shook her head.

"What do you want?"

"I want you to tell me what's going on. Everything."

Ann sighed. "We still need to eat something."

"I'm not that hungry," Maggie said. "I was too worried all day."

"Worried about what?"

"You." Maggie looked down.

Ann *pishawed*. "You don't have to worry about me," Ann said. "I took out Yaldabaoth, remember?" She held her arms up and pretended to flex her muscles. "I'm all powerful."

In the recent past, Ann thought an act like that would have made Maggie laugh, but it didn't. She didn't even crack a smile.

"Maggie." Ann focused on the girl. "What in the world is going on?"

Maggie lifted her chin from her arms. "Nothing," she said, but she couldn't stop the stupid tears from coming to her eyes. She couldn't tell Ann she was so worried she had actually thrown up in the trash can in Ann's office while Pinky whined and sighed next to her and pawed at her.

"I'm okay, girl," Maggie had told her, patting her head. She hadn't had lunch either, so all that came out was yucky foamy yellow stuff. It made her head hurt, the force she'd guessed. And afterward she'd lain back on the couch and stared at the ceiling. She tried watching something on Ann's laptop, but her mind wandered to Ann. What was Ann doing? Was she safe? What if Teresa was waiting for her somewhere to *get* her? She couldn't even *think* the word *kill*. It made her heart and tummy hurt. Pinky had followed her while Maggie paced up and down Ann's office. And when Pinky got tired of that, she jumped on the couch and watched Maggie. Pinky must have known Maggie was feeling nervous. Maggie had patted her head and rubbed her ears a lot to make Pinky not worry about her, but that was what Pinky did. It was her nature, Ann had said so when Maggie had started back to school a few weeks after The Night.

And now, here Ann stood asking her what was going on, and Maggie couldn't get the words out to tell her.

"Maggie," Ann said. "We've been to hell and back—literally. You know you can tell me anything."

But she couldn't. The knowledge of it would be a burden. Ann would have questions, and Maggie didn't have answers. She looked up at Ann, at the worry creasing her forehead.

"Tell me, Maggie. Please. Let me help you with whatever is burdening you."

Maggie jerked her head up when Ann said *burdening*. Did she know how Maggie was feeling? How Sally Opperheim told her she was that very thing?

"Sally Opperheim told me one time that everything I touch turns to shit," Maggie blurted out. She gasped and covered her mouth when the bad word came out. "Sorry." Her cheeks grew hot.

"It's okay." Ann leaned on the counter with her forearms. Maggie was surprised at her light tone. "You were quoting someone." She gave Maggie a little wink.

Maggie let out a whoosh of air. "She also told me I'm a burden."

"A burden?" Ann's eyebrows frowned, all traces of worry gone. She also straightened. "Why would she say that?"

Maggie shrugged. "Because she is—was—mean." Maggie looked up. "What happened to her? What happened to Glory?"

Ann took a deep breath, filling her lungs completely. She let the air out and leaned down on her forearms again. She wanted to sit after being on her feet all day, but standing seemed like a better option.

"I shouldn't tell you everything," Ann said. "Rachel tells me all the time I treat you too much like an adult."

Maggie shrugged. "I can handle it."

She had that bratty tone, like she did the time she'd breathed on Ann's hand to show her—no, to *prove* to her—Ann was The One. All that was missing was a snooty crossing of her arms and a lift of her chin. She'd exhibited that sort of body language before too.

"Raghib called me," Ann said. "Your *baba*." She felt stupid using the word, but it's what Maggie called him.

Maggie tensed, lifting slightly from her arms.

"But don't worry," Ann hurried on. "No one is after you this time." She didn't want to tell Maggie about Yaldabaoth possibly being alive.

Despite what Raghib had said about Messengers of the Light only wanting the babies. In the end, they wanted the babies because they wanted Yaldabaoth, and they wanted Yaldabaoth because they wanted to kill Sophia. Her throat clenched. Maybe Maggie wasn't as safe as Ann thought.

She touched Maggie's wrist. "They want Teresa and her babies."

The Blighted Womb.

The words jumped into Ann's head. Derrick had told her Teresa was barren, her remaining ovary malformed, and yet, she'd somehow gotten pregnant—again.

"Remember the passage the book showed us at the bank?"

Maggie nodded.

Ann went to the living room and grabbed her notebook

off the table. She gave Pinky a pat on the head and returned to the kitchen to show Maggie what she'd discovered. What the book had shown her.

"I think Glory and Sally are the first of the Logismoi."

"When did the book show this to you?" Maggie's eyes traveled over the page in Ann's notebook.

"A couple nights ago." Ann shrugged. "I actually asked it to show me, and it did. I think it maybe was a coincidence?" She wasn't entirely sure, now that she said it.

"The Blighted Womb." Maggie looked up at Ann. "What does that mean?"

"It's like when something is ruined, I guess." Ann wasn't sure how to explain it to Maggie in terms she would understand, but that seemed close enough. Ann cleared her throat. "But look at these pairs." She pointed to the ones she'd identified—possibly—as Glory and Sally.

Maggie nodded. "I think you're right."

"When you drew Glory, you saw her the way I saw her when I found her in the woods, but *you* hadn't actually seen her." God, she sounded so stupid. "It was like when you drew . . ." Ann didn't want to trigger anything negative.

"Ruthie, and Sheriff McMichael, and Yaldabaoth using their zoe," Maggie said in a soft voice. "After I dreamed about them."

"But you didn't dream about Glory, right? Sophia showed you?"

Maggie nodded.

"You drew the Luminaries, too," Ann said in an equally soft voice. "Why did you draw them?" She *really* wanted to know why Maggie drew the abyss.

She watched a plethora of emotions cross Maggie's face before the stubborn look came back and she gave a decisive nod.

"Eleleth told me that if I lose anyone else I love I will return to the abyss. I don't know if she meant me or Sophia is the thing, but I don't want Sophia to go there either." Maggie's words rushed out. She touched her mark.

"Is it hurting now?" Ann asked.

Maggie shook her head. "I just . . . feel her . . . there. I think in my heart. I didn't feel her before like that. Not until after the Luminaries told me what happened in Tartaros."

Maggie's recent behavior made so much sense now. Her stomachaches and apparent anxiety. Ann mentally smacked herself for not seeing the symptoms she herself had suffered before. Maggie was worried she would lose Ann and return to the abyss.

Maybe she does *need therapy*, was her first, knee-jerk thought, followed swiftly by, *Jesus Christ, hasn't this kid been through enough?*

"I think the nightmare I had the other night was because Sally was taken," she said. "It makes my mark hurt."

"The book said only the Mother of Angels can stop them." Ann squinted. "Isn't *Wisdom* the Mother of the Angels?"

Maggie nodded.

"Isn't *Wisdom* Sophia?"

Maggie's honey-colored eyes looked tired. Stressed.

Ann needed to help Maggie. Put her at ease. Soothe her. That's what a good guardian would do. To do that, to prove to Maggie she was there to protect her, Ann needed Teresa Hart back behind Mountain View's walls.

CHAPTER THIRTY-SEVEN

The town hall did not go as expected. Ann told the townsfolk to start locking their doors again if they weren't already, report anything suspicious or strange, and to be home and shut in by ten every night.

At the mention of a curfew, the younger crowd erupted into cries of unfairness. Ann held up her hands to silence them.

"This is all for your safety, and it will only be in effect until we apprehend Teresa Hart."

"We should be out there looking for her!" someone in the crowd cried out. "*You* should be." He pointed at her.

The immediate group next to him shouted agreement, which spread through the mob like a bad flu.

"Listen up," Sully shouted. His size and bellowing voice shut down the crowd. "We're doing everything we can to find Teresa Hart. Rest assured—"

"Where's Duke? He'd be out there looking. He probably *is* out there looking."

Duke must've made his rounds campaigning to have this sort of reaction. Ann scanned the crowd as the gathered residents also turned their heads looking around for him. He wasn't there.

"Yeah, your dad abandoned us," someone else shouted. An old grizzled voice. "Maybe it's time we get some fresh blood running this place."

Ann bristled. She took a step forward, but Sully stopped her.

"Ms. Masterton? Did you have a question or comment?" Sully asked.

Ann looked up. Ronnie Masterton stood at the podium placed in the center aisle for those who had questions.

She nodded, bumped the microphone with her cheek, grabbed it like it might fall off the podium it was attached to, and cleared her throat.

"As some of you know, my daughter was missing a few days ago. She came home safely thank the lord, but something isn't right about her. She's different."

"Different how?" A blond woman stood and asked.

"She looks pale," Ronnie looked at the woman. "Pale a-and—"

"Like her skin doesn't fit right?" the other woman asked.

Ronnie closed her mouth tight but nodded.

"My Sally's the same way." The woman made her way to the microphone. "Susie Opperheim," she said. "Longtime resident of Harmony. My Sally spent the night outside the other night. I didn't know until I found her out there the next morning looking bewildered. She was real dirty. Just black muck all over her face, down the front of her dress."

The crowd started to mutter and shift around uneasily.

Sally Opperheim.

"Yeah, that's how my Glory looked when she came back home."

Ann looked up at Sully standing sentinel by her side.

"Has the report come back from the lab on that black substance?" Ann asked him.

"It was inconclusive." He shrugged one shoulder.

Ann cleared her throat. "Anyone else have a child with the same thing going on?" If others had children with the same issue, she might be able to figure out how many potential Logismoi Teresa had already taken.

As if reading Ann's mind, Susie Opperheim shrieked, "Do you think Teresa Hart is doing something to our kids?" into the microphone. The crowd erupted in gasps and more murmurings.

Ann held up her hands. "Please everyone, calm down. I don't know what's going on with Ms. Masterton and Ms. Opperheim's children. Perhaps a trip to the *doctor* is in order. But until we know, please obey the new rules we've set out."

Teresa Hart *had* to be behind this. The Blighted Womb, feeding her children—Ann couldn't finish her thought. It sickened her.

By the end of the meeting the sun had started to set, and Ann felt no one would obey the curfew. She needed to get home. The meeting had lasted far longer than anticipated.

CHAPTER THIRTY-EIGHT

The moment Ann got to the house, Rachel grabbed her messenger bag and hurried to the door. Ann stopped her.

"Everything okay?" Ann asked.

"Yeah, I just have to go." Her eyes shifted over Ann's shoulder and back.

"Thanks for watching her," Ann said. Rachel nodded and left. The young dispatcher wasn't much for touchy-feely, and Ann wasn't typically one to give touchy-feely, but this was unusual. She seemed almost flustered.

"How was it?" Ann asked Maggie. "Everything go okay?"

Maggie looked sullen. Pinky came out of the master bedroom with halting steps, ears back, tail down. The tip of her tail wagged. No wiggles. No tail lashing.

"What's going on?" Ann asked.

"Pinky growled at Rachel," Maggie said with a sigh. "So Rachel yelled at Pinky and called her a bad dog."

Pinky did not like being called a bad dog.

"So I yelled because I didn't like it that Rachel called Pinky a bad dog, because she's *not* a bad dog, she's a really good dog. So Pinky hid in your room because we were both yelling."

Oh for Pete's sake. The dog was *a marshmallow.*

"Why did Pinky growl at her?" Ann asked, as if Maggie spoke dog and could tell her. "I mean, what happened before Pinky growled? How vicious was the growl?"

Maggie crossed her arms tight over her chest.

"You're not in trouble," Ann said quickly. "I just need to know how it all happened."

"It was like this." She went over near the front door. "This happened after you left—I'm Rachel."

Oh, she was going to reenact it.

"Hi Maggie, hi Pinky," she said in a high, bright voice. Pinky wiggled over to Maggie. "Rachel reached down like this to pet Pinky." Maggie bent over at the waist. The effect was lost, since she wasn't as tall as Rachel. But Ann could see how that sort of body language might be intimidating to a dog.

"Is that when Pinky growled?" Ann asked.

"No." Maggie shook her head. "She put her bag down." Maggie mimed pulling the bag off over her head—she was quite good at this—and put it on the table.

"When did Pinky growl?" Ann asked.

"I'm getting there. Ann, you be me. Sit on the couch at the end."

Ann did as directed.

"Rachel came over, and she sat right in the middle." Maggie did just what she said and sat on the center cushion.

"And what did you do?"

"I said, 'Hi Rachel.'" Maggie leaned back on the couch and held her hands up in front of her.

"What is that?" Ann asked.

"I'm Rachel again. I'm texting on my phone." She did

this for a few more seconds. "And then I—Maggie—reached over and put my hand in front of the screen. Rachel gave me a really serious look."

"Is *that* when Pinky growled?"

Maggie shook her head. The play-by-play was tedious. Ann shifted forward onto the cushion and placed her elbows on her knees. "Can we skip ahead to the part where Pinky growled at Rachel?"

Maggie took a deep breath and looked at her lap. "I made her mad."

"What did you do?" Ann reached for Pinky. The dog, still not her usual self, came over to her.

"She didn't stop texting. She doesn't usually do that when she's with me. Sometimes we play games, and sometimes we play with Pinky out back, but today she just wanted to sit on the couch on her phone while I watched movies."

Ann narrowed her eyes. That was very unlike Rachel. She seemed to really enjoy hanging out with Maggie.

"She *looked* okay, though, right?" Rachel had rushed out so quickly, Ann had hardly gotten a good look at her.

"Yes. She wasn't like Sally. Or Glory." Maggie continued her story. "Anyway, I asked her who she was texting, and I joked that it was her *boyfriend*, and she snapped at me that it wasn't my business who she was texting." Maggie frowned. "She was really kind of just weird tonight. Annoyed."

"Is that all you did to make her mad? Ask her who she was texting?" Ann rose from the couch to start something for dinner. Probably a frozen pizza. Maggie followed her to the kitchen.

"Um, no. When she got up to go to the bathroom, she left her phone on the coffee table." Maggie pointed to the coffee table like the phone was still there. "She was texting someone named LMCM. That person told her to hang in there, and sent a picture of a kitten hanging from a tree. It was really cute. Before that, Rachel told LMCM that she was having a really hard time with her assignment."

"Assignment?"

Maggie shrugged. "Oh, and then she was also texting someone named Patrina."

"Patrina?" Ann closed the freezer. It was such an unusual name, it had to be the Patrina from Mountain View.

"That's what it said. P-A-T-R-I-N-A." Maggie closed her eyes while she spelled the name. "Patrina asked Rachel if she was watching the little rug rat again. Ann, what's a rug rat?"

"It's just a teasing thing to call kids." Ann waved it off like it was nothing. "What else did they talk about?"

"A surprise in the back room at Paul's shop." Maggie shrugged. "That's it. Rachel said she was going to miss the meeting tonight because she had to babysit me and she was tired anyway and just wouldn't make it."

Meeting. Ann's initial thought was AA, but Rachel did not exhibit signs of an alcoholic. Maybe it was some other support group. She had lost someone important to her when Sheriff McMichael died. Ann recalled her taking it pretty hard. She hadn't considered what their relationship had been at the time. Ann barely knew the young woman back then.

"When Rachel came out of the bathroom. I was still holding her phone, and she yelled at me for dis-disre-something her privacy."

"Disrespecting," Ann offered.

"That's when Pinky growled. Rachel sort of rushed

toward me and snatched the phone and I cried out and Pinky jumped between us and growled."

Maggie's shoulders slumped. She looked down. "Are you mad I snooped?" She peered up at Ann with her golden eyes.

"You did disrespect her privacy, but I'm not mad." Ann put the frozen pizza in the oven. "I am wondering if we should maybe give Rachel a break from babysitting, though. I think I depend too much on her sometimes." And Sully. She thought about his behavior earlier as well.

Maybe Ann herself needed a support group. One for single mothers in law enforcement.

She now had a lead, though. A weak lead, sure, but better than nothing. She needed to check out this Paul person's shop. If he was linked to Patrina, who worked at Mountain View, maybe there was something there. It was a thin hunch, but it was all she had to go on.

In order to check out Paul's shop, she'd need Maggie to go to the Daycare Place. She wasn't going to leave her alone. Not with Teresa Hart out there.

CHAPTER THIRTY-NINE

Ann got Maggie off to bed with Pinky cuddled up next to her.

"Want a story?" Ann asked.

"You know I can read, right?" Maggie asked with a crook to the corner of her mouth.

Ann rolled her eyes and smiled. "Of course, I know you can read, but I thought kids liked to be read to when they go to sleep."

Maggie shrugged. "I guess you're right." She snuggled down into the blankets and pulled them up to her chin.

Ann sat at the head of her bed, back against the headboard, one leg slung on the little bed, the other foot on the floor like someone who had too much to drink and needed to keep the room steady. A one-foot-on-the-floor kind of night, she used to call it. She'd gotten that term from—

Ugh. Duke Westley.

"I'm ready," Maggie said, as if able to tell Ann was distracted.

"Okay, here we go."

She'd pulled some sort of Children's Treasury out and picked a random story. Maggie fell asleep before she even reached the second page, with Pinky snoring beside her.

Ann closed the book and carefully got up, hardly disturbing the bed at all. Pinky lifted her head.

"I'm going downstairs," she whispered to the dog. "You can come with me if you want."

Pinky let out a giant dog sigh and rested her head across Maggie's legs. Ann left the door open a crack.

At the bottom of the stairs, she turned to the kitchen for a glass of water. As she passed the front door, someone rapped lightly. She jumped and whirled toward the sound.

A low woof came from upstairs followed by footsteps. Ann looked up. Pinky stood at the top, ears perked, eyes intent on the door.

"Stay," Ann said. She peeked through the peephole.

Duke Westley stood on her front porch looking off to the right. He turned his face back to the door. Ann jumped away as if he could see her through the tiny one-way hole. He knocked again, this time a little harder. Pinky let out a low grumble.

"Good girl. Stay." Ann took a deep breath and opened the door.

Duke jumped back as if she might hurtle out at him and attack. He grinned, but not in his usual arrogant way. It was almost like George Riley's sheepish grin with a slight duck of the head.

"What are you doing here at this hour?" Ann asked.

He looked at his watch and raised an eyebrow. "It's only eight."

Ann looked at her watch. He was right. She'd had a long day—knocking on doors, holding the town hall, consoling Maggie.

"Can I come in?" Duke asked. "There's something I want to talk to you about." His tone was not the usual full-of-arrogance-better-than-thou. It was almost kind.

Ann leaned against the doorframe and crossed her arms. She looked him up and down. He wore a nice pair of slacks and a white button-down shirt. His hair was tousled in the way he used to wear it in high school. Lately she'd only seen him with a slicked-back, all-professional, all-business, all-I'm-here-to-steal-your-job hairdo. His cheeks and chin were freshly shaved.

She sniffed and waved her hand in front of her face. "Are you going on a date or something later?"

"A date?" He looked confused.

"You bathed in aftershave."

"Oh, that." He laughed a nervous laugh and cupped his chin. Ann didn't know him well enough to know any of his tells—not like she knew Derrick—but she knew enough about him to know he was nervous. Something was up and this was bound to be unpleasant.

"If you're going to talk to me about the election, you can get the hell out of here."

"I'm not here to talk about the election, Ann." He cleared his throat. "In fact, I think I'm going to pull out." He coughed a laugh. "That's what *he* said."

Ann straightened from the doorframe. Pull out? She stepped aside and motioned him in. Interesting development.

Pinky wagged her tail at the top of the stairs and looked at Ann.

"Free," Ann said.

Pinky blasted down the stairs and wiggled all over Duke. She collapsed at his feet for belly rubs, tail thumping the floor. She had apparently forgiven Duke for scaring her the other day.

"Hello again, you vicious beast," Duke said, crouching low to scrub her chest. "Sorry I spooked you the other day."

"Quiet," Ann whispered. "Maggie's asleep."

Duke looked up at her, his eyes and brows soft. His lower lip trembled. He coughed into his fist. "Sorry." He stood. Pinky pawed at him for a second, then gave up, got a drink of water, and plodded up the stairs. She didn't go to Maggie's room, though. Instead, she flopped onto the floor, paws hooked over the tread of the top step, and gazed down at them.

"Drink?" Ann asked. Whatever he needed to talk to her about probably required an adult beverage. She pulled out two glasses and a bottle of whiskey. She sloshed a couple fingers into each of them.

"Whiskey?" Duke said with a grimace. "Got any red wine? Malbec or a Zinfandel?"

"Wine?"

"Wine's not for sissies anymore," Duke said, doing a poor job hiding his offense. "Whiskey will do—if that's all you got."

"I have beer in the fridge." She nodded toward the kitchen with her chin. While he retrieved one, she shuffled Maggie's drawings into a pile and put them on the coffee table, then took a seat in the dining room.

Duke cracked a beer open and joined her.

"Why are you dropping out of the race?" Ann asked.

"Right down to business. You really haven't changed, Ms. No-nonsense. I see, I see."

Ann took a sip of her drink and raised her eyebrows.

"Listen," he started. As if she weren't sitting here raptly awaiting his explanation. "This town loves the shit out of you. You solved that case last year. Your dad and grandpa were both sheriff. I don't stand a chance." He took a long pull of his beer.

Ann nodded. "You're probably right."

Duke laughed through his nose. "It was just stupid of me to come here thinking I could take what's rightfully yours."

"Not rightfully. Anyone can have this seat." Ann sat back in her chair and propped her foot up on the empty one Maggie usually sat in. She took a sip of whiskey, relishing the smooth burn of it. The heat it produced in her belly.

"Per my previous statement. No one stands a chance." He sat back, too, relaxing into their conversation. His nerves seemed to be at bay for the moment, so talking about leaving the race wasn't what made him that way. "You're Harmony's sweetheart, for God's sake. You and Derrick. The king and queen of this little shit place."

"Hey now, don't call my town shit."

"It was my town, too, once," he said all melancholic. "I ran this place."

Ann scoffed. "Into the ground. Besides, you didn't have *anyone* convinced of the hotshot you thought you were."

He chuckled.

Ann tossed back the rest of her drink and pulled the one she'd poured for Duke toward her.

Duke laughed. "You've gotten feistier." He pounded his beer and crushed the can with his big paws, just like he did when they were teenagers. At least he didn't smash it against his forehead. She wondered if he could still do that.

"What's the real reason you're here?" Ann asked, trying and failing to sip her second drink.

She suddenly thought of Derrick and the last time they'd sat together at this table. She'd found Maggie out in the cold and snowy weather without a coat. Derrick came to Ann for help, and they'd ended up drinking way too much Sailor Jerry Spiced Rum with a chaser of too much reminiscing.

"The real reason I'm here . . ." Duke examined his thumb. "Can I have another beer?"

"Knock yourself out," Ann motioned to the kitchen with a flourish of her hand. While his back was turned, she knocked back the second whiskey and poured a third.

He came back, chugging the beer as he walked. He sat in Maggie's chair. Ann moved her foot off of it and sat up straighter. He crushed that can, too, and put it with its fallen brother.

"I . . . the reason is . . . I came to tell you . . ." He groaned and threw his face toward the ceiling. "Why is this so hard?"

Ann's heart rate picked up.

"You don't have to tell me," Ann said.

Please don't tell me.

"I have to tell you. I can't go on pretending." Duke cleared his throat, tossed back *her* whiskey, coughed, grimaced, wiped his mouth on the back of his hand. "Remember how you used to hang out with us guys, the jocks, like you were one of us?"

"It was because I was with Derrick." But really, she had always preferred to be "one of the guys."

"Remember the night before you left? When we were at the abandoned funeral home?"

Ann nodded. After she'd broken the news to Derrick she was leaving for the academy and after their ensuing fight, she'd gone to their old hang out. Duke was there drinking alone. They'd kissed.

Ann's throat went dry.

"Ann, I-I love you. I have loved you since before you and Derrick got together, and while you were together. And after you left him, I thought—and we had that thing at the place, but then you left." He grabbed her hand in both of his.

Ann jerked it out of his warm grasp as if he'd burned her. She leaped out of her chair, knocking it over backward. Pinky bolted down the stairs and put herself between Ann and Duke, full mohawk hackles raised.

"Jesus, Ann, you're acting like I shoved a dead rat in your face." He'd done that once. Maybe he thought it would be funny to remind her. When she didn't laugh, he backed away from her and Pinky. His face distorted into an offended scowl. The arrogance returned.

"I get it. Hotshot detective turned shit-town sheriff. You think your shit don't stink. You think you're better than everyone else."

"That's not—" She was going to say true, or fair, or something, but Duke's sudden one-eighty threw her for a loop.

"You know what, I'm not dropping out of the race. I'll win this seat and you'll have to answer to me." He poked himself in the chest. "I'll be the best goddamn sheriff this town's *ever* had."

"Duke—"

He looked her up and down with an ugly scowl. "You must think you're too good for the likes of me. Maybe you are." He jutted his chin at her. "I'm just King Derrick's lowly sidekick goon, anyway. Yeah. I know you called us all goons."

"You need to go. Now."

He sneered at her down his chin and didn't move. Ann

leaned and touched Pinky's shoulder. Pinky growled low and menacing in her throat.

"Ready," she whispered. Pinky's muscles bunched, the growl deepened, reverberating through her body. Ann felt it in her fingertips.

Pinky was not trained to attack. She wouldn't—*couldn't*—hurt a fly. But Ann had trained her to growl on command with words that made it *sound* like she would attack on command. And *one* word made it sound like she was trying to control an out-of-control dog. "Easy."

Pinky growled and lunged forward, snapping her jaws.

Duke took a step back and laughed. "That dog won't touch me. She's a fucking pussy." He mock-lunged at Pinky. She yelped and scurried behind Ann's leg.

So much for that.

"Ann?" Maggie said from upstairs. "Why's *he* here?" She came down the steps and stood at the bottom.

"He was just leaving," Ann said. "Weren't you, Duke?"

Duke turned toward Maggie, held out his hand. Maggie automatically took it—she was a polite kid, after all—but then jerked her hand away. "Nice seeing you again, little lady. Ann's right. I was just on my way out."

He glared at Ann, hand on the doorknob. She saw the real pain in his eyes and for a second wondered if her reaction *had* been a little over the top. Was she supposed to be appreciative that he *loved* her? Was she supposed to get all giddy and silly like some stupid cheerleader?

She was not that girl. Never had been and never would be. She had no interest in him whatsoever. Just because they shared a kiss the night she left Derrick, the night before she left Harmony, didn't mean anything. It was one kiss. She had been weak and miserable and angry at Derrick for not being supportive of her decision.

Duke slammed the door behind him. Maggie gasped. Pinky ran to her side and pressed against her legs, nearly knocking her off balance.

"Sorry he woke you up," Ann said. She put the cap back on the whiskey, cleared up his empty cans, and finally looked at Maggie. She was rubbing the spot over her heart. Her mark.

"Sophia didn't like his touch." Maggie grimaced.

CHAPTER FORTY

Cassie poked her triangular head over the edge of the crib at eight.

"Now?" Though the sun had gone down behind the tall peak, it wasn't quite full dark yet. Luckily, she had a disguise. But it was summer. People stayed out later in the summer, drinking and having backyard barbecues, women laughing high-pitched, drunken squeals. The very thought of it made Teresa wince and grimace with distaste.

Cassie climbed up the rail and perched on it, holding it with her back claws and her little hand-paws. Her long tail wrapped around the opposite rail, keeping her from toppling out.

Teresa went to the crib and peeked in at Amanda. Sound asleep.

She lifted Cassie under the armpits. The little triangular shaped head nuzzled under Teresa's chin, the smooth fuzzy flesh warm.

Teresa put Cassie on the bed where she hopped up and down gently.

"No jumping on the bed." It was as automatic as

reciting her mother's rules had been. She tried to think when the admonishment had come into her list of automatic phrases, but she couldn't remember jumping on the bed as a kid. She'd been better behaved than that.

Teresa lifted her chin and sniffed. "Go ahead. Jump all you want."

While Cassie hopped around, Teresa went to the dresser.

Lory had left some eyeliner, mascara, and some rouge in a little pharmacy bag on top.

"Give yourself that cat eye Patrina was talking about. No one will recognize you at all." She had touched Teresa's arm in a motherly way. A friendly way. Teresa had resisted the urge to hug her, to feel that human connection she craved that was different from the parasitic relationship she had with her babies.

She pulled her hair into a low bun, stretched the wig cap over it, and put the wig on.

It really was a fine piece. Once she had it in the right position, she couldn't even tell it wasn't her real hair.

She took Lory's advice and did her best with a cat eye. It was uneven, but her cheekbones appeared higher, transforming her face from the vanilla housewife-widow to a youthful and maybe borderline gothic—dare she say— chick. The dark liner made her blue eyes pop.

She dusted some blush on the apples of her cheeks, then mixed a little with some lip balm and put it on her lips.

The final touch was a double coat of mascara. She looked like Elizabeth Taylor. Just like Patrina had said.

"I'm a different girl," she whispered. She turned to Cassie. The little gargoyle stopped jumping abruptly and bounded to the end of the bed. She lifted a little paw-hand toward Teresa, head cocked.

"I'm still mama." Teresa took Cassie's little hand and kissed it. Cassie sniffed at her hand. Seemingly satisfied that Teresa was still herself, she continued jumping.

Teresa pulled off her frumpy sweat suit and opened the closet. Lory said she could borrow or have whatever she wanted.

In the closet among Lory's old clothing, she found a sixties-style little black dress with a slim skirt, tucked waist, and modest neckline. It accentuated her best assets and concealed the post-pregnancy pudge around her middle. And, it had pockets.

On the floor of the closet she found a pair of combat-style boots only a half size too big.

Cassie hopped off the bed and went to the door. Teresa opened it, and together they left through the back.

It was a warm night. Teresa was glad she'd ditched the sweats.

She followed Cassie to the old cemetery. The lost souls bobbed and bounced. Cassie chased them, but they were always just out of her reach.

On the dirt road, they headed into town. Cassie took to the air, drifting from vortex to vortex. Teresa followed at a casual pace.

In town, the diner still had lights on, and the local watering hole, Flynn's, had music bumping out its open door. Teresa hurried past, one eye on the sky where Cassie soared.

At the end of the block, across the street, a muscular man charged down the sidewalk, muttering. His hands were clenched into fists. High above, Cassie circled back.

This must be their mark.

"Excuse me." Teresa jogged across the street, her hand raised as if she were calling a cab.

"Can I help you?" the man asked in a deep voice. He was attractive. Extra tall. Broad at the shoulders. He looked her up and down. "You look like—"

"Elizabeth Taylor," she said with a coquettish hand to her chest and a roll of her eyes.

"No, I was going to say Morticia Addams."

Teresa dropped her hand.

"I'm kidding. I think she wears black lipstick, doesn't she?"

She let out a peal of girlish laughter—the kind that made her wince and grimace and wonder who that girl's mother was to let her laugh so carelessly.

He held out his hand. "Duke Westley."

The name seemed familiar, and Teresa knew she'd seen it somewhere around town during their nightly escapades. She remembered. It was a sign in someone's yard.

"You're running for sheriff," Teresa said. "Against Ann Logan." She couldn't stop her voice from souring at Ann's name.

Duke grinned. "Care to join me for a drink?"

"Sure, but let me make a call first. I'll meet you at Flynn's in five?"

"Sure. See you then." He strutted across the street to Flynn's.

Teresa waved Cassie down. They were in the alley between the pawn shop and real estate office. "Stay here. I'll bring him out in a bit and we'll get him in here."

Cassie backed away into the shadows and crouched behind a box. Teresa went into Flynn's and looked around. She spotted him at the bar with two glasses of red wine in front of him. He turned and spotted her.

She sauntered in. The anonymity of the outfit and wig gave her courage to *be* a different person. This brunette wig, this little black dress, these combat boots? She *felt* like a different person. A stronger person. Someone who could seduce a big-muscled man into an alley to steal his soul.

Duke talked too much about himself, told dirty jokes to the bar tender, had too much wine, and agreed with people about the bullshit curfew.

"When I'm sheriff, there won't be *any* curfews." He lifted his glass to cheers and whistles.

Teresa nursed a single glass, small sips here and there. She couldn't drink too much. She still had to breastfeed the babies. He didn't seem to notice as he pounded glass after glass for himself.

When his attention was on her, she touched his arm and threw her head back and laughed at everything he said, grateful for the secure fit of the wig. They talked about life and eventually love. Duke told her about Ann shoving him away from her when he'd told her how he felt.

Duke was on the second bottle at this point. Teresa pulled him close by the shirt collar.

Teresa slid off her barstool.

"Let's get out of here," she whispered in his ear, pressing her chest against his arm. He groped her buttocks.

Apparently, Ann breaking his heart wasn't enough to break other parts of his body.

"I'll meet you outside," he growled in a husky voice.

She sashayed out of the stuffy place into the fresh air. It helped clear her head. She hurried across the street to wait to beckon him over.

"Cassie, my sweet girl," Teresa whispered into the alley. A little peep came from above. Teresa looked up. Cassie perched on the roof of the real estate office. "Get ready. He's coming."

Duke stumbled out of the bar and looked around.

"Over here." She waved.

He perked up, looked both ways, and crossed toward her. As soon as he reached her, his hands went to her hips. His lips crushed hers with deep desire. Her body couldn't help but respond. Her back hit the brick wall behind her. She pushed him away and whirled teasingly deeper into the alley. Duke's face twisted into a grin of sexual malice. He followed Teresa, hands fumbling at his belt.

The second he passed Cassie up on her perch, she swooped down and dive-bombed him, wrapping her little hands under his chin like a strap on a helmet.

"What the fuck," Duke hollered. He flailed his arms, reached up, grabbed her little arm, and twisted it until she let out a pained and animalistic shriek.

Something boiled inside Teresa. An almost painful feeling in her heart. A savage rip of ventricles and arteries. Hot pokers jabbed at all of her pulse points.

"Don't you hurt her!" She lunged at him, hands outstretched.

Caught off guard—and incredibly inebriated—Duke lost his balance, and they toppled to the concrete ground.

"Your eyes," Duke said.

The glint of the street light at the end of the alley flickered on a broken bottle. Teresa caught her reflection in it. Her eyes glowed with yellow fire. She grabbed the bottle and jammed it into his left eye.

Duke bucked under her, throwing her off to the side. She cried out, but kept a grasp on the bottle, now coated in blood.

"Jesus Christ, you fucking lunatic!" He covered his eye with his hand. Blood—black in the moonlight—poured from between his fingers. She had to get his other eye or risk it all right now. If he got away—she couldn't think of that.

Duke turned to run. But he stopped.

Teresa peered around him.

Three figures blocked his escape.

A gang? Were they there to rob him, rape her, kill the little monster laying so still on the cold ground? Teresa wanted to go to Cassie, but the fire within her forbade it. She had to finish this.

Duke turned back toward her.

"A setup? What do you want? Money?" He pulled his wallet out and threw a wad of cash on the ground at her feet. Teresa kicked it away.

The three at the end of the alley stepped closer, boxing him in. It was her or them.

"You hurt my baby," Teresa growled.

"Your . . ." Duke looked at the little creature laying on the ground, wings laying every which way.

While he was distracted, she lunged again and caught him in the cheek with the broken bottle.

Duke backhanded her. Teresa hit the opposite wall.

She saw him again, in her mind, wrenching Cassie's little arm. Heard again her baby's pained animalistic shriek.

The fire raged inside her. Similar to when she'd injected herself with the zoe and ravaged Yaldabaoth. But sex would not cure this ailment. She needed the slithery sickening texture of a soul sliding down her throat, no matter the horrific aftertaste.

She pushed off the wall, bottle lifted above her head, and slashed downward across his face. The glass snagged his left eye, the one she'd stabbed before, and tore it clean out of his head. The optic nerve snapped. The eyeball flew somewhere behind her.

Duke staggered backward. Two of the three figures

caught him and held his arms, and it was then, with the pale moonlight filtering down, she recognized them.

It was Glory, and the girl with the curls, both grinning sadistically with mouths stretched far too wide, so wide, dark liquid trickled from the corners. The third was the lady cop. She moved a lot slower than the others, grabbing onto Duke's shirt sleeve with one hand, not even really trying.

Glory and Curls shoved him forward.

Teresa lunged and jabbed the bottle into his other eye. Duke fell to his knees. Teresa twisted the bottle and made a scooping motion, pulling out his right eye.

The three backed away from her. She held up the bottle in case they decided to attack, or get the soul first, or chase her away. But they didn't. They shied away from her in fear, then scurried out of the alley in different directions.

Teresa slurped the soul as fast as she could. It left a salty taste in her mouth and the feeling of snorting pool water up her nose at the back of her throat.

Cassie stirred behind her. Teresa went to her side and lifted her little arm. She moved it gently. Cassie hissed and snatched it back, like a wounded animal.

Teresa lifted her. "Tuck your wings, little one," she said. Cassie did. She found an old musty blanket by the box Cassie hid behind and covered her little monster with it. "I know it's stinky, but I need to hide you."

Before hurrying home, she grabbed the beer bottle and smashed it—eyeball and all—into the bottom of an empty trash can.

CHAPTER FORTY-ONE

Cassie turned back into a baby the moment they arrived. She bawled as the shreds of gargoyle skin drifted down around her and evaporated like melting snow. Lory flew into the room.

When Teresa lifted Amanda from the crib, Amanda reached for her sister and whined.

"It's not broken," the older woman said. "But I think her elbow might be dislocated.

As a former obstetrician, Teresa knew about nursemaid's elbow, caused by toddlers who held hands with their parents, reaching above their heads, sometimes hanging their full weight, putting pressure on those delicate joints.

"Can you fix it while I nurse her?" Teresa asked, wincing at how excruciating it would probably be for poor little Cassie. If Lory couldn't fix it, Teresa could. She'd fixed several in her time as an OB.

Lory nodded gravely. "Yes. It's going to sound like I'm murdering her while I do it. Well, you're a doctor. You know how it is with this injury." Lory waved her hand.

Teresa nodded without correcting her—*was* a doctor—and moved to sit in the rocker to nurse Amanda. But Amanda pulled away from Teresa, tears pouring down her cheeks, a silent sob crumpling her little face.

"Bring her closer," Lory said. Teresa did.

Amanda touched Cassie, and Cassie's cries lessened. The pair locked eyes.

"Closer," Lory said. Teresa gently lay Amanda next to Cassie. Their foreheads touched. Lory let out a grunt and Cassie let loose a sharp yelp, but then stopped crying.

Amanda patted her sister's cheek while Lory flexed her little arm.

"Right as rain," Lory said with a satisfied smile. She sat on the end of the bed and looked up at Teresa. "Who did this to her?"

"Duke Westley," Teresa said in a hushed voice, as if saying his name might summon the man—like her scuffle with him, her fight really, had seemed to call forth the other three to assist.

"Oh, that buffoon?" Lory waved her hand dismissively. "He's trying to run for sheriff. He'll never win." She spoke with pride.

Teresa raised an eyebrow. She needed to be wary around Lory, to not trust her so much.

"It's a shame you never really knew your daughter," Teresa said. She heard the sneer in her own voice.

Lory turned her head and looked at Teresa with regret or sadness or some other more powerful and complicated emotion.

Lory tickled Amanda and stood. "I'll leave you to rest now. I can tell you've been through something traumatic tonight."

She paused in the doorway. "You really do look like

Elizabeth Taylor with that on." She smiled and closed the door behind her.

Teresa slid the wig off and fluffed her hair. She lay down next to the babies, still in their own little twin land with their foreheads together, eyes locked. Amanda's hand rested on Cassie's cheek.

Teresa watched Cassie's eyes drift shut. As soon as they did, Amanda shifted and reached for Teresa.

After feedings and diaper changes, Teresa lay the babies together in their crib. She watched them fall asleep, then slipped out to the bathroom.

Her reflection startled her. She'd never worn dark eyeliner before. Some of it had smeared and run a little, giving her what might be considered a smoky eye—or a poor attempt at one.

I look like a raccoon.

Teresa reached for the bottle of face wash. It was the same one from Lory's bathroom.

She washed her face and patted it dry, and only then did her hands start to shake with the gravity of what had happened in that alley. She'd smashed the bottle, but her fingerprints were still on the glass. And Duke's body. She shook her head. At some point he would get up and walk away, but after how long? What if his body was discovered before then? He would be found along with the broken glass and—

Oh God. His eyes, too.

How long would she have to consume souls? She imagined until Cassie and Amanda could eat them on their own, but she would still have to help them.

Teresa lurched to the toilet and threw up at the thought of having to do this until they were—what—fifteen, sixteen? Eighteen and no longer minors?

There has to be a limit.

There was a limit. Shadow Eve had told her.

Souls of the eight.

Teresa sighed. Four down. She was halfway there. Tomorrow, the babies would be around eight months old.

***

In the middle of the night, a tapping clacked—and screeched—against the window.

"Probably just a tree—"

Did I lock the back door?

She flung back the covers and checked on the babies. They were both there, snuggled together. It made her want to cry.

Teresa crept down the hallway to the back door and checked the lock. It was engaged. Movement caught her eye through the lace curtains.

She held one aside and peered out. She dropped the curtain and stepped back with a strangled whimper.

They were out there. Glory and Curly—with their insane smiles, teeth bright in the moonlight—just standing there, staring at the house. Where was the lady cop?

Teresa backed away and scuttled to her room. Inside, she ripped the curtain back and yelped.

The lady cop's face pressed against the windowpane, leaving a black smear where her lips touched. She flung her arm up, fingertips sliding down the glass. When her hand hit the edge of the sash, she tapped it with her fingernail.

It all at once reminded Teresa of Ruthie scratching and clawing at doors and windows. But the lady cop's movements were so lackadaisical, as if her arm weighed a hundred pounds and it took every ounce of effort to lift it up to touch the glass. What did they want?

Me, Yaldabaoth's voice spoke in Teresa's mind, skittering across her scalp.

"Why do they want you?" Teresa asked.

I created them. The children want their father.

"You're dead."

Am I?

Teresa backed away from the window, letting the curtain fall across the glass. It swung, sickeningly showing that face, then darkness, then the face again, before stilling, like some horrific peep show.

The backs of her legs hit the mattress. She sat hard, bouncing.

He *was* dead, wasn't he? That's how they got out of Tartaros, wasn't it? Teresa had been dazed the night of the betrayal. She'd hit her head twice that night, once against the windshield when she took Derrick, and again when Yaldabaoth, after announcing his betrayal, threw her from him.

All she could remember was telling Ann, huddled over a still figure with Maggie, to walk out the door to get out.

She tried to remember if Yaldabaoth was there. All this time she thought he was dead. Had she even seen him? His body? His remains? She recalled the sound of rending leather, but what did that mean?

And Lory told her she could talk to him.

Was it some sort of master-slave bond? Could he call to her from Tartaros?

Teresa shook her head. It was a hallucination. Even if it wasn't, maybe he meant he was still alive in one of the babies. She got up again and peered down at their sleeping figures nestled close together, heads touching. Cassie had her thumb in her mouth. A new self-soothing habit. Maybe from being injured. Maybe from seeing Amanda do it.

Which one of them would have Yaldabaoth in them? Cassie? Surely. She turned into a tiny monster on command, just as Yaldabaoth could hide his true nature—the lion-snake-man hybrid—on command, transforming into that dark and intensely attractive man.

Maybe she just read far too much into his voice in her head. Plus she was tired, and the screeching tap grated on her nerves. She left the room again and went out onto the back porch.

"You need to leave," she said. "Get out of here."

The lady cop came around the side of the house at a lethargic pace, but she didn't come closer. She gave Teresa as wide a berth as possible without running into the raised beds in the garden, lush with growing vegetables and flowers.

Teresa took a step closer. The three shied away from her, but their faces didn't register fear.

"Go on, leave." Teresa flung her arms at them. They stumbled and groped at each other, manic grins still stretching their faces. They disappeared into the night.

They feared her. A swell of power came over her. This time *they* feared *her*.

Teresa turned to go back inside, but movement caught her eye. Rebecca huddled in the trees just on the edge of Lory's property.

"I know what you're doing," she said from across the garden.

Teresa didn't fear this woman. Not anymore. Not after overpowering—for the most part—a grown man. She clenched her fists. If Rebecca even tried anything to get

Cassie and Amanda, Teresa would do more than rip her eyes out.

"What is it you think I'm doing?" Teresa asked, not even lowering her voice.

Rebecca stepped out to the edge of Lory's yard. Her long black hair framed her face and draped over her chest.

"The eight Logismoi, of course," Rebecca said. "You're feeding them the eight."

Goosebumps broke out on Teresa's arms. Of course *Rebecca* knew what was going on. She was a Messenger of the Light.

"What happens after?" Teresa asked. "Once they're fed?"

"How many so far?"

"Four," Teresa said.

"They'll be eight years old then." Rebecca looked off to the side.

"Eight *months* old, you mean," Teresa said.

Rebecca jerked her head back in Teresa's direction. "Months?"

"Yes. They seem to age about two months each time I feed them."

"I must have misinterpreted the text. I assumed they would age by two years," Rebecca said. "I thought they would be sixteen years old at the end. This is quite different than expected." She was lost in thought for a couple seconds, then looked up at Teresa. "Whatever you do—now that you have begun, you cannot stop. You must feed them all eight."

"Or else what?" Teresa asked. She knew there was an "or else" attached. There always was.

"Or else they'll both die." Rebecca backed away, turned, and ran into the darkness.

CHAPTER FORTY-TWO

THURSDAY

Ann had planned to go to Paul's, but her phone rang early in the morning.

"Cindy didn't show up today," Sully said. "Did she call you? Is she still sick?" His voice sounded frustrated but worried.

"No. I don't know." Ann stood from her place at the table where she and Maggie were devouring pancakes again. Her mind automatically went to last year when Sheriff McMichael didn't show up and George Riley—rest his soul—asked for her help. McMichael had shown up eventually. At the bottom of a pit with two other dead bodies on top of him.

"The thing is, I saw her the other night, the night before she called in sick, that is." He cleared his throat.

"At the station?" Ann downed her coffee, moved the phone from in front of her mouth and whispered to Maggie, "You need to go to daycare today."

Maggie's face fell. She dropped her fork onto her plate. She slouched out of her chair and stomped up the stairs, Pinky at her heels. At least she hadn't protested.

Sully had responded, but Ann wasn't paying attention.

"At the station?" she asked.

He made an impatient huffing sound. "No, at her house. She didn't seem sick at all. I think something else is going on."

"I'll drop Maggie off at daycare and swing by. We can go to her house together to see if she's home." Ann hung up after Sully okayed the idea. She climbed the stairs and paused outside Maggie's room. Thumping and muttering came from beyond the door. Ann pushed it open a crack and peeked in.

Pinky lay on the bed, head cocking and tilting with each tantrum-like throw of something.

"I don't want to go to that horrible place," Maggie whisper-yelled and chucked a shoe into her closet where it made a satisfying *thud* against the back wall. "Sally Opperheim will probably be there, won't she?"

Pinky tilted her head the other direction. Maggie slumped onto her bed and draped herself over Pinky who shifted and sniffed and snorted in Maggie's ear. Maggie giggled.

"I wish I could just stay here with you," she groaned.

Ann knocked on the door and went in.

Maggie lifted her head. "How can you send me back there with Sally Opperheim the way she is?"

Ann wondered the same thing but had no other choice. "Just stay away from her. I'll tell the ladies at the front desk to keep the two of you apart. You can just sit at a table away from her and draw." If Sally looked the way Maggie described her, Ann wondered why her mother would even take her to daycare, but then she thought about her own reason for doing it. Sally's mom might not have any other choice either.

"I don't want to draw anymore." Maggie started to close up. "I don't want to go to the Daycare Place. I want to stay here with Pinky." Her face brightened. "Or, I can go with you to help."

"You can't come with me. My work is dangerous."

Maggie's head shot up. "You said it wasn't."

Shit.

They argued until Ann finally told Maggie she didn't have a choice in the matter. She would go to daycare—end of story, end of discussion.

Maggie stomped into the bathroom and slammed the door.

Was Ann being too hard on her? Was sending her there —where Sally Opperheim might be—a bad idea? Ann dropped her face into her hands. She didn't know. What would her dad have done in this situation? Ann remembered going to work with him plenty of times, but it wasn't until she was ten or eleven even. Before then she always went to her dad's friend's house to be looked after. Always the same lady.

Ann recounted the events of the previous evening. Maggie had talked so fast and animatedly, she didn't get a chance to interject to ask questions. Rachel's texts. Pinky's behavior. Sophia not liking Duke's touch.

Ann remembered when Pinky had growled at Raghib the night Ann left Maggie with him and how that had panned out. Until Ann got a handle on what was going on, Maggie either *did* have to come with her or go to the Daycare Place. Like it or not.

The latter was preferred and probably safer, of course.

But with her mark not giving her clear signs as to when Maggie needed her, and with Sally Opperheim potentially being there, Ann wasn't entirely sure that was true.

At the Daycare Place, Ann gave strict instructions to keep Maggie away from Sally. And much to Ann's relief, the redhead told her Sally wasn't coming today.

Rachel didn't even acknowledge her when Ann walked into the station. In fact, Rachel's eyes flicked up, and she shrunk down a little. Her saving grace was Pinky wiggling over to her for some pets. Rachel turned her full attention to the dog.

Ann let it go for now. "I'm leaving Pinky here while we go check on Cindy."

Rachel made a grunting affirmative noise.

Sully jumped to his feet, ready to go. They took the station vehicle with Sully in the driver's seat.

Cindy's house was a cute little cabin in the middle of a copse of evergreens. A big blue spruce stood sentry over her driveway. Sully parked the Jeep, but he didn't get out right away. Ann paused with her hand on the handle.

"I came by here the other night because I like her," Sully said, not looking at Ann.

So much like George Riley. Ann swallowed a knot in her throat but said nothing. She climbed out and donned a pair of nitrile gloves.

Ann pounded on the door and peered in one of the windows at the front of the house. Dark. No movement. "How did she seem when you stopped by?"

"She sounded a little funny. Her voice was different. Could have just been because we were talking through the door." He shrugged. "Or because she was coming down with something." Sully stayed near the Jeep with a kit in his beefy hand. "She said we would talk the next day. I told her I like her." His cheeks flushed. "Maybe that's why she called in sick. To avoid me." He looked down at his shoes.

"No. You heard her on the phone. She is definitely sick." Ann patted his arm. "Lethargic, at least. *Really* lethargic, actually."

Ann moved to the side of the house and looked in the windows. "Her badge and gun are on the table. Furniture's all upright. Nothing seems out of place. Have you tried her cell?"

Sully pulled his phone from his belt. "I'll try it again." He poked the screen and held it to his ear.

From inside the house, a spot on the kitchen counter lit up along with a faint but unmistakable cell phone ring tone.

"Looks like her phone's on the kitchen counter," Ann called to Sully. She kept her voice even, despite her heart pulsing in her throat. The ringing stopped and the light went out on the screen.

Ann rejoined Sully. "She might just be sleeping. If she's sick, I mean."

Sully pounded on the door with the side of his fist. It shook in its frame.

"I don't know, Sheriff," Sully said. "I have a bad feeling about this. What if something's wrong with her? Like those girls—"

"Let's go in." A tremor of anxiety wriggled through Ann's gut. She pushed it aside.

"Do you think—"

"I don't think anything, but we need to get inside and make sure she's okay." Ann got the ram from the back of the

Jeep, but Sully and his linebacker size had already made short work of the door. He fingered the splintered frame.

"I'll fix it for her." His cheeks turned red along with the tips of his ears. He reached inside and turned on a light. "Cindy? You home?"

Ann followed him inside. "Don't touch anything else."

He looked over his shoulder at her and swallowed audibly.

Ann surveyed the living room, which leaked into a dining room where her badge and gun lay. The whole space was about the size of Ann's own living room.

Something shriveled lay on the floor by the dining table. Ann's heart lurched higher into her throat. Her lungs squeezed.

It better not be the same crispy stuff from last year.

When people went missing during the events leading up to The Night, the key indicator that linked the victims was a dried crispy substance. Results from the lab were inconclusive, but it was close to human umbilical cord.

Ann inched closer and kneeled.

"What is it?" Sully asked over her shoulder.

Ann lifted one of the multi-colored crispy things. "Dried flower petals, I think?" She handed a red one up to Sully. There were yellow, pink, and purple ones, as well.

"There should be a crystal vase," Sully murmured. "The photo and the description on the florist's website showed a crystal vase with the flowers. That's why I got that one. The vase was real pretty." He looked at Ann with wide eyes. "Someone stole the vase."

"The vase is not what we're here for." Ann couldn't keep herself from thinking the worst. No one stole the vase. Someone stole Cindy, and maybe that person had touched the vase, so they took it with them.

"Start dusting for prints," she told Sully. A short hallway led to darkness at the back. "I'll check the bedroom." Ann moved inches at a time and turned on a hall light. "Cindy? Are you back here?"

Two doors on either side of the hall and one at the end. She opened the one on the left. Bathroom. The one on the right was a linen closet. She gripped the knob on door number three and pushed it open.

A tidy little room. Bed made, uniform draped along the back of the chair in the corner.

"She's not here," Ann called.

"Maybe she got called away for a family emergency or something," Sully said from the doorway.

"But her phone is on the kitchen counter," Ann said.

"Musta been a real bad emergency?" The hope in Sully's voice stopped Ann from any further naysaying. "Come back out here." Sully led the way. "Pictures are knocked over on this sideboard here." He pointed them out. "Signs of a struggle?"

They had flimsy cardboard stands attached to the frames. The kind that fell over if you looked at them too fast. She wasn't going to rule anything out, but she figured they likely fell on their own.

They processed Cindy's place, leaving fingerprint dust everywhere. Cindy would either be horrified at the state of her house—it had been clean and tidy when they'd arrived, with the exception of the flowers and the photos—or pleased she got to clean it all over again if she came back.

When she came back, Ann corrected herself.

"We need to call for help on this," Ann said.

"State police?" Sully loaded the kit and prints into the Jeep and closed the door.

"Let's start with Pine Valley," she said. "They have a

decent detective over there now. She graduated a year behind me."

Sully nodded.

"If they can't help, then we'll call someone else."

They got in the Jeep and drove back to the station, both silent for all five minutes of the drive.

CHAPTER FORTY-THREE

Sully processed the fingerprints while Ann called Pine Valley. The detective there apologized, but they could not spare anyone. They were short-staffed themselves, what with Cindy running off to Harmony. They hadn't backfilled her position yet. Ann told the detective Cindy was the one missing. She said she would see what she could do, but it wasn't promising.

Ann called the state police after that and was promised a call back within twenty-four hours.

"Jesus fuck, she's possibly been missing for forty-eight already!"

"That's the best we can do, ma'am."

She hung up and went out to the bullpen. "I don't want to call CBI, but I might have to if I can't get any goddamn help."

The door to the station opened. Mr. Proust, Harmony's oldest resident and lifetime local, shuffled in, watery eyes taking in the bright fluorescents. He grinned at Rachel and raised and lowered his eyebrows at her.

"Mr. Proust," Ann said in greeting. "How can we help you?"

"Town hall yesterday, you says to let you all know if anything seems fishy," Mr. Proust said. "Whell, I saws somethin'." His watery eyes twitched around. The nearer he got, the stronger he smelled, and he smelled like a bar.

"Been to Flynn's today already?" Ann asked him.

"That's beside the point, missy." He straightened a little. "I saw a man get attacked in that there alley between the real estate office and that good-for-nuthin' Emerson's Pawn shop."

"Go on," Ann said. These old timers liked to weave a good yarn. They also liked to take forever doing it.

"Big fella. Walked over there. Creature sitting up on the roof swooped down and knocked him into the darkness."

Ann's shoulders slumped. "A creature?"

"Wing-ed thing. Tail. Looked like one of them gargoyles on the roof of that old church or whatever it is out by Old Harmony. You seen those spires from the road out that way."

Ann hadn't been to Old Harmony since she was a kid and certainly did not remember an old church. But it sounded like something Maggie might like to see.

She wanted to ask him how much he'd had to drink leading up to that moment. "Thank you for the information, Mr. Proust." She patted his shoulder.

"Well ain't-cha gonna write it down?" He poked her in the breast pocket of her shirt where she kept her notepad. Ann grabbed his bony hand and managed to halt the involuntary reaction to twist it sideways.

"Time for you to go home."

He grumbled as he went. Ann watched his hunched back as he shuffled out.

Gargoyle? Big fella. The only other big fella she could think of off the top of her head was Duke Westley.

And Sophia didn't like Duke Westley's touch.

"Sully," Ann said. "Come with me."

If it had been red, it would have been a bloodbath. But the substance in the alley was black. Just like the stuff in the clearing.

Sully taped off the alley while Ann took pictures and jotted notes. They took samples of the black stuff and collected anything they thought would help their case.

"Must've been the same drug, or whatever Glory was on," Sully said, eyeballing a cotton swab coated in the black goo. He dropped it inside a vial and closed the cap.

Ann wondered who around town she would see this time with ill-fitting skin and when Cindy would show up with her skin sagging at the seams. She also wondered if it wasn't time to bring Sully in on all of the not-so-believable occurrences in Harmony.

CHAPTER FORTY-FOUR

The babies were now eight months old. The cloud had blasted out of Cassie at daybreak with such force, tears leaked from her eyes.

"Mama," she said, her little hands grabbing. Teresa lifted her.

"Chashy," Amanda's little voice said, so quiet, Teresa wasn't sure she heard correctly. "Chashy."

Teresa peered down into the crib just as Amanda gripped the rails and pulled herself to a stand.

"Look at you," Teresa said. "We need to get out for some fresh air." She plunked Cassie on the bed, lifted Amanda, and got them changed into fresh diapers.

They spent the day in Lory's backyard on a blanket in the grass. Cassie and Amanda loved the sunshine. They smiled up at butterflies that fluttered overhead and played little games only their twin world would understand. Teresa relished the sun, let it pour onto her face.

Lory brought a playpen up from the basement and put it in the living room. It was still there when Teresa came out of her room later in the afternoon.

The sympathizers were all situated on the living room furniture as if waiting for her.

Everyone was there, except one.

"Where's Rachel?" Teresa asked.

"She's working," Patrina said. "If she's not working the dispatch desk at the sheriff's station, she's babysitting the sheriff's kid."

Teresa had not been aware of Rachel's occupation.

"She works for Ann Logan?" Teresa asked.

"Rachel is one of us." Lory bustled into the living room with a tray of cookies. She set it on the coffee table. Paul swiped one and stuffed it into his mouth. "There is no need to worry about her working for Ann. She's our insider."

Teresa looked at her skeptically.

Trust no one, Raghib's voice from the visitor room said in her mind.

Well, she would have to keep an eye on this girl. Teresa turned to Patrina.

"Patrina. Would you like to help me bring the babies out?"

Patrina jumped to her feet at the mention of her name, and when she heard Teresa's request, she clapped her hands delightedly and bounded to Teresa's side. She followed Teresa down the hall, right on her heels like an excited puppy.

"Oh my gosh. I've been waiting my whole life for this. Well, not my *whole* life, but ever since I held one of them the night they were born—oh, thank you for picking me to help!" she gushed.

"You can carry Amanda," she said, pointing to the smaller of the two, though she was starting to catch up to her sister's size. Teresa didn't trust Cassie to not get grabby with eyeballs.

"They're so big," Patrina said. "How are they so big already?"

"Mother's milk. Fattens them right up, doesn't it baby?" She reached down, lifted Cassie, and nuzzled her. Cassie let out a delighted squeal. "Does wonders for the growing young."

Patrina lifted Amanda, cradling her head, even though she didn't need to. They could pull themselves up to stand now, for heaven's sake.

Out in the living room, they placed the babies in the playpen. Everyone *oohed* and *aahed* and cooed at the babies as they resumed their play from earlier, completely ignoring the people peering down at them.

"I just want to eat them up," Patrina said with an adoring smile, clasping her hands under her chin.

"What do you suppose babies taste like?" Paul asked her in a voice he seemed to think was too low for Teresa to hear. He shoved another cookie in his mouth. Patrina smacked his arm with the back of her hand and gave Teresa an appalled look.

"I'm sorry for Paul's—whatever it is." She rolled her eyes.

Indecency? Lack of brain-mouth barrier?

"I always wanted kids." Olivia's eyes glistened with tears.

They all looked at her. She wiped at her cheek, though no tears had fallen, and blinked rapidly.

"Hunter doesn't want them." She looked up at Teresa. "He even had a vasectomy in *secret* to avoid it happening on accident. He said he didn't trust me to take my birth control pills—like I would sabotage his *life* by skipping them on purpose or something." Her shoulders hitched, but she took a deep breath and collected herself.

Patrina touched Olivia's arm. She opened her mouth to say something, then shut it. Teresa could only imagine what it might have been. She had her own ideas, like, maybe Hunter didn't deserve Olivia. Teresa didn't know the redhead very well, but she did recognize some sort of emotional abuse going on between them the last time Hunter had been at the house.

Teresa suddenly felt a silent kinship toward Olivia. She knew what it was like to crave a child. She'd battled infertility herself until Tiffany's miraculous conception. She reached over and touched Olivia's hand, gripping the top of the playpen.

"You can babysit any time," Teresa said.

Paul cleared his throat. "Where is Hunter, anyway?" He cleared his throat again. A nervous tick perhaps?

"He said he's done with this—with us." She looked up sharply—at Paul?—then quickly back down at the babies, reaching for them without really trying. "I mean 'us' the group of us, not 'us' like me and him."

"Maybe it should be 'us' you and him," Paul said in a low voice.

Olivia's cheeks reddened, but she otherwise didn't show any sign of hearing him.

"Is he trustworthy?" Teresa asked Lory. "He's not going to turn around and tell the sheriff where I am, is he?" Her throat clenched, and she choked on the last words.

"He's harmless," Olivia said. "He's just as guilty as the rest of us, anyway, and knows it. He never even threatened to turn on us, even with—well, even so." She sniffed and turned from the babies and sat down next to Paul. She was supposed to sit on the other couch. Her assigned seat was on the couch with Rachel, Levi, and Hunter. Levi sat all alone on the other couch now.

Paul settled back into the cushions and put his arm along the back. Olivia didn't lean away. Paul's fingers touched her opposite shoulder just barely. There was definitely something between them. Teresa wasn't sure if they were a thing behind Hunter's back already or if they were getting to that point.

Before she could speculate further, the front door burst open. Hunter stood in the doorway.

CHAPTER FORTY-FIVE

"You." Hunter pointed.

Paul and Olivia leapt to their feet. They both had flushed cheeks. Paul held his arms out, blocking Olivia, fists clenched, but his eyes were wide and wild. Olivia cowered behind him, hands clasped together at her chin. Worry knitted her brow and surprise widened her eyes.

"Now Hunter," Lory blocked the wide entry to the sunken living room and held up her hands. "Be reasonable."

Hunter's eyes, full of rage, of malice, flicked to her.

"They are *fucking*, Lory." He pointed into the room at no one in particular. "Behind my back. They are *fucking*." He gripped something in his other fist.

Teresa positioned herself closer to the playpen, ready to protect her babies. She recognized the thing in Hunter's hand. It was a pregnancy test.

She glanced down. Cassie's little triangular head with the almond eyes peered up at her.

Now? With all of these people around?

She took a deep breath.

Lory held her arms straight out to the sides. She shifted from side to side when Hunter tried to go around her.

Hunter growled a frustrated sound. "Get out of my way, Lory. I'm not here to hurt *you*."

"I won't let you hurt *anyone* in my house, Hunter. You need to calm down and be civilized." Lory's voice came out firm, but there was a fearful waver to the ends of her words.

"This is childish." Hunter lifted one of his big hands and shoved Lory. Levi jumped up. But Lory stuttered her feet under herself, turned, and flopped against the soft couch. Levi righted her fully and pulled her behind him.

"Hey," Levi yelled. "You need to get out of here."

"Or what? You'll call the cops?" His angry eyes found Teresa, looked her up and down. "You wouldn't dare. Not with *her* here." He stepped down into the living room. Levi ushered Lory back and away. Hunter threw the white thing at Olivia. It bounced off her lifted arms.

"Care to explain this, you slut?" Hunter took another step forward.

Cassie shot out of the playpen and latched onto his face, sending him reeling backward. His heels struck the step, and his arms wind-milled. He landed hard on his back.

Teresa duly noted the screams and shrieks. She raced toward Cassie's beating wings. An eyeball flew to the side, hit the wall, bounced, and rolled to a stop by the basement door.

Hunter's screams far surpassed the shrieks of the men and women in the living room. Teresa put a hand on Cassie's shoulder to stop her.

Hunter's fist lashed out. Teresa caught him by the wrist —surprised by her reflexes and strength—and wrenched it until he cried out. He covered his empty left eye socket with his free hand, but between his fingers, Teresa could see the silvery glimmer of his soul.

"Hunter," she said in a level tone. "Calm down."

Spittle flew from his lips. That black fluid leaked from his left nostril. It was less viscous than blood, like mascara tears dripping down the side of his face.

"What the fuck is that thing?" His remaining eye swiveled, looking for Cassie, who had crouched next to his head, just outside of his peripheral vision.

"You are going to die," Teresa whispered to him, placing a hand on his cheek. "You really should not let your anger get the best of you like this."

What had Mother said to her whenever she threw a tantrum? Nothing. That's what. Mother acted like she didn't exist. Gave her the silent treatment, even hours after she'd calmed down, even after she'd apologized.

Teresa nodded to Cassie. Her little hand lashed out, snatching the remaining eye with deft skill. Hunter cried out again. Teresa pinned his arms with her knees, still surprised at her own strength, and sucked the soul out of his eye sockets.

It tasted angry, like the pure heat of a hot pepper without the mouth burn, and like stomach acid when it singed the back of her throat. It burned all the way down into her belly.

After she finished, she turned, still squatting over Hunter. Cassie peered at her. Teresa stroked her strange little head, the flesh soft and smooth under her palm.

Someone in the living room made a strangled sound.

Teresa lifted Cassie into her arms and stood. She cleared her throat.

Olivia pulled out of Paul's arms and rushed to Hunter's side. She screamed and sat back presumably at the sight of his eyeless face, at his deflated skin bag body. She crawled around on the floor and located the eye by the basement door, crawled back to him, and tried to stick the eye back in its socket, going as far as lifting the deflated skin and tucking it inside like a pocket.

"Where's the other one? Where's the other one?" Her face glowed with redness, her eyes rolled around wildly in her head.

Paul went to her.

"He's gone, Oli. He's gone."

She fought him, trying to pull out of the grip he had on her wrists. Finally, she succumbed and fell against him, pressing her face into his shoulder.

The whole thing had taken a matter of seconds. The rest of the room remained frozen in time while Paul and Olivia rocked in the foyer by Hunter's deflated body.

Teresa watched them with mixed emotions. Hunter had been abusive. Maybe not physically, as far as she could tell, but verbally and emotionally. She was better off without him. She could also see that Olivia had loved him despite those tragic traits.

Patrina had gone pale, her mouth agape. Levi still protected Lory behind his back. She peered out from behind him. Both of them looked at Teresa in shock.

"My babies," Teresa said breathless and choking on the burn from Hunter's soul. She cleared her throat, squared her shoulders, and lifted her chin. "These children of Yaldabaoth require more than the milk I can offer them in order to thrive," she said. "Hunter was a necessary sacrifice."

"Sacrifice," Paul whispered behind her.

Teresa turned.

"Yeah. Yes." He nodded with wide eyes. He whispered 'yes' and 'a necessary sacrifice' over and over.

Olivia pulled away from him and gave him a ghastly look.

"I have to go," she said in a screechy voice. She stood, shaking.

"Why don't you go sit with Paul," Teresa said. "Now." She nodded at Paul, and he guided Olivia back into the living room. She wept quietly on the couch but did not move to seek comfort from him.

"How many?" Lory stepped out from behind Levi. "How many have you taken now?" Her voice rode the edge of hysterical shock.

"You knew about this?" Patrina's shrill voice asked.

Lory turned to her and motioned for her to calm down.

"I'll explain everything," she snapped. She turned back to Teresa. "How many?"

Teresa glanced down her nose at the older woman.

"Hunter makes five."

CHAPTER FORTY-SIX

Maggie thumped around in her room upstairs. Probably throwing a small tantrum, though larger than the one she'd thrown that morning. At least the girl was semi-private about it. Ann wasn't sure how she'd handle a child throwing themselves around, beating their hands and fists on the floor.

"I didn't do anything to *you*," Ann said when Pinky slinked up the stairs. The dog cast a furtive look at Ann, then continued up. Great. Now they were both mad at her. Why was she the bad guy for trying to do the right thing?

All she did was tell Maggie she had to go to the Daycare Place again the next day.

"*Again?*" Maggie's voice held flabbergasted outrage.

"Nothing happened today," Ann explained in a calm and even voice. "Sally wasn't even there, was she?"

"She'll be there tomorrow, I just know it," Maggie said.

"Even if she is, just stay away from her."

Ann needed to check out Paul's shop, since she hadn't been able to with one confirmed crime scene and one potential. Cindy's house hadn't had any other prints besides Cindy's herself.

Ann sat on the couch and tried to keep the sense of helplessness that crouched on the periphery of her mind from jumping in and taking over.

She had too many *things* to deal with. To work through. Teresa Hart at large. Maggie and Sophia and these Luminaries. Cindy missing. The kids with weird skin.

She looked at her notes again, at the pairs, but her mind kept drifting to the alleyway and Mr. Proust. She could still feel the poke of his finger against her breast pocket, as if that knobby thing poked straight through her notebook. She rubbed the spot.

Dirty old drunk.

Was the big fella he saw Duke? Ann picked up her phone and found him in her contacts.

"Duke Westley," he said in greeting, as if his phone didn't have caller ID. As if he didn't know it was Ann on the other end.

Ann thought about hanging up, but he knew it was her. He could just call her back.

"Hi, Duke." Ann paced. "I just wanted to follow up on our conversation the other night." She hated how professional she sounded, but it was for the best, wasn't it?

Duke laughed, but not his usual laugh. It sounded joyful. "Oh, Ann. Don't you worry. I understand completely. I know I'm not for everyone. What is it some people say? I don't suit everyone's tastes?"

"Um, okay." She could hear the smile in his voice. And for a brief second, in her mind, saw him with a mouth stretched in a too-wide grin, like Glory and the way Maggie described Sally.

"No need to apologize," Duke said.

"I wasn't going to—"

"Oh, I think you maybe were." He chuckled. "But there's no need. No need. To apologize." A pause. Then he said it again quickly. "No need to apologize."

"Okay, I won't."

"Good. Because there really is no need."

Ann narrowed her eyes. He was being weird.

"No need at all." Another pause. "To apologize."

Was he trying to *get* her to apologize now? Was this some sort of manipulation? But he sounded too . . . cheery. Too unlike himself. Not his usual egotistical, arrogant, prideful—

She narrowed her eyes at the living room and stopped pacing. She went to the list, but before she could read the pairs of sins and virtues, the book flipped open.

"I'll see you around then," Ann said.

"Bye, Ann." His voice dropped at the end like he was running out of batteries. The line went silent.

The book had landed on a page with an illustration that looked like some sort of schematic.

A rectangle with two circles on either end. Two lines arched over it like a rainbow. The ends of the arch connected to the two circles. Eight smaller circles arched below the rectangle. Within that semicircle were three symbols. The Egyptian *Ankh*, the *Sa*, and one Ann had never seen before. It was basically a stylized snake.

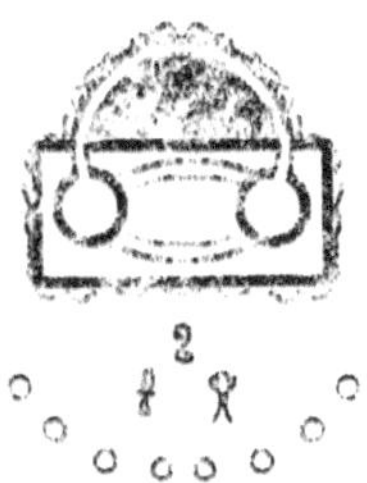

The text above and below it transformed. Ann's eyes devoured the fragmented text.

Light and dark, life and death. The children of chaos. The children of the mother-father.

The Blighted Womb. Mother of the Angels. Father of Death. Together shall gather. The Devotion of Consanguinity shall unloose the balances of halves and wholes.

The eight Logismoi shall lend the suffering. The Children of Chaos shall unite. The Perfect Soul shall be resurrected.

The Gateway to Tartaros shall open.

Pinky blasted down the stairs in a rumble of paws that sounded like a whole pack of dogs. She halted in front of Ann, poked the book, reared up like a horse, and ran back up.

Ann followed her to Maggie's room, where Maggie lay sprawled on the floor, eyes glowing blue-white with Sophia. Pinky nosed Maggie's limp form and looked at Ann with a wheezing whine and concerned wrinkles on her forehead. Ann pulled Maggie onto her lap and held her close.

"What's happening?" she whispered. "Maggie?" Maggie's form flopped. A dead weight.

The light sucked back into her pupils returning her eyes to normal.

"Ann," Maggie shouted. Her eyes focused.

"What happened?" Ann lifted Maggie in her arms, stood, and carried her to the little twin bed.

"I saw two ladies who looked the same. Exactly the same." Her words rushed out. Her eyes were tight. "They looked like my mom. My *real* mom, I mean."

"Your mom? You remember your mom?" Ann didn't know. She'd never asked. She thought bringing up Maggie's past might upset her. Just like they hadn't been back to the diner, just in case, and they rarely spoke of The Night or of Derrick or of Raghib.

Maggie nodded. "Only a little bit. Her smile mostly. She always smiled at me. Even when she was mad. Like she couldn't help it."

"What was your mother's name?" Ann asked.

"My dad only ever called her *Habibi* when he talked to her or *Amek* when he talked to me about her. But those aren't really names. They were like nice names he called her. Like when you call me Mags or kiddo."

"Nicknames. What do the nicknames mean? Are they real words?"

"*My love* and *your mother*." Maggie lifted her hands and covered her face. "I guess *Amek* isn't really a nickname." Maggie curled into a ball. "My mark hurts again."

Ann went to the hall closet and got the expired ointment. She applied some to Maggie's mark, but she wasn't sure if it would help. It wasn't Maggie's body causing the pain. It was Sophia.

"You saw your mom and someone who looked just like your mom?" Ann asked.

Maggie nodded. "Two of my mom."

"What about your grandpa or your dad?"

Maggie shook her head. "Nope. Just the two of them."

"What were they doing?" Ann asked.

"They were fighting, I think. But at the end they hugged." Maggie's brows furrowed. "One of them glowed during the hug."

Ann tried to figure out what it meant, but she had no idea. She also wanted to tell Maggie that the book showed her something, but she didn't want to burden her.

Burden. They both feared burdening the other. Ann would have laughed at the strange irony of it, but couldn't. Maggie was in no shape for laughter.

"Stay with her, Pinky."

Pinky thumped her tail and positioned her head across Maggie's body protectively. Ann eased the door shut behind herself and returned to the living room.

She scanned the list.

I am hubris and humility. She wrote Duke's name next to the pairing.

CHAPTER FORTY-SEVEN

FRIDAY

"Just look at the state of you," Teresa's mother said in her acerbic voice. She pointed to the hall bathroom in Teresa and Derrick's house.

Teresa walked toward the open door in slow motion. Red light poured out of it. She didn't remember changing the bulbs to red. Derrick must have done that for some reason.

When she looked in the mirror, she wore Yaldabaoth's face. She screamed.

"What is it, my sweet, do you not miss me?" Her lips said in his voice.

Her scream in the dream turned into the shriek of the black cloud bursting out of Cassie's open mouth. Teresa launched out of bed and opened the window.

She ran to the back door in time to see the tail end of it disappear into the bushes.

She went back to her room and lifted Cassie—now ten months old—from the crib, carried her out to the living room, and plopped her into the playpen. She did the same with Amanda, who was awake when she returned. She nuzzled Amanda's fuzzy head before putting her inside.

Lory was in the kitchen making oatmeal. When she turned, her face was drawn.

"Good morning," Teresa said. "How did you sleep?"

"Not well, to be honest." Lory nodded her head toward the coffee pot. "Coffee's ready."

Teresa poured herself a cup with a splash of cream. She sat at the table.

From her profile, Teresa could see Lory's mouth pulled down at the corners. The skin around her eyes was red and puffy.

"Are you upset about what happened?" Teresa blew on her coffee and took a quick sip.

Lory looked at her. A tear slid down her cheek, but she smiled. "No. Not upset. Just shocked, I think." She wiped the tear away. "I guess—well I guess I didn't know what it was you did. To collect or"—she gulped—"eat the souls. I didn't realize it required . . ." she pointed to her eye and seemed to pale. "It was just shocking, is all."

"You were a Messenger of the Light," Teresa said with barely veiled contempt. "I thought you all were—I don't know—brainwashed into being tough or something."

Lory placed brown sugar, dried fruit, and a small carafe of milk on the table, followed by two bowls of steaming oats. Teresa was so hungry, this meager portion likely would not be enough.

"I wasn't." Lory prepared her oatmeal with the fixings on the table. "Brainwashed, that is. I was a member before they started using those tactics on new recruits. I was in it from the start, I guess you could say. Born into it. We were supposed to be tough, sure. Ruthless, of course. But, well, I guess I've gotten soft." She stirred her oatmeal absently. She lifted one shoulder and met Teresa's eyes. "Maybe I should start my own group. Maybe I can help rehabilitate members who decide to leave." She let out a mirthless laugh and sipped her coffee.

Teresa stopped stirring milk into her oats. Lory laughed and dismissed the idea with a wave of her hand .

"My sister on the other hand, she—I don't really know who she's with anymore." There seemed to be sadness in her voice. "She probably wonders the same of me."

Teresa put her spoon down and folded her fingers together on the table. "Go on."

Lory lifted her coffee mug with both hands. She took a careful sip. Another tear dripped down her face.

"It's just bad history. Bygones or what have you." Lory shook her head and lifted her spoon, but she didn't eat.

Teresa stared at Lory's face. The woman looked up at her, then quickly away again. She sighed.

"She betrayed me by stealing my husband's love. I betrayed her right back."

"What did you do?"

"It's a long story."

Teresa leaned back and looked into the living room. Amanda and Cassie played quietly in the playpen, both gurgling and cooing. Every once in a while, a recognizable word popped out, like *look*, or *here*. They shared the toys well. They called each other Chashy and Mumba.

"Mumba, Mumba, look." Cassie had the stuffed kitty in her chubby hand. She bopped it on Amanda's nose. Amanda let out a delighted squeal.

"We have time." Teresa shoveled a large spoonful of oatmeal into her mouth.

Lory kept stirring her oatmeal. She sighed. "Quite a few

years after I was hit by a car and woke in Egypt—Ann would have been in her twenties by then—I saw Bram. In a market in Nag Hammadi. I knew then that he was there looking for *her*. For my sister." She spat the words. "He found her all right. I'd been keeping an eye on her. She's my twin sister, after all. I had hoped to mend things with her. I missed her. I went to her house one time. She had married into the Protectorate."

Teresa pushed her empty bowl away. A motion her mother would have chastised her for doing. She leaned her elbows on the table and resisted the urge to say, "and how did that make you feel?" to prod Lory along.

"Anyway, I knew from watching she and her husband that they were having troubles getting pregnant. But then she and Bram met up, and magically, a few months later, there was an undeniable bulge in her belly. Nine months later she gave birth." Lory met Teresa's eyes.

"Another betrayal, it sounds like," Teresa said.

Lory frowned. "I never thought of it like that." She stopped stirring the hot cereal. "Why didn't he look for *me?* Sure, I was supposed to be dead, but the rings—they keep us alive until the contract is fulfilled." She shifted her eyes from the wondering middle distance to Teresa. "That's how I survived getting struck by a car."

It was worse than she thought, then. Teresa felt bad for making Lory so sad.

"She really is just despicable," Lory said in a low voice, her eyes glistening. She gave Teresa a small smile. "So is he, as far as I'm concerned." She wiped at her cheeks, sniffled, and started eating.

Teresa waited a few mouthfuls before asking, "How did you betray her back?"

"I told the Messengers of the Light where to find my

sister and the baby. I didn't know if they would care where she was or not, but apparently they did." Lory put her spoon down again. She nudged the still half-full bowl of oatmeal away. "I don't know what happened, but I do know my sister's daughter was gone, and her husband had been killed. And they, the Messengers, had disfigured her."

CHAPTER FORTY-EIGHT

Maggie sat at a table as far from Sally Opperheim as she could get. She sat with her back to the wall with a view of the entire playroom and pretended to draw with crayons.

Once again, Sally handed out the toys to the littler kids, sharing and grinning with that wide smile. As the day went on, she looked worse and worse. Her skin was like wax after it had melted and cooled a little and someone had reshaped it over her skull. Her eyes grew sunken and pale, as if the bright blue they'd been before had leaked away. Faded.

Ann had told Maggie to stay away from her, so she did. Even when Sally waved her over wanting to play. Maggie felt sort of bad for her. She played by herself in the corner with the only toy left. A wooden car with wobbly wheels. It had a string tied to the front. It looked homemade.

Sally sat on her knees, pulling the car back and forth by the string. Sometimes she drove it around behind her, but whenever she did, it was like she lost track of it. She had to really work to get it back around and would say *whoops* and laugh each time, her mouth never moving from that big smile.

Sally seemed perfectly satisfied playing with this old rickety toy. Before, she would have had all of the best toys hoarded around her. Every once in a while, something black dribbled out the corner of Sally's mouth, and she made a horrific slurp to suck it back in. She used the cuff of her shirt to dab at her face.

"Hey Maggie," Sally called in a thick and slow voice. "Want to play with this c-c-car with me?" The word came hacking out of her, like a stuck hair ball. Black spittle speckled her chin. She swallowed, her throat convulsing.

"No thanks." Maggie worked hard not to grimace.

Sally lifted her wrist and dabbed at her mouth. Her shirtsleeve was wet with inky fluid.

The day progressed this way. Every so often, Sally would try to get Maggie to come play with her. Once, she came closer to Maggie. Maggie cringed away from her, not because she was drippy but because her mark hurt when Sally came closer.

Maggie looked to the exit. She suddenly wondered if Ann was okay. Ann's mark hadn't been alerting her as usual, and Maggie's had changed.

I'm *supposed to protect* her *now*. She thought. *Or go to the abyss.*

Her mark throbbed a few times. She took it to mean yes from Sophia. There was no other reason for it that she could tell. It had to be Ann or Pinky. And one of them must be in trouble.

Or both of them.

Don't lose anyone else.

Return to the abyss.

She needed to get out of there.

A few minutes later, Not-Olivia unlocked and opened the back door so they could go out and play. Maggie knew

Not-Olivia would take a "ciggies break," because she always came back from recess and smelled bad. Only Olivia would be there to watch everyone.

Maggie had twenty minutes to figure out a plan and get out of there. Then she could find Ann and prove she could help so Ann would never have to send her back to this place ever again.

Sally tripped on her way out because her feet weren't operating correctly. Olivia ran to her side.

"Are you okay, Sally?"

"Yes," Sally said in that slow voice. She made the slurping sound.

"Your mom will be here to take you home soon, okay?"

"Oh . . . kay . . ."

Olivia turned to Not-Olivia. "Not sure why Mrs. Opperheim even brought her today. She's obviously sick." She wiped her hands on her pants.

Not-Olivia shrugged. "Some people don't care, I guess. I'm going out front." She waved her box of ciggies at Olivia.

Olivia held her elbows and gazed around, the corners of her mouth turned down, her eyebrows swooped upward toward the middle. She looked sad. Maggie was sad for her to see her like that. She wondered if it was because of her hair.

Maggie backed away from Olivia to the side of the building and ducked around it. A chain-link fence towered above her head, but Maggie had seen kids climb fences in movies before. It didn't look that hard.

She stuck the toe of one shoe into a hole and reached as high as she could. The wire cut into her hands, but she used her legs to boost herself up.

Climbing was a lot harder than it looked, and at the top,

she would have to figure out how to get over and down the other side.

"Maggie! What are you doing?" Olivia reached up and snagged Maggie by the legs. Maggie let go and fell into Olivia's arms. She slid to the ground. "What on earth?"

Maggie turned and tried to climb again, but Olivia stopped her again. Maggie let out a frustrated growl.

"Just let me go, please," she shouted, tears in her eyes. "I have to help her."

"Help who?" Olivia asked, holding Maggie's arms.

Maggie shook her head and wiped her cheeks.

"Is someone in trouble?" Olivia looked through the fence and back at Maggie.

Maggie shook her head and shrugged. She didn't know. But she had to make sure, and she needed to help Ann so Ann wouldn't get hurt. She pulled away from Olivia and stomped inside.

CHAPTER FORTY-NINE

Ann walked into Harmony Gifts and Apothecary. It was located in the same place where the Harmony Five and Dime used to sell cheap toys, dry goods, an assortment of things.

This store, however, held shelves and racks of Harmony-branded memorabilia. Drinkware, coasters, keychains, pens, candles encased in glass, postcards, T-shirts, hats—all with Harmony, Colorado, emblazoned across them along with a neat map of the town or an illustration of the mining bear on Harmony's welcome sign. She stepped farther into the store, and the tourist merchandise gave way to packs of tarot cards, bundles of sage, pendants, bowls with symbols carved on them, and candles of every color.

She'd dropped Maggie at the Daycare Place around eleven before heading to investigate the shop. Maggie didn't give Ann any problem about going to daycare that morning. Ann spoke to the redhead at the front, asking her to keep an eye on Maggie and make sure she stayed away from Sally Opperheim and vice versa.

"I'll do my best." She'd looked drawn and sad. Tired maybe? Ann didn't trust she'd do her best. All she could hope was that Maggie would listen to what Ann had told her and stay away from Sally Opperheim.

Ann wandered deeper into the store. A spice rack at the end of one aisle caught her attention. It had to be a joke, right? Eye of Newt? Come on. She was about to open the little jar when someone walked up behind her.

"Welcome to Harmony Gifts and Apothecary!"

Ann turned. The man's excited demeanor changed but came back quickly.

"Oh hi, Sheriff Logan." He cleared his throat. "What brings you in today?"

"I'm looking for a burn remedy." Ann had prepared ahead of time. The website mentioned homeopathic medicines made on site. "I've tried over-the-counter salves to no avail."

"For you or someone else?" the man asked. "I'm Paul, by the way." He held out his hand. "I don't think we've officially met in person like this before." He had a broad smile and dark, sparkling eyes. He was extremely cheery.

"Nice to meet you," Ann said. "It's for a child. She's seven."

"Children can be tricky," Paul said. "Sensitive skin, unknown allergies. Let me see what I can find for you." He went to a desk toward the front of the store and opened a book.

Ann wandered down the center aisle. Maggie had said Rachel's text talked about the back room of Paul's shop. She did her research that morning and found only one business license that had been granted in the past few months. It was for Harmony Gifts and Apothecary. The owner: Paul

Ramthorp. Patrina Ramthorp was listed on the license as well.

At the end of the aisle, Ann spotted a door off to the right with signs reading PRIVATE and EMPLOYEES ONLY. She glanced toward the front of the shop. A stack of books blocked Paul's line of sight. Ann opened the door and peeked inside.

It was a whole other room. A display of jewelry and a carousel of different postcards and brochures sat just inside. Ann slipped through the door.

One brochure talked about the Teresa Hart Tour. Every Tuesday and Thursday night at midnight! Join us at the town square.

Jesus H. Tony Cook-Robin was right. They'd been conducting a tour right under her nose.

Maybe it *was* time to move on from law enforcement. Let Duke take over as sheriff.

Except Duke wasn't really Duke anymore, was he? She wasn't one hundred percent sure, of course, but it made sense. His behavior the other night coupled with his humility on the phone . . .

Ann pulled one of the brochures out and folded it into her pocket. She moved to the jewelry rack. The pendants were some kind of clear resin encasing something brownish pink.

She pulled one from the display and held it up to the light. She turned to put it back on the hook.

Jewelry made from Teresa Hart's placenta.

Ann jumped back with a strangled sound lodged in her throat. It couldn't really be that, could it? It was a marketing scheme for the people drawn to town because of the case. It had to be. Ann backed away from the display and slipped back into the store proper.

"Oh, there you are," Paul said, coming around the corner a couple aisles down. "I found a recipe for a burn salve for children," he said. "It'll take me about an hour to mix it. Payment up front." He smiled. He smiled a lot. Ann searched his face for any sign of ill-fitting skin, but he looked like a normal guy. No black goo oozing from the corners of his lips. His skin fit correctly, sagging in the right places for a guy who was a touch overweight.

Ann paid Paul and left the shop.

CHAPTER FIFTY

After breakfast and the illuminating conversation with Lory in which she'd divulged a few more secrets, Teresa had played with Cassie and Amanda, helping them to stand. They'd be taking their first steps soon. With their rapid development, she hadn't spent much time helping them learn the skills they ought to in order to be in the top percentile for their ages. She'd missed tummy time completely, as well as any attempts to crawl.

A part of her was saddened by how quickly they were growing. They'd be a year old after just one more Logismoi.

The only thing she was happy to miss was the teething. So far, they'd been quiet, happy babies. All throughout her pregnancy, she'd been worried about postpartum depression and about what had happened with Tiffany.

It was the crying that did it.

Now, Cassie's wings flapped as she hopped on the mattress. Sleep clung to Teresa's brain, trying to drag her back down into its depths. She sat up.

It was four in the afternoon. She'd slept for three hours. They'd all slept for three hours.

Cassie crawled over on all fours and climbed onto Teresa's lap.

"You're getting quite heavy." She got up, lifting Cassie with her, and put the little gargoyle on top of the dresser. Teresa donned her wig and put on some eyeliner and mascara. Not the heavy cat eye like before. Something a little more sensible.

After checking on Amanda, Teresa opened the door and lowered Cassie to the floor. The little gargoyle leaped down the hall to the back door.

Out in the late afternoon air, Teresa took a deep breath. The fresh air helped her wake up a little.

Teresa followed Cassie into the woods. It was too light out to see the lost souls, but she still thought of them. She wondered if this was where the black clouds went. Did they become those pretty green lights? Blast through the window and out into the woods to join their brethren in their lostness?

Out on the road, Cassie veered to the right into town as usual. She didn't ride high like she did in the dark of night. Teresa gazed upward, watching her daughter float across the treetops. She moved with such grace.

Teresa felt more like herself in a pair of mom jeans and a button-down shirt. The little black dress had made her act, well, slutty.

They reached the town square—a roundabout that branched off like a compass rose.

A man across it waved. "Nice afternoon for a walk," he called.

"It is. Have a good one." Teresa waited for him to walk away before looking up. She didn't see Cassie right away, but then her daughter's winged form—looking very much like a giant bat—took flight again from the tree tops overhead.

They went to the left and back into the woods to the old residential district.

Cassie landed in the driveway of a familiar house, and Teresa halted. She gulped. It was Sheriff McMichael's house. Even though Teresa knew Olivia and Hunter now lived there—well, only Olivia now—she couldn't help but feel a cold trickle of fear along her spine. Then she gasped as it dawned on her. Olivia must be next. A small measure of sadness came to her. She'd felt a momentary kinship with the girl last night. But her infidelity to her husband, despite how horrible he was—well, she deserved what she got.

Teresa went to the front door and pressed her ear against it. Muffled voices spoke within. She crouched, holding Cassie's little clawed hand to keep her near, and tried the knob. The door opened.

A laughing scream came from within the house. Teresa frowned. Apparently Olivia had gotten over her grief. Paul's familiar voice said something after the laughter stopped.

Teresa kept low and crept inside. Cassie crawled along beside her.

A light from the living room cast a warm glow over the two figures at the dining room table. On her back, Olivia lay on the table top with her legs spread wide. Paul stood between them, hips pumping away, completely oblivious to the pending interruption.

Teresa stood. Olivia screamed and grabbed the nearest thing to cover herself—Paul's arm.

"It's her, Teresa's here, she's going to—"

"Yeah, yeah, that's good. She's going to rip our eyes out. Yeah." His pumping doubled in speed.

"Paul," Teresa said.

Paul looked over his shoulder and did a double take. He jumped back and covered himself futilely with his hands. Olivia scrambled to the far edge of the table, casting around. She found a T-shirt and pulled it over her head, mussing her spiky hair.

Cassie gripped Teresa's calf. Teresa looked down at her. She had her thumb in her mouth and held Teresa's leg like a shy little child.

"Which one?" Teresa asked Cassie.

"I'm willing. I'm willing." Paul raised his hand. "Please. Let it be me. I'll be a necessary sacrifice. Like—like Hunter!"

Olivia let out an appalled sound and glared at him.

Cassie looked up at Teresa, pulled her thumb out of her mouth, and pointed at Paul, who let out a sort of strangled-surprised sound. He took a step backward, despite his apparent excitement to be next.

Cassie didn't put her thumb back in her mouth, though. She moved her finger in a sweeping arc to point at Olivia. Olivia screamed.

Both. Two for one. Like a goddamn *shoe sale*.

Cassie launched at Paul. He laughed and caught her. They toppled backward.

Teresa advanced on Olivia. A stack of opened mail sat on the table. A letter opener gleamed from a pile of ripped envelopes. Teresa grabbed it.

Olivia backed away, hands held up in front of her.

"Please, Teresa. I'm pregnant."

Teresa looked Olivia up and down. She wore Paul's T-shirt and nothing else. Her naked legs trembled.

"You cheated on your husband," Teresa said.

Just like Mother.

She lashed out with the letter opener, but Olivia dodged to the side and shoved Teresa. Teresa sprawled onto the table, scattering the mail every which way. She spun around.

Olivia took off out the front door, running barefoot.

Teresa took chase, sneakers crunching on the gravel. Olivia reminded Teresa of women in horror movies who don't watch where they're going. The dumb bimbo who trips and falls repeatedly, who can't help but emit a high-pitched scream every so often like a homing beacon. Teresa gained on Olivia both times she fell. The second time she got up, she ran aimlessly into the woods.

Teresa lost sight of her, but then a blood-curdling scream ripped the air.

She found Olivia cowering on the ground on her backside in front of Hunter, her shirt hiked up to her waist, bare butt on the ground. Her feet bled.

"We can raise the baby together, Olivia." Hunter's voice was lower and gravelly. His mouth didn't move. It just hung open. Black ooze dripped from it.

"Hunter? Hunter?" Each time she said his name, her voice became shriller. It hurt Teresa's ears.

Hunter was a big man. Teresa thought so every time she saw him stand up and move around. Even more so the night before when Cassie'd snatched his eyes out.

He reached a hand down toward Olivia.

"Hunter? How—your eyes—" Olivia stammered. She placed her hand in his, just the tips of her fingers. He gripped them and pulled her to her feet.

His mouth closed and stretched into an impossibly wide grin. His skin wasn't snug against his bones like it was before, with his chiseled jawline and T-shirt stretched across his chest.

It suddenly dawned on Teresa. The black cloud had gone into the bushes where they'd hidden Hunter. It must have something to do with his ambulatory state.

"I'm sorry I said I hated your hair." Hunter stroked the side of Oliva's face.

Olivia turned around and saw Teresa. She screamed and jumped behind him.

Hunter looked up, eyes intent on Teresa. He backed away from her. Olivia moved with him.

"She's mine," Teresa growled. "Give her to me."

Hunter reached behind his back and pulled Olivia out by the arm. He flung her forward. She let out a surprised cry and fell to the ground, bare butt in the air.

"I'm patient. I can be kind," Hunter said. Teresa realized he was talking to Olivia. "I can raise the baby as my own. I can tell people the baby is mine." His words weren't pleading, they were just stated like facts. "I am patient."

Teresa took a step toward Olivia. Hunter took a step back, lifting his hands, his shoulders hunching protectively around his ears. He curled in on himself, but that smile remained.

Olivia flailed her arms and kicked her legs. She got to her feet and ran back to Hunter.

"Hold her," Teresa said.

He wrapped his arms around Olivia and leaned his cheek against the top of her head. "We will raise the baby together," he whispered through his smiling teeth. "I will be patient and kind and loving. I love your hair. I think it is cute and edgy, like Paul said."

Olivia cried and struggled in Hunter's arms. Tears ran down her fear-distorted cheeks.

Teresa still held the letter opener. Hunter squeezed Olivia tighter. He closed his eyes, trembling against Olivia.

"Hunter, please let me go." Olivia's voice was barely audible, it quavered so much.

Teresa did it fast. She jabbed the letter opener into Olivia's left eye, then her right, effectively blinding her. She screamed bloody murder. Hunter moved his hand to cover her mouth. He shushed her like he was trying to calm her down.

Teresa levered the implement under the eyeballs and dug them out the rest of the way with her fingers. Black liquid poured out of Olivia's eye sockets, a stark contrast to her porcelain skin. The soul glimmered inside.

Teresa slurped. She was pleased to find it didn't taste as horrible as the others. It had a rosewater flavor with a tinge of saltiness. The aftertaste, however, was musky. Like—she covered her mouth—like the smell of sex.

The moment the deed was done, Hunter released Olivia and backed away into the dark woods. His footsteps crashed away through the brush.

Teresa wiped her mouth on the back of her hand and adjusted her wig. There was still Paul. Her belly ached with fullness, but she couldn't waste him.

She hurried back to Olivia's house.

Cassie perched on the table where Teresa had found them fornicating, playing with one of his eyes. She gripped it in her hand, squeezed it until it popped up into the air, and caught it again. She purred.

Paul's body lay still. The soul glistened in his sockets. She wondered what he would taste like and hoped it wasn't awful. Her stomach ached.

She bent over him.

"I'm willing," he whispered.

Teresa jumped back with a scream.

"He's alive?"

Cassie turned and lifted one shoulder.

"I'm a willing sacrifice," his lips whispered.

Teresa bent over him and looked into his empty sockets. The soul rose to meet her lips. She opened her mouth and slurped it.

The flavor of black licorice with a handful of various flavored chips filled her mouth. The dill pickle potato chip flavor at the end almost did her in. She covered her mouth and sat in a chair next to Paul's naked torso. Olivia's discarded skirt covered his necessary parts.

Cassie still played with the eyeball. It made a sick sucking sound each time she squeezed it.

Teresa put her head on her folded hands and counted. Paul was number seven.

Yaldabaoth's voice laughed. That sadistic and sensual laugh that sent thrills and chills alike throughout her body.

Teresa's stomach roiled with acid.

Heat spread over her, through her, starting from the pit of her stomach. It had been a long time since she'd drank brown liquor, but she would never forget how it felt when she did. How it burned all the way down into her belly. That's how this felt. Only instead of whiskey, it had to be pure fire, and it burned up her throat. She thought she would vomit, but the fire surged out across her shoulders, down her arms. It spread from her sour gut down to her womanhood to her thighs to her feet.

Yaldabaoth's voice chuckled in a sickening echo, pricking her scalp.

Seven bloods, seven souls.

Goosebumps broke out over her body, despite the heat coursing inside.

Seven? No. Not seven. Not this time. It was supposed to be eight.

Her skin ignited. She lifted her head. Her veins glowed with red-white light. Like they did that night she'd injected the zoe into her leg to get past Ruthie and Sheriff McMichael and Derrick. The night of her babies' conception. The night of Yaldabaoth's betrayal.

The glow intensified, as did the heat. It burned. It seared. She cried out and ran to the bathroom, desperate to douse her body in cold water.

She turned on the shower and caught sight of herself in the mirror.

Her right eye glowed gold along with the red of her skin. She looked like she was made of heated metal. Teresa jumped in the shower under the cold water, but still her skin, her bones, her muscles, everything burned.

She screamed.

Cassie peeked around the edge of the curtain and held the eyeball out to her.

"No," Teresa growled, her voice savage and deep. "I don't want your eyeball."

Cassie cringed behind the doorjamb.

"What's happening to me?" Teresa moaned.

A sacrifice. A vessel. You are mine. I am yours. Yaldabaoth's voice again, outside of her and inside of her at once. She'd never heard those words before. "Bound together as one. Seven bloods. Seven souls. The mother-father of the Children of Chaos."

"No." The word ripped out of her. She clawed her way out of the shower. No. No it couldn't be.

The burn in her skin began to lessen. The glow diminished. Her right eye no longer glowed, but it remained yellow.

Like a lion's eye.

Like Yaldabaoth's eyes.

I am here within you. The sensation in her scalp when his voice traveled through her mind, trickled down to her breasts, to her stomach. Lower. *Together we shall rule.*

"No," Teresa shouted. She snatched a metal nail file from the countertop and held it near her eye. She had to dig it out. If she dug it out, he would go with it.

Her hand refused to move. Was he controlling it? No. It was her own weak will unable to force her hand to harm herself. She threw the file against the shower wall and glared into the mirror.

"I have harnessed *you*," Teresa growled through her teeth at her reflection. She looked into that yellow eye. "*I* am in control of *you*." Spittle spackled the mirror. "You have *no* power over me. *I* have power over *you*."

She tore away from the mirror, unable to look at that yellow eye any longer.

Outside, Teresa stumbled along after Cassie, feeling half drunk and twice full, with a dull ache all over her body like her skin was dry and itchy on the inside. Twice she had to stop and lean against a tree. They went through the woods and finally came to the dirt road. Cassie crossed over into the old cemetery.

At Lory's house, Teresa quickly took the wig off and lifted Amanda. She hoped nursing her would ease the tightness of her belly.

CHAPTER FIFTY-ONE

Ann flung the door to the station open and charged inside. Pinky ran in with her ears back, bypassed Rachel and Sully, and scampered to Ann's office. Sully looked up from some paperwork on his desk. Rachel jumped to her feet.

"Are either of you aware of a secret tour that happens *every Tuesday and Thursday* night?" she shouted.

Ann flung the brochure for the tour on the nearest desk and stabbed it with her finger. She glared at Sully. He said he'd only stopped patrolling *lately*, but it would appear he hadn't been doing it for a while.

Sully picked up the brochure and stood. He cleared his throat, looked resolute.

"When I signed on with you, Sheriff, I told you I would work hard to serve and protect this community. I told you I would do whatever it takes to keep this town safe."

Ann crossed her arms.

"I have been working morning till night seven days a week. Cindy backs me up when I can't be around, but Sheriff, Ann, everyone has a breaking point."

Ann lowered her arms.

"I have been operating on four hours or less of sleep a night. Sometimes I go on patrol in the middle of the day so I can get a couple extra minutes in. I don't think you meant for it to be this way. I fully believe we were to share the schedule and switch weeks for night patrol, but something happened about a month ago, and it seems I took everything on."

Ann felt her face flush. She swallowed hard. School ended about a month ago. That's what happened. "Sully—I'm—"

He held up his big hands. "No. Don't apologize. I had every right and every duty to stand up for myself and tell you what was going on. The truth is, I stopped doing night patrols three months ago. I kept it from you because I didn't want to burden you with this. I know things have been tough for you for a while. I can't imagine what balancing a kid is like along with a demanding job, so I did all I could until I couldn't." He plowed onward. "It started as one night a week, then two, then three. Nothing bad ever happened, so three became seven just like that." He snapped his fingers. "I just stopped doing it. I have no excuse to give. I shirked my duties." Sully removed his badge from the front of his uniform and unholstered his gun.

"Do not put those on this desk unless you mean it." Ann held up her hand in a halting gesture.

Sully paused.

Ann smoothed her fingers over her eyebrow. She sighed. "You have gone above and beyond for this department." She cleared her throat and moved so she could address both Sully and Rachel. "I have leaned heavily on both of you. Asking you, Rachel, to babysit and not even paying you to do it." She took a deep breath. "I haven't been pulling my own weight around here."

"You have Maggie to care for," Rachel blurted with a knowing look in her eyes. Ann understood she likely meant Sophia.

Ann stopped her from saying more. "That isn't an excuse. Plenty of people raise children alone. I just don't know how to do it." And she didn't trust just anyone with Maggie. Not after Maggie's own grandfather had betrayed her. "I don't know if I'm cut out for any of this anymore, actually." She let out a mirthless laugh.

"Of course, you are," Rachel said in a soft voice.

"Teresa Hart is on the loose, and we have people popping up sick with some weird disease that I think is linked to her—again." Ann looked at Rachel then at Sully.

"Care to explain what that means?" Sully asked.

Ann motioned for Sully to follow her to her office. They settled in chairs across the desk from each other. Rachel stood in the doorway, leaning against the frame. Ann filled him in on everything that had happened in October. From seeing the vision of Maggie in a clearing in Salida, to Maggie's somewhat sentient book, to the missing persons turned homicides, the bodies in the woods, and how it all wrapped up nice and not-so-tidy in the underworld of the Bible's secret texts where she found her inner strength to defeat Yaldabaoth.

Sully listened with rapt attention. When she finished telling the sordid tale, an hour had passed. Rachel had moved to the other chair in front of Ann's desk. Sully didn't say a word for a few long seconds. He looked at Rachel, who gave him a shrug and raised eyebrows, then back to Ann.

"You think these sick kids are because of Teresa Hart?" he asked.

"Fairly certain." Her voice came out small.

Sully rapped his knuckles on the desk and pulled his

lips into a thin straight line. He looked at Rachel again who nodded.

"You saw Glory in the woods, Sully," Ann said. "I know you tried to justify it or explain it away with drugs or something else. I would have done the same a year ago."

"And this book. It *tells* you what's going on?"

Ann lifted a shoulder. "In its cryptic way, yes."

"So, what has it said about what's going on?" He swallowed hard. "This time, I mean."

Ann started with the passage they learned at the bank, and when she reached the end with what she'd read the previous night, Rachel sat back and looked at her hands in her lap. Her cell phone beeped.

Which reminded Ann that Rachel had been texting Patrina.

"What is your relationship with Patrina Ramthorp?" Ann nodded toward the phone in Rachel's hand. "That's her texting you, isn't it? Maggie told me what happened." Ann rose from her chair. "Are you aware her brother, Paul, has necklaces in his gift shop made from Teresa Hart's placenta?"

Rachel held her hands out, palms forward, face shocked. She paused and cocked her head. "Ew, really?"

"Sully, cuff her. She's under arrest for harboring a known fugitive."

"Let her explain—"

"I trusted you with Maggie," Ann said through her teeth. "How could you do this to us?" She turned to Sully. "Cuff her. Now. And take her to the holding cell."

"I know where she is." Rachel's voice came out high and panicked. "I know where Teresa is." Tears spilled out of her eyes.

"Where is she?" Ann asked.

"She's at Lory Magan's house. That's where—" she sucked in a gasping breath. Her face crumpled. She covered it with both hands. "That's where we meet . . . to talk about the tour."

Like a book club. How quaint.

"I trusted you with Maggie. You were the *only one*, Rachel. The only one I *ever* trusted here." Ann stopped talking. The anger building up behind her eyes pushed the tears out.

She sat heavily in her desk chair. Pinky jumped off the couch and came over to her, the tip of her tail wagging. Ann bent over and pressed her forehead to Pinky's.

"Sorry, Rachel." Sully's cuffs clinked, then ratcheted shut. Rachel didn't resist. Ann peeked at her. Rachel kept her eyes downcast. Tears continued to drip down her cheeks as Sully led her to the holding cell.

Ann followed them back. After Sully closed the door and locked it, Ann gripped the bars.

"What were you thinking? Who are you? What the fuck is going on?" She knew her questions weren't exactly professional. She took a deep breath.

"I'm sorry, Ann. I don't know what I was thinking. After Sheriff McMichael, I just . . . I don't know . . . I was close to him and his wife Lisa. They were like family to me."

Frank and Lisa McMichael had been family to Ann, too, before she left. She didn't realize Rachel had been so close to them. It made sense, though. Rachel had taken McMichael's death pretty hard last year. She even took his cat—Remy—home with her.

"I guess I wanted to just understand her more. Why would she take lives like that? How she *could*—I wanted answers."

Ann softened her tone. "Is Lory Magan dangerous?"

Rachel shook her head.

"What does she want from Teresa?"

Rachel shook her head again. "I don't know."

"What do you all meet about?" Frustration began to creep into Ann's jaw. She asked the question through her teeth.

"We usually just meet up and talk about the case and how to make the tour more exciting. And then Teresa showed up." Rachel lifted her hands and gripped the bars near Ann's hands. "I'm so sorry. I should have told you the second she showed up."

"Did you tell them *anything* about Maggie?" Ann asked in a low voice.

"No," Rachel blurted. "They know I babysit the sheriff's kid sometimes. I mostly just went and listened in and-and-and tried to make sense of it all." She slumped onto the bench in the cell. "I'm so stupid."

Ann left Rachel to stew in her self-inflicted self-loathing. She needed to go to Lory's house. She needed to search it top to bottom. Teresa Hart was there. She was responsible for what was going on. Responsible for the people—

Ann paused in the hallway. A scratching came from the bullpen.

Cindy, who must have come in during the share-it-all session, stood facing the wall. Every once in a while, she hefted her arm. Her hand flopped up and smacked against the wall, then dragged down, fingernail scraping the plaster. A spider clung to the wall just out of reach. Black sludge dripped from her open mouth and plopped onto the floor.

Pinky growled at Ann's side.

"Jesus Christ," Sully shouted. He wasn't one to use profanity of any sort, certainly not the Lord's name in vain.

He rushed around the bullpen desks toward her but halted. "No, not you. Not you. Please." He reached for her, and Ann couldn't help but see the pain that crossed his face at the sight of her. He pulled his hand back and covered his mouth.

"Cindy?" Ann tried to get her attention. "You okay?"

Cindy didn't respond.

Ann searched her mind for which pair Cindy could be. She'd been a hard worker, but now she was—

Lazy. Sloth. "Idleness?" Ann guessed, remembering the pair from the poem.

Cindy froze. She stood there for a couple of beats, then turned around an inch at a time until she faced Ann. Her skin sloped sideways off her face, exposing bone underneath. The skin seemed to pile up on her shoulder like drips of wax from a candlestick.

"Sully!" Ann shouted. She didn't know what to do. "Call an ambulance." Or did they need a priest? The Logismoi were demons, were they not?

As if on cue, Cindy vomited black bile all over the floor before collapsing headlong into it.

CHAPTER FIFTY-TWO

Maggie sat at a table by herself the rest of the day. Sally had gone home after recess, and Olivia had gone home early, too. Before she left, Maggie had heard Olivia and Not-Olivia yelling. Not-Olivia shouted at Olivia that she couldn't just leave to go see her *boyfriend* in the middle of the day. Olivia said that's not what she was doing. She had said she didn't feel well. Not-Olivia had yelled they could get shut down for not having enough adults on the premises. Olivia must not have cared, because she left anyway.

It was almost 5:30, and at 5:30, most of the parents arrived, and when the parents arrived, it got crazy. Kids ran around screaming while their parents or other guardians tried to wrangle them. For some reason, the other kids never wanted to go home when their parents showed up. Even the ones who cried every morning when their parents left them.

They didn't know the first thing about being left behind. Or, rather, taken away.

Maggie sighed and watched the second hand tick around the clock face.

The first parents arrived a couple minutes early. It

wasn't crazy enough yet. She waited until more arrived at the same time, hoping the rest would all show up at once.

Not-Olivia saw them out. A few minutes later, more parents or guardians showed up. This was her chance.

While Not-Olivia helped the kids gather their things, Maggie went to the book on the counter, found her name, and signed herself out, copying Ann's signature as best she could. She slipped out between two adults. One of them grabbed her by the shoulder.

"Hey, there, where are you going?" the man asked.

"My mom's out front," Maggie said, hoping and hoping he didn't recognize her as The Sheriff's Kid. Maggie tore out of his grip and ran to the door and out into the early evening.

She wasn't sure where to go, but she needed to stop whatever was going on before Ann got too involved and got hurt.

That morning, before Ann dropped her off, Maggie had asked her what she was doing today, and if it was dangerous. She had that tight panicky feeling in her chest again. Ann told her she was just checking out a few places in town to ask some questions, catch up on some paperwork. Ann had spoken in short, quick sentences, a way she talked when things were starting to get to be too much. Maggie had learned small details like that. Ann told her one time she would be a good detective.

"You did the right thing telling me about Rachel's texts," Ann had said, her voice softening. She'd given Maggie a pat on the head like she was a good dog. She had patted Pinky on the head right after in the same way.

Maggie figured Ann was probably somewhere to do with Patrina or LMCM.

"Where should I go?" Maggie whispered. "I need to

stop this." Whatever *this* might be. She danced from foot to foot trying to decide.

"Magdalena?" a woman's voice called. "Is that you?"

Maggie knew who it was before she turned. She would never forget that voice.

From the opposite side of the street, the woman shrieked with delight, holding her hands up to her face. One side of it was melted with some sort of scar. The other, though, was just as Maggie remembered.

The woman had long black hair. It framed her face like curtains. She was older than the other mothers she knew back in Nag Hammadi, but prettier than all of them. She didn't have that scar last time Maggie had seen her.

"*Ami?*" Maggie's vision tunneled like she was looking through a paper towel tube pretending it was a telescope. A wave of dizziness washed over her. "Mama?"

Maggie knew the truth about her parents. It wasn't what her baba had told her. He gave her a lie to help her feel better about leaving them. He'd told her they were dead, but Maggie was old enough when she was taken from them to remember the chaos and terror. Baba pulling her away from her parents. Her mother's hands reaching for her, her nails scratching the backs of her hands.

Hearing her mom's voice call her name, and that shriek, brought back a scrap of memory from that day she'd forgotten until now.

Her mother screaming, "She is Sophia! We must give her to them."

Maggie didn't realize, but it was the last time she'd heard her mother's voice.

Her mom looked both ways and stepped into the street.

Maggie ran away toward the town center and the roundabout. She ran without knowing where to go, but just to get away. She reached the square—which was actually a circle—and made a fast decision to lead her mom away from Forest Parkway where the sheriff's station was. Away from there and away from Ann, just in case she was part of something bad that might get Ann into trouble and hurt or worse.

Her mother called after her, begging her to wait, but Maggie knew better. Maggie sprinted as fast as she could. She darted into the woods. She could lose her mother there. Hide somewhere and wait.

The sun disappeared behind a thick cloud, darkening the area inside the dense forest even more. She dodged tree trunks and jumped over bushes. She didn't recognize where she was until she saw toppled grave markers. The abandoned funeral home loomed in the distance.

CHAPTER FIFTY-THREE

No pulse. She's not breathing.

Sully's voice in her head, repeating over and over.

She's dead.

She lost another deputy. Sully's hands slick with that black substance.

"Go wash that stuff off," Ann shouted at him, in case it was contagious. "Goddammit Cindy."

She helped Sully get Cindy's body into a body bag and called the coroner, who, of course, was not in at the moment. Ann had done a few things for Harmony since she became sheriff, but they still had a lack of resources.

"What's going on?" Rachel called from the holding cell at the back of the station.

A feeling of overwhelm encroached on Ann's chest, squeezing her lungs until they burned. Things were piling up and she couldn't get a handle on any of it.

"I have to get Maggie from daycare," Ann said in a low voice to Sully. She was ashamed. Ashamed she had to leave him with the mess on the floor. The mess of the woman he cared for.

"I'm sorry, Sully. About Cindy." She patted him on the shoulder and left.

After loading Pinky into the truck, Ann climbed in and beat the steering wheel with her fists.

Pinky whined and nosed her armpit. Ann put her arms around the sturdy dog, comforted by her scent and the warmth and strength of her.

"You're a good dog, Pinky," Ann said. "I don't tell you that enough." She patted Pinky's head, put the truck in reverse, and drove to get Maggie.

The windows of the Daycare Place were dark, and the front door was locked when Ann arrived. She jerked on the handles and let out a frustrated yell before panic pounded in her chest.

She dialed the phone number, but no one picked up. Her vision swam. Maggie was gone. Maggie was fucking gone.

"Goddammit. I was fifteen minutes late." They would have called her, wouldn't they? They would have called her if someone tried to pick Maggie up who wasn't authorized. The only authorized people were herself and Rachel. And Rachel was locked up in the holding cell.

"Pinky," Ann shouted, her voice cracking. She opened the truck door. "Pinky." Her voice was high and tight with desperation. "Find Maggie."

Pinky bellowed and leaped out of the truck. She took off. Ann ran after her.

Running was her thing. Or it had been. She hadn't been out for a good hard run in a while.

I'm off my game in every way, she thought. *I should have just given this job to Duke when he first showed up.* Even citizens of her own town were ready for someone new.

Pinky sprinted off into the distance.

"Pinky!" Ann shouted after her. "Wait!"

Pinky didn't listen.

So many things she should have done differently. She should have been rational. She should have strapped Pinky's vest on with the body cam and tracker. Or a leash at the very least. She shouldn't have trusted Mountain View to hold Teresa. Should have had her transferred somewhere with higher security, better tech, somewhere not right outside Harmony, instead of keeping her close in order to check in on her from time to time. She should have never trusted Rachel.

She should have never come back.

"Then humanity would be gone." Ann picked up her pace and kept running in the direction Pinky had gone, hoping she could catch up to the dog, and if she didn't—

Don't think about that.

At the roundabout, Ann paused and doubled over, hands on her knees. Pinky was nowhere to be seen. She couldn't even hear the jangle of the dog's tags.

CHAPTER FIFTY-FOUR

Maggie ran to the backside of the abandoned funeral home and crouched in the shadows between an overgrown bush and a rusty barrel.

Her breath came in sharp bursts, and she worked hard to take a few deep inhales.

Ann would be so mad at her. She would be so mad Maggie couldn't even think about it. But it had to be this way. Sophia was the one to stop it. The book said so.

Maggie pressed her back against the old house, hoping there weren't spiders. Even if there were, she would rather deal with spiders on her than her mother. Maggie wiped her hands on her pants, all at once feeling her mom's tight and desperate grip on her. If only that grip had been to keep Maggie near. Not to give her to the Messengers of the Light.

"Maggie?" her mom's voice called from somewhere nearby. "Maggie please come back. Please come to me, my girl."

I'm not your girl anymore.

Footsteps crunched through the bushes, snapping twigs. They were slow and hesitant.

Maggie huddled deeper into the shadows, but she felt like anyone could see her. She wasn't hiding well enough. She peeked around the edge of the bush, then around the edge of the barrel. She didn't see anyone. She got her feet under her in a squat.

On the count of three . . .

She counted to three and took off into the woods, straight away from the side of the funeral home.

"Maggie!" her mother called.

Maggie didn't stop. She didn't look over her shoulder. Ann told her once that you couldn't see in front of you if you were looking behind.

She came to a ditch. A deep ditch. It had a different name, but she couldn't think of the word. She slid down mostly on her butt with one leg extended. The bottom was covered in rocks and pine needles that muffled her footsteps as she followed it to the left.

She could barely hear her mother calling her name over something crashing through the bushes behind. Maggie ducked down behind a fallen log and pushed herself partially under it. She squeezed her eyes closed as dirt fell in her face.

"Please, please, please," she mouthed the words. The sounds grew louder. A cold nose snuffled her ear.

Maggie shrieked, then clamped her lips shut and grabbed Pinky's ears.

"Pinky, oh Pinky," she whispered into the dog's fur, gripping the loose skin of her neck. Tears leaked from her eyes. She gripped Pinky's face and looked into her amber eyes. "I think I messed up."

CHAPTER FIFTY-FIVE

The black cloud blasted out of Cassie shortly after Teresa finished nursing them. As if the sheer volume had been too much for her, too.

It came in two parts. The first one blasted out so fast and fierce it knocked her backwards. Her legs kicked and her little arms flailed.

Teresa opened the window and let it out, then rushed to Cassie's side.

"Are you okay?"

The second one slammed into Teresa's face, knocking *her* backward. It stung, like a thousand bees with their stingers pointing at her. She grabbed her face.

The clouds vanished out the window. Teresa touched her cheeks. They didn't seem to be bleeding or cut or anything. Cassie and Amanda were both four months older. Fourteen months now.

She gathered Cassie into her arms, blinking back tears. Amanda crawled over to her and gripped her shirt to stand. She bent her little knees and bounced.

"Chashy," Amanda said. Cassie looked at her. She bent her legs and bounced and giggled with delight. "Yump."

Teresa gasped a sob and covered her mouth.

"Mama." Cassie patted Teresa's face. "Mama, eye." Cassie pointed at her own eye.

Teresa knew Cassie was talking about the yellow eye. She took a deep breath, swallowed the tears and grief for the lost months of nurturing and caring for helpless babies, raising them, teaching them.

"That's your father." Teresa lifted her chin. "That's all he gets. One eye."

Teresa couldn't believe she had almost stabbed herself in that eye. It probably wouldn't have even done any good. Yaldabaoth had his ways. This was his way to prove to her he had some shred of power. But he had no power over her. She was the vessel. Louise *had* said something about this. He was essentially allowed in the material world *because* of her.

Cassie looked at Amanda who still bounced, gripping the shoulder of Teresa's shirt in her chubby fist and giggling with glee. The only way to tell the two of them apart, now that Amanda had caught up to Cassie in size and weight, was the mark on Amanda's neck. The mark of Yaldabaoth.

Teresa wondered if he would one day have power over her as well.

Lory burst into the room. "To the basement. Quick."

She helped Teresa gather the babies, one in each arm. They were heavy. Their weight pleasant. And the strength she'd gained after each soul helped her hold them tight.

Yaldabaoth's power, she thought with a frown. She carefully made her way down the stairs while Lory closed the door behind her.

CHAPTER FIFTY-SIX

"Pinky," Ann called. She listened for the jingling of Pinky's collar tags. "Pinky, come!"

Nothing. The sun disappeared behind King Mountain. The days were shorter in Harmony because of that peak.

"No need to apologize," Duke's voice said from behind her.

Ann whirled around.

He stood in the middle of the street that led to the library and Maggie's elementary school. It also led to Lory's house if she took the partially hidden trail off the sidewalk.

That's where she needed to go. Lory's house. Apprehend Teresa. Get her put back where she belonged—

She needed to find Maggie.

"Did you see Maggie run by here?" Ann asked Duke, unable to keep the hope out of her voice.

Duke didn't respond. He just stood there, still. A breeze came through and wafted his scent toward her.

He no longer wore cologne. He smelled like semen. That strange musky chlorine smell.

"Duke?" Ann took a step closer.

In the fading light, his skin had a sickly pallor. Sweat beaded on his forehead and upper lip, and a roll of loose skin puddled at the base of his neck.

Black fluid trickled from his mouth. He slurped. The front of his shirt was stained with it.

"Damn," she whispered.

"No need to apologize," he said again.

"I'm not."

"But you were going to."

Ann stepped to the side to pass him, but his arm shot out. He grabbed the front of her shirt, bunching it in his thick fist. His scent made her gag.

"We wait," he whispered through his wide smile. "We wait to lend the suffering."

Ann grabbed his hand, dug her thumb between his metatarsals, and twisted. Duke's wrist bent sideways, then twisted completely around before he let go of her shirt. She didn't even feel any bones. It was as if he had no substance inside that skin.

Ann pushed past him and halted.

The redhead from Maggie's daycare, Paul from the apothecary, a big guy she didn't know, the girl who must be Sally, and Glory all stood in a row blocking the way to Lory's house.

They didn't make any move toward her, but she could see the labor of their breaths in the movement of their shoulders.

A sickly smacking came from behind her. She glanced over her shoulder. Cindy dragged herself along the ground. The body bag she and Sully had zipped her into stuck to her legs.

Duke bent to help Cindy. He gripped her under the floppy skin of her armpit. She dangled to the side like a rag doll.

She didn't have a pulse. She was dead.

There were seven. Teresa had been busy.

With Pinky off to find Maggie—Ann knew Pinky would cross the ocean to find her girl—Ann felt she could sort of focus on stopping Teresa from getting the eighth Logismoi. To do that, she needed to get to Lory's house, but the seven blocked her way. Two of them were hulking males, probably weighing around 250 pounds each. Duke and the other guy. Paul was no featherweight either.

Maybe they were slow. Cindy was slow. Cindy would slow Duke down, too, tucked under his arm like a giant football.

Ann really only had to contend with the other five.

She plotted her course through them and took off at a sprinter's pace, ducking and dodging defensively. A heavy weight tackled her. She plummeted to the ground.

His loose flesh sagged around her with the impact before it sprang back to normal human shape. His stench permeated the air. He smelled like heat. There was no other way to describe it. Ann's eyes watered with the odor. The weight of him lifted off of her, but he kept a grip on her arm. He pulled her to her feet effortlessly.

"We wait to lend the suffering." He started walking, pulling Ann along behind him. She wrenched and struggled, but his grip only tightened. She tried maneuvering to gain leverage to twist his arm, but it did no good. He kept hold. The black fluid dripped from the corners of his mouth. He didn't even try to slurp it back. It just dribbled down his chin onto his shirt.

The others followed behind.

The only reason she stopped trying to get away was because they turned off the sidewalk down the semi-hidden path to Lory's house.

CHAPTER FIFTY-SEVEN

In the clearing at the front of Lory's house, the thing shoved Ann forward. She stumbled and fell onto all fours. She jumped to her feet and whirled around, ready to defend herself. The seven just stood there.

Ann backed away from them and stumbled up the few steps to Lory's front door.

She banged on it with the side of her fist.

Lory appeared, breathless. She swiped a hair off her forehead.

"Oh, hello Sheriff—"

Ann shoved her way inside. Lory fell against the door, but righted herself. Ann turned and peered out past Lory.

The seven were gone. For a second, she wondered if she was going crazy. But no. She could no longer explain away things with stressed hallucinations like she had tried to in the past. She'd seen Duke. She'd heard him. She'd felt him and that other man touch her. The dampness of his soft flesh—she could still feel it on her wrist. Could still smell them.

"Close the door," Ann said, in case they were lurking in

the shadows. Lory closed it. Ann rushed to the window and peered out.

"You didn't see them?" Ann asked. "Before they left?"

"See whom?"

"The . . . I don't know . . ." Ann turned. She held her fingers to her forehead.

"What's going on?" Lory asked, eyes wide with alarm.

"I don't know." The Logismoi—that's what they were—had thrown her off her game. She was here to find Teresa. Her mind swirled. What to say now? What to do? She'd pushed her way inside to get away from those *things,* and they weren't even there when she turned around.

"Do you need some water? Here, please, sit." Lory guided Ann to a chair in the living room. She bustled back into the kitchen and brought Ann a glass of water.

Ann drank it, tilting her head all the way back. She set the glass on the coffee table next to a familiar wooden figurine. She picked it up. It was an angel holding a child in a protective embrace. Just like the one from Ann's own mantle, but without the face drawn on it.

"Where did you get this?" Ann asked, holding the figure out toward Lory like a cross against something evil.

"It was a gift," she said with a shrug. "Have you seen those before?"

"I have a whole bunch of them," Ann said. "I have one just like this. I dr—"

"Drew the face on it," Lory said in a soft voice.

Ann dropped the angel. It thumped onto the rug. Her mouth went dry despite having just chugged sixteen ounces at least.

The voice without the Southern accent. The eyes. Her smile. Ann's body turned cold.

"M-Mom?"

Lory nodded.

The front door burst open. Ann jumped to her feet. A woman with long black hair came in out of breath.

"I lost her—" Her eyes landed on Ann. "Annie?" she said in a surprised voice.

Ann's eyes shot from Lory's face to this other woman's. Half of her face was marred with a horrible burn scar. The other half looked exactly like Lory's.

They had the same voice. Mostly the same face. They were the same person. They were both her mom, yet that could not be.

Ann had lost her mom when she was six in a hit-and-run accident in Crested Butte. She would never forget that day. She would never forget the way her mom had smiled down at her right before the car took her.

Seeing these women—especially the one with black hair —reminded her all over again.

It had been a special day. The sun was out, big fluffy clouds filled the bright blue sky, but not enough to blot out the sun. Cups of hot cocoa warmed their hands.

Ann's mom looked up the street. Her mouth pulled down in a slight frown. Ann looked in that same direction, but didn't see anything worth frowning about.

Her mom looked down at her and smiled. She crossed the street, Ann in tow, right in front of a car. The car didn't slow. It sped up.

At the last second, Ann's mom had shoved Ann away and—

"You told me to run." Ann looked from Lory to the other woman. "One of you did."

"Sit down before you faint," the dark-haired woman said.

Ann didn't sit.

Lory frowned at this other woman.

"Who are you?" Ann asked the dark-haired woman. "And who are you?" She asked the blond one, Lory.

"Lory Magan," Lory said. "It's—" she laughed. "It's a silly anagram for Mary Logan."

A fucking anagram. If it had been a cipher puzzle, she'd have figured it out no problem. But an easy anagram?

Ann didn't know how to react. She once again doubted her ability to serve this town. She questioned whether she had what it took anymore. Harmony made her soft. It made her forget her training. It made her into a country bumpkin sheriff, not a seasoned officer of the law, let alone a detective.

She tugged at her shirt collar until two buttons popped off and clattered onto the floor. She looked at this blond woman with the medium skin tone—the same as her own—and her brown eyes and her smile. She looked at the dark-haired woman, whose eyes, though the same color as Lory's, seemed more intense as they looked at Ann. Determined. Earnest.

"And you? Who are you?" Ann asked.

Before the woman could answer, the basement door opened and Teresa Hart stepped into the room.

CHAPTER FIFTY-EIGHT

Teresa had waited in the basement, listening to their muffled voices through the door for long enough. Something inside her—well, Yaldabaoth of course—had told her they needed to keep Ann there.

To draw my mother.

"My mother is dead," Teresa had snapped in a whisper.

Not your *mother.* Mine. *Sophia.* His voice still tickled the underside of her scalp.

She'd plopped the babies into the playpen—Lory had moved it back down there at some point—where they immediately gripped the edges to pull themselves up to standing. They could walk now, she knew. The way Amanda had bounced on the bed. She had the leg strength, and if they were approximately fourteen months old, they could surely walk.

Cassie, of course, could always fly.

Teresa stepped into the room. Lory and Rebecca were there, standing together, faces side by side—

"You," Teresa said through her teeth. She looked at Lory. "*Rebecca* is your twin sister?"

Movement out of the corner of her eye from the living room. Teresa turned as Ann lunged to her feet. Teresa grabbed her and gripped Ann's right bicep as tight as she could. Teresa lashed out and grabbed Ann's wrist in her other hand and wrenched her arm behind her back. Ann grunted with the pressure of Teresa's fingers gouging into her flesh. She bent over double, probably trying to lessen the pain of her shoulder about to pop out of its socket.

Maybe Ann was number eight. Wouldn't that just be wonderful?

Teresa forced her toward the basement and ripped the door open. Ann pushed back against her despite the horrific angle of her arm. She grunted, presumably in pain.

"I'll throw you down the stairs if you don't cooperate," Teresa said, all at once reminded of Louise's threat to Maggie the night of The Betrayal.

But it hadn't been a betrayal, had it? Because Yaldabaoth didn't leave her. He was inside her. He was slithering around inside her skin now, occupying the same space.

Maggie had stopped struggling with that threat.

"So fucking throw me," Ann hissed, still resisting.

Teresa pushed her.

***

Maggie's mark lit up with urgent burning pain. Sophia stirred in her chest.

If you lose another, you will return to the abyss.

Maggie looked at Pinky. "I think Ann is in trouble." An overwhelming sense of emotion overpowered her. She burst into tears. "I don't know what to do."

You must go to her. You must save her, Sophia whispered in her mind.

Maggie crawled out from under the fallen log and stood. Pinky let out a soft *woof*.

"Pinky, we have to find Ann. Can you find her?"

Pinky looked at Maggie, her tail swishing back and forth. She put her nose to the ground and sniffed and snuffled.

Maggie followed Pinky back to the edge of the deeper woods right by the abandoned funeral home where she'd hid between the bush and the barrel. She grabbed Pinky's collar.

"Stop. Stay."

Pinky obeyed. She sat at Maggie's side and looked at her for the next command. Pinky rarely did what Maggie told her to do, probably because she usually said things like, "Get that ball," or "Find my shoes." Nothing as simple as the commands she *actually* knew.

Maggie listened hard for any voices or movement. What would Ann do in this situation? She would be careful. She would make decisions based on hunches and instinct.

Maggie didn't have hunches or instinct yet, but she thought of the time when Ann had told her she would make a good detective, and it gave her strength.

"Find Ann," Maggie told Pinky when she felt like the coast was clear. "But be quiet." She told Pinky to be quiet because she knew sometimes Pinky bellowed—as Ann called it—when she took off to find Maggie. Maybe when she actually had to sniff it was different. Maybe she was more focused.

Teresa had kept a grip on Ann's arm. Something popped. A pained growl ripped out of Ann's throat, and she acquiesced. Teresa managed to get her down the stairs. Lory and Rebecca followed.

Teresa shoved Ann to the floor, wishing it was concrete and not this plush carpet.

Ann fell forward and twisted at the last second. She landed on her shoulder and cried out. It was probably dislocated.

Teresa leaned over the edge of the playpen where Cassie and Amanda were bouncing and giggling at each other.

"Cassie," Teresa said. "Is it her?" Teresa pointed at Ann.

Cassie followed the line of Teresa's arm with her gaze, then looked up at Teresa and grinned with four upper teeth. So many teeth. Teresa took in her baby's smile. Amanda smiled, too, as if copying Cassie.

"Chashy," Amanda said. She smiled at her sister. Cassie turned and smiled back. They laughed gleefully, taking turns smiling at each other. Touching each other's teeth.

"Tie her up," Teresa said to Lory and Rebecca. "We need her to draw Maggie."

"How will Maggie know—"

Teresa lifted a hand and silenced Lory. She spoke with certainty, though she didn't know how she knew these things. "She'll know. Don't you worry. She will know."

CHAPTER FIFTY-NINE

Pain stabbed Ann's shoulder. A wicked, throbbing pain. Teresa pulled both of her arms behind the chair and bound her wrists with rope, tied her ankles to the chair legs, and slapped a strip of duct tape across Ann's mouth.

She fought to maintain control of her thoughts. To compartmentalize. She could unpack her mom and aunt—according to Teresa's revelation—being there, and the Logismoi manhandling her, and anything else later. Right now, she needed to get out of this situation, arrest Teresa Hart—and her mom and her aunt for that matter—and get them all into custody.

And Maggie. Where the hell was Maggie? Ann's mark had only given her that one warning at Mountain View, which she'd mistook for acid reflux, despite multiple times when it should have done more to communicate with her. It made her worry that her ability as Maggie's Protector was faulty.

Of course, the way her shoulder throbbed with stabbing pain would mask any feeling she had in her chest.

Ann's breath came hard and fast through her nose.

Anger boiled inside her, and under that fierce anger lay anxiety like she hadn't felt since before The Night. It dampened her armpits and made hot and cold flare and flash throughout her core.

It was a panicky sort of anxiety that tightened her chest and filled her head. It was mostly because she'd never been in a situation like this, and it was also because of how stupid she felt for being there.

The only thing that gave her any sort of solace was she knew what was going on. Because of the book.

Lory, or Mary, and the other woman—her twin, Ann's aunt, Rebecca—argued. Ann discerned from the argument that Mary didn't have a clue what was going on, but Rebecca did.

"How could you be so stupid as to not memorize the most important passages?" Rebecca hissed.

Their voices sounded the same, but Ann was trained to pick up on slight nuances. Mary's voice had a slightly higher pitch, like a mother talking to a child. Rebecca's had a certain grit in it.

Part of Ann's anger was at her mother. She'd stepped in front of that car on purpose. How could she do that to Ann? To her dad? Bram had been so heartbroken after Mary's death. He never took his ring off.

That very ring lay heavy against Ann's breastbone. She suddenly felt it was important that she had it with her. It brought her something. A small sense of strength perhaps.

"How many?" Rebecca asked.

Ann glanced over. She was addressing Teresa.

"Seven," Teresa said. "I can only feed them when they're hungry." She motioned to the babies who stood in the playpen looking up at her.

This was impossible. Teresa Hart's babies shouldn't be

that big. They should be infants. Newborns. Tiny and wrinkled. Ann didn't know much about kids, but she knew that much. They didn't turn into *babies* in a matter of days. She thought it took months before they stopped looking like grumpy old man monkeys.

It had to be the Logismoi.

"One more then." Rebecca moved over to the table at the back of the room. She pushed the bowl of plastic fruit off of it. The bowl hit the floor. Plastic fruit tumbled out. She whipped the cloth off the top of it, revealing a stone altar. Ann couldn't see the top from where she sat, but she figured it likely had two circles on each end connected by arching lines.

Rebecca moved her hands over it. "One goes here, the other here." She pointed to the ends of the altar. "The eight will gather. Then, we need the father of death—Yaldabaoth." Rebecca turned to Teresa. "That's you, if I'm not mistaken?"

Maggie followed the sniffing Pinky past the abandoned funeral home, and they made their way through the woods with the lost souls. Maggie knew where they were before she spotted the hidden entry to the abandoned funeral home's basement.

Louise's house loomed in the near distance with lights on inside.

Maggie grabbed Pinky's collar again. "You have to stay here and stay safe," she whispered to the dog. To her bestest friend. She hugged Pinky tight. "You have to be a good dog and stay here. Stay."

Pinky licked the tears off Maggie's face and sat.

"If I call you, you come, okay?"

Pinky yawned. It ended in a soft howl.

Maggie ran to the back door of Louise's house. She knew where it led. They had come out that door on The Night, before going into the tunnel to the abandoned funeral home's basement. She'd had ropes around her wrists that dug into her skin. She had scars from that night.

She hoped *this* night would not leave any marks.

The back door was unlocked.

At Rebecca's proclamation, Ann's eyes widened. She struggled against her bindings, and cried out from behind the tape when her shoulder flared.

Teresa came over. She smacked Ann. Not hard.

"Stop struggling. It's futile." She leaned down to peer into Ann's face.

Ann startled at Teresa's eyes. One was blue. The other was yellow. Not just any yellow. It almost glowed yellow. Like a predator's eye. Her yellow eye moved a fraction of a second behind her blue eye, like they were on separate tracks but tied together.

Raghib was wrong. Ann's dad wasn't alive in Tartaros carrying Yaldabaoth inside him. Yaldabaoth had gone inside Teresa.

Ann's heart broke a little. The hope of seeing her dad again dissipated. He was gone. He was really gone.

But that meant—*Jeezus. Yaldabaoth was out and Maggie was missing and if he got her and killed her—*But if Yaldabaoth was out here . . .

Her mind was a jumbled mess. She couldn't think straight.

Ann mumbled, "Why do you want to open Tartaros?" beneath the tape. It came out as hummed intonations, not words.

"What was that?" Teresa ripped the tape from Ann's face.

Ann cried out as the top layer of her skin tore away with it, numbing and burning at the same time.

"I said, why do they want to open Tartaros if you're already out here?"

Teresa took a step back. She looked toward Mary and Rebecca. A cruel grin spread across her face.

"Oh, Ann," Teresa said with a tone of condescension.

"What?" Ann forced her voice to come out strong and petulant, but she felt weak and fragile inside, like a wrong move might shatter her.

"Don't you know?" Teresa stood upright and looked at Lory and Rebecca.

Ann followed her gaze. They both wore identical expressions of shock on their faces.

"Mary and Rebecca both love your father," Teresa said. "And they think he's alive and in Tartaros."

CHAPTER SIXTY

Teresa didn't bother with the tape. Ann could ask what she wanted. Besides, if Maggie—no, *Sophia, Mother*—needed help finding them, she needed Ann to be able to call out to her. Even if she had to use force to get Ann to do so.

A cruel relishing of this situation coursed through her. Teresa wasn't sure if it was her own glee or Yaldabaoth's at getting another shot at Sophia.

A door opened and closed upstairs.

Teresa froze, as did Lory and Rebecca.

"Hello?" a female voice called. "Lory?"

Teresa rushed over to Ann and slapped a hand over her mouth. "Not a word." She gouged Ann's shoulder. Ann squeezed her eyes shut and grunted.

"It's Patrina," Lory whisper-yelled to Teresa. "She thinks we're all meeting here like usual. I didn't tell anyone not to come."

Teresa laughed inwardly. Most of the followers were eyeless sacks of flesh.

"I'll go," Teresa said. She lifted Cassie from the crib.

"Chashy," Amanda said in her husky voice. She reached

for her sister. Cassie reached for Amanda over Teresa's shoulder.

"Mumba," Cassie called, stiffening and arching her back. Teresa nearly dropped her.

"I'll come with you," Lory said, quickly lifting Amanda and holding her close to Cassie. "They want to be together."

Teresa climbed the stairs first. Cassie cooed at her sister over Teresa's shoulder. Amanda giggled.

"Patrina?" Teresa said. "We're meeting downstairs today. Too much going on—"

"Is my brother here?" Patrina asked. "I can't find him. He won't answer his phone. Is he here?"

Something flashed in Patrina's eyes. Almost as if Teresa could see the soul lurking there behind her eyeballs.

"Paul's in the basement with everyone else," Teresa said. "Why don't you carry one of the babies. I know you love to hold them." Teresa moved to hand Cassie over, but Lory intervened and all but thrust Amanda into her arms.

"My back. Can you take her?" Lory held her hand to her lower back as if an eighteen-pound baby was too much for her. Teresa shrugged.

"Oh I'd love to," Patrina held out her arms, worry about her brother momentarily forgotten. "Hello, little angel."

She's not an angel, Teresa thought. Angels didn't require the consumption of souls to thrive.

Lory led the way down the stairs.

"No pinching," Teresa heard Patrina say to Amanda. "Yes, those are my eyes."

Teresa halted for half a second. Would Amanda? No, Cassie was the one.

"Ouch, baby. No, no."

"No grabbing, Amanda," Teresa said. "They're in that grabby stage."

"How are they so big?" Patrina asked.

"Good genes," Teresa said.

"We don't see any babies at the institute," Patrina said. The institute. She meant Mountain View, of course. Teresa never heard anyone call it the institute. It made it sound like something it wasn't. A research facility or something. Not a poorly operated *insane* asylum. Teresa knew they didn't call them that anymore, but Mountain View seemed so far removed from modern medicine she only ever thought of it as an insane asylum.

Lory reached the bottom of the stairs. Teresa and Patrina moved slower and more carefully due to their precious cargo. Patrina even slower trying to keep Amanda's hands off her face.

At the bottom, Teresa lowered Cassie to the floor. Cassie stood on her own but was a little wobbly. Teresa expected Cassie to burst into her gargoyle form, but she didn't.

Maggie had barely closed the back door behind her and crept a few feet down the hall, when the front door opened and a woman came in and called out.

Maggie had nearly answered her out of habit but clapped a hand over her own mouth. She'd tucked herself into the entry to a bedroom.

Inside was a bed and a crib and a dresser with a dark-haired wig on it. Maggie ventured farther into the room and peered into the crib. There were two blankets. A pink one and a purple one.

More voices sounded from the front of the house. Maggie peeked out and ducked back, covering her mouth with both hands this time. The breath from her nose blasted in and out.

Teresa Hart. Her adoptive mom. Who'd tried to raise Yaldabaoth to kill her last year. Who'd brought about the events of The Night. Teresa was there in this house. Maggie peeked again, just to be sure. She was there, holding a baby in her arms. A brown-haired woman stood by the front door, and a woman with blond hair stood next to Teresa, also holding a baby.

Light and Dark, Life and Death, Sophia whispered in Maggie's mind.

Maggie backed away from the doorway and huddled in the corner.

Fear riddled her insides. Her organs trembled. Her bones jumped around inside her skin.

Teresa Hart. Here. Did Ann know?

Maggie gasped. Did Teresa hurt Ann? Maggie's face crumpled. She covered her face with her shirt and wept.

Do not be afraid, Sophia's calm and soothing voice said. *Do not be afraid.*

"I can't help it." Maggie hitched in a few breaths and wiped her tears with her shirt. "I'm only seven." And she didn't know what to do. She was so scared, all she could think about was how her teeth chattered, how her knees and elbows trembled. She couldn't hear anything beyond her own gasping. She sucked in as deep a breath as she could and listened.

The voices out at the far end of the hall faded away. She waited, just in case, before peeking out of the bedroom. The entryway was clear.

That's when the screaming started.

Amanda finally found purchase in Patrina's face. She had pinched Patrina's cheek with one hand, and with the other, gouged her little fleshy baby fingers into Patrina's eye socket.

Patrina screamed, but still she held onto Amanda, as if her instinct to protect the baby from falling overpowered her own self-preservation.

Ann cried out.

Lory and Rebecca both shied away in apparent horror.

Teresa watched, pride and a small sense of sadness for Patrina filling her. Patrina had always been so nice to her. So gracious. Teresa pulled Amanda from Patrina's grasp. Patrina's hands went to her empty eye socket.

"Oh my god!" she cried. "Oh my god, my eye!" She screamed again. Teresa slapped a hand over her mouth.

"Your brother was a willing sacrifice," she said in a low voice.

Patrina's remaining eye widened. "No, please. Not me. Not me, please."

Teresa pushed Patrina against the wall by the stairs. She fought Patrina's waving hand and managed to get her forearm across Patrina's throat, cutting off her air. Her waving hands went to Teresa's arm. Strangled sounds choked from her throat. Teresa lifted her free hand and gouged her index finger into the inner corner of Patrina's eye. She had to use more force than she thought she would need, but she curled her finger around Patrina's eye and popped it out. It dangled from its optic nerve.

Patrina's screams came out as wheezing air. She slid to the ground, her knees giving out from shock.

Teresa slurped the silver soul from Patrina's sockets.

Maggie ducked back into the dark and quiet room. The screams were muffled. That meant they were in the basement. She didn't want to go down there. That place had horrible memories. Mr. Bram, so thin and dirty. The smells. The thought of seeing that place again was far worse than the thought of seeing the inside of the abandoned funeral home, or the passageway under the forest to get to it, or even Tartaros itself. Seeing Mr. Bram like that—tied up, smelly, and weak—when he'd always been so clean and always smelled like soap and some man's perfume or something?

That's probably where Ann was, now.

Maggie sucked in a gasp. The screams hadn't been hers. There's no way Ann would scream like that. It was too high-pitched. Maggie imagined Ann would grunt and groan and yell. She wouldn't scream. She was too tough for screaming.

"It'll be a bit before it happens," Teresa said.

"Before what happens?" Lory asked. Her face looked drawn and gray.

"Before the cloud explodes from one of them. Since Cassie nursed first, it'll come out of Amanda this time." Teresa shrugged. She hadn't yet worked out why most of the time Amanda fed first and the black cloud came out of Cassie, but when Cassie fed first it came out of Amanda.

"Of course, with the last two, it happened pretty quickly. Probably because it was two at once and extra filling."

Lory covered her mouth.

"We'll need to make sure the cloud can get out of here," Teresa said. Patrina's still and empty form lay at the bottom of the stairs. A pang of guilt and sadness filled her once again. The part of her Yaldabaoth hadn't numbed yet. The compassionate part of her that still recognized humanity and the goodness in people.

Ann couldn't come to terms with what she'd just witnessed. A baby ripping the eye out of one of the nurses from Mountain View? Teresa tearing out the other one? And what the hell did she slurp out of that woman? The silvery substance had floated up to her as if drawn by some gravitational pull.

Patrina's body had emptied like a water balloon running out of water. All that was left after Teresa sucked the last of it was a deflated flesh bag.

Teresa had immediately fed one baby and then the other, as if this was business as usual. Of course, if this was the eighth and final Logismoi, by now it *was* business as usual.

Then the babies napped. Everyone else seemed to be waiting.

Exhaustion tugged at Ann's will. She wasn't ready to give up, but she needed to save her energy for whatever might happen next. She hoped to everything holy that she may or may not believe in that Maggie did not come to find her. That Maggie and Pinky were somewhere safe.

Ann closed her eyes. She wished she had the pain compass like she had before. The one that had guided her to Maggie after Raghib had taken her.

Her eyes popped back open. Where the hell was Raghib in all this? She was surprised he wasn't here in cahoots with these women.

These women. Her mom and her aunt.

Suddenly, a shrieking sound filled the air. Ann turned her head in time to see one of the babies with her head thrown back. A black cloud swarmed out of her. Like a thousand flies, only instead of buzzing they screamed and wailed.

The cloud finished blasting out of the baby. It moved like a thing crawling across the ceiling, then dropped into the eyeless woman's mouth.

It filled her up. It filled her up and she sat up, but her skin didn't quite fit right.

Oh god.

Black fluid leaked from the corner of her mouth. Demon eyes, like the eyes Glory had in the clearing, glared out at them all.

Her face didn't smile like Glory or Duke or the others, though. It sagged into a hateful sneer. A sneer so loathsome, the skin under her eyes pulled away exposing her occipital bones.

Maggie sat on the floor in a dark corner of the room trying to get her fear under control. She wished Sophia would talk to her more. Sophia was wise and could, or maybe should, tell Maggie what to do and how to feel better and how to be brave. She took a few deep breaths and focused her thoughts on what would happen if she didn't act.

"I will lose someone I love. I will return to the abyss," she whispered. She took a few deep breaths.

The last one stalled in the back of her throat when another sort of distant scream came from the basement. A scream made up of the fear and trembling from a nightmare. It made her mark burn. Maggie covered her ears until it stopped. She crawled to the door and peeked out into the hallway. She took three steps down the hall when the door opened *again*.

Only this time, her mark ignited so hot she had to rush back to the bedroom where she doubled over, clenching her heart. She bit her knuckles and waited for the pain to stop.

Logismoi, Sophia's voice whispered.

CHAPTER SIXTY-ONE

Upstairs a door opened again. Feet tramped above, then clobbered down the stairs. The seven joined their eighth. Teresa took a step toward the babies, blocking them from the eight people she'd taken over the past few days.

Lory whimpered. Rebecca stepped closer to Teresa.

"What the fuck," Ann whispered.

They were in various states of disrepair—or decomposition might be a more likely description.

Duke—who no longer looked like the handsome man Teresa had seduced into an alleyway—held the lady cop under the arms where she sagged like one of those gaudy inflatable lawn decorations. Curly grinned at her, as did Glory. Both of them had skin sagging and puddling around the area where neck and shoulders met. Olivia and Paul didn't look too horrible. Just a little puffy. Like the places where their skin should have hugged their bones had air under it. Hunter looked just the way she'd seen him earlier. Patrina's evil grin peeked out from the back of the group.

"Eight Logismoi," Rebecca said. "They look a lot

different than I expected them to." She cleared her throat. "And smellier." She let out a cough bordering on a gag.

"What exactly did you expect?" Teresa asked.

Rebecca shrugged. "Definitely not *this*." She moved away from Teresa. Teresa followed her movement. "The babies go here and here," Rebecca said again. She hadn't finished her instructions from before. "They will do something . . . join hands maybe? I'm not sure. But they'll do something to create an opening. See these arches?"

Teresa peered down at the two circles and the arches.

"What about these?" She pointed to the three symbols at the bottom.

"That's the father of death," Rebecca said, pointing to one that looked like a stylized snake. "That's the mother of angels."

"And the third?" Teresa prompted.

Rebecca shook her head. "I don't remember that one."

"So much for *memorizing* the passages," Lory said with sarcasm.

"Devotion of consanguinity," Ann said.

Teresa turned to her. "Devotion of what?"

"Oh yes, that." Rebecca looked at Lory. "Devotion of Consanguinity. Ancestral love, for lack of a better term. Or, to modernize it, sibling love."

Lory scoffed again. "Good luck with that one."

"These two have enough sibling love to open a thousand portals," Teresa said, lifting Cassie from the crib to set her on one of the circles. Lory rushed forward, blocking Rebecca, and lifted Amanda to place on the other.

"Who is the mother of the angels?" Teresa asked.

Ann laughed.

"Wisdom is mother of the angels," Lory said. "Sophia."

She scowled at Rebecca distorting her otherwise pleasant face.

"Don't scowl like that. It'll give you wrinkles." Teresa reached forward and smoothed her thumb in an upward motion between Lory's eyebrows. It was something her mother did to her when she was younger. Teresa snatched her hand back.

"Rebecca was supposed to bring Maggie." Lory lifted her chin.

"She got away," Rebecca said, dejected. "She's fast."

Ann laughed again. "Because we hike above ten thousand feet and she *loves* to run."

Teresa detected more than a hint of pride in Ann's voice.

"When did you two join forces, anyway?" Teresa asked Lory.

"The day Rebecca was in the house." Lory shrugged. "We may be angry at each other, but our bond is still strong." Lory smiled at Rebecca. Rebecca did not return it.

"And why is *she* here again?" Teresa threw a thumb in Ann's direction.

"To draw the mother of the angels." Lory took on an explaining tone. "There's a story in the book about—"

"I don't care about the stories from your stupid book." Teresa went to the altar where Cassie and Amanda had crawled closer to each other. They no longer sat in their circles. They just wanted to be near each other. The circles were too far apart for them to hold hands like Rebecca said. Maybe if they were sixteen like Rebecca had thought they would be.

"Look what these *things* are doing to my carpet," Lory said. "This is not what I expected *at all*."

The eight were leaking black fluid onto Lory's white rug, destroying it. One of them—the lady cop—was on the ground now, having oozed out of Duke's grip. Her skin had sagged so much it barely hung on her face. Teresa grimaced.

CHAPTER SIXTY-TWO

Maggie willed the pain in her chest to go away until it lessened from a brutal searing to a dull ache. She took deep breaths and told herself she could do this. She had the courage. Only then did she creep down the hall to the doorway to the basement.

She stood at the top of the basement steps and looked down into the lighted space below. Last time she'd peered down these stairs, there wasn't white carpet at the bottom.

She took a deep breath and tiptoed down the first steps. About halfway down, the wall became open wooden frames. She stopped right before that part and sat on the stairs. She peeked into the room.

Two babies sat on an altar. Maggie didn't like the look of it. Those babies should not be on there like that. Teresa moved into her view. Maggie sucked in a gasp and covered her mouth again.

Maggie's mom and a blond lady joined Teresa. Maggie couldn't see Ann, if Ann was even there, from where she sat and peered.

"Someone needs to find Maggie," Maggie's mom said.

"I'm here," Maggie called.

"No! Run!" Ann yelled.

Maggie didn't run. She rose and stepped down the rest of the stairs. At the bottom, she moved around and through the Logismoi with their bad fitted skin and their stink. She wasn't afraid of them. They didn't want her. It was a feeling. Probably from Sophia.

"Hi, Maggie." Sally Opperheim waved fanatically with a grin so wide it actually split her upper and lower lips. Black ooze dribbled from the wounds. Her skin was even worse than earlier that day. It sagged around her eye holes like those dogs with the really long ears and short legs.

"Hi, Sally." Maggie said in a low voice. She looked up at the blond woman, then to her mom. Her mom had pulled her long dark hair into a loose bun. The two women had the same face, except for the scar.

"Maggie," Ann said in a breathless way Maggie had never heard her use before.

Maggie jerked toward the sound. Tears glistened in Ann's eyes. Maggie all at once saw Mr. Bram in her face and traces of the blond woman and Maggie's own mother, but everything was also distinctly Ann. Maggie ran to her and hugged her, just like she had with Mr. Bram. And just like Mr. Bram, Ann struggled against her ropes, but she stopped and hissed with pain.

A low rumble started. Maggie looked up toward the sound.

The eight blasted out of their skins as black clouds wailing and shrieking and buzzing like the agonized cries of a gagillion flies. Their empty husks fell to the floor.

The babies were torn from each other by some force

that dragged them to the center of two circles on the stone altar.

The black clouds swarmed the low ceiling above. One peeled away and dropped down. It struck the baby on the left in the chest like it meant to flow through her—like ghosts in cartoons—but it never came out the other side. The second did the same to the baby on the right. Again and again it happened, alternating babies. The babies screamed, their faces red and mouths wide open. They reached for each other, straining against whatever held them in place.

The empty skins dissolved into bubbling stinky black goo.

Bye, Sally, Maggie thought, surprised to feel sad. Sally had been awful before, but the last few times Maggie saw her—well, Maggie would have forgiven her, she knew, if Sally hadn't been infected with a Logismoi.

"Eight perfect pairs. The Children of Chaos shall resurrect the Perfect Soul," Maggie's mom said.

The babies stopped crying. Maggie looked at them. They had moved from their circles and now held hands, trying to get closer to each other.

A face shimmered between them. Not male or female, but both at the same time. Its mouth opened wider and wider until that's all it was. A big open mouth. A roar started. The force from the altar pulled the babies apart again, expanding the mouth. Inside was empty darkness.

The abyss.

"I haven't lost her!" Maggie shouted. She saw Pinky in her mind, keeping her stay like a good dog.

What if someone had found her and hurt her?

"Pinky!" Maggie shrieked.

The roar grew louder. The blond woman and Maggie's mom screamed. Maggie looked over at them. They leaned forward, away from the portal, reaching their hands. The portal pulled at their clothes and hair, trying to suck them inside.

Ann's chair shifted toward the gaping hole. Maggie moved behind her and started working at the ropes around her wrists. They were too tight.

Another scream. Maggie looked. The blond woman lost her footing and flew backward into the dark opening.

Teresa, huddled off to the side of the altar, was out of the path of its suction.

Maggie moved to Ann's feet. The knots were looser, she got them undone. Ann kicked the ropes away. She stood and kicked the chair. It flew toward the portal, hit Maggie's mom in the chest, and they both went through. The playpen went next.

Ann sat on the floor. "Get behind me," she said.

Maggie shook her head. "We need to get out of here."

"It's too strong." Ann worked her hands under her butt and managed to slide the rope past her hips, under her knees, and get her hands in front of her, crying out in pain as she shifted her arms around. She used her teeth to loosen the knots at her wrists. Maggie helped her with them. The ropes flew into the portal.

Ann grabbed onto Maggie, and Maggie grabbed onto Ann. They were both trying to save each other.

It was no use. Maggie's feet lifted off the ground. She held onto Ann's hands, but Ann's arm was hurt. She couldn't keep her grip on Maggie's one hand.

"I won't let you go," Ann shouted at Maggie.

Maggie's hand slipped. Ann cried out and reached forward with her hurt arm, but it was useless. Her grip wouldn't hold. Her eyes, wide and full of panic, stayed locked on Maggie's.

Maggie held onto Ann's hand with both of hers, but her grip slipped.

Maggie flew backwards. Ann's face registered shock before the darkness of the abyss took Maggie into its cold grasp.

She flew for only a few seconds. She landed in a heap and rolled to a stop, eyes closed. Her hands touched sand. She opened her eyes on stone walls, torches in sconces.

It wasn't the abyss at all. She sat up and looked around. A dark pool of water reflected the torches. The blond woman and Maggie's mother lay on the stone floor not too far from her. Her mother lay very still. Ann's chair lay folded on the ground. The playpen had thrown up stuffed animals all over the place and collapsed on itself.

"Welcome back to Tartaros, kiddo."

Maggie turned her head and let out a surprised scream.

Smiling that special smile of his, Mr. Bram sat with his back against the wall. Only *he* could make such a serious situation less serious.

A noise came from the other side of the cave. Ann flew through the hole open on the wall. Maggie rolled out of the way just in time.

Ann landed with an *oof*.

Maggie scuttled to Ann's side and put a hand on her.

"I'm okay," Ann said.

Maggie stared at the portal, waiting for Teresa to come flying through next.

Instead, a fawn-colored bundle of energy shot into the cave. Pinky landed on her feet, slid to a stop, and shook off. She spotted Maggie and wiggle-bounded over to her.

"Pinky! You heard me!" Maggie collapsed on the dog, her heart swelling with love and affection.

"Annie!" Bram shouted.

Ann jerked her head in Bram's direction. "Dad?"

"Please tell me you have my ring."

CHAPTER SIXTY-THREE

Teresa gripped the edge of the altar and pulled herself up. At the side of it like this she seemed to be safe from the pull of it. The portal—still open because of the babies on the altar—sucked air and anything it could get. The carpet even started ripping up at the edges of the room. Teresa did not want to get sucked inside.

Do not let it take you, his voice prickled her scalp with icy fear.

Yaldabaoth did not want that either.

Something clattered down the stairs. Teresa looked up just in time to see the fawn-colored pit bull, Brent Winter's pit bull—Pinky—leap into the air. The suction from the portal grabbed the dog. She let out a yip and got sucked inside.

Teresa touched Cassie, but Cassie was frozen solid like stone. She pulled Cassie away from the center of the circle. Her skin softened. She pulled harder, and with a popping sound, Cassie released from the magnetic hold of the altar.

The opening collapsed on one side, and a ghastly groan

issued from it. Teresa hurried to pull Amanda from the other circle.

The portal closed. The sudden closure made her ears pop. The ensuing silence was deafening.

Amanda's cry cut that silence to shreds. Cassie joined in, mouth open wide, head thrown back. Teresa cried, too. A soft whimpering weeping.

Take them out of here. Take them far from this place. Get our children somewhere safe, Yaldabaoth's fearful voice pleaded in her mind.

He would not be able to exert his will over her as long as she was in charge. She didn't know if that was true, but she felt it was true. She believed it was true.

She had faith in the fact that it had to be true.

She would do as he said. This time. Only because she, too, wanted to get away from here. If they had gotten out of Tartaros before, they could get out again. Like it or not, Teresa was a fugitive.

Holding Cassie on one hip, Teresa went to Amanda and hefted her up onto her other hip.

"Hold on tight." She side-stepped around the black goo on the carpet, climbed the stairs, and ran out the front door and into the night.

CHAPTER SIXTY-FOUR

The portal closed as Ann got to her feet, Maggie fussing over her trying to help, and limped over to her dad. She pulled her necklace over her head, unclasped it, and pulled her dad's ring off the chain.

He took it in the two remaining fingers on his left hand, thumb and forefinger, and jammed it onto his right ring finger. He gave it a sharp twist.

Lory—Mary—Ann's mom cried out and lifted her left hand. The ring on her ring finger glowed.

"Bram, no," she said.

"What's happening?" Ann asked.

"I'm invoking the Luminaries." He struggled to his feet. Ann helped him up.

"No," Maggie cried out. "No don't, please don't." She gripped Ann's good arm and pressed her face against it.

"Why, Bram?" Mary cried. "Why would you do this to me. To *us?*"

"A contract is a contract," Bram said. "You broke your end of it, Mary, so I'm breaking mine."

"We can resolve this ourselves. The Luminaries need not be involved." Mary's voice shrieked.

Rebecca groaned now and sat up.

"*Ami.*" Maggie tucked herself behind Ann even further.

Bram went to Rebecca's side.

"Rebecca," he said in a soft voice, cupping her face. "What happened to you?"

"Messengers of the Light." She pressed her face against Bram's palm. "After *Mary* told them where we were—Maggie and I—I sent her away to the Protectorate. They tried to get her location out of me."

"You . . . sent her? With Raghib?"

Rebecca nodded. His eyes darted to Maggie and back, widening in apparent surprise. He gulped, his Adam's apple bobbing visibly. He turned to Mary, and his face fell into a scowl.

"No, it's not how it sounds." Mary held up her hands.

"It's exactly how it sounds." Rebecca glared at Mary.

"What the hell is going on?" Ann shouted.

The pool of water rippled.

"There's no time right now, Annie," Bram said. "The Luminaries are coming."

Maggie whimpered. Ann's mark stung. She crouched next to Maggie and pulled her close.

The pool churned like someone had turned on the jets in a hot tub. A rumble shook the cave. The water boiled, and four figures rose from its depths.

They glowed like shining gold. Four luminous creatures. Two male, two female. They wore robes of snowy white light.

They had great wings on their backs. Wings made of light. They looked like Sophia's angel who once lived within

Ann, who gave Ann the power to stop Yaldabaoth last year, but she didn't really stop him, did she?

Failed again.

Maggie and Rebecca both dropped to one knee in genuflection.

"They came from the abyss," Ann heard Maggie whisper. "How did they come from the abyss?"

"There is much that is unknown about the abyss," Rebecca said in a low voice.

"Who invoked the four Luminaries?" one of the females asked in a powerful voice.

Bram stepped forward. Ann reached her good hand to stop him. The Luminaries were beautiful and frightening at the same time.

"I did." Bram held up his right hand. The ring glowed blue-white. "Our contract was broken long ago."

"Bram, please." Mary groveled on her knees. "It doesn't have to be this way. I'm sorry for what I did. Please forgive me."

The Luminaries looked at Bram to Mary and back to Bram.

"Explain," they said at once, their voices echoing and shaking the cave.

"Mary tried to kill Ann," Bram said. "She tried to end the Protector when she was merely six years old. The contract states—"

"No," Ann said. "No, she didn't."

Bram turned to her. The Luminaries flicked their gazes to her.

"Mary threw me aside." Ann bowed her head, feeling like she should. "She threw me out of the way of the car and let it hit her instead."

"It's true," Mary said. "I was supposed to hold her with me, but I pushed her. I told her to run."

Mary rose and approached Ann, held out her hands. Ann rose. "I loved you, Ann. Like a daughter. I did."

"What do you mean, *like* a daughter?" Ann asked, taking a half step back. She shifted her eyes to her dad and back to Mary.

"I'm not your biological mother. Though, technically a maternity test would prove otherwise, since we're identical twins and all." She looked at Rebecca, then Bram.

"Annie, listen to me." He took her hand. Ann glanced at the Luminaries. They looked bored now. Bored with these mere mortals, she was sure. Their petty squabbling. The taller male pulled out a pocket watch and checked the time, held it to his ear, wound it, and leaned over to the shorter male who pulled a watch out, too. She wondered for a second what time zone they were on.

"Mary and I were brought together under the contractual obligations of the Luminaries."

Ann closed her eyes trying to wrap her head around those words.

"These rings? They were created by the Luminaries and filled with light from the Entirety," Bram said.

"What exactly was the contract?" Ann smoothed her fingers over her eyebrow and wondered how much more *weird* she could handle.

"It started as a means to bring the Protectorate and Messengers of the Light back together," Bram said. "Mend the grievances of the previous decades."

"First they would be granted perpetual life until carrying out the terms," the tall male Luminary jumped in, his voice booming around the cave. He waved his hand in a continue-and-get-on-with-it gesture.

Bram laid it all out. How they were to bring a child into the world, raise her to be the Protector, train her in the ways of the Protectorate and her duties as the Protector. How Mary failed to get pregnant.

"Rebecca and I are identical twins." Mary reached for her sister. But Rebecca ignored her outstretched hand. Rebecca rose from her bow, gripping her ribs, and took a faltering step toward them. Ann backed away from everyone.

"I carried you, Annie," Rebecca said. "I carried you for nine months and I raised you until you were weaned. You were *my* baby for a full year." A tear slid down her cheek. "I loved you so deeply, and I fell in love with you and with Bram during that time. We were together so much, how could I not?" She smiled over at him.

"Ami?" Maggie rose now. "But Ami, you are *my* mom."

Rebecca eased herself into a squat. "Yes, my little Magdalene." She reached for Maggie, who didn't move toward her.

"I, uh," Bram cleared his throat and smoothed his fingers over his eyebrow, his tell for discomfort matching Ann's. "One of my last trips back to Nag Hammadi I found Rebecca." His cheeks flushed, and he looked at Rebecca. "I looked for you every time I went back. I was on my way to see you when Louise . . ." He held up his mangled hand.

Rebecca smiled at him. Bram went to her side now.

Rebecca still addressed Ann. "My husband and I struggled to get pregnant for so long we gave up. I wanted another child after having to give you up to Mary. For so long I yearned to have a child of my own. I loved Bram so dearly, when I saw him, well, it was quite a reunion." She smiled shyly. Bram raised and lowered his eyebrows in a lecherous way that made Ann look away.

Mary made a disgusted sound and crossed her arms.

"Wait." Ann held up her hand. "That would mean that Maggie and I—"

"Are sisters," Rebecca finished, looking up at her. "You are the Devotion of Consanguinity."

Maggie backed away from all of the adults. Ann could only imagine what this was doing to her mind. Her eyes glistened with tears. Her chest hitched. She went to Pinky who wagged her tail and licked Maggie's face. Pinky, always an anchor, a rock, steady for the girl when the madness around her was too much.

"But you wanted to give me to the Messengers of the Light," Maggie said. "Ami, you told Baba to give me to them. You told him I was Sophia—"

"My husband was Protectorate Allegiant. The Messengers of the Light assassinated him. His father—your baba—Raghib came to help me. I told him to give you to the Protectorate for safekeeping. Even though he, himself, was a Messenger."

"But you scratched my hands." Maggie rubbed her hands as if feeling the scratches again. "You wouldn't let go. You wanted to give me to—"

Rebecca shook her head and held out her hands toward Maggie, who, though just feet from her, shied away behind Pinky. "I wanted him to take you, but I also *didn't* want him to take you." She laughed and wiped the tears from her cheeks. "You were my child. *My* child. Not one I begot for my sister. I thought I would have you forever. I wanted you to be taken to safety, but I physically could not let you go."

"This is all very—whatever it is," the tall male Luminary said with a flop of his hand. "But, Barbelo, it is time for you to come back home now."

At the mention of Barbelo, Rebecca's eyes glowed with the same light of the Luminaries.

"Rebecca?" Bram looked at her.

Before she could respond, Mary stepped toward the Luminaries.

"You knew *she* was the one to create the Protector and manifest Sophia and you still forced us together?" Mary shrieked at the Luminaries. "Why not just let Bram and Rebecca be together then?" Mary shouted. "Save me the heartache—" Her voice broke and she covered her mouth, face contorting with grief.

"We sent the Barbelo, true," the tall male said. "She chose who to inhabit. Perhaps she was confused by your identical appearance." He smiled as if it were amusing.

"Mary," the tallest one said.

Mary stepped forward, eyes lowered.

"Your time on his realm is over."

Mary cried out. She looked to Bram, to Ann, back to the Luminaries. "No, please." But Mary's skin had already begun to age. Maggie hid her face against Pinky. Ann crouched next to them and pulled Maggie against her, covering her ear and pressing Maggie's other ear against her not injured shoulder. Mary screamed. Her body aged to bones in seconds and those bones turned to dust and returned to the earth.

"Barbelo," the Luminaries said in unison. "Aeon of the aeons. It is time to return to the Entirety."

"Ami, don't go." Maggie let go of Ann and ran to Rebecca.

"I must, little angel." Rebecca stroked her hair and kissed her in the middle of her forehead. "Sophia," Rebecca said, but it wasn't Rebecca's voice. It was another ethereal voice made of many voices like Sophia's but different. Deeper, more mature. Her eyes glowed.

"Barbelo," Sophia responded.

"You must complete your purpose." She pressed her forehead to Maggie's. They stared into each other's glowing eyes for long seconds.

"I shall."

Rebecca's eyes stopped glowing. She stood and stopped before Bram and took his hands. She kissed him on the mouth. She came to Ann next. Her face, no longer obscured by a scar, crumpled with grief.

"I wish I could have known you," Ann said. Rebecca hugged her.

"Take care of Maggie. She is more special than anyone can ever know." She pulled away and stared into Ann's eyes for a fraction too long, but Ann didn't look away. Barbelo glowed within Rebecca's pupils. Blue-white coursed up Ann's left arm. Her mark tingled. She nodded.

Rebecca went to the edge of the pool. One of the Luminaries touched her forehead. Her physical body fell away, leaving behind an angel of light. The angel slid beneath the surface of the pool and disappeared.

CHAPTER SIXTY-FIVE

"Where did she go? What is the Entirety?" Maggie asked through her tears, voice hitching.

"All that came before the creation of the material realm," Eleleth said. "Sophia included. She was the last being created within the Entirety. It was her desire to create another like herself that brought forth Yaldabaoth."

"And now, so much more evil stalks the earth because of *you*." The big mean one from before pointed his finger at Maggie.

Pinky growled and lunged between them with full mohawk hackles, as Ann would say.

The Luminary stepped back and bumped into the tall female Luminary.

"Harmozel." Eleleth tried to hold in a laugh while helping him stand straighter. "You fear this little creature?"

"The little creature protects the Mother," the mean one said. The others had a good chuckle.

The mean Luminary leaned down. "It is okay, little creature." The Luminary stuck his hand out for Pinky to sniff.

Pinky sniffed the Luminary's hand. Her hackles relaxed and her tail swished. He smiled.

The Luminaries all bent to pet Pinky with their glowing hands.

"This little creature deserves something special." Eleleth looked up from rubbing Pinky's belly. "She stood up to you, Harmozel." She looked at the tallest one.

The tall Luminary bent and peered at Pinky. Maggie clutched her dog. They wouldn't take her, would they?

"She already holds within her the brightest light from the Entirety." His eyes flicked to Maggie's. She met them without fear. "How about . . . as long as Sophia is on this material realm in need of protection as powerful as this creature can give, this little creature shall live?"

Maggie smiled. "Yes, please." She hugged Pinky and looked at Ann. "What about my Protector?"

"Your Protector has fulfilled her duty by protecting you from Yaldabaoth and restoring life through the angel within her. Your growing courage has weakened the strength of her ability to protect you. Now, it is time for Sophia to restore the balance within the material realm. Without balance, this realm shall destroy itself. Chaos will return to take back what was created from it."

Eleleth bent to Maggie's level. "The humans, and the little creature, surround you with love," she said. "This love will protect you from returning to the abyss before it is time."

Maggie looked over her shoulder. Ann and Bram—her sister and her dad?—came nearer and embraced her. Maggie wrapped her arms around Pinky and squeezed her eyes shut.

"By the light of the Entirety," Eleleth's voice said. "You shall be restored."

The cave rumbled and vanished. When Maggie opened her eyes, they were back in the basement. Teresa and the babies were gone.

"We need to find Lisa," Bram said as soon as they'd gotten their bearings. His fingers had been restored. Ann's shoulder no longer hurt.

"Lisa?" She did a few arm circles, testing her rotator cuff.

"Lisa McMichael."

"Wait, what? She died years ago." Ann froze. "Didn't she?" Lisa was Sheriff McMichael's wife. She was Protectorate, according to Sheriff McMichael's little black book. She had died in a bus crash in Egypt. Allegedly.

"Faked," Bram said. "Just like the rest of us."

"The rest . . ." All along, the Protectorate were out there while Ann floundered being Maggie's Protector.

As if reading her mind, Bram came to her and embraced her. "They couldn't help you, Annie. You had everything you needed." He pulled away and pointed to his heart and nodded knowingly, turned, and climbed the stairs out of Louise's—Lory's—*Mary's* basement. Ann motioned for Maggie and Pinky to follow. She took up the rear.

Lisa McMichael was in the living room reading a home decorating magazine. She looked up and grinned at Ann.

"There you are." She set it down and got to her feet. "Rachel said you'd all be here."

"Rachel?" Ann took a breath. "She's a no good, backstabbing—"

Lisa laughed, cutting her off. "She did her duty well I see." Lisa said. "Frank and I wanted to pass on the Protector lineage, but we never had children. Rachel's been, well, she's been part of our family since you left, Ann. Since she isn't blood, we had to suffice with swearing her in as Protector Allegiant."

"I locked her up." Ann felt dazed. "She betrayed me—us." She indicated Maggie. "She was consorting with Teresa Hart. Harboring a homicidal maniac!"

Where had Teresa gone?

Lisa touched Ann's arm and shook her head. "No, dear, she was doing her duty. She was completing an assignment I sent her a few months ago. I wanted her to collect intelligence on Lory Magan. I knew she was an ex-Messenger. I wanted to know what she was doing here, especially after the events of last year." She nodded knowingly at Bram, then at Ann.

Assignment. The text messages. LMCM. Lisa McMichael. Ann touched her eyebrow. It was plain as day. Well, now it was.

"Rachel's locked up at the station." Ann gupled.

"My car's out front." Lisa led the way out.

<hr>

Ann unlocked the door to the holding cell and let Rachel out.

"I'm sorry I couldn't tell you," Rachel said. "I was sworn to secrecy." The younger woman, though not the touchy-feely type, wrapped her arms around Ann and hugged her hard. Her body shook with sobs. Emotion welled within Ann. She didn't want to let it out. Not yet. Not until she could be somewhere alone to process.

Her mom—*moms*—her dad home. Maggie her sister.

Rachel. Lisa McMichael. And Pinky just being Pinky wiggling around to everyone.

Teresa Hart still at large.

No. There would be time for that, but it wasn't now.

Rachel said a string of things that Ann could not understand through her bawling.

"It's okay," Ann said, patting Rachel's back. "You're one of us now. I mean, officially." She pulled away and smiled.

Rachel's puffy face smiled back at her. She laughed, and a snot bubble popped in her nostril.

"Oh, god." She wiped her nose on her sleeve. "I'm so gross." Rachel turned away and disappeared into the bathroom.

Ann, exhausted, found Maggie and Pinky on the couch in her office. She crouched. Pinky licked her face. Ann allowed it and petted the dog's head.

She had never felt like a mother to Maggie, but she had always felt *some* sort of affection toward her. She thought it was because she was Sophia's protector. Like a love out of duty. But she realized now, it was the love of a sister.

"Hey, sis." Ann felt foolish saying it, but Maggie grinned. "Can you believe it?"

"I can," Maggie said with a nod. "I think I could feel it. I just didn't know what it was."

"Now the real work begins," Ann said. "I am here for you. However you need me. Sister, guardian . . ." Ann cleared her throat. "Mother, if you want." She opened her arms, and Maggie stepped into them. "I'll protect you, even still. I promise." She felt Maggie nod against her cheek.

"I know." She pulled away and pressed her forehead against Ann's. "And I will protect you."

CHAPTER SIXTY-SIX

Cassie flew overhead while Teresa ran through the woods with Amanda in her arms. She leaped over low shrubs, dodged tree trunks. The lost souls seemed to flee from her when she reached the old cemetery.

Still she ran, holding Amanda close. Cassie soared overhead. She dipped down out of sight.

"Cassie," Teresa yelled.

Amanda lifted her head. "Chashy," her little voice called.

Teresa nearly tripped. She caught herself and stumbled the last few yards out of the forest, leaped over the ditch that marked the boundary when she hunted souls last year.

On the road, she looked around, back and forth, gasping for air. Spinning, searching the road, the sky, the trees for Cassie. It was so dark. A cloud cover blocking out the full moon slid away. Cold blue moonlight lit the area.

"Mumba!" Cassie called. She'd never spoken before while in her gargoyle form. Teresa spun in the direction of her little voice just as she flew across the moon.

A shot rang out. Her winged form tumbled to the

ground. Teresa screamed and watched with open-mouthed horror.

"Get her in the van," a somewhat familiar man's voice shouted. "Make sure she isn't injured."

Teresa took two steps toward them, two more. She started to run.

Car doors slammed. Brake lights ignited. An engine turned over. Headlights facing the opposite way broke the darkness pointing toward Harmony. A white van with a red stripe.

"Chashy!" Amanda yelled. She reached her little hand out. Teresa sprinted toward the van as best she could without jostling Amanda too much.

The van took off, throwing gravel and fishtailing.

"No!" Teresa cried. Someone grabbed her from behind. She almost lost her hold on Amanda, but Amanda gripped her shirt and clung to her with her chubby but strong little legs.

"Teresa, no," a gravelly voice growled in her ear. Raghib.

"Let me go," Teresa shouted, struggling against him as much as she could without losing her grip on Amanda.

"Chashy," Amanda cried. "Chashy."

"We must go, quickly."

"I can't leave her," Teresa shrieked. A hysterical desperation shattered her lungs. Her breath came sharp and ragged. Her voice broke when she screamed her daughter's name. "Cassie! No. Please." She turned and started running again, though the van was gone. Raghib grabbed her and held her tight against him.

"We will get her back. But right now, you must come with me." His hand gripped hers. He pulled her in the opposite direction the van went.

Teresa stumbled along behind him.

"Chashy," Amanda wailed. "Mama, Chashy."

Teresa cried and kissed and shushed her daughter gently. "It's okay. We'll get her back. It's okay."

Amanda cried. Big wet loud sobs. Teresa's heart broke, and her own sob erupted from her chest.

After what had to be a mile or two, maybe more, Teresa slowed. "I can't," she said, gasping through her sobs. Amanda whimpered. Fat tear drops glistened on her cheeks.

Raghib tried to take Amanda, but Teresa wouldn't let her go.

"We're almost there," he said. "Please. We must hurry."

Teresa picked up her pace to a slow jog.

A sign loomed. *Welcome to Old Harmony*.

Teresa followed Raghib. Amanda had quieted, only letting out small little whimpers as her head lolled on Teresa's shoulder. Occasionally she whispered Cassie's name. Every time, Teresa's heart broke all over again.

Ruinous buildings lined a narrow and overgrown dirt road, from what she could make out in the gloomy darkness.

Thunder rumbled. Lightning flashed in the clouds way up high. It started to rain, tentative at first, then a full-on deluge.

"You must go to the church," Raghib yelled over the crashing rain. "You can find sanctuary there." Raghib pointed up a path.

The silhouette of a church spire rose up out of the trees. At first she thought it was an extra-tall tree, but the lightning flashed, illuminating it.

Teresa hugged Amanda close, huddled over her against the rain, and ran up the path.

The church in front of her was a ruin. No one could live

there. The roof was caved in, and most of the exterior wall had crumbled. But Teresa kept going.

She was a few yards away when electricity crackled across her skin. The hair rose on her arm. For a second, she thought lightning might strike her dead. The rain stopped. Teresa looked up at the sky, and the church before her was in perfect condition.

"How—" Teresa looked over her shoulder and back.

It was a massive church. Something out of a European town. Gothic with its spires and gargoyles.

Another sob burst out of her. Her little gargoyle was gone.

She stepped up the stairs toward the big wooden door and lifted the heavy iron knocker. While she waited, shivering and trying her best to keep her baby from catching a chill, she huddled close to the stone wall.

A smaller door inside the big arched door opened.

A nun peered out.

"Please, I need sanctuary," Teresa said, feeling strange using that word. She showed Amanda to the nun.

"Come in, come in," the nun ushered her inside where it was warm. Her habit wasn't the traditional black and white. Instead, it was black and red.

Teresa dripped rain water on the stone floor and shivered with a chill and adrenaline and distress from losing Cassie.

The nun peered at Teresa in the gloomy entryway. Their eyes met. The nun's eyes widened.

"Come with me." The nun held out a hand and ushered Teresa down the corridor, skirts sweeping along the floor as she went.

They entered a massive room. At the far end were four thrones with three steps leading up to them.

Another nun in red robes sat in one of the middle two chairs. She stood and looked down her nose at Teresa.

Teresa shrunk under that cold and scrutinizing gaze. But then, the woman's face pulled into a grin.

"Welcome home," she said, lowering her chin with a welcoming smile. "Yaldabaoth."

EPILOGUE

When they had come out of Tartaros and Teresa Hart was gone, Ann's first instinct was to get the K9 unit from Pine Valley on it, stat, but she had to let Rachel out of the holding cell first. After Rachel blubbered all over her, and after Ann made sure Maggie was okay, she called Pine Valley. The K9 team arrived within two hours.

Bram and Lisa took Maggie back to the house while Ann took the Pine Valley search team out to Lory's basement to start the search.

The team searched the house. In a room with a crib in it upstairs, they found a bloodied vase containing two eyeballs, as well as some discarded clothing. Ann assumed the clothes were Teresa's and gave them to the team for the dogs to sniff. She collected the vase in an evidence bag for testing, though she suspected she already knew whose eyes they were.

Down in the basement, she looked around. From an outside perspective, she thought it probably appeared to be the usual messy basement. Stained carpet. Furniture thrown every which way.

Ann swallowed hard to stop from thinking about what happened mere hours ago. She had high hopes the dogs would find Teresa and she could put this whole thing to rest.

They found nothing. Teresa's scent had vanished in the little ghost town of Old Harmony near a ruin of a cathedral. Despite the dogs' inability to locate her, they searched the surrounding area to no avail. Teresa was gone.

Now, a few months after Teresa disappeared, Ann stood at that very site, wondering where she could have gone. She stepped into the courtyard of the ruin and gazed upward toward the collapsed roof, at the remains of gargoyles stationed at its four corners, protecting it from all directions.

How could Teresa's trail be lost here with no sign of her within?

Ann often pondered this while searching the ruin. She went there at least twice a week.

"Back again?"

Ann whirled around. She hadn't heard Lisa McMichael arrive. Hadn't heard her even come through the woods. Ann's heart pounded. It could have been anyone.

It could have been Teresa sneaking up on me. Ann needed to get her head clear. Get her awareness levels back up to detective standards. She needed to remember her training. She also needed to remember Lisa McMichael had been a trained operative for the Protectorate. She likely had stealth mode down to a science.

"Sorry to give you a fright," the older woman said.

Ann relaxed under Lisa's matronly smile.

"I just don't understand," Ann said, motioning around. "She couldn't have just disappeared."

"There are many ways to disappear without a trace." Lisa referred to the Protectorate, Ann knew. How they all faked their own deaths—well, most of them. Some actually had died—to avoid assassination from the Messengers of the Light.

"I have a feeling you are here not only to search for Teresa, but perhaps to find other answers." Lisa raised her eyebrows. "Or maybe to just . . . get away?" She touched her fingers to Ann's shoulder and gave it a light squeeze.

Ann looked down. The truth was, with her dad home caring for Maggie, Ann felt... incomplete. Lost even. Like she had no purpose anymore.

She wasn't sure what she'd expected. The Luminaries had made it clear their work was unfinished. Well, Sophia's work was unfinished. Ann didn't know what that meant for *her*, personally. They said her duty as Sophia's protector had been fulfilled.

Ann knew these feelings were not what Lisa was talking about. It wasn't the complex feelings Ann was having. It was the fact that the house, with Bram home, was a little too . . . full.

"He knows," Lisa said, as if reading her mind. "He knows he's disrupted your life."

"Disrupted is a little strong," Ann said. "He hasn't done that." What was it then? Ann walked around the courtyard, eyes on the overgrown weed infested ground, while Lisa waited, arms loosely crossed, the definition of patience.

Ann got to keep the master bedroom. Bram didn't see any point in uprooting her from the room she'd moved into. He took the guest room upstairs just down the hall from Maggie—his other daughter, Ann had to keep reminding herself. Close to her in case she had nightmares. Ann touched her mark.

"I don't even know if she's scared anymore," she whispered. "I don't know how she needs me . . . *if* she even does need me." With Bram home, Ann's life had an almost untethered feeling. Like she could even leave it behind. Return to detective work in Salida or somewhere else. Pine Valley maybe.

"She needs you," Lisa said. "So does Bram. More than you know."

Ann wasn't so sure. Bram and Maggie had become close over the past few months, he being her primary caregiver now. It gave Ann the freedom she needed to run the sheriff's department, give Sully the time off he needed, and get back to normal life. But normal life was too, well, normal. She didn't want normal life.

Ann returned home, leaving Lisa at the roundabout. The older woman had moved into the house where the Perfect Soul had been resurrected, where the gateway to Tartaros had been opened. Louise's, then Lory/Mary's house, and now Lisa's. She could have moved back into the house she'd shared with Sheriff McMichael, but she said that house wasn't a home without him.

She'd kept the altar so she could study the markings on it.

Pinky bounded to the door the moment Ann opened it, tail lashing, body bending in half back and forth. She flopped onto her side when Ann crouched to rub her chest and belly.

"Hello?" Ann called. "You guys home?" No one answered. Ann stood. Pinky rose to a sit and pawed at her leg. Pinky wasn't freaking out, so Maggie must be okay. "Where's Maggie?" she asked Pinky.

The dog jumped up with a woof and ran to the back door. Ann opened it.

Bram and Maggie were in the back yard. Pinky gave a sharp bark and rushed Bram.

"No, no, no," Bram cried out, backing away. He stumbled and fell onto his butt at the same time Pinky lunged toward him, tackling him onto his back. She stood over him, tail upright, head low, peering at Bram who held his hands up in a warding off gesture.

Maggie giggled, which seemed to release Pinky. The dog wiggled over to Maggie, tongue lolling.

"What the hell was that?" Ann rushed to Bram and helped him to his feet. He grumbled obscenities under his breath. "And why was she inside if you two are out here?"

"She thinks I'm attacking Maggie," Bram growled.

"Dad was showing me some self-defense stuff," Maggie called from the grass where she sat petting a now-content Pinky. She'd only just started calling him that after weeks of referring to him as Mr. Bram. "I don't blame her. You kind of were attacking me." Maggie closed one eye and grinned.

"What was he showing you?" Ann asked. At that same time, Bram grabbed her around the shoulders from behind. She shoved her butt against his hip, grabbed his arm, and flung him over her shoulder. He landed on the ground flat on his back.

Pinky barked.

"Stay," Ann told her. The dog obeyed.

"That," Bram said from the ground, air wheezing out of his lungs. "Is how you do it, Mags."

"Try again, old man." Ann crouched in a fighting stance.

Bram waved her off. "No, no." He got up, bent over his knees. "I trust you remember everything I taught you."

"Plus, you know, Academy training." Ann winked at Maggie who grinned at her. "You okay, dad?" He was still doubled over.

"Just getting my wind back."

He had been acting a lot older since their night in Tartaros. Ann wondered if the broken contract meant he would age more rapidly. Not as rapid as Mary, of course, who had withered away to crypt dust in a matter of seconds, but perhaps his age would catch up to him. He wasn't old by any standards—in his sixties—but she still wondered if his life being part of a secret organization might catch up to him in the form of arthritis or other age-related issues.

He stood upright with a groan and stretched his back.

"Maybe you should leave the self-defense training to me?" Ann said with a lift of her eyebrows.

Bram waved her off again. "Got any ibuprofen?" He grinned and hobbled inside.

***

Later that night, Bram put Maggie to bed. Ann could hear Maggie reading *him* a bedtime story, shortly followed by his raucous snoring. Pinky came down the stairs with her ears back, as if his snores personally affronted her. Ann patted her up onto the couch. The dog leaned into her and flopped down as close as she could get without actually being *in* Ann's lap.

A minute later, Maggie peeked around the wall at the top of the stairs.

"Come on," Ann said, motioning her down to join them on the couch. Maggie grinned and rushed down.

"His snoring," Maggie said. She covered her ears.

"I know," Ann said. "There were times when I lived up

there in your room, and he was down here in the master . . . I swear I could hear him through the floor."

Maggie sat next to Ann, but didn't cuddle close to her like she did with Bram. Ann didn't mind.

Their relationship had evolved over the past few months. Ann didn't have to be her parent anymore, which was a huge relief. But she still had to be a big sister, which she didn't know how to be. She settled with treating Maggie like a close friend. A friend who held Wisdom and the fate of humanity within her.

"Is . . . Sophia—"

"Sophia—"

They both started at the same time. Ann let out a breathy laugh. Maggie tucked a stray curl behind her ear and gave Ann a shy smile.

"Go ahead," Ann said.

"Sophia hasn't stirred in a while," Maggie said. "Not since we were in Tartaros. That's what you were going to ask, right?"

Ann nodded.

"What do you think it means?" Maggie asked.

Ann shrugged. "My hope would be it means all is well in the world. For now."

Maggie nodded. "For now," she whispered.

Silence settled between them.

"Have you had any nightmares lately?"

Maggie took a deep breath. "They aren't . . . scary . . . but I have been dreaming." She shifted and turned, pulling her knees up to her chest, and leaned back against the arm of the couch. She lowered her chin onto her knees and didn't meet Ann's eyes.

"I dream about the Luminaries sometimes," she said. "About what they said. How you fulfilled your duty as my

Protector." Her voice came out thin like she wanted to whisper.

"Don't worry about that, Maggie," Ann said. "You have all of us now. Me, Dad, Pinky. Even Ms. Lisa and Rachel."

"I know," Maggie said. "But I need . . . I need you." She lifted her chin and met Ann's eyes. "I need *my* Protector."

A warm feeling flooded into Ann's heart, as if Maggie saying those words had filled in broken cracks and holes that had formed inside her chest over the years. All the times she stuffed her feelings into the back of her mind in the past year. All the times she broke someone else's heart and as a result broke her own. They filled in with the feeling of Maggie's love.

"Maggie," Ann said, tears in her voice and in her eyes. "The Luminaries said all the love around you will keep you safe." She opened her arm and Maggie crawled over to her and nestled close. "And the truth is . . . I . . . I love you, kiddo." She gave Maggie a squeeze.

The book, sitting on the coffee table ever since the night in Tartaros, flipped open. Ann cried out. Maggie jumped. Pinky shot off the couch, ears back, tail tucked.

The pages fluttered and flipped. They stilled. A bass sound pulsed twice.

Ann and Maggie looked at each other. The bass faded to silence. They leaned forward and looked at the text.

Want to read the lost prologue that launched this book off the ground? Want to see alternate cover artwork concepts and designs? Visit https://claireLfishback.com/tgos-bonus to get some fun bonus goodies!

One of the best ways to show how much you enjoyed it is to give a star rating or, even better, a review on Goodreads or your favorite online retailer, even if it is only a sentence or two. Or, just tell a friend or two about it, or share it on social media! Word of mouth recommendations help exceptional readers like you find great books.

Thank you for reading!

ACKNOWLEDGMENTS

This is dedicated to my twin sister, Melissa Sirevog, but I would be remiss to not say why. Thank you for nights of drunken brainstorming, for beta reading, and for being my inseparable and balancing half. I could not have written this book without your ingenious ideas and what ifs and validation when I sent you pages and pages of texts on my thoughts about different plot points and characters and *things*. I literally could not have done it without you. Thank you also for coming up with the ideas that helped me determine the title for this book.

A special thank you to my other beta readers: Rachel Haag, Rachel Whetzel, Amanda Keil, and Amy Drayer (author of the Makah Island Mysteries, check 'em out). You all brought different eyeballs to the table. I am forever grateful for you helping me make this book what it is today.

An additional shout-out to Rachel Haag who was willing to hear all the spoilers and cheered me to the finish line twice a week while she helped me fix my brain, and also for tweaking the title from Gorge to Gorging.

Thank you to Julie Barr of Elevation Physical Therapy

for answering my questions about what dislocating a shoulder is like. And for laughing when I call her up for an appointment for some new weird injury I've managed to sustain.

Thank you to Karen of Magpie Place in Salida for providing a lovely place for us to stay—our new home away from home—where I started writing this book.

Thank you to Jessa Forest (author of the amazing Slaughter Chronicles) for helping me pick a font. Seems trivial, yet so important!

A big fat thank you to my amazing editing team, Jennifer Chesak of Wandering in the Words Press and Michael Mann. You guys took what I thought was a decent draft and helped me make it a solid draft I'm so very proud of, all against my aggressive timeline! Thank you thank you thank you!

The care and feeding of a writer is a massive task. Thank you to my patient and supportive husband, Tim, who, during the writing and editing of this book became a "book widow" and struggled to find things to watch on Netflix that I wouldn't also want to watch. For 12 years of husbandly service at the time of publishing this. For the care and feeding of this writer, including vegetables so I won't die. And for making me laugh and smile every single day.

Thank you to Kira for all the couch cuddles during the writing and editing of this book (and anytime else). Thanks for not pushing my Mac off of my lap and onto the floor in an attempt to get *even closer* to me. If you have a pibble, you understand.

And most of all, thank *you* for taking the time to read this book.

ABOUT THE AUTHOR

Claire L. Fishback lives in Morrison, Colorado with her loving husband, Tim, and their pit bull mix, Kira. Writing has been her passion since age six. When she isn't writing, she enjoys drawing, reading, hiking, baking, and adding to her bone collection, though she would rather be stretched out on the couch with a good book (or poking dead things with sticks).

Please visit www.clairelfishback.com and sign up to stay up to date on the latest releases and more!

www.ingramcontent.com/pod-product-compliance
Lightning Source LLC
Chambersburg PA
CBHW051310190726
48290CB00001B/94